Into the Midnight Wood

Into the Midnight Wood

—A NOVEL—

ALEXANDRA McCOLLUM

DUTTON

An imprint of Penguin Random House LLC
1745 Broadway, New York, NY 10019
penguinrandomhouse.com

Book design by Lorie Pagnozzi

LIBRARY OF CONGRESS CATALOGING-IN-PUBLICATION DATA

Names: McCollum, Alexandra author
Title: Into the midnight wood: a novel / Alexandra McCollum.
Description: New York: Dutton, 2026.
Identifiers: LCCN 2025005706 (print) | LCCN 2025005707 (ebook) |
ISBN 9798217045587 trade paperback | ISBN 9798217045594 ebook
Subjects: LCGFT: Fantasy fiction | Romance fiction | Novels
Classification: LCC PS3613.C373 in 2026 (print) |
LCC PS3613.C373 (ebook) | DDC 813/.6—dc23/eng/20250331
LC record available at https://lccn.loc.gov/2025005706
LC ebook record available at https://lccn.loc.gov/2025005707

Printed in the United States of America

1st Printing

The authorized representative in the EU for product safety and compliance is
Penguin Random House Ireland, Morrison Chambers, 32 Nassau Street,
Dublin D02 YH68, Ireland, https://eu-contact.penguin.ie.

Hast du nicht alles selbst vollendet,
Heilig glühend Herz?

Did you not achieve it all yourself,
Sacred glowing heart?

—GOETHE, "PROMETHEUS"

Into the Midnight Wood

Chapter One

Meredith Schwarzwelder might have been a nightmare to live with, but at least he paid his share of the rent on time.

It had become something of a coping mechanism for David Carew to remind himself of this fact several times per day. It was what he reminded himself now as he attempted to decipher the smudged ink of the hastily scrawled note on the kitchen table. In fact, if David were to draw up a list of points for and against his housemate, the *For* column would have a single point in his favor:

#1: He pays the rent on time.

The *Against* column—against what, precisely, David wasn't sure; just against him generally—would have taken a lifetime to write out.

#1: He has an absurd name.

Meredith was a good, fine Welsh name, of course, if a bit out of style as a man's name these days. David had nothing against that. *Schwarzwelder*, too, was a perfectly acceptable surname, even if some clerical meddling of the distant past had led to the nonstandard phonetic spelling. But to combine the two—that was pure absurdity. One simply couldn't go around mixing languages and nationalities in such haphazard fashion. It was a frivolous name, befitting a frivolous person.

#2: He is a frivolous person, an irredeemable eccentric.

Every quirk of speech and manner that David had taken for affectation upon their first meeting five years ago, he now knew to be authentic. The simple truth was that Meredith was genuinely, incurably strange.

Exhibit A: The note.

Ran down to the shops. Bednarek stopped by early, and he says, can you clean up the garden because there's people coming later. Also, don't worry about the hallway ceiling. Says me, not Bednarek. Back soon.

Love, Meri

The *i* was dotted with a heart. A *heart*. A grown man, a sensible man, did not sign his name in such a fashion. And yet—

The note continued with the addendum:

P.S. Don't worry about the linen cupboard either.

P.P.S. The bread is out.

David closed his eyes, took a deep breath, and ran a hand through his wavy dark hair. He ought to go and investigate what, precisely, had happened to both the hallway ceiling and the linen cupboard, but he wouldn't. Not yet. He would deal with that and the garden and Mr. Bednarek, the landlord, after he finished his breakfast. He needed a moment to drink his tea and read the morning paper and go through the daily process of reconciling himself to the reality of living with the singularly most bizarre person he had ever met.

"I think Schwarzy's having it off with Mrs. Jupiter," said Brian.

David's eyelid twitched. He made a noncommittal sound without glancing up from the finance pages.

"Schwarzy! And Mrs. Jupiter!" persisted Brian.

Brian was the third occupant of Midnight Cottage, so named for its location at the edge of the Midnight Wood.

Mrs. Jupiter was the witch who lived down the lane.

"I heard you the first time." David wasn't surprised. He'd seen the way Meredith spoke to her, leaning over the garden gate and winking and saying things like *Nice weather, isn't it, Mrs. J?* and *How's the chickens, Mrs. J?* and *Want me to show you the spot where the sweet woodruff grows down by the sycamores, Mrs. J?* Sooner or later, she'd been bound to take him up on it.

Sooner or later, most people did.

#3: He flirts with everyone in his path, whether man, woman, or other.

"It's hardly decent," said Brian.

Privately, David agreed, but he merely sighed and folded his newspaper. "Mrs. Jupiter is a widow, Brian. She's allowed to have it off with whomever she likes."

True or not, it was hardly the scandalous news his housemate seemed to take it for. David bit into his English muffin (the last from the half-forgotten package in the cupboard, its staleness not disguised by a thick layer of marmalade), took a sip of tea, dabbed at his moustache with a paper napkin, and was just turning his attention back to the newspaper when Brian spoke again.

"Yes, but *he* isn't, is he?"

"What, widowed? Or allowed to have it off with—"

"Stop *saying* that," demanded Brian. "It's vulgar. But yes. The latter."

David didn't bother pointing out that Brian was the one who'd introduced the phrase to begin with, and once again took up the newspaper without comment.

#4: He is, apparently, having it off with Mrs. Jupiter.

"I saw them, you know," Brian went on. "Yesterday. In the Midnight Wood."

With a huff, David dropped the paper back to the table. "Yes, and?"

Brian scowled and picked up his plate, set it back down, and began to pick at his undercooked freezer waffle. "He was *clinging* to her."

Unmoved, David took another drink of tea. "He clings to everybody. He clings to *me* if I let him. I wouldn't worry."

#5: He clings.

#6: And he stares.

At David, at his own reflection, at the sky, in the direction of anything with the slightest hint of sparkle, and, at times, at nothing at all.

On the verge of taking another sip of tea, David paused with his cup in midair. The gears in his mind had begun to turn; suspicion crept in. "Why *are* you worried?"

Brian didn't reply. David's suspicion grew stronger.

"You've been here, what, three weeks now?" David asked.

That question elicited a tight-lipped nod of affirmation.

David Carew did not consider himself a cruel man, but it was better for all concerned, he told himself, to confirm what he suspected, to rip the Band-Aid off and get it over with.

"All right," he said. "Suppose they are."

Perhaps he was being cruel, but he pressed on anyway. "Suppose they are," he repeated. "Schwarzy and Mrs. Jupiter, screwing each other senseless in the back garden right this minute." (He could have said *making love*, he reflected, but that implied a certain delicacy of feeling, and in any case, Brian needed a reality check. Judging by the way he flinched at the phrase, he needed it badly.) "What difference does it make to you?"

Brian's cheeks had gone pink, and his nervous fingers had made considerable headway in the task of shredding his waffle into a heap of crumbs on his plate.

So that was it, then. David should have known from the outset. "You slept with him, didn't you?"

Brian opened his mouth in what was probably meant to be righteous indignation and closed it again. He raised an index finger, frowned, and subsequently lowered it.

#7: He slept with Brian.

"I *told* you not to," said David severely. "I did tell you, the first day you moved in."

"I didn't mean to!" said Brian in despair.

David raised his eyebrows and set down his cup. Very seriously, he asked, "Do you mean to say it wasn't consensual?"

"N-no, it was." Brian took on a dreamy, faraway look. "It was *very* consensual."

David forestalled any further reminiscences with a raised hand. "That's quite more than I need to know." Something else occurred to him. "I thought you were straight." He'd thought—hoped—that fact would prevent any complications of this nature, but he was neither naive nor ignorant of Meredith's effect on people.

"So did I! I mean, I am!" insisted Brian. "I was. Oh, I don't know!" He threw down the last bit of waffle and lowered his face to his hands, from behind which he said indistinctly, "Schwarzy's got me all confused."

"Yes," said David, "I can see he has." If his tone was rather dry, Brian was too distraught to pick up on it.

"It isn't my fault," said Brian. "He gave me *the eye*. He does that, you know. To everybody." He raised his face and repeated, in an accusatory tone, "*You* know."

"I don't know," said David flatly. "He's never given me, as you call it, *the eye*. Not so that I've noticed." Or perhaps David was immune to Meredith's supposed charm. In any case, he was the only person in the shared rental house who'd ever lasted more than three months.

#8: He's driven away every other occupant of Midnight Cottage without exception.

With a few, it had been this exact scenario. With others, it had been the inability to withstand the psychic distress of living with a person who was chaos distilled—of the distinct possibility of coming home at any given time to find the drawer pulls off the kitchen cabinets or the wineglasses stacked precariously in the bay window or a trail of Chihuahua-sized pawprints in India ink leading down the back hallway.

True, the proximity of the reality-distorting Midnight Wood might have played no small part. The interior of the forest disregarded the laws of time and space, and was home to innumerable strange plants and dangerous creatures. At times, faint strains of music seemed to drift out on the wind at night but vanished the moment one tried to listen more closely. Paths appeared to shift the moment one turned one's back, trees and hills and valleys never quite staying in the same spot one had last left them. It was a most unsettling place, and David never set foot inside the Wood if he could help it.

Meredith regularly went for nighttime walks there.

It was said that prolonged exposure to the Midnight Wood, even at a distance, could drive one mad. That, David knew, was nonsense. He himself had lived there for five years and was perfectly sane. So was Mrs. Jupiter, and she had lived there longer still. For that matter, so had Meredith, and while *sane* was perhaps not the first word that came to mind to describe him, certainly he was no *more* mad than he had been upon their first meeting.

Brian was speaking, David realized, and had been for some time.

"—and I won't take that lying down, I can tell you."

"Sorry?" said David. "Won't take what lying down?"

Brian slammed his teacup down onto the table. "There you go again," he hissed, "making everything *vulgar*."

"Yes, all right, my apologies," said David in the most placating tone he could muster. He had witnessed enough impending departures to recognize the signs, and this time he aimed to prevent it, if possible. Brian was a tolerable housemate: he was quiet in his comings and goings, adhered to an adequate standard of cleanliness, and for the most part kept to himself (although, as it turned out, to a lesser extent than ideal). David would much prefer convincing him to stay over taking a gamble on a new, unknown housemate.

"Have you spoken with him?" he asked.

"What good will that do?" Brian scooped up a handful of waffle bits, rose from his chair, and pitched them into the trash can. "He has *betrayed* me, David."

David turned over the newspaper, which he'd long since abandoned any hope of reading. "Does he know that? I mean, he's . . ." He made an inarticulate gesture that encompassed the utter futility of attempting to explain Meredith to the uninitiated. "I expect he did give you his speech? *No plans to fall in love*, et cetera?"

The color drained from Brian's face. "How do *you*," he said through gritted teeth, "know about the speech? Don't tell me you—"

"What?" David stared across the table in disbelief at the very suggestion. "Good God, no." He'd had to overhear Meredith's little recitation in bars and in clubs and, on occasion, in the living room of Midnight Cottage so many times he knew it verbatim. It was what Meredith told everybody who succumbed to his charms, earnestly explaining the parameters of a potential encounter to the interested party or parties. "I know it because we've lived together so long, nothing more."

Brian planted both hands on the table and leaned forward, attempting to loom over David. "Do you really expect me to believe that?"

Then again, David decided, all things must come to an end. Perhaps Brian's tenure at Midnight Cottage had, regrettably, run its course.

David pushed back his chair and rose to his full height. He stood six foot three with the muscle to back it up (even if he had put on a few extra pounds after the past few years at a desk job) and could out-loom Brian—and most people, for that matter—by sheer natural aptitude.

"Yes," he said. "I do." In fact, he was far less offended by the accusation of lying than he was by the very idea that he would ever so much as *consider* going to bed with Meredith.

For a long moment, the two of them glared at each other over the breakfast table.

It was Brian who looked away.

"Fine," he snapped. "You know what? I don't care. You can have him."

"I don't *want* him," protested David, but Brian had already stormed out of the kitchen. David made a half-hearted effort to follow.

By the time he rounded the corner into the living room, Brian had already ascended the stairs, and stopped at the top to call down, "I won't be sticking around here any longer, I can tell you that much. And!" he added with indignation. "We're out of bread."

He turned his back and vanished from the landing; a moment later, an upstairs door slammed.

"Right," said David to the empty room.

Under ordinary circumstances, the interior of Midnight Cottage was a pleasant, cozy space. Its hardwood surfaces had become polished with age and acquired a warm, honeyed patina, and the wide bay window let in both sunlight and the ever-present view of the adjacent forest. In combination, it gave the effect of bathing the living room in a faintly yellow-greenish light, a comforting hue that put David in mind of green glass bottles and the pages of old books and sunlight filtering through foliage on a summer's day. A large potted fern hung from the rafters of the sloping ceiling, overfilled bookcases flanked the window seat on either side, and the sofa's slipcover bore a sensible yet subtle herringbone pattern of David's choosing, though the effect was somewhat ruined by the atrocious color-wheel throw pillows Meredith had brought home one day, insisting they were *vintage*.

Right now, however, the palpable resentment radiating from behind Brian's closed door seemed to permeate the entire cottage. David retreated to the back deck, closed the door behind him, and lowered himself into a weathered Adirondack chair that creaked in distress at the addition of his weight. That was an improvement—nothing to disturb him out here, no sound apart from the distant twitter of birds in the early-spring chill. At last he could enjoy the remainder of his tea in peace.

He took a drink and found it had gone quite cold.

David set his half-full teacup on the deck rail, leaned back in his chair, and pressed his hands over his eyes. All he wanted, really, was to wake up in a house—in a world—blissfully devoid of Meredith Schwarzwelder and the chaos he left in his wake.

#9: Living with him makes any semblance of a normal, quiet life impossible.

Housemates fled in the night. Dates and boyfriends—David's, not Meredith's—were tempted astray. The sum total of his actions, direct or indirect, intentional or not, made day-to-day life a parade of indignities and irritations that, while individually minor, were cumulatively unbearable.

Perhaps Brian wouldn't be the only one to leave Midnight Cottage this spring.

As it happened, David had been saving up for a down payment on a house of his own for some time. Over the past few years, he'd watched the number in his bank account steadily increase, yet he'd stayed on at Midnight Cottage, for a number of perfectly sensible reasons. The rent was low. His first-floor room afforded both space and privacy. Aside from its proximity to the Midnight Wood, the location was ideal, just on the outskirts of Bingham Junction. The nearer side of the city was accessible both by bicycle and on foot, which appealed to David's athletic inclinations, and Cleveland lay only a short drive to the northwest. And, he reminded himself doggedly, in spite of the perpetual problem of retaining a third housemate, in spite of *everything*, Meredith did pay the rent on time.

In actuality, the time of *anyone* living at Midnight Cottage might be drawing to a close; David had grown increasingly suspicious of late that Mr. Bednarek intended to sell the property. Over the past month, the landlord had undertaken a number of long-overdue repairs and renovations—reshingling the roof, evicting a nest of treacle wasps from the rain gutters, taking away the remains of the trellis where the writhing jasmine had once grown after vines and frame both had been gnawed to bits by a passing herd of satyrs. Then, of course, there was the ongoing debacle of the upstairs bath, which joined both the linen cupboard and the hallway ceiling on the list of things David was not going to spend time thinking about.

Well, he'd given it a fair shot. He'd stayed longer than he'd meant to, he'd put up with a great deal more than could be fairly expected of him, and if he'd been looking for a sign, this was it: the injustice of cold tea.

If David was honest with himself, he might admit, too, that he had not been able to dispel the new and as-yet-nebulous discontent that had lately begun to surface in the back of his mind. Leaving aside the continual thorn in his side that was his housemate, David felt no great unhappiness in his day-to-day life. His work as an accountant paid well enough and did not require him to spend an undue amount of time speaking with other people. He took vacation once or twice a year to visit family back in Wales or old university friends now spread across the country. He had a modest yet promising stock portfolio. Yet he was nearing thirty, and beginning to feel as though he didn't have all that much to show for it. At that age, his father had already completed his PhD, married, and had a child on the way. David himself was no academic, and tended to regard children as a rather noisy and troublesome variety of pet, though he was fond, in an abstract way, of his two small nephews. And while he'd prefer being single over clinging to an unsuitable match, still he had the vague feeling that there ought to be something or someone more in the picture. Even his best friend, Harriet, who'd persistently sworn off relationships, had a few months ago joined a dating app and consulted him for advice on composing her profile.

Inside the house, a door slammed, startling the sparrows from a nearby dogwood tree and bringing David back to the reality of the present situation.

He might as well go and get bread, he supposed, if it kept him occupied and out of Brian's way for a time. Rising from his chair, he stretched and, with a last uneasy glance back at the house, started off. He followed the footpath down the hill and to the west, past Mrs. Jupiter's cottage and toward town. A few patches of snow remained in the shade at the edge of the Wood, where the trees towered dark and foreboding. In the sunny spots nearer the path, crocuses and snowdrops had already begun to bloom.

David had reached the second bend in the lane when, over the crest of the next low hill, there came into view the distressingly familiar figure of the person responsible for all of the morning's trouble: Meredith Schwarzwelder.

Chapter Two

David watched the approach of the slim black-clad figure in the distance. Rather, mostly black-clad: with its wide black and white stripes, Meredith's absurdly oversized sweater billowing in the spring breeze gave him the effect of a great magpie flapping its wings.

Yes, a magpie was just about right, David decided, the way he always came swooping in with a jangle of bracelets and rings that he'd scavenged and traded and otherwise acquired from God knew where.

#10: He has the most inexplicable and disorderly sense of fashion.

It wasn't only the jewelry or the sweater that annoyed David. It was everything about Meredith from head to toe, from his perpetually disheveled hair to his chipped nail polish to his indecently tight trousers that left nothing to the imagination—from the vacant half grin displaying slightly crooked front teeth right down to the mismatched laces of his modded Doc Martens (under which there was a high chance of finding mismatched socks as well). And as an added affront, lately he'd taken to wearing muttonchop sideburns that didn't suit him at all.

A white Chihuahua trotted at Meredith's side, her lead looped around one wrist; from his other arm dangled a basket. Spotting David, the dog yipped in excitement and darted forward.

"Morning, David!" called Meredith. "And Bianca says good morning, too."

Bianca was the Chihuahua.

#11: His accent.

David didn't know where to begin with Meredith's accent. It had *layers*, like a fine perfume or a wall that had been painted over many times. Or—here David settled on a more familiar comparison—rather like a spreadsheet running numerous functions at once.

The base was itself a mélange, as if someone had taken the accent of the Rust Belt cities lining the Great Lakes, the so-called Pittsburgh dialect that bled into eastern Ohio, and the odd few markers of Appalachian speech that persisted into the northern foothills and whisked them all together into a precarious and improbable meringue of twisted vowels and swallowed consonants.

That combination was overlaid with an obvious effort to correct certain peculiarities of pronunciation—an overemphasis of the letter *T*, a deliberate and distinct rounding of the *O*. As a finishing touch, there were sprinkled in bits of other accents, words and phrases and pronunciations borrowed from people he'd known and places he'd been—Toronto and New York and a hint of the cadence of old East London. The result was a soft, vaguely plaintive singsong that was somehow less grating than it had any right to be.

(David had never before heard someone manage to sound both American and British *at the same time*, yet Meredith had somehow accomplished it. Most people split the difference and guessed he was Canadian, but David knew better: Meredith was from the nearby hills to the southeast, much as he might try to disguise that fact.)

At last they met on the path. To David's chagrin, but, unfortunately, not his surprise, Meredith leaned in to give him a one-armed hug and a kiss on the cheek. It was only an air-kiss, the briefest touch of cheek to cheek, although on occasion Meredith did get carried away and give him a brief peck. David minded this less in practice than in principle—he had no objection to the gesture itself, only to its sheer extravagance. Such affection was hardly necessary toward a housemate one saw every day, but of course Meredith greeted nearly everybody that way, and somehow had the unerring ability to gauge whether they'd let him.

#12: They almost always let him.

"Morning," muttered David morosely. "You're up early."

Come to think of it, it was unusual to see him out and about at this time of day. Meredith was a nighttime creature, strange and pale under the sharp early sun. His windswept hair, somewhere between dishwater blond and mousy brown, hung to his shoulders in loose waves and shimmered faintly in the morning light. So, too, did the fuzzy material of his sweater and Bianca's rhinestone collar.

#13: He persists in outfitting his dog in this humiliating fashion.

"I went down to the shops," said Meredith, and added, "The bread is out."

"Yes," said David. "I know." And then, because although ordinarily the answer should be obvious, but with Meredith, nothing was ever obvious, he asked, "You picked some up, then?"

#14: One must regularly ask such questions of him.

"No," he said, quite cheerfully.

#15: Because this is the answer.

"I—" David wiped a hand over his face and contemplated this for a moment. "I think I'm going to kill you."

Meredith giggled. He was always giggling at things that, to David, weren't funny at all, just as he went around with a foolish grin plastered on his face no matter the circumstances.

"I got rolls," he explained, holding out the basket. "And soap, and oranges, and straight pins for Mrs. J, and Bednarek asked me to pick him up a pound of coffee, and—"

David stared.

"Rolls isn't bread," protested Meredith.

That was enough to snap David out of his disbelief. "You watch your language, young man."

He actually wasn't sure of Meredith's exact age, and had never had the inclination to inquire. From early on, though, it had been clear to David that he himself must be the elder of the two by at least a few years, and he'd turned twenty-nine that winter.

Meredith giggled at that admonition, too. "Yeah, all right, rolls *aren't* bread, are you happy? Actually, no, you don't look happy at all. Is it the rolls?" he inquired anxiously. "I thought you liked the little buns with the egg glaze and the—"

David pinched the bridge of his nose. "It is *not the rolls*."

#16: The man is impossible to have a conversation with.

Trying again, he said, "Brian's flown into a jealous rage."

"Has he?" said Meredith with apparent interest, but at that moment, they passed by Mrs. Jupiter's cottage as she came around the corner from the back garden with a basketful of brown eggs, surrounded by a swarm of mismatched cats. Mrs. Jupiter was a heavyset woman with dark brown skin and braids twisted into a towering, elaborate updo atop her head. She wore a great many pieces of crystal jewelry that David suspected were more for style than function, though she was a well-respected witch by all accounts.

"Good morning, Mrs. Jupiter," called David.

She smiled. "Good morning, Mr. Carew." And then, with a different sort of smile that showed quite an immodest number of teeth, she said, "Morning, Meredith."

Even though there was no discernible change, some shift occurred, some indication of intimacy that made David feel like an obscene voyeur when Meredith returned, "Morning, Liz." He rummaged in his basket and presented her with a card of bright new pins. "Here's them sewing pins you wanted, by the way."

Mrs. Jupiter beamed. "Thank you, my dear, most kind of you. If you'll forgive the imposition, I do have another favor to ask—if you happen to have a moment, that is."

"Actually," said David, "we were in the midst of quite a serious—"

"Course we do," interrupted Meredith. "Anything for you, Mrs. J."

Unbelievable.

(David wondered whether the reversion to her title was an intentional downgrade or merely force of habit.)

"Oh, thank you," said Mrs. Jupiter. "You remember the stray that showed up on the doorstep this morning?" *Stray* was a euphemism. People often abandoned unwanted pets at the edge of town. The lucky ones found their way to Mrs. Jupiter; the rest wandered into the Midnight Wood, which, as far as David was concerned, was hardly a stroke of good fortune for them.

Bianca had been one of Mrs. Jupiter's rescues, but as a witch, she specialized in cats. As the Chihuahua had been unable to see her way to a peaceful coexistence with housemates of the feline persuasion, she'd ended up being adopted by Meredith. (Currently, she uttered a low growl from between his ankles as she turned her baleful gaze on an orange tabby.)

"Do you mean the big round stripey one?" asked Meredith.

"That's the one. She's having kittens," said Mrs. Jupiter, "and having a pretty rough time of it. The trouble is, I'm fresh out of bloodroot—type A—and nearly out of slattern's comb. I didn't want to leave her to go hunting for it myself."

"That's all right, Mrs. J, you can count on us," said Meredith brightly. He leaned down to unclip Bianca's lead from her collar, straightened up, and ran a hand through his hair, getting his rings tangled with his bangs, as usual. (He'd once confessed, after an evening of smoking false prophet's balm, that he cut his hair that way to conceal a scar, but the subsequent half-second display of his forehead had revealed no evidence of one.) Stowing the lead in his shopping basket, he handed it over to Mrs. Jupiter. "I'll just leave this with you for the moment, if you don't mind. C'mon, David."

David opened his mouth to protest at being roped into this little expedition, then reconsidered. Though there were countless sensible reasons to avoid setting foot in the Midnight Wood, Meredith still remained cheerfully oblivious to his own role in Brian's imminent departure—a most unsatisfactory state of affairs, and one that David intended to rectify at once.

Mrs. Jupiter inclined her head. "I owe you a debt of gratitude," she said. "Do be careful, you two. And be sure to stick together. The Midnight Wood is no place to walk carelessly."

"Oh, *I'll* be all right," said Meredith. "I always am."

#17: He always is.

David fought the urge to roll his eyes, but it was true. Meredith could go prancing through the Midnight Wood unharmed, whereas other people—well, it was best not to consider what sometimes happened to other people.

"By the way," called Mrs. Jupiter as they started along the overgrown path toward the edge of the Wood, "it's a bit late in the season for imitation wintergreen, but if you happen to come across any, would you mind bringing it back?"

"Not a problem, Mrs. J!" called Meredith.

Without so much as a backward glance, he stepped into the darkness of the Midnight Wood, and David, against his better judgment, followed.

ALTHOUGH THE SKY had been bright and clear on the footpath only yards away, inside the Midnight Wood it was dark as night.

That was because it *was* night.

It was always night in the Midnight Wood. Time moved differently there; hours could go by inside the Wood while mere moments had passed outside its boundaries, and vice versa. It was darker even than in the true nighttime, as the moon had not yet risen, though a sprinkling of stars against the black velvet sky illuminated the scene below.

Though it was nearly as bad as David remembered from the very few—and brief—occasions upon which he'd entered the Wood in the past, he had to admit there was a strange kind of beauty to his surroundings. Hemlocks and balsam firs and white pines towered overhead; the still-bare branches of birches and tulip poplars and black walnuts stretched toward the night sky. Massive outcroppings of lichen-encrusted rock punctuated the rolling hills.

The place was permeated by the dank, herbaceous scent of loam and poison plants. Eerie birdcalls echoed through the darkness, answered by the shrill and dreadful chirpings of night creatures lower to the ground.

Despite the darkness, Meredith seemed to find his way by effortless instinct, taking circuitous routes to avoid treading on flowering plants. David kept close behind him.

"So," he couldn't help asking, "you and Mrs. Jupiter, then?"

"Oh, yeah, last night she took me out into the back garden and—well, I tell you, afterwards I didn't know which way was up." Then Meredith took on a furtive look. "Only don't tell anybody about that. It's a secret."

"You've just told *me*," David pointed out.

"Yeah, but you and me, we tell each other all our secrets."

"Do we," said David.

"Nearly," said Meredith, and fell back to walk alongside David, linking one arm through his.

"You're clinging again."

"I'm *cold*."

"It's not my fault you didn't dress properly."

"I dress more properly than anyone," proclaimed Meredith, but released David as the path narrowed, forcing them back into single file as it wound its way through a dense thicket of brambles.

A screech sounded in the nearby treetops, and a shadow swept past unseen with a swish of bat-like wings.

David shuddered. "I can't imagine how you go walking about in here on your own, or why you'd want to."

"It's a good place to meet people," said Meredith with a shrug. "A while back, for instance, I stumbled upon a group of sycamore dryads up on the hilltop there. And dryads, you know, they're quite skittish at first, not that one can blame them, but in the end, we had quite a nice time together."

David had the horrible suspicion this was a euphemism. "You don't mean to say—?"

"Well, you see," said Meredith, ducking under a low branch, "they were having a bit of a get-together, and once we got to talking, they invited me to join them, and one thing led to another—"

"You mean to tell me," said David, having to step well out of his own path to bypass the same branch, "you come skulking around here nights on the off chance you could have your way with a wood nymph?"

#18: He has been consorting with the sycamore dryads in the Midnight Wood.

"Oh, hardly that! Besides, if anything, it was the whole lot of them who had their way with *me*. Not that I'm complaining, mind you."

"I do not wish to know of your sordid entanglements with the sycamore dryads."

"All right," agreed Meredith. "All right. Forget the dryads. There are plenty of other nice people here. Like the Moon Calf and the Night Horse, they have a lovely little cottage together just the other side of that ridge."

"Do they."

#19: One can never tell when he's being serious and when he's completely making things up.

"They do, they invited me to tea only last week."

"The Moon Calf," repeated David skeptically. "Right. And what does he do, exactly?"

"The Moon Calf prefers to be called *it*, actually. The kids are reclaiming that one these days, you know." For a moment, a faraway look came over Meredith as he ran his fingers over the needles of a nearby pine bough. "Although I don't know that I'd care for it so much myself. But," he rushed on brightly, "the two of them are in charge of the moon, of course! The Moon Calf puts it up and then the Night Horse takes it back down again. And the other day—or night, I suppose—" Meredith continued, "I met a Chinese panda down by the waterfall."

"There are no Chinese pandas in these woods," objected David.

Meredith gave him a withering look. "He was on a tourist visa. *Honestly*, David."

David couldn't quite muster a response to that.

"We had a lovely chat," Meredith continued, "and I took him down to the brook to meet the Most Weasel, and then we all—"

"What in heaven's name is a Most Weasel?"

"Why, it's the opposite of a least weasel, of course."

That was simply too much for David to accept. "Oh, come on. There's no such thing!"

Meredith turned to face David, hands on hips. "Well, you just hadn't better go telling *him* that. I can't think how he'd take it. I mean, really," he said in indignation, "how would you like it if somebody came around insisting *you* weren't real?"

They'd reached a stretch of path surrounded on either side by plants with glossy green leaves and ostentatious white blossoms that shimmered in the starlight, and David took the opportunity to change the subject.

"Is this one of the things Mrs. Jupiter wanted?" he asked. "Slattern's comb, wasn't it?"

"Nah, this is maiden's drawers, can't you tell the difference? But there's some bloodroot just over there."

David joined him in uprooting a few of the plants. Bianca ventured after them, but halted after a few steps at finding the leaves still wet with the morning dew. She gave one paw a dainty shake to rid it of the offending moisture, then returned to the path to regard them both with a distinctly judgmental air.

"There, I think we've got enough, don't you?" said Meredith. David followed him back to the path in silence, trying to collect his thoughts. Surely there'd been something he'd meant to tell him, something important, but now his mind was awhirl with weasels and dryads and—

David stopped in his tracks, disoriented. "Weren't those firs in the opposite direction before?" In fact, he was certain the entire grove had rearranged itself in the few moments their attention had been elsewhere.

This didn't appear to concern Meredith in the least; rather he lit up with excitement and seized David by the hand to pull him along. "Oh, David, come see! This is one of my favorite spots!"

David resigned himself to being dragged through the grove of firs and into the glade beyond. Running ahead, Bianca tried without success to clamber onto a large flat stone that rose to waist height at the far edge of the clearing, surrounded by flowers still in bud and shaded by a mossy rock overhang. Some distance away stood a massive black alder ringed by high hawthorn bushes.

Meredith lifted the Chihuahua and set her down on the rock. "There you are, precious, how's that?"

Crossing the clearing to join them, David gave a little shiver as he passed through the shadow of the alder. No more than a momentary chill in the dark and damp, yet he found himself struck with a sense of foreboding as he gazed up into its branches.

Of course Meredith would like it here.

"I fell into some thornbushes just like that once, you know," he remarked, breaking into David's thoughts.

"What, here in the Wood?"

"No, no, this was ages ago. I was trying to hide in a tree," he added with a rueful laugh.

"I—" David tried to process this, and couldn't. Meredith was not, by any stretch of the imagination, what one would describe as athletic. "I'm sorry, but you don't strike me as the tree-climbing sort."

"Yeah, well, didn't make it very far, did I?" Meredith wandered over to the hawthorns and began to toy absently with the jagged edge of one leaf. "I'd just got past the first branch, and then the next thing I know, I've fallen right back down again." With a sharp hiss of pain, he jerked his hand away, a tiny trickle of blood staining one fingertip.

David winced in sympathy at the sight of the long, cruel spikes adorning the hawthorn branches, even if the result had been rather a foregone conclusion the moment Meredith was within arm's reach of them.

Before he could point it out, however, Meredith asked, "You were about to tell me something earlier, weren't you?"

"*Was* I?" At this point, David had become so sidetracked that he might as well have forgotten his own name.

Bianca leapt from the rock, and David followed as she and Meredith both started off for the opposite side of the clearing.

"Something to do with Brian? Jealous rage?" prompted Meredith, then leaned down to pluck a plant with a spiky periwinkle blossom. "*This* is slattern's comb, by the way."

David groaned as it all came back to him. "Oh, yes. Jealous rage indeed, with a side of identity crisis. I'm fairly sure you've just cost us another roommate."

Meredith at least had the decency to look dismayed. "Brian's gone?"

"He hasn't yet, but I think he's about to."

"Oh dear." Meredith straightened up with a handful of flowers, frowning. "Was it about the fan blades?"

"The—what?"

"The fan blades. I only thought—"

"It was *not* about the fan blades." David took a deep breath. He did not want to know about the fan blades.

"Shall I speak with him?"

"Best not to just now," said David. "But did you really have to go and sleep with him, too? How many roommates does this make now?" As soon as the words left his mouth, he realized that he very much did not want to know the answer to this question.

"Technically," said Meredith, blinking wide blue eyes at him, "we didn't sleep together, exactly. I only—"

"That's quite far enough," interrupted David, though Meredith's aborted hand gesture had already insinuated far more than he needed to know.

"I didn't *mean* to, only he kissed me. People are always going and kissing me," he said, and managed to make it sound like a complaint. "They should know better, really."

"Schwarzy," said David thoughtfully, "I really think I might kill you."

Meredith only giggled—*again*—and then, contrite, tried to stop himself, pressing his hands over his mouth, to no avail.

"Do you know," David went on, "I don't think he even knows your first name?" That, too, might have been cruel, but he was in no mood for gentleness.

That did the trick, though Meredith looked more shocked than anything. "Oh! But of course he does. He must."

"Must he? I haven't heard him say it once."

"But *how*?"

"*You're* the one asking? I should think it would've come up when the two of you—" David grimaced and let the sentence end there. "It's not as if you help matters. You don't introduce yourself properly."

#20: He never *introduces himself properly.*

David hadn't learned Meredith's first name for over a month when he'd moved in. True, perhaps a portion of the blame could be laid at the feet of Mr. Bednarek, who was in the habit of addressing him only by nickname, even when making introductions to new tenants.

And this, he'd say with a sweeping gesture, *is our Schwarzy*, in much the same way one might say, *And this is the kitchen garden.*

And Meredith never elaborated, just invariably grinned his foolish grin and gave a wave and said, *Yeah. Hi.*

"Anyway," said David, "it doesn't matter now. The damage is done."

"But I really did tell him," said Meredith in distress. "I told him the same way I always do: *I'm not in love with you, I've got no plans to—*"

"Yes, yes, I know," David interrupted. He'd heard it more times than he could count and was in no mood to do so again now.

Meredith reached out and caught him by the elbow. "I'm sorry, David."

"I know. I know you are."

He always was, not that it made things any better.

To David's surprise, as they came around the next bend in the path, daylight shone through the edge of the Wood quite close by. In just a few moments more, they emerged in Mrs. Jupiter's back garden next to the henhouse.

Meredith strode up to the open kitchen window and rapped lightly on the sill. "Mrs. J?"

He collected the bloodroot from David, and handed it over along with his own supply of slattern's comb when Mrs. Jupiter appeared in the window.

"I do appreciate this," said Mrs. Jupiter, returning Meredith's over-full shopping basket to him. "The two of you must drop by for tea soon, but for the moment, I had best see to finishing this potion."

With that, she vanished from view, and David and Meredith started up the hill toward Midnight Cottage.

"I really am sorry about Brian," said Meredith. "I didn't mean to make any trouble for you."

David's first instinct was to point out that it was much too late for that, but he relented. "Well, never mind. I'll go and see if I can't calm him down. You make yourself scarce for a bit." He doubted Brian would change his mind, but they might at least part ways amicably.

"Here, I'll take this down to Bednarek." Meredith took the bag of coffee and handed his basket over to David. He started away, turned back after a single step, and threw an arm over David's shoulders as he leaned in to grab a poppy seed roll from the basket, ignoring his aggrieved sigh. "Say goodbye, Bianca."

Bianca, of course, did no such thing.

"See you in a bit!" Meredith raised his roll in a mock toast and sauntered off with his little dog in tow, leaving David feeling once again as though he'd just weathered a bewildering and infuriatingly good-natured hurricane.

Chapter Three

Not quite half an hour had passed by the time Meredith returned, but within that half hour, enough had happened to solidify David's plans of leaving Midnight Cottage for good.

Having once more retreated to the relative safety of the deck, he lay back in his chair, closed his eyes, and mentally composed an email to his real estate agent—or, strictly speaking, the email he *would* send to his real estate agent once he had found one. Which he would do, just as soon as—

That thought was interrupted by two sets of footsteps—one canine, one presumably human—ascending the stairs from the garden to the deck, Bianca's claws clicking rapidly against the wood.

"David?"

He kept his eyes firmly closed. Perhaps if he didn't acknowledge him, Meredith would go away, would simply vanish back into the ether of whatever nightmare realm was to blame for his existence.

"David."

He couldn't abide the way Meredith said his name, either, with a torturously elongated Midwestern *A*, and of course the way he had trouble with his middle *V*'s, dragging them out nearly to *F*'s in words like *Cleveland* and *haven't* and—

"*David.*"

David gave in and sat up. "*Yes?*"

"Oh, I thought perhaps you were asleep."

David glowered at him, which Meredith paid absolutely no attention to. Instead, he made his way to the corner of the deck behind David's chair, while Bianca promptly bounded over to take up residence beneath it.

"You really shouldn't sleep out here," Meredith continued, moving aside the basket of rolls and oranges (in fact, tangerines) that now rested next to David's abandoned teacup. "You'll be carried off by vultures."

"Vultures."

"Vultures," repeated Meredith firmly, perching on the deck rail and picking absently at the peeling paint. "I'd go and rescue you, of course, but best to avoid the whole situation altogether, if you ask me."

David hadn't asked him, and decided it best to change the subject. "I thought I told you to take your time."

"I did. Me and Bednarek had coffee," said Meredith, causing David to despair at the state of his grammar, "only he wasn't in a chatty mood."

"Didn't you have coffee with Mrs. Jupiter this morning?" If there was a touch of nastiness in David's tone, well, Meredith deserved it.

"Nah, didn't want to wear out my welcome there. Matter of fact, I—" He broke off as he caught sight of the adhesive bandage newly adorning David's forehead. "What happened to you?"

David batted away his reaching hand. "Don't go touching it, would you?"

Meredith only continued to regard him with dismay.

"What happened?" David echoed with a grim laugh and plucked another wisp of white wool from his sleeve. "*You* happened. You left your—your *fur* all over me—"

"It's mohair," Meredith protested.

"—and Brian got the wrong idea about that, too."

"Oh, no!"

"Oh, yes. As if," said David in indignation. "I mean no offense to you, Meredith, but you are the last person in the world I would be interested in sleeping with."

"Oh, none taken," he said cheerfully. Then a thoughtful frown crossed his face. "Wait, last even after the women? Or—"

"I'm not going to answer that." David might be gay, but very possibly Meredith Schwarzwelder might indeed rank below every woman on earth, if it were to come to that.

"Suppose not. Would you like an orange?" he asked, offering the basket.

"No, I would not like an orange, you hopeless *goldfish*." What David would like was for Meredith to keep a thought in his head for longer than thirty seconds at a time, but he knew by now that was a lost cause.

"I do like goldfish," agreed Meredith. "And koi. The way they sort of glitter in the water when the sun hits just right." Then, after this latest mental detour: "Wait—what happened with Brian?"

"I was trying to tell you. He threw a saucer at me."

"Oh! That's not on!"

David agreed, but there was no use reiterating it. Again he waved off the reaching hand. "Don't. It's just a scratch."

"He ought to have thrown it at me."

"Yes. He ought. But he didn't, did he?"

#21: He avoids having crockery thrown at him even when he deserves it.

"Where's he gone?" asked Meredith. "I'll go and sort him out."

"Like hell you will." David was fairly sure Meredith couldn't sort out so much as a geriatric butterfly. "Anyway, he's gone. Loaded up half his room into his car and took off." An accusatory note crept into his voice. "I don't think he'd even unpacked all his boxes to begin with."

Meredith looked like he was about to cry.

"There, it's all right," said David, hoping to forestall the possibility of being seized in a tearful hug, which was not an infrequent occurrence. "I'm not hurt, not really. Anyway, we'll have to tell Mr. Bednarek."

Mood apparently restored, Meredith selected a tangerine from the basket and began to peel it. "Oh, yes," he said. "Bednarek says there's a man coming to look around later."

"What do you mean, *to look around*?"

Meredith shrugged. "Somebody called Maitland Cartier."

If David had accepted a tangerine, he would have dropped it in shock. "*Maitland Cartier* is coming here?"

The name failed to elicit the proper reverence from Meredith. "Yeah, why, do you know him?" he asked, eating a slice of tangerine. "Friend of yours?"

"Maitland Cartier, a friend of mine?" If only. Maitland Cartier, the property developer, was one of the most revered yet elusive figures in the world of finance. "He *owns* the Corner Store." And about half of Bingham Junction, not to mention a number of other concerns throughout northeast Ohio and western Pennsylvania.

David liked his present job well enough—he'd been head of accounting at the Corner Store for some time, ever since his unfortunate predecessor had to be taken away following the Incident with the fax machine. He did not, however, like having to continually explain that he worked not at *a* corner store but at *the* Corner Store, the flagship location of a midsized regional department store chain. He also did not particularly like Steve Corner, general manager and grandson of the owner. Former owner, rather, following the recent sale of the business to Cartier.

David could tolerate all that for the time being, but what he'd really set his sights on was someday working for Cartier directly in his head office, preferably sooner than later. Rumor had it that Elaine Contreras, Cartier's longtime VP of finance, was on the verge of announcing her retirement. If true, that would leave an opening for her replacement, and Cartier was known for promoting from within his own ranks.

In his current position, David had a foot in the door already, and if all went well at the Corner Store's upcoming charity auction that David was helping to organize, Cartier would have no choice but to take notice of him. Of course the door would open wider still if David was able to obtain one of the highly coveted spots on the auction's exclusive VIP list. That would gain him admission to the VIP lounge and, more importantly, a chance to speak to Cartier face-to-face.

If Cartier was coming to look at Midnight Cottage, the only logical supposition was that he was interested in purchasing it—further confirming David's suspicions about Bednarek's plans to sell. Yes, David decided, he was ready for a change of surroundings in more ways than one. It was time to say goodbye to the Corner Store, to Midnight Cottage, and to Meredith.

Meredith, whose attention had turned to the half-full teacup next to him. He picked it up, gazed at it thoughtfully, and then flung its contents out into the flower bed.

David was appalled. "Don't do that!"

"Why not? 'S only tea."

"We do not dispose of things by throwing them into the garden," said David severely. "I swear, I've met wolves with better manners than you."

"So've I, Maurice Wolkowitz invited me to dinner a while back and had so many little forks laid out, I hadn't the first idea where to begin. Course *he* managed it well enough, even with the paws."

"From the outside in," said David automatically.

"What?"

"The forks. You start from the outside—never mind," said David. "The cutlery was not the point here. Nor were the wolves." He had quite forgotten the point. In any case, if Meredith was going to go about flinging tea into the garden, which he apparently was, David would have to get him safely out of the way before Cartier made his appearance. If Meredith did such a thing in front of Cartier, he'd surely ruin David's chances with him forever. "Aren't you working today?"

"Later." Meredith licked a stray drop of tangerine juice from his fingers. "Nobody wants to get tattooed at eight in the morning, or if they do, I'm a little scared of them."

"Why not? It's a good sensible time for an appointment."

"You *would* think so."

Choosing not to dignify that with a response, David closed his eyes and settled into his chair once more, tipping his head back to rest against the deck rail. As Meredith was sitting behind him, however, he found himself reclining against his thigh instead.

David didn't bother to move; it was more comfortable than the railing, but only just.

"Orange?"

David opened one eye as a black-nailed hand came into his field of vision bearing a segment of tangerine. "No, tha—oh, all right."

He leaned forward and let Meredith feed him the fruit. Briefly, David wondered whether five years of the Midnight Wood—and of Meredith—hadn't warped his ability to gauge normal behavior after all, but soon rejected that idea. After everything Meredith had put David through that morning alone, feeding him tangerines was the least he could do to make up for it.

"Really," said Meredith, "Brian thought—you and I." He giggled. "Really, I can't imagine."

David hummed in agreement, by now well accustomed to Meredith's disorienting habit of catching hold of an idea again minutes or hours after the subject had faded from the conversation. "How anyone could get such an idea is beyond me."

Wordlessly, Meredith offered David another tangerine segment, which he took. For a moment, he relaxed. The wind had dropped off to a pleasant light breeze, the air had warmed, and the sky stretched bright and cloudless overhead. Meredith had fallen into a meditative silence, a state in which he was almost tolerable. Still, something nagged at David in the back of his mind, some forgotten phrase—

He sat up. "What have you done to the hallway ceiling?"

"Do you like it? It isn't finished, but—"

David didn't wait for the end of that sentence before he was on his feet to investigate and making his way down the hall, Meredith trailing at his heels, and Bianca after him.

"I'm doing a fresco," Meredith announced, shedding his sweater to reveal a clinging black T-shirt. He tossed it carelessly over the back of an armchair before beginning to remove his rings and bracelets, letting them clatter one by one to the breakfast table. (Bianca, losing interest in the proceedings, trotted off to her basket next to the bookshelf.) In response to David's look, he went on, "Bednarek says it's all right. He says he meant to have the ceiling redone anyway, so it's no great loss if it doesn't turn out. And if it does, it'll be a conversation piece."

There was no question that Mr. Bednarek was planning to sell, then. David ought to point it out to Meredith, but he was so excited going on about his fresco, and if he couldn't put the pieces together himself—

Something else occurred to David. "But you work in ink and watercolor. Aside from live subjects, I mean."

"I'm broadening my horizons, David. You ought to try it sometime." Meredith went to the coat closet and retrieved a paint-spattered stepladder, which he dragged into place beneath the beginnings of his fresco. "Anyway, it's *The Virgin and the Unicorn*."

"Isn't that Italian Baroque?" asked David.

"Yeah!"

"Schwarzy, you're a surrealist."

Meredith returned to the closet, where he turned out to have stashed his painting supplies for easier access, balanced precariously above David's best overcoat. "Yeah, I figure it'll be a fresh take."

"A fresh take," repeated David skeptically. "Right. Well, I'm going to go tidy up the garden, if you're quite done throwing things into it."

"Put on some music on the way out, would you?" asked Meredith, inspecting his plaster knife. "None of them French ladies, though."

#22: He lacks a proper appreciation for the chanson réaliste.

"*Language*," said David. Emerging from the hallway into the living room, he called over his shoulder, "Just for that, I'm playing Edith Piaf for the next twelve hours straight."

"Oh! You *wouldn't*!"

No, David wouldn't, if only for the sake of not wearing out his Piaf records, but for the moment, he'd let Meredith suffer in suspense.

He had fully intended to tidy up the garden, and to put on music, but he didn't even make it to the record cabinet below the bay window's bench seat before getting sidetracked. Meredith, as usual, had left the place in absolute shambles.

#23: He never puts anything back in its proper place.

Scowling to himself, David retrieved the throw pillows that had been stuffed behind the sofa, plucked a whisk from a vase of tulips, and collected an empty beer bottle from the bookshelf. He reached for the jar of abandoned paint water on the end table, but then, on second thought, left it for Meredith to deal with.

As David returned from the kitchen, the landline telephone rang. Suppressing the urge to scream in frustration, he picked up the call. "Midnight Cottage."

"Meredith?" asked a female voice doubtfully.

Good God. David couldn't handle a second jealous lover in one day. "Ah, no, this is his roommate. I'll just get him, shall I?" Covering the receiver, he called down the hall, "There's someone on the phone for you."

"Put it on speaker for us, would you?" Meredith called back. "I'm up to the elbows in plaster."

"I didn't think frescoing involved so much direct contact."

Meredith began his unsteady descent down the stepladder. "Yeah, well, had a bit of a mishap there."

"He's coming," David told the caller. "I'll put you on speaker."

"Uh, hello?" said the woman. "Mere?"

"Genevieve?" said Meredith in astonishment.

Genevieve? mouthed David. Meredith shook his head as he emerged into the living room, dripping bits of plaster onto the floor. David gestured at him irritably and grabbed the roll of paper towels from where it balanced atop the shade of a table lamp.

"So you *are* home," said Genevieve. "Good. I'll be there in twenty minutes."

David sank to the floor and began wiping up plaster.

"I'm really quite busy," said Meredith.

"Not too busy for me."

"But I've only just got started on the unicorn," he protested, "and I haven't even touched the virgin yet."

#24: He never stops to consider how these things sound.

"Gross," said Genevieve. "Look, whatever, finish up your freaky three-way and at least be dressed by the time I get there."

"But—"

"See you!" she said, and hung up.

"So. Genevieve, is it?"

"She is my cousin, David," said Meredith with dignity—which he immediately lost by running a bewildered hand along his jaw, leaving a streak of plaster down his face. "But what in the world she wants, I can't imagine."

Chapter Four

"You've never mentioned any cousins before," said David.

"Oh, yes," called Meredith from the kitchen, the rest of his words lost under the sound of running water as he rinsed the plaster from his hands in the kitchen sink—

#25: He rinses the plaster from his hands in the kitchen sink.

"What was that?" asked David as Meredith returned to the living room.

"I said," said Meredith, slathering lotion onto his hands and tattooed forearms, "I've got loads and loads of them."

#26: He is fanatical about hand lotion and leaves bottles of it all throughout the house.

"That many," said David.

"Absolute bucketfuls of cousins," Meredith confirmed. "Genevieve's my favorite, though. Have we got anything to serve with tea?"

"I think there's some of the marble cake left that you made Tuesday."

"You don't think it's gone stale?"

"If it has, that's all the more reason to—"

"Oh!" Meredith's cry of recollection interrupted David's pragmatism. "The Battenberg!"

"I beg your pardon?"

"I was making a Battenberg cake. Am making," he amended. "Baked the sponge last night when I came back from Mrs. J's, I just have to finish it—oh, but the hallway."

"I'll take care of the hallway," said David decisively. "You handle the cake and put the kettle on." As much as he hated being left to deal with the fallout of Meredith's various art projects, even less could he abide the thought of failing to offer proper refreshments to a guest. (His mother, rest her soul, would have been horrified at the very idea.)

David hid away the stepladder and plaster, shoving them unceremoniously back into the coat closet. (Placing them in Meredith's room would have meted out the appropriate comeuppance but would also have required carting them upstairs.) He cleaned the hallway floor and returned to the living room, tuning out the various curses and expressions of dismay emanating from the kitchen, and finally managed to put a record on. He chose neither Edith Piaf, as threatened, nor any of Meredith's collection, which he classified disparagingly under the nebulous heading of *postpunk*. Instead, he chose a Vivaldi record, long abandoned by some housemate of the distant past, set to low volume.

"Oh, kill me *dead*," Meredith lamented from the kitchen, "the marzipan's gone all wrong."

"Sure it's not just you?"

The indignant reply was drowned out by the knocking at the front door. Bianca leapt up and yipped ferociously at the as-yet-unidentified intruder, rushing across the hardwood floor to precede David into the front hall.

"*No*, Bianca," David ordered, and pointed back to the living room. "Go on."

With a tiny grumble that David was sure held resentment, she obeyed and retreated.

He answered the door and found himself face-to-face with a blond woman who was very buxom, extraordinarily beautiful, and carrying a designer handbag that could have held Bianca several times over. If David had had the slightest bit of attraction to women, it would've been all over for him.

"This is Midnight Cottage?" she asked.

"It is, yes. You must be Genevieve." At her look of suspicion, David clarified, "We spoke on the phone. Do come in. Schw—er, Meredith's just in the other room." He supposed he'd have to resort to his proper name now that there were multiple Schwarzwelders in the house. "I'll get him, shall I?"

As he escorted Genevieve into the living room, he took the opportunity to surreptitiously study her face. The resemblance between her and Meredith was so strong the two of them could have been brother and sister. They had the same broad cheekbones and wide jaw, lending a certain soft roundness to the cheeks. (While he was apparently attempting to create the illusion of prominent cheekbones with the ill-advised sideburns, she had accomplished the effect rather more successfully through a severe use of contouring makeup.) Both, too, had the faintest aquiline curve to the nose, though Genevieve's eyes were a brighter and more piercing shade of blue, and she was a true golden blonde, even if nature had been enhanced by a few carefully placed platinum highlights. And while Genevieve's figure couldn't be described as anything but ample, Meredith was decidedly skinny—not exactly of a slight build, but what David's mother would have called rawboned.

As Meredith had still not emerged to greet his guest, David excused himself and continued into the kitchen, where steam wafted from the spout of the floral-patterned teapot. He inhaled the calming aroma of fresh-brewed tea—and then faced the decidedly less calming sight of Meredith holding a butcher knife, even if it was only to slice the sad and misshapen marzipan-covered lump on the plate in front of him. (He fancied himself a hobby baker, and while the results were most often passably edible, they were just as often aesthetic monstrosities.)

"Oh dear," said David.

"I did try," said Meredith mournfully. "I suppose it's the sort of thing one can't rush."

David decided it best not to comment further. "Your sister is here."

"She's my cousin."

"Oh, yes, you said."

"I haven't got a sister."

Of course Meredith was an only child. That explained a great deal.

"Anyway, she's waiting. I think you've got as far as you can hiding in here."

"I'm not hiding! I was making the tea."

#27: He is most certainly hiding.

Why he was hiding from his supposedly favorite cousin, David couldn't imagine, nor would he venture to guess; he'd long since given up trying to make sense of Meredith's motivations.

"Of course," agreed David. "Go on, then. I'll get out of the way and let you two catch up."

Meredith caught at David's sleeve. "Don't you dare," he hissed. "Don't you dare leave me alone with her. I need you for moral support."

"Moral support," repeated David skeptically. "For what? Afraid she'll criticize your cake decorating?"

"I mean it! You don't know Genevieve, she's a blond bulldozer. Whenever she wants something, she'll run you right over if you stand in her way."

It was not without a certain wistfulness that David's thoughts drifted to the house listings waiting for him just a few rooms away. "You don't even know what it is that she wants."

"*Please*, David."

#28: He can put on the most unfairly effective puppy dog eyes.

David relented. "Oh, all *right*." After all, he'd have plenty of time when Meredith finally left for work, and he did owe David a proper cup of tea after the earlier fiasco. Besides, with any luck, in a month or two he'd be out of here. No more cousins being sprung upon him, no more frescoes on the ceilings, no more nonsensical talk of vultures and unicorns and goldfish.

In short—and best of all—no more Meredith.

"Come on, then." David took up the tea tray and shepherded Meredith, bearing the attempted Battenberg, into the living room. Genevieve had settled onto the sofa and shrugged off her rose pink overcoat, which was adorned with a generous amount of cat hair (and which Bianca regarded from afar with an expression of disdain).

"Genevieve!" Depositing the cake plate on the table, Meredith leaned in for the usual business of embrace and air-kiss. "It's been ages."

"It has," she agreed. "You're a hard one to pin down."

She, too, spoke in that same odd mix of accents, David noted as he poured the tea, but without the alterations and embellishments that characterized Meredith's speech.

"What brings you to the neighborhood?" Meredith asked, automatically reaching for the first cup.

David swatted his hand away. "Guests are served *first*."

Undeterred, Meredith took a slice of cake and draped himself over the armchair, sprawling out across the seat and letting one knee dangle over its upholstered arm.

#29: He appears physically incapable of sitting in a chair in any respectable fashion.

"I actually wanted—oh, thank you," Genevieve interrupted herself, accepting the tea from David. "I'm sorry, I didn't get your name."

"This is David," said Meredith, an odd note of pride in his voice. "He's lived here five years, can you imagine?"

"You've lived here longer," said David irritably. He wasn't sure what there was to criticize about having a stable living situation. He wasn't, in the end, sure that it *was* a criticism, but it certainly sounded like one. Then again, with Meredith, one never could tell.

"I know! Nobody else has stuck with me for so long," he said in admiration.

Not for much longer, if David had his way.

He placed the next cup on the end of the coffee table nearest Meredith, poured one more for himself, and joined Genevieve on the sofa. Bianca hopped up next to Meredith, squeezing herself into the space between his side and the arm of the chair.

Genevieve took a polite sip of tea and cleared her throat. "Okay, I'm just going to say it. No offense to you, Dave—"

"David," he corrected automatically.

"—but this is probably better off as a private conversation."

So that was Meredith's game.

#30: In spite of all his airy manner and vagueness, he really can be quite crafty at times.

"My apologies," said David, "I'll just—"

"Nonsense," said Meredith without any apparent concern. "Anything you want to talk to me about, you can say in front of David." He leaned forward to swap his cake—which he set down on the as-yet-unpaid electric bill—with his teacup. "We haven't any secrets."

"I see," said Genevieve.

David rather wished he wouldn't say such things, and that she wouldn't believe him.

Fixing her intense blue gaze on Meredith, she said without further preamble, "We need to talk about the wedding."

"Oh, yes?" he asked brightly, and took a sip of tea. "Whose wedding?"

Genevieve stared in disbelief, a reaction David was all too familiar with himself. "Florian's, *obviously*."

The change that came over Meredith was astonishing. He froze, teacup in midair, and never had David seen that foolish grin drain away faster.

"Florian's getting married?"

David had no idea who Florian was, but judging by Genevieve's response, it was evident this had been the wrong answer.

"Oh, now that's just too much, even for you," she scolded. "I figured you'd still be sulking, but pretending you don't know about it is just childish."

"I *don't* know about it," said Meredith. "I've not heard so much as a peep out of Florian or anybody. And I do not *sulk*."

#31: He does, on occasion, sulk.

Genevieve set her teacup onto its saucer with a forceful *clink*. "I mean it, Mere, cut the crap. Florian already told me how you threw a tantrum because he asked Jayceon to be his best man—"

"I never did!"

"—and refused to be a groomsman over it—"

"I tell you this is the first I've heard—"

"—but to not even attend your own brother's wedding?"

David fumbled with his own teacup as he set it down, earning a sharp look of disapproval from Genevieve.

Meredith had not once, in the entire time they'd known each other, mentioned the existence of a brother.

"And not even RSVPing is rude as shit, excuse my language. If you're not going to go, at least grow up and have the—the *decency* to say so instead of just ghosting them."

David would be lying if he didn't admit to a certain satisfaction at seeing someone finally put Meredith in his place, even if he himself hadn't been privy to the exact events that warranted it.

"Bit hard to RSVP to something one hasn't been invited to," said Meredith, now falling into a definite sulk.

Genevieve folded her arms. "I know for a fact Adalynn sent you an invitation weeks ago."

"Who?"

That elicited another incredulous stare. "Uh, Adalynn, Florian's fiancée? Your future sister-in-law?"

The name rang a faint bell in David's memory, but Meredith waved away this information. "Well, I've never met her, and she certainly never sent me any such thing." As Genevieve looked to be on the verge of rebuking him further, he turned to David. "David, you tell her. You'd know if it had come, nobody else bothers checking the mail around here."

#32: Nobody else does bother checking the mail around here.

David had no interest in being dragged into this dispute. "It's been weeks, how should I remember what came in the post for *you*?"

It was true he didn't recall seeing such a thing, but it was equally true he simply mightn't remember, and quite plausible that Meredith had, in fact, mislaid his mail. Still, a tiny hint of doubt sprouted in the back of David's mind. Meredith had an astounding capability for remaining blithely unaware of a great many things, but for all his faults, in all the time they'd known each other, David had never had reason to believe him an outright liar.

"Perhaps it was lost in the post," he suggested.

That seemed to diminish Genevieve's ire. "That could be," she allowed. "Our letter carrier at home did have some trouble with a gang of renegade sorcerers a few weeks back." She rummaged in her oversized handbag, pulled out a battered half sheet of card stock, and held it out in offering. "I'll let Adalynn know, but for the time being, here."

Meredith leaned in to view the invitation, and David did the same.

It read:

Together with their families

Adalynn Cartier and Florian Schwarzwelder

request the pleasure of your company

at their wedding

Saturday, the thirteenth of May—

David stopped reading.

Adalynn Cartier.

Adalynn Cartier.

The only child of Maitland Cartier. *That's* where he'd heard the name, or, rather, read it: Cartier had been profiled in February's issue of *Accounting Monthly*.

"Your brother," David choked out, "is marrying *Adalynn Cartier*?"

#33: His brother is marrying Adalynn Cartier.

Meredith only gave a bewildered shrug. "S'pose so. Why?"

#34: And he fails entirely to appreciate the gravity of this fact.

"Do you two know each other?" asked Genevieve. "Adalynn and I have been best friends since college."

"Not personally, no," said David, composing himself as well as he could. "Her father owns the company I work for." His mind was racing. If Meredith went to the wedding—if David could find a way to get to the wedding himself—

Genevieve, now somewhat mollified, took a slice of cake. "I'm sorry I came down hard on you about RSVPing, but after everything—well, never mind. You *are* coming, obviously?"

Meredith fidgeted and reached for his bracelets, but as he hadn't put any of his jewelry back on following the business with the fresco, his wrists were bare of any adornment save his tattoos. (One arm was covered in delicate black filigree; the other bore a full sleeve of various botanicals that David had never bothered to look at closely, done in shades of black and gray with a few tiny color details so minimal one was always surprised to catch sight of them.)

"Well, you see, I really haven't the time."

"This is your *brother's wedding*," Genevieve emphasized. "And it's not for another six weeks. That's plenty of time."

"I'm telling you, I'm well booked up. I've got a *waiting list*."

Genevieve wrinkled her nose. "Who'd book with *you*?"

David couldn't tell whether she was teasing or not.

"People do," said Meredith indignantly. "Lots of people."

This was true. David knew because he'd eventually, out of sheer frustration, insisted on taking over the convoluted nightmare of Meredith's taxes.

"I'm sure you can rearrange your schedule."

"I can't!"

"Mere, you need to go to this." This time, there was no question Genevieve was dead serious as she leaned forward over the coffee table. "I know you and Florian have never been best friends, but I haven't seen your face at a family gathering since Grandpa died. My mom was about to call and give you a piece of her mind—"

At this, Meredith visibly blanched.

"—but I told her I'd handle it."

"But—" he began weakly.

No. No, there could be no *buts*, not where the daughter of Maitland Cartier was concerned.

David stood. "Meredith. Could you come help me in the kitchen." It was not a request. It was also the barest pretense, but the situation was too dire to waste time on a more plausible excuse. Without waiting for an answer, he caught Meredith by the wrist and pulled him to his feet. "Do excuse us for a moment."

"David, what's got into you?" asked Meredith with wide eyes once they were safely in the relative privacy of the kitchen.

"What the hell are you playing at?" David demanded.

"What do you mean?"

"Not fifteen minutes ago, you told me you were an only child, and now, all of a sudden, you've got a brother? Whom you somehow didn't know was getting married?"

"I *didn't* know," insisted Meredith. "And anyway, I told you no such thing. I said I hadn't got a sister. You always go making assumptions."

"That," said David, "is not the point. How can you possibly turn down a chance to attend Adalynn Cartier's wedding? How can you refuse to *participate* in Adalynn Cartier's wedding?"

"But Florian never asked me, I swear it!"

David waved away that protest. "Look, it doesn't matter."

"It matters," said Meredith, "a great deal." He appeared on the verge of tears—over a ridiculously small matter yet again.

#35: He cries at anything.

Horror films, baby birds, sad news stories, free jazz. (To an extent, David could sympathize with him on the final point.) He even teared up when cut flowers had passed their prime and needed to be thrown out, and every time "Solsbury Hill" played on the radio.

Very well, David could make a small concession to placate him. "Yes, all right. Clearly there was some miscommunication." That, too, was altogether too likely.

This failed to have the desired effect; rather, Meredith took on an expression of hurt bewilderment.

Well, David had tried. "In any case, of course you must go. If you can still arrange to be in the bridal party, all the better." Surely, as a groomsman, Meredith would be afforded a plus-one.

"I don't want to be in the bridal party."

"Of course you do." David felt a pang of sympathy for Genevieve. Really, she'd had her work cut out for her. "Everyone likes weddings. They constitute an important social ritual and provide an atmosphere of conviviality."

"All that?" asked Meredith doubtfully.

"And need I reiterate—the father of the bride is *Maitland Cartier.*"

"But I don't *care* about Maitland Cartier."

#36: He does not care about Maitland Cartier.

"But I do," said David. "If you've no care for yourself, at least consider my position. If I want to make any headway with Maitland Cartier, I must go to this wedding, ergo *you* must go to this wedding and find a way to get me there." What exactly he would say when face-to-face with Cartier was something he could work out later, after an invitation had been secured. The important thing was the opportunity.

"But isn't he coming here today anyway?"

"That is quite a different matter." If luck held, David would have a chance to meet Cartier when he arrived to inspect the property, but a brief chance encounter was nothing in comparison to his daughter's wedding. "Now, get back out there and settle things with your cousin."

With an air of defeat, Meredith slunk back to the living room. "All right," he told Genevieve, not without a lingering trace of sullenness. "I'll go, if it matters that much to you."

"I knew you'd come around." She rose, put on her coat, and gathered up her handbag. "I'll let Adalynn know. Give your brother a call, okay?" Stepping around Bianca, she went on, "Thanks for the tea, but I really have stayed longer than I meant to. And, Mere? I'm glad you changed your mind. It'll be good to see you with everybody again."

"I don't know about *that.*"

She rolled her eyes. "Trust me, nobody cares about you being gay half as much as you do yourself."

"I'm not!"

Genevieve's neatly penciled eyebrows rose. "That's the story you're gonna stick with, huh?"

Meredith frowned, and one hand traveled once more to the opposite—and still bracelet-less—wrist, but before he could reply, Genevieve pulled him into another hug. "We'll talk soon, okay?"

At that moment, the front door banged open, and Brian strode into the room as the two drew apart, startled.

"Really!" he cried in outrage. "This is disgraceful!"

"Brian—" began Meredith, taking the opportunity to fully extricate himself from Genevieve's embrace.

Brian glared at him. "Don't you even speak to me or I'll scratch your eyes out!"

"I don't *want* to speak to you," said Meredith, turning his back, then looking over his shoulder to continue, "not if you're going to go throwing teacups at people. I will not endure violence to teacups. *Or* to David."

It would have been touching if it weren't so absurd.

"It was a saucer, actually," David corrected.

"I've only just moved out," Brian fumed, "I've *only just* come back for the rest of my things, and you've already—you've—" He gestured toward Genevieve in inarticulate fury. "Brought this blond floozy into the house!"

Genevieve advanced a step toward him. "Excuse me?"

Brian's accusation compelled Meredith to begin giggling, which achieved nothing in the way of diplomacy, even as he tried to compose himself. "She's my cousin, Brian."

"That's disgusting!"

"No, no, you misunderstand—"

Genevieve's gaze swept over Brian, leaving her clearly unimpressed. She turned to Meredith. "Is this one the virgin or the unicorn?"

"*You said you wouldn't tell!*" Brian seized a stack of unopened mail from the hall table and flung it at Meredith, who tried to bat away the ineffectual barrage of envelopes.

"Oh! But I didn't!"

"Stop throwing things," implored David, though he doubted it would do any good.

"Right. Okay then," said Genevieve. "Dave, nice meeting you. Mere,

I'll be in touch. Move it, unicorn boy." With that, she barreled right toward Brian in the living room doorway, making him scurry out of her path. A moment later, the front door fell shut behind her.

David attempted to calculate whether there was enough space for him to edge past Brian and escape to his own room, and determined it an unlikely prospect.

Meredith, meanwhile, attempted to reason with him. "Now, look here, I had quite a nice time with you. It didn't have to turn out like this. You didn't have to go and—" He gestured at the fallen letters.

"*You* didn't have to go and sleep with Mrs. Jupiter, and half the rest of town!" seethed Brian.

"But I told you," said Meredith earnestly. "I did tell you I'm not in love with you, I've got no plans to fall in love with you, and we needn't—"

"*I thought you'd change your mind!*"

Meredith turned a helpless look upon David, who remained stone-faced. He had no assistance to offer in this situation, and really, Meredith had brought it upon himself. He tried again: "I never gave you any reason to think anything of the kind."

"No, I suppose not," said Brian viciously. "I can't imagine what I *was* thinking, wasting my time on some—some little *hillbilly harlot* like you!"

#37: This is not an altogether inaccurate description.

Unfortunately, it was also not one that Meredith could face with the solemnity and penitence Brian seemed to expect. He made a heroic effort to keep a straight face, but made the mistake of catching David's eye across the room and promptly dissolved into giggles.

"And now you have the audacity to laugh at me!"

Brian seized hold of the nearest object, the jar of paint water on the end table, and threw it full force at Meredith.

Chapter Five

Meredith yelped in surprise as the paint water splashed over him. The jar hit the floor and shattered at his feet.

David stepped between him and Brian, looming magnificently. It was some of his best work; what he'd done across the breakfast table earlier paled in comparison.

"*Out*," he thundered.

Brian shrank back, but, with surprising tenacity, insisted, "I told you, I've come for the rest of my things."

"Then get them," said David, "and get out."

Giving David a wide berth, Brian stomped up the stairs.

"You," David told Meredith, "don't move from that spot. Just keep well out of his way until he's gone."

There didn't seem much danger of him doing otherwise. With an absent frown, he stood rubbing at one wrist and dripping dejectedly.

David sighed. "I'll get you a towel." As he went to fetch it (and found the contents of the linen cupboard piled inexplicably atop the clothes dryer), he reflected that Meredith wouldn't have ended up drenched in his own paint water if he hadn't left it sitting out to begin with.

Still, David couldn't bring himself to say so aloud. (Not just now, anyway. Later, perhaps.)

He returned to find Meredith looking so intolerably forlorn that he tossed the towel into his face and said, "Dry yourself off, you hillbilly harlot."

That got a laugh from him, which somehow returned everything to normal—even if the normal state of affairs was hardly any more satisfactory.

"That was quite unfair, really," said Meredith, attempting to pat himself dry. "One can't help where one's from."

#38: That's *the part he's concerned about.*

"Oh, well," he went on, "at least black won't stain, and I did want to change anyway. This doesn't quite suit the mood anymore, does it?"

#39: If allowed the opportunity, he'll go changing his outfit whenever the urge strikes him.

David retrieved broom and dustpan, shooed Bianca away, and swept up the broken glass. One particularly large and jagged piece had ended up beneath the sofa, and he knelt to reach for it.

"David?"

That pensive note had returned to Meredith's voice—never a good sign, but being otherwise occupied, David attached less importance to it than he might have. "Hmm?"

"I'm not going."

Retrieving the glass shard, David sat back on his heels. "What? Not going where?"

"To the wedding."

David was so astounded that he remained in his crouched position, gaping up at Meredith in disbelief. "I beg your pardon?" Surely he had misunderstood.

"I am not going," Meredith repeated, now attempting to scratch both wrists at once, "to Florian's wedding."

David shot to his feet. "You just said you would, not five minutes ago!"

"I—I've changed my mind."

#40: He is utterly unreliable.

"You *lied*," he accused. "You lied to Genevieve." And to him. Perhaps he'd been quite wrong in his assessment of Meredith after all. David was rarely wrong about such things, and the possibility that he had been annoyed him as much as losing his chance at impressing Maitland Cartier.

"She never would've left otherwise," said Meredith. "And I *didn't* lie. The way you were so—well, I suppose you swayed me, and for a moment I thought perhaps—oh, I don't *know*," he said with a hopeless, flailing gesture.

"You fail to understand the importance of this opportunity. To attend—what is the *matter* with you?" David interrupted himself as Meredith clawed at his own wrists.

"She said I was gay!"

David quite failed to see how one related to the other, but the non sequitur did make it difficult to maintain the proper state of vexation. "What of it?"

"You know I'm allergic to labels," said Meredith reproachfully.

"Nonsense," said David.

"I am, I'm breaking out in hives as we speak, look."

"You're allergic to cats. Did you see her coat? It was covered in enough fur for a half dozen kittens."

"And I'm not gay."

"Well, strictly speaking, no," began David. The business with Mrs. Jupiter—to say nothing of the sycamore dryads—had made that obvious, in case there'd been any doubt, which there hadn't. "I'm certainly not claiming you as one of ours, but it depends, really, how you define—"

Meredith sneezed. "Oh, stop, you're making it worse," he pleaded. "You *know* I'm allergic, you've seen it."

#41: He sincerely believes this.

David, however, was not so convinced. His skepticism must have shown on his face because Meredith insisted, "You have. The first time we went to—oh, I forget the name, that little satyr club that ended up getting shut down by the health department, remember?"

Unfortunately, David did. He'd spent the entire time awkwardly sipping a beer on the sidelines while Meredith danced—neither particularly well nor with any trace of self-consciousness—with whoever caught his eye. The night had ended with him propositioning a rather attractive lumberjack type and subsequently being informed that said lumberjack "didn't do bisexuals," whereupon Meredith, to all appearances entirely unperturbed, had replied that this was perfectly all right because he himself was straight.

Astonishingly, the man had ended up asking him home after all, though David had found himself somehow relieved when Meredith didn't take him up on it.

"Yes, and as I recall, you kissed three different men—"

"*And* two ladies."

"—and two ladies," David agreed, "before telling that bearded fellow you were straight."

Meredith waved a dismissive hand. "Just wanted to throw him off balance a bit, that's all. He deserved it, really. He called me bisexual!"

"Well, yes, but—" *But you are* hung in the air unspoken. "I mean to say, that's hardly an insult."

"It *was*, the way he said it," muttered Meredith darkly. "And I'm allergic to that sort of thing. It gave me hives! You *saw*. Left me all covered in horrible spots like some sort of leper."

"Now, look here, young man, Hansen's disease is quite a serious matter," said David. "And by your logic, you're half to blame yourself, going and calling yourself straight just to prove a point."

Meredith was quiet at that, though whether he was actually giving the matter due consideration or simply sulking was anyone's guess. "All right," he conceded at last, "so I'm not straight."

"Yes, I gathered that."

#42: He acts as if this were not already abundantly clear.

"But I'm not gay, either. And I don't like people going and pinning labels on me, all right?"

"Understood. But—" Here David faltered, trying desperately to regain the thread of whatever conversation Meredith had derailed them from. Right—the wedding, of course. "*But the wedding.* Label-induced or not, a case of hives is no excuse to miss your own brother's wedding. Especially when he's marrying a Cartier."

"Oh, *Cartier,*" said Meredith in exasperation. "Really, David, why don't you—"

He broke off at the sound of footsteps on the stairs, and for once had the sense to keep silent as Brian came stomping back down bearing an overflowing cardboard carton, glared at the two of them, and made his final departure without another word. The moment he was out the door, Meredith darted up the stairs, calling back over his shoulder, "Be back in just a moment."

#43: He is never back in just a moment.

In Meredith's absence, David cleared away the tea things, sent a text message to Harriet to make plans for the afternoon, and formulated several sensible arguments that would make Meredith understand the necessity of attending Adalynn Cartier's wedding.

He'd intended to launch into these the moment Meredith returned, but when he descended the staircase, David could only stare. "What the hell are you wearing?"

"What are you talking about? I wear skirts all the time."

#44: He wears skirts all the time.

#45: The skirt, however, is the least of the problems.

It was houndstooth check, quite short (though he'd had the decency to wear leggings underneath), and clashed hideously with the green argyle sweater he'd chosen to accompany it. The sweater's lower pair of sleeves, useless on him, were tied into a jaunty bow at his waist, which irritated David. (Naturally, Meredith had not bothered to pick up the previous sweater that still hung abandoned over the back of an armchair in plain view.)

"Besides," added Meredith, drifting to the kitchen table to begin the lengthy task of replacing all his jewelry, "the prime minister wears dresses, too."

"Ah, yes," conceded David, "but she came out as a lady last year, so that's a bit different, isn't it?"

"She wore them well before that," returned Meredith. "And anyway, haven't you read Günter Grass? He's got this whole bit about how skirts are masculine, it's hilarious." He paused to consider. "Only it don't work so good in the English."

"Language," admonished David.

"Yeah, in the English language," agreed Meredith, sliding his final ring into place. "'S what I'm telling you."

"Never mind," said David. "You know I couldn't care less about the skirt. But what the hell is that sweater?"

"Do you like it?" Meredith looked far too pleased with himself and turned as if to model the ridiculous garment. "Belinda Fairfax gave it to me."

"Who?"

"Oh, really, David," said Meredith reproachfully. "You met her only last week when you came into the shop." In a conscientiously hushed tone, he added, "She's just moved here from Rhode Island, you know."

"Ah. That explains the sleeves."

"Yeah, I figure it's sort of avant-garde."

"Is it."

Meredith grinned, David's sarcasm apparently lost on him. "Yeah! Kinley says this sort of thing is about to be in. Not that I mind either way, really."

#46: He never minds about anything.

Kinley was one McKinley Hendricks, Meredith's best friend and the owner of the only other tattoo shop in town. By all rights, they should have been rivals, but as they specialized in different styles, the issue had failed to arise.

"And anyway," Meredith went on, "it's not as if you've got room to talk, the way you go around with them funny fisherman sweaters all the time."

"There is nothing humorous about Gansey knits," said David severely, possibly due to the fact that he was currently wearing one in a tasteful and flattering shade of charcoal gray. "They are a classic style from a rich cultural tradition, and furthermore—" He stopped, realizing he'd allowed himself to become badly sidetracked.

Meredith, now wrapping several slices of cake, said, "I'll take some of this down to Mrs. J. With only the two of us in the house now, we're never going to finish it ourselves. Come along, Bianca."

David suspected this to be a ploy to avoid the conversation altogether, but he was not so easily deterred. Pulling on his heavy woolen peacoat, he followed Meredith and Bianca out of the cottage as they started down the hill; during the past hour, the sky had clouded over and the wind picked up a slight bite, a last reminder of winter. "*About the wedding.*"

"I'm not going," said Meredith placidly.

"Listen to me," growled David. "In all the time we've lived together, I've never asked you for a single thing except to pay your share of the rent on time. I am asking you for this now. Consider it a favor, if you like."

"You ask me for all sorts of things," objected Meredith. Deepening his voice in imitation of David and putting on what could only be called a travesty of a Welsh accent, he went on, "*Meri, put the kettle on. Meri, quit leaving your clothes lying around everywhere. Meri, clean up those ink stains before I have your head on a platter.*"

"Why've you given me that ridiculous accent?" demanded David. He'd left Wales for Washington state with his parents at age nine, and he most assuredly had no such accent.

"That's what you sound like."

"That is *not* what I sound like," said David, "and I have certainly never called you—look, none of this is the point."

Meredith stopped abruptly on the footpath, forcing David to stumble in order to avoid trampling Bianca. "What is the point, David?"

David took a deep breath, quieting the slow-simmering anger that had been building inside him all morning. Why Meredith had to be such a difficult person, he didn't know.

"The point," said David, "as I have already explained, is to speak with Maitland Cartier."

"If you want to speak with him so bad, why not just go to his office and schedule an appointment?"

"Ah, but it's not that simple," said David. "Mr. Cartier is a busy man. It's not as if he personally oversees the Corner Store. And seeing him in the context of a social occasion—in the casual, relaxed, dare I say *joyous* atmosphere of his daughter's wedding—is a different thing altogether."

"You mean you want him to take notice of you."

It sounded a bit pathetic and embarrassing, put like that, but there was certainly no harm in ensuring that he was top of mind for Cartier when he began the search for a replacement finance VP. "I want to work for him," he corrected.

"But you already work for him."

"Not directly. There's a difference."

Meredith folded his arms, failing to look the least bit convinced. "I know, Bianca, it's sad, isn't it? He really doesn't know how to switch off business mode." He started down the path once more.

"Listen." David tried another approach. "Mr. Cartier is a well-known patron of the arts. As your soon-to-be uncle-in-law"—he was not at all sure if that was the proper relation—"he'd be kindly disposed toward you, perhaps inclined to finance a venture such as opening your own shop."

"I don't want my own shop," objected Meredith. "I'm happy enough working for Thao at the Lost & Found, and if I wasn't, I'd go and work for Kinley. I mean, think of all the paperwork, can you imagine?"

"You've simply no head for business." David intended that as a criticism, but Meredith didn't take his meaning at all.

"No, I haven't," he agreed. "You know that, you've just done my taxes."

"Yes, and your recordkeeping is abysmal."

"Yeah."

"You let half your customers pay you in Canadian francs!"

Meredith shrugged. "What can I say? The Canadians flock to me."

"They think you're one of their own," David agreed, and realized once more they'd gotten entirely off topic. "*The Canadians are not the issue.*"

"Oh, speaking of—" began Meredith.

Speaking of what, David had entirely lost track at this point.

"—you're going to kill me again—"

"Again? You'd have been killed several times over by now if I had my way."

Meredith only giggled at that. "Yeah, I know, only I've forgotten what you want written down if I don't charge somebody."

David groaned. "Just materials, but it hardly amounts to anything since you can't deduct—never mind." Explaining the specifics would do no good. "Don't tell me you've gone and done it again."

"This guy needed a cover-up," said Meredith, as if that made it perfectly acceptable not to bill for his time.

"So what?" David failed to see how that was anyone's problem but the client's own. "Tell him to come back when he can pay like everyone else."

"Nah, I mean, he *really* needed a cover-up."

For once, there was no trace of amusement in Meredith's expression; David's curiosity was piqued in spite of himself. "What of?"

"Some old Nazi shit." Then, bouncing back to his usual mindless good cheer, he said, "Perhaps Mrs. J will let us see the new kittens."

#47: He can go from taxes to Nazis to kittens in the span of sixty seconds without batting an eye.

"Now, you may not want to get your hopes up there," David cautioned. "From the sound of it earlier, things may not have gone well."

"Oh, I know, one mustn't go counting one's kittens before they've hatched," said Meredith, "but Mrs. J will make sure they're all right, no question of that."

David himself wasn't so sure, especially when their knock at her front door went unanswered.

"That's all right, she'll be back soon enough." Meredith slipped the wrapped cake into the hanging basket on the witch's front door. "Well, I expect you've got something or other you'll be wanting to get back to, but it's such lovely weather out, I feel like a walk myself. In the Wood," he added pointedly.

The weather was not lovely at all, and even if it had been, this was a transparent effort to get rid of him. Under ordinary circumstances, David wouldn't be willing to venture into the Midnight Wood a second time in one day—it was hardly the sort of place where any sensible person went for a leisurely stroll—but he was determined to settle this matter for good. The two of them were going to Adalynn Cartier's wedding, one way or another.

"Wonderful," said David, "that's just where I was planning to go myself."

Chapter Six

David walked side by side with Meredith through the dark forest, feigning as much appreciation of their surroundings as he was able. In fact, he told himself, it really wasn't so bad after all. Stars twinkled here and there through the dense canopy of foliage, and it didn't take long before his vision adjusted to the gloom.

On the other hand, he had no idea where they were going, and the landscape looked nothing like it had only a few hours before. The silence between them held an awkward, brittle quality that only seemed to intensify the longer it went on.

Very well, David would be the one to break it.

They'd reached the bank of a creek, and Bianca splashed through the clear shallow water. As Meredith searched for a narrower spot to cross, David began, "Look, I just think—"

"Bianca, wait!" called Meredith. When the Chihuahua darted ahead into the underbrush, he hopped over to the opposite bank after her, and David followed, crossing the water in a single stride.

"Bianca, really, you mustn't—*oh!*" Meredith cried in dismay. "Oh, *no*."

David reached him as he sank down to crouch on the forest floor. "What is it?"

Meredith looked up at him, eyes shining with tears. "Oh, *David*, look."

On the mossy ground in front of him lay a small white mouse, quite dead.

"It's only a mouse." David meant the words to sound comforting. They didn't.

"It's a Midnight Mouse." Meredith's voice trembled. "They're an endangered species, you know."

"Ah. I hadn't realized."

"They keep the time here," he explained. "Without the Midnight Mice making their rounds, the clock would go all wrong."

In David's opinion, the clock was already all wrong, time not proceeding in an orderly fashion at all, but it seemed in poor taste to say so just now.

He made another attempt at consolation. "These things happen. Nature. Cycle of life and all that."

"We ought to bury her."

"Don't you dare," said David. "We haven't got a shovel, and the last thing you need is to pick up some disease off a dead rat." Surreptitiously shifting his weight to one foot, he stretched the opposite ankle in an effort to dispel the faint ache that often accompanied rainy weather—the result of an old sporting injury.

"Suppose not." Meredith rose to his feet, plucked a large frond from a nearby fern, and pressed it into David's hand. "Help me find a few more of these, would you?"

Resigning himself, David half-heartedly collected a handful of fronds while Meredith picked an assortment of stolen-breath and vicar's shame and the odd white violet. Once he'd fashioned them into a ragtag bouquet, he took the fronds from David and knelt once more.

"Oh, now, is this really necessary?" asked David.

Taking no notice, Meredith arranged the ferns with care to cover the mouse and laid his collection of flowers before the makeshift grave.

"Do you want to say anything?" he asked.

David shook his head; he'd already contributed more than enough to this travesty. All he'd wanted was to spend his Saturday morning with a cup of tea and the paper, and now here he was, however unwillingly, standing vigil over a dead mouse.

#48: He insists upon holding an impromptu funeral for a rodent.

"One feels one ought to," said Meredith apologetically, "only I don't know any prayers. No, all right, I've got something."

David half expected Meredith's idea of a funeral oration to involve Bauhaus lyrics, and very nearly said so, but just managed to hold himself back.

Instead, Meredith recited:

"Die Vögelein schweigen im Walde.
Warte nur, balde
Ruhest du auch."

He spoke the lines with such solemnity that an unexpected stab of shame lanced through David's gut, and he was glad he hadn't voiced his thoughts aloud.

As Meredith knelt, head bowed, David relented and rested a hand on his shoulder. "There, it's all right," he said softly. "Come on. You've done the best you can."

Meredith stood, and for a moment, the two walked along in silence.

"I didn't realize you knew so much German," David said at last.

"I don't really," said Meredith. "Just bits of song and poetry and the like. That one they read at my grandfather's funeral."

David recalled Genevieve's words: *I haven't seen your face at a family gathering since Grandpa died.* This could be the opening he needed, but he had to tread carefully. "How long ago was that?"

"Oh, some time," said Meredith vaguely. "Just before you were around, actually."

He fell back into silence as they walked along. (As they made their way over the crest of a hill, David was almost sure he did see a cottage in the distance nestled among the pines.)

"Oh, look, there is some imitation wintergreen yet after all." The dell below was filled with a sea of shiny dark leaves, and Meredith made his way down the gentle incline to kneel at a cluster of plants bearing round white berries.

David leaned against the trunk of a nearby hemlock and reached out to take a handful of berries from Meredith.

"Do you suppose she wanted the whole plant?" he murmured half to himself. "I didn't think to ask. Suppose we'd best take one back just in case."

As he carefully freed the delicate roots of the plant from the loose soil, Meredith surprised David once more by asking, "Do you get on with your family?" As soon as he'd spoken, he waved away the question. "What am I saying, course you do. You go and visit them every Christmas."

"Oh, I suppose so," said David. "About as well as anyone." Truth be told, he didn't have much family. His sister, twelve years older, in Cardiff. A few scattered aunts and uncles seen infrequently at holidays. "My mother passed away when I was still at university, and my father moved back to Swansea not long after." It was not without a pang of guilt that David realized he couldn't recollect the last time he'd actually phoned him.

Meredith stood and rested a hand on David's arm, rubbing his knuckles over his elbow in what David supposed passed for a gesture of comfort, and likely rubbing soil into his coat sleeve as well. "I'm sorry."

Shrugging off both the touch and the sentiment, David said, "It was a long time ago. Why do you ask?"

"Oh, I don't know. I suppose . . ." Meredith trailed off and leaned down to pick a few more imitation wintergreen berries.

David seized upon this opening. "Do you not, then? Get on with *your* family."

"It's not that, exactly."

Perhaps this roundabout approach might get him somewhere. "Go on."

Meredith shrugged. "Nothing to go on about, is there? We're just not close. I do my own thing, they do theirs, that's all." With the toe of his boot, he nudged the disarranged soil back into place.

"What about your brother?"

"Florian?" Meredith drew his sweater closer around him as a biting wind swept through the Wood, rattling branches and making the treetops sway erratically to blot out the stars above. "What about him?"

"Well, for instance, what did he do?"

"Oh, he works in our dad's construction firm. I expect he'll take it over someday, if he hasn't already. We . . . haven't talked much in a while."

Aside from the conversation about the bridal party that might or might not have taken place, but perhaps he wasn't counting that.

"No. I don't mean what does he do for a living," David clarified as they started through the Wood once more. "What *did* he do so that you won't even go to his wedding?" If he could get to the root of the matter, he'd be that much closer to resolving the whole issue. Unless Meredith was simply being contrary for its own sake, in which case—

"It's not—he didn't—" Meredith floundered. "It isn't that he *did* anything exactly, not any one thing in particular, it's just—like Genevieve said. We don't really get along. You know," he went on, apropos of nothing, "it'll be time for the sweet woodruff soon. I want to make some decent May wine this year, last spring's was a bit of a disaster."

#49: Everything he touches is a bit of a disaster.

Not to mention he was clearly avoiding the subject.

"In other words," said David, "you've no good reason for boycotting this wedding."

"I don't want to go," said Meredith. "Isn't that reason enough?"

"In this case, no, it isn't." With a concerted effort, David clamped the lid down on the simmering frustration that now threatened to boil into rage. "It would help me, and it certainly wouldn't do you any harm. It's the least you could do."

"I told you, I won't."

So it was sheer contrariness.

"This is Maitland Cartier we're talking about!"

"Who *cares* about Maitland Cartier? Just because you're a bit in love with some—some CEO or something—"

"How dare you!" The frustration finally boiled over. "I am not in love with Maitland Cartier. I *admire* his work ethic and aspire to join in his entrepreneurial vision," said David in outrage. "*You*, on the other hand, are the most selfish person I have ever met."

"Oh, yeah?" Meredith, too, had acquired a certain viciousness in tone, and though the foolish grin remained in place, there was an unnerving sharpness to it that put David in mind of broken glass. "Am I?"

"You are, as a matter of fact," snapped David. "You never think of anybody but yourself. You're governed by whims and you don't give a thought to the consequences of your actions and you've caused me no end of trouble with your utter *promiscuity*." The low rumble of distant thunder ground across the sky, and something scurried through the nearby undergrowth, but David was too incensed to be worried by it.

"Yeah, all right," said Meredith. The sharp, sneering quality had gained a definite foothold in his expression. "Feel any better?"

"*No*, I do not." David was only getting warmed up. "You leave me to clean up all your messes while you won't lift a finger the one time I ask for your help. You're refusing a perfectly reasonable request with no justification whatsoever, you've got no ambitions, and your taste in music is rubbish. You don't pick up after yourself, you keep leaving all your eyeliner pencils in my bathroom, and your sideburns look *stupid*!"

That succeeded in knocking that sneering smirk off his face. "I—"

David was not to be stopped now. "Do you know what? I understand exactly why you don't want to see your family. Any time you run into trouble, you haven't any recourse that isn't putting on that empty-headed act and charming or fucking your way out of it—"

"Oh!"

"—but you can't do that with them, and you can't do that with me. And by the way, houndstooth doesn't go with argyle!"

There was a rustle overhead, and a fallen pine cone thumped into the loam at David's feet. Then, all at once, rain pelted down, startlingly loud against the canopy of leaves above, though it did shield them from much of the downpour.

"Oh, yeah? Well—well—" Meredith was near furious tears now. "Well, *I don't like your moustache*!" Turning on his heel, he flounced off in the opposite direction, crashing through the underbrush, Bianca bounding along after him.

Very well. If Meredith wanted to be difficult and go storming off alone through the Midnight Wood because he was unwilling to face the truth, so be it. Good riddance. David had plenty of better things to do.

He started back in the direction from which they'd come. For an uneasy moment, he questioned his route in the darkness and rain, but no, there was the patch of imitation wintergreen they'd found—Meredith had hung on to the plant, but David still had a handful of berries in his coat pocket—and here was the creek. Its surface rippled with the odd raindrop, though the initial intensity of the downpour had already abated.

Idly, David bent and took up a small flat piece of shale from the creek bed, turning it over in his hand as he walked along. He didn't need Meredith's help. Not to find his way in the Midnight Wood, and not with Maitland Cartier.

His frustration threatened to bubble up again, and he pushed any thought of Meredith firmly from his mind, replacing it instead with a visualization of his goals: One day, perhaps a month from now, waking up in his own house, alone, and drinking his tea uninterrupted—free of tangerines and unsuitable pattern combinations and Meredith. A few weeks further on, somehow meeting Cartier at his daughter's wedding. Gracefully turning casual conversation into an offer of the VP position at Cartier's head office. Perhaps he'd even have a handsome son of marriageable age whom he'd be eager to introduce him to.

No—Cartier had no son, David knew. A nephew, then. A big, muscular, outdoorsy type who played football and went kayaking and had warm dark eyes—

It occurred to David that he ought to have reached the edge of the Wood by now. Somehow the path he'd been following had quite vanished.

No matter. He'd been heading in the right direction; he was sure of it. He picked up his pace—not because he was by any means uneasy, but because he had important and pressing things to do, regardless of the passage of time here.

Was that a rustle in the nearby trees? A crack of a branch? No, surely his mind playing tricks on him.

"Meredith?" he called.

There was no reply.

David attempted to console himself once more with thoughts of Maitland Cartier and his possibly imaginary nephew, to no avail. Branches whipped at him. Briars caught at his clothing. Tree roots tripped him up in the dark. All the while, rain continued to fall. Realizing he was still holding on to the bit of shale from the creek, David tossed it away.

Instead of the expected rustle of its landing among dry leaves, he was met with a soft *thwack* as though it had just struck the flesh of a living being.

"Meredith?"

Silence.

David looked around wildly, broke into a run, dodged around the broad trunk of an ancient oak, and nearly crashed into a dark figure half hidden in shadow that was very definitely *not* Meredith.

Even if it had been a long time since he'd set foot on a rugby field, David could move fast and turn on a dime when he had to. It served him well now as he took off in the opposite direction. The figure pursued, crashing through the underbrush with a high, cackling laugh that filled David's heart with an icy dread.

David darted between trees, leapt over a fallen log, splashed through a pool of stagnant water. He hoped he was gaining distance, but didn't dare look back, didn't dare stop to think. A tiny flash of white crossed his path, and then, too late, David discovered that the rock beneath his feet was no gradual incline, as he'd thought, but terminated in a sharp drop-off where the opposite end jutted out of the earth.

This time he was not able to stop so quickly. In spite of his best efforts, his boots slid over the mossy surface, and he was falling, grasping in vain at the rock face, at the nearby branches that tore at him as he plunged through them. He landed hard, and something cracked as pain exploded through his arm and shoulder.

The sounds of his pursuer slowed, then seemed to recede into the distance. David groaned and tried to sit up, without success. His head swam, and for a time, he could only lie among the crushed plants and broken branches in a daze.

Then approaching footsteps sounded anew, and his heart sank. He was sure *something* was broken, and he was in no condition to flee, let alone face whatever was coming for him.

"David?" called Meredith.

He groaned again, this time for an entirely different reason.

"*David!*" With a distraught cry, Meredith ran to him, Bianca trotting close behind, and David forced himself to his feet. "Oh, you're hurt. I never meant—"

"It's nothing." David steadied himself against a nearby tree with his good arm and found an awkward posture in which the pain in his shoulder was just bearable. "I'm all right." He was not all right, but he could walk on his own, and admitting it here when there was nothing to be done was unlikely to help matters.

Meredith reached out and brushed a stray lock of hair from David's eyes. "You're bleeding," he said, and made it sound like a reproach. "One of the Mice found me and said you were in trouble."

#50: He talks to mice, or imagines he does.

David leaned back out of Meredith's reach. "Just took a bit of a spill, that's all. Come on, let's get out of here." He started off through the trees in what he hoped was the right direction; it appeared to be since Meredith followed without correcting him.

"She said something was after you," he persisted.

"Of course there wasn't." David didn't want to linger on the figure he'd seen, or, more likely, imagined he'd seen. And imagination it must have been, even if he did feel quite foolish now—the Midnight Wood was known to play tricks on one's mind. "I suppose," he admitted grudgingly, "I just got a bit worked up, being alone in the dark."

"The Wood can do that to you," said Meredith with sympathy. "You sure you're all right?"

"Fine," said David. The concern was surprising, and his anger at their earlier row began to dissolve.

Until Meredith next spoke.

"Give us your coat, then. I'm freezing."

"Schwarzy?" said David thoughtfully.

"Yeah?"

"*Get fucked.*"

Meredith gasped. "Oh! You're so *mean* to me."

"I'm not giving you a thing after the way you've behaved," said David, "and anyway, my arm's broken."

"You just said you were fine!"

"A necessary falsehood, to boost morale."

"My morale does not feel very boosted."

"Yes, clearly, as you shattered the delicate illusion. Come on."

"We'll get Mrs. J to fix you up," said Meredith. "She'll know just what to do. Does it hurt very much?"

"Yes. Stop talking."

Thankfully, he did. Soon the daylight—such as it was—filtered through the trees at the edge of the Wood, and presently they emerged a short distance from Mrs. Jupiter's cottage. Though the sky remained overcast, the rain had faded to a half-hearted drizzle.

Of course there hadn't really been anything after him in the Wood, David told himself firmly. He'd simply been spending far too much time with Meredith, whose wild imagination appeared to be contagious. David had been preoccupied with Pressing Concerns about his future, at the expense of paying proper attention to his surroundings, and had let his nerves get the better of him, that was all.

Just coming down the path beneath identical dark umbrellas were Mr. Bednarek—a pudgy, bald-headed man in a black overcoat, with a face rather like that of a dissolute cherub—and a small, elegant, silver-haired man whom David recognized from his photograph as none other than *the* Maitland Cartier. What he was doing by the Wood, David couldn't guess—perhaps taking the scenic route after visiting the cottage? David had missed his chance there, and there was no one to blame for it except Meredith, for dragging him on this ridiculous outing to begin with.

There was no way he could meet Cartier in this state—coat torn, trousers filthy, bits of dead leaves sticking in his hair, one cheek scratched and bleeding, not to mention the current unnatural position of his shoulder making him look like a shuffling monster out of a horror film.

Perhaps if he hung back in the shadow of the Wood, the two would pass without taking notice of him.

"Aren't you coming?" asked Meredith.

"Wait." David made a grab for him with his good arm, but Meredith eluded him, already starting down the path. "That's him!"

"Who? Oh, *him*," said Meredith, face lighting up in realization. He waved and called out, "Bednarek!"

"What do you think you're doing?" David hissed.

"Helping you meet Cartier like you wanted, what do you think?" asked Meredith, unperturbed.

The landlord turned. "Ah, boys, glad to see you."

As they met on the path, Meredith leaned in to embrace and air-kiss Bednarek and then, to David's horror, Cartier, who looked momentarily taken aback, but allowed it without comment.

#51: He just air-kissed Maitland Cartier without a second thought.

"This is Mr. Cartier," explained Bednarek. "He is dear friend and business associate. I give him the tour. This," he said to Cartier, "is Mr. David—"

"David Carew, sir," he said, ignoring Meredith pulling a face at him and extending a hand weakly despite the tremendous pain. "Delighted to meet you. I admire your work very much."

Cartier smiled and gave him a firm handshake that nearly drove David to his knees. "A pleasure."

"And this," said Bednarek with an expansive gesture, "is our Schwarzy."

"Yeah. Hi."

In the back of his mind, David wondered what it would take to make Meredith introduce himself properly, but this wasn't the time to experiment.

"We shall just be on our way," Bednarek said. "So glad we could all meet, yes."

"Wonderful to meet you in person at last, Mr. Cartier." David ought to say something profound and impressive, but between the pain and meeting his idol, his mind had gone quite blank.

"Nice meeting you, too, Daniel." Maitland Cartier reached over and clapped him on the injured shoulder, and David fainted.

Chapter Seven

As David blinked slowly back into consciousness, he recognized his surroundings as the cozy interior of Mrs. Jupiter's cottage. Copper pots and bunches of dried herbs dangled from the rafters, and the shelves lining the walls were crammed with all manner of books and jars and boxes. Outside the open window, wind chimes tinkled gently in the breeze, and a cauldron bubbled on the hearth, filling the room with a scent very like—but not quite—that of mulled cider.

He was laid out on the chaise longue, a cat purring at his feet. For a moment, he was almost comfortable—and then his initial fuzzy perceptions sharpened into pain. The memory of his last waking moments came flooding back, and a familiar voice faded into his awareness.

"—and I had to go and catch him. You're quite heavy," complained Meredith from the overstuffed armchair, where he was curled up with a cup of tea and a calico cat in his lap. (Though he appeared to be suffering no ill effects from the latter, that proved nothing; David knew for a fact that Mrs. Jupiter put an anti-allergy enchantment on all her cats.)

Wincing, David sat up. "Not everyone can be built like a malnourished eel, you know," he said testily. Perhaps he had gone a bit softer around the edges than he'd been a few years ago, but underneath was still solid muscle.

"Yes, well, we can't all be rugby forwards, either, can we?" returned Meredith.

Mrs. Jupiter cleared her throat, putting an end to their squabbling. "Here you are, Mr. C, drink up." She handed him an oversized cup patterned with large cheerful polka dots, which he instinctively distrusted.

"And this'll fix me up, will it?"

"Oh, go on, David, she's gone to the trouble of making it up for you," Meredith implored. "*Honestly.*"

"Do *you* go drinking anything somebody hands you just because they say so?"

Meredith shrugged. "Yeah, usually."

"I'm afraid it doesn't taste very nice," said Mrs. Jupiter, rummaging among the sundry items on the far shelves, "and it will hurt. But it'll fix your shoulder straightaway."

After due consideration, David drank. It did hurt, nearly as much as the knowledge that he'd utterly humiliated himself in front of Maitland Cartier.

"Thanks," he managed to choke out after his bones had finished healing.

Mrs. Jupiter returned with a green ceramic jar in hand. "The two of you really ought to stick together. It seems you get into no end of trouble when you separate. Here, stay still." She peeled the bandage from David's forehead and smeared a liberal amount of strong-smelling ointment onto his various cuts and scrapes.

It seemed to David that sticking together had been the cause of the trouble to begin with, but, thinking better of contradicting a witch, he confined himself to a wordless huff of dissent.

Mrs. Jupiter's eyebrows rose. "What did happen to you, if I might inquire?"

David shook his head, but Meredith piped up, "There was something after him! The Mice said—"

"It was nothing," interjected David hastily. At Mrs. Jupiter's sharp inquiring look, he went on, perhaps just as much to convince himself of it, "I, er, thought I saw something and lost my head for a moment, but it was just a trick of the light. Or darkness, rather."

Mrs. Jupiter's curious gaze lingered on his face for longer than he liked, but at last she applied the final bit of ointment and said, "There. You'll want to leave that at least an hour, then you'll be as good as new."

With one of those unfair pleading looks, Meredith wordlessly held out his hand to display the nearly imperceptible scratch from the thornbush earlier.

Mrs. Jupiter shook her head in mock exasperation but daubed the excess salve onto his so-called injury. "And thank you both again for bringing back those herbs this morning, by the way."

David had forgotten entirely about the herbs. He wished he could forget about everything else. Still, out of politeness, he asked, "The cat's all right, then?"

"Tabitha has six new kittens," said Meredith with obvious, if inexplicable pride.

"You named her," said David flatly, "didn't you?"

"I did! Tabitha because she's—"

"A tabby," David finished. "Yes. How clever."

#52: He is terrible at naming things.

Meredith deposited the calico cat onto the armchair, moved over to perch on the arm of the chaise longue, and prodded David in the shoulder with one fingertip. "Does it still hurt?"

David stared up at him for a long moment. "Do you suppose that'd help if it did?"

"Oh."

That was all. Just *oh*, just like every time one forced him to confront the logic of his own actions.

#53: Not that it ever seems to do any good.

On the walk back to Midnight Cottage, David fell into a state of melancholy befitting one who had experienced such an ignominious disgrace. Maitland Cartier must think him a fool, a weakling, a joke. It no longer mattered if he attended Adalynn's wedding; nothing could repair the damage done.

Cartier would find some other replacement to bring into his inner circle, someone more competent, more confident, practically perfect and unquestionably better than David in every way. Perhaps Rick Pangolin, the charismatic new head of HR, or, worse yet, Steve Corner himself—no matter whether either one had any qualifications for a finance position.

(Fleetingly, David recalled the final argument he'd had with Charles, his college boyfriend, who'd once told him with a kind of contemptuous pity that David was the most unremarkable man he'd ever met. He'd laughed it off at the time, but perhaps there was a grain of truth to it.)

Now the visions turned to Corner moving into Cartier's headquarters, standing in a spacious office with floor-to-ceiling windows and a distinguished-looking desk of dark polished wood. Cartier joining Corner for weekly business lunches, chuckling over finance in-jokes with him, giving him the occasional fatherly advice. Cartier inviting Corner for a round of golf and introducing him to his very handsome and less-imaginary-by-the-minute nephew who'd just happened to tag along.

Meredith, of course, remained blissfully unaware of David's dismal ruminations. He'd acquired a blue glass bottle from somewhere—presumably Mrs. Jupiter—and, quite enamored of his new possession, occupied himself turning it this way and that in the sunlight, until at last he lost interest. "David?"

David didn't reply, too deep in visions of his future crumbling.

"David." Meredith stopped, and after another couple of steps on autopilot, David did as well, turning to face him.

"What?"

Meredith dropped his gaze to the ground, to his mismatched bootlaces. "I'm sorry about earlier. That was going too far." He looked up to meet David's eyes, and his own were brimming with sincere contrition. "I didn't mean what I said about your moustache."

#54: This is his idea of an apology.

"It doesn't matter now," murmured David hollowly. "It's all over." He turned and continued to trudge up the hill toward home.

Meredith, hurrying to catch up with him, said, with a touch of desperation, "I'll go to the wedding."

"All right," said David. "That's nice." Cartier was probably laughing at him right now, or scrubbing his hands in disgust at having had contact with such a base creature as himself.

"Did you hear me? I said I'll go to the wedding. And you'll come with me."

This time, the words registered, but they brought him none of the triumph they would have an hour ago. David shook his head. "It doesn't matter anymore," he repeated. "There's no coming back from this. He's lost all respect for me."

Meredith frowned. "I don't think it's as bad as all that."

As much as David dreaded knowing, he had to ask. "What did happen, when I, er—"

"Fainted? Nothing really. I caught you somehow, and then me and Bednarek dragged you into Mrs. J's."

David pressed his hands to his face and steeled himself for the worst. "And Mr. Cartier? What did he say?"

"Not a word," Meredith reassured him. "Just stood there looking a bit awkward about the whole thing, and then Bednarek hustled him off as soon as he could."

David couldn't stop a groan escaping his throat. "Why couldn't you have just let things be?"

"I was trying to help. I—I'm sorry," Meredith faltered. Linking his arm through David's, he leaned in to rest his head against his newly healed shoulder as they proceeded up the hill. "I'll make it up to you, I mean it. We'll go to Florian's wedding, and I'll see you get to talk to Cartier like you wanted. It might not be my idea of a good time, but I'll live."

David gave a grudging hum of acknowledgment. It might not be enough to repair the disastrous first impression he'd made, but it could be a start. He ought, he supposed, to apologize for his own remarks as well. Granted, they were mostly true, but he had gone a bit far in the way he'd said it. Perhaps there was something in all those rumors about the effects of the Midnight Wood. David considered himself a clearheaded and rational man, but that had not been, he had to admit, the behavior of one.

Before he could, however, Meredith jumped to a new topic. Brightening up considerably, he asked, "Did you see what Mrs. J gave me? Look!" He held up the blue bottle—upon closer inspection, in fact an old-fashioned vinegar cruet.

"Wonderful," said David. "One more bit of sparkling junk to collect dust."

"Oh! That's unkind," said Meredith. "Mrs. J doesn't give out junk. And it's magic, too."

"Is it."

"Yeah! She says if you fill it up and leave it sit for a fortnight, it'll make pipe-cleaning solution, I think. Or was it grenadine? Or a potion for disintegrating . . . spheres?" he said uncertainly. "Well, anyway, suppose I didn't quite catch that part, but it is a pretty bottle, isn't it?"

David had no opinion one way or another on the aesthetics of the thing, though he must admit to a touch of misgiving at the idea of

Meredith being entrusted with such an item. Then again, none of its purported functions seemed particularly dangerous—or, for that matter, particularly plausible—and chances were that Meredith would forget its existence the moment it was out of his sight anyway.

"—AND HE *DECOUPAGED* the shelves of the linen cupboard, can you believe it?" David demanded. "Do you know how long that takes to dry? And then—"

Harriet Albert held up an arresting hand over her half-finished coffee. "Stop. You are *so* obsessed." She and David had been good friends for years, ever since meeting in their university's finance club, and when she'd moved across the country for a job offer in Cleveland, he'd eventually followed. They still made time to catch up regularly, though their face-to-face meetings had become less frequent over the past few years.

"I am not obsessed," said David. "And anyway, the man doesn't allow anything else. He's like a—like a Christmas tree covered in baubles and twinkle lights that's *also on fire*. It demands attention. One can't look away. Only this particular Christmas tree stands there going, *Ooh, don't these flames sparkle so nice on my tinsel.*"

Harriet's eyebrows rose until they were hidden by her wispy black bangs. "You seriously need to get out of there. Or get out more in general. It sounds like the two of you get stuck in your own little world."

"He's always in his own little world," lamented David, lifting his coffee mug halfway before setting it back down, "and is constantly trying to pull everybody else into it."

"Of course," Harriet suggested, eyes twinkling, "you could just sleep with him already and get it out of your system."

David's jaw dropped. "Excuse me? I do *not* want to sleep with him." He understood why people did, he supposed. Meredith wasn't unattractive, if one's tastes ran that way—which David's didn't, and neither did he go in for one-night stands.

"We are talking about the same guy, right? The blondish goth Canadian?"

"That's the one." David recalled now; Harriet had once met him briefly when she'd visited Midnight Cottage the summer before. "He isn't, by the way. Canadian, I mean."

A dreamy expression came over Harriet's face as she sipped her coffee. "You could do a lot worse, you know."

"Excuse me? Since when are you interested in men?"

"I'm not interested," she protested. "I'm just making an observation."

David pointed a warning finger at her. "Don't you even think about it." The last thing he needed was for Meredith to go seducing his best friend, or vice versa. "And in any case, in spite of what you seem to believe, I have never once felt the slightest romantic or sexual inclination toward that—that absurd, jangling, brainless little walking disaster."

"Ob*sessed*," whispered Harriet, and laughed at his sour expression. "Okay, okay, that's the last you'll hear of it from me. Here's what you really came for." She took a business card from her handbag and slid it across the table. "Leonard Flood, my real estate agent. Go ahead and give him a call."

"Thanks." That was exactly what David needed to get himself out of Midnight Cottage, even if he would keep his plans to himself on that front for the time being. Just until the moment was right to break the news, he told himself. It was too soon after the business with Brian, and he could ill afford to jeopardize his still-precarious invitation to Adalynn Cartier's wedding.

When David returned to Midnight Cottage, a late-model diesel pickup sat parked alongside David's own cargo van and Meredith's ancient

Cadillac, both rarely driven. Though the truck was spattered with mud, its new paint gleamed, and the bed was outfitted with a well-maintained toolbox and ladder rack. Another workman summoned by Bednarek, no doubt.

Perhaps this was the long-anticipated return of the plumber who'd come to see to a minor leak in the upstairs bath the previous week. He had rendered the facilities entirely unusable, left under the pretext of obtaining the proper alchemical solution, and failed to return that day or any other. (Plumbing repairs of the ordinary variety were already well beyond David's area of expertise, and adding magic into the mix only reinforced his conviction that it was a job best left to professionals.)

Or perhaps someone for the exterior repairs—the deck was still in need of repainting, and David was not so sure the treacle wasps had been entirely eradicated.

He made his way around back to check whether any further repairs were in progress. He found the deck itself unoccupied, but the sliding doors stood open, the faded gingham curtains billowing in the chilly breeze—undoubtedly Meredith's doing.

#55: He's always going and leaving windows open no matter how unsuitable the weather.

As David crossed the deck, voices carried from inside. The television? No, a real conversation. His curiosity piqued, he lightened his step as he approached the open door. He didn't, of course, intend to eavesdrop, although he was curious.

It was a man's voice, one he didn't recognize, and speaking rather forcefully, though David could make out only a few snatches of conversation: ". . . *wanted* you involved . . . Genevieve . . . screw this up for me."

Meredith's reply camc low and indistinct.

David was on the verge of opening the door properly and stepping inside when Bianca began to bark furiously. He froze, but not in time to stop a floorboard from creaking beneath his foot.

"David?" called Meredith, and his tone was so strange that it gave David pause. No, this was not a conversation he was meant to have overheard, and, suddenly well aware of the mistaken impression one might get from his current position, he silently backed away from the door and off the deck.

David hurried back around to enter through the front door and made sure to close it loudly and obviously behind him.

"Meredith?" he called as he stepped into the living room, knowing full well he'd find him there. He had, in David's absence, changed yet again, this time back into the striped sweater of the morning, which appeared to be his current favorite, not that David took deliberate notice of such things. In any case, he was more interested in the stranger standing next to him a suntanned, straw blond man with a neatly trimmed beard and a well-worn flannel shirt, a weathered ball cap in his hand.

"Oh. Hello," said David. "Pardon me for interrupting."

"Hey, no worries," said the blond man with an easy smile. "I was just on my way out."

When Meredith made no move to provide introductions—

#56: He never introduces other people properly, either.

—the stranger admonished, "Aren't you going to introduce your friend?" Extending a hand, he said, "Florian Schwarzwelder."

David rather admired how Florian was able to take a firm approach with Meredith, though of course he'd had far more practice.

"'S my roommate," muttered Meredith sullenly, "David."

"David Carew," said David.

Florian had a strong handshake and a rather nice smile. He was quite handsome, actually, though certainly neither available nor interested. He was taller than Meredith, though not by much, and while the brothers were of a similarly slim build, Florian had some obvious muscle. There was a difference, too, in the face; Florian's narrower features lent something of the sly and fox-like to his expression—if one were of a fanciful temperament, which David certainly was not.

"So you've been keeping my little brother in line, huh?" said Florian with a laugh.

David managed a laugh as well, because he was supposed to, but internally he quite despaired at this. "Ah, well, I try."

#57: Nobody can keep him in line.

"Congratulations, by the way," said David. Managing to sound as if he were only casually aware of the fact, he added, "I hear you're getting married."

"Heh. Thanks." Florian's cheeks flushed as he rubbed the back of his neck. "Anyhow, I'd better get going. It don't pay to stand around talking." Putting his hat back on, he pointed a finger at his brother. "Saturday, don't forget."

Meredith made a vague sound of acknowledgment. Florian appeared satisfied with this and nodded to David. "See you around, Dave."

With that, he made his exit.

"What's Saturday?" asked David as soon as the door had fallen closed. "And what are you doing home? I thought you said you were working tonight."

"Oh, yes," murmured Meredith vaguely. "I *had* someone booked for a long session, but they've gone and rescheduled for Tuesday and I've had to rearrange everything. S'pose I could've gone in anyway, but . . ." He made a listless half gesture approaching a shrug and drifted back to his usual spot in the window, sitting on the bench seat properly for once, feet on the floor. Bianca emerged from beneath an armchair to nose at his ankles with a whine, but he appeared lost in his own world, gazing down at his hands and twisting one of his rings, a bit of green sea glass entwined in decorative wire.

"They say a magpie in the window foretells death, you know."

"Hmm?" said Meredith absently, and then, with an effort, turned to David. "What?"

"Death," repeated David.

"I *heard* you," said Meredith. "Where's a magpie?"

"You, you're a great big magpie with your stripes and sparkles."

"Oh." He considered a moment. "But, David, I haven't got wings."

"The wings are incidental. Can't you grasp metaphor?"

"Not really, no."

Harriet had been right, David decided. About him needing to leave Midnight Cottage as soon as possible. Most assuredly not in her other suggestion.

Meredith drifted off in thought once more and leaned back against the windowpane, but straightened up at once with a wince. "Do you feel like a cup of tea?"

David had meant to retreat to his room to look through some house listings, but Florian's appearance—surely on wedding business—had bolstered his spirits and seemed to have straightened out Meredith quite a bit, which *also* bolstered his spirits. "Oh, I suppose I could spare the time for a quick cup."

When Meredith only continued to stare blankly at the wall, David scowled and said, "Suppose *I'll* put the kettle on, then."

As he waited for the tea to steep, it occurred to him that he hadn't previously put much thought into what sort of person Florian might be. Had he done so, he would've expected someone much more like Meredith, not anyone so normal and sensible. He wondered fleetingly, and not for the first time, exactly how one ended up with a person like Meredith Schwarzwelder.

Not immune to a bit of introspection, David took stock of his reflection in the door of the microwave oven and magnanimously gave due thought to Meredith's earlier criticism. No, he decided, there was nothing the matter with his moustache. Meredith had simply been in one of his moods.

David carried two cups of tea back to the living room and handed one to Meredith, who spent a moment staring right through David in the most unnerving manner before finally accepting it.

"You shaved," said David in surprise, only now taking a proper look at him for the first time since arriving home. The offensive sideburns were gone; without them, he looked younger, softer.

"I didn't mean—" David began, but Meredith waved a dismissing hand.

"Nah, you were right. The look didn't suit me."

It hadn't, but David couldn't help but feel a twinge of guilt. Searching for a new topic, he remarked, "It's funny how you and Genevieve look more alike than you and your brother."

"Oh, yes. We take after our mothers' side," said Meredith, gazing into the depths of his teacup. "Florian favors our dad."

"I see," said David, and asked again, "What's Saturday?"

"Adalynn's coming to take me shopping." Meredith raised his teacup, didn't drink from it, and lowered it with a frown of confusion. "Got to match the others, you know."

David brightened further still. "So you are going to be a groomsman, then."

"S'pose so," murmured Meredith, and then, looking up at David, confirmed, "Yes. I thought you'd be pleased."

"Naturally," said David. "Naturally. Very right and proper."

"Yeah," echoed Meredith, frown lines still etched between his eyebrows. "Right and proper."

Chapter Eight

On Monday morning, the note on the kitchen table read:

Went out early for an appointment. Bednarek says, there's somebody coming later to look at the room. But she's a psychic, so don't worry about the time, she'll stop by when we're both here.

Love, Meri

P.S. There's risotto in the fridge.

P.P.S. Don't worry about the light bulbs.

David put the light bulbs firmly out of mind and went to work. He'd had a mercifully quiet Sunday: Meredith had shut himself in his room upstairs, evidently seized by artistic inspiration, while David had had quite the encouraging meeting with Leonard Flood, a most sensible and professional man, and had managed nearly the entire time to avoid staring at his tentacles.

Now, in his office on the topmost floor of the Corner Store, David surreptitiously browsed real estate listings, emailed a few of the likelier possibilities to Mr. Flood, and checked the Cartier Property Investments website for updated job postings. He scrolled wistfully through the shared guest list for the auction, briefly considered the odds of getting away with adding his own name to the VIP section, and discovered that he had only viewing access to the document. He drank a cup of tea, responded to an accounting meme sent to him by Harriet, and took a walk through the furniture department to contemplate the potential decor of his future living space. (He made particular note of the enchanted self-alphabetizing bookshelves—a practical choice, and far preferable to the disorganized state of the shelves in his living room now.) He had a brief inconsequential conversation in the break room with Rick Pangolin from HR and made a second cup of tea.

At that point, David resigned himself to returning to his office and completing some actual work, which consisted chiefly of reviewing expenditures for the Corner Store's upcoming centennial celebration. That kept him occupied until he received a phone call from Mr. Bednarek in the early afternoon.

"Mr. David! I have for you excellent news," proclaimed the landlord.

"Is that so?" asked David, one eye on his email as he refreshed his inbox.

"Indeed! I make arrangements, the plumber comes tomorrow."

"That is good news," agreed David. Though the weekend had had its share of hiccups, things were looking up now. In fact, successes were rolling in one after the other—an email appeared from Leonard Flood, confirming not one but two house viewings for the following day. Then a less promising possibility occurred to him. "That would be the same plumber who was out last week, or . . . ?"

"That one?" The landlord's tone darkened. "Never! I desire no further dealings with that incompetent ass clown."

"I see Meredith has been helping you with your English again, has he?"

#58: He is unmistakably the source of the more colorful additions to the landlord's vocabulary.

"He is nice boy, no?" said Bednarek fondly. David could partially see his beaming expression on the other end of the telephone. "But I call new plumber, all will be well, I assure you."

"Right," said David, though he still had his doubts.

"Unfortunately, I am called away on another matter," said Mr. Bednarek. "I do not wish to impose, but perhaps is possible that you arrange to work from home in the morning, yes?"

"Not a problem, Mr. Bednarek. It's Dan Quayle Day tomorrow, the office is closed."

"Ah, yes, your charming American holidays," enthused the landlord. "Wonderful!"

At half past three, David went for a late lunch at the Corner Café in the annex off the lobby. Over coffee and a sandwich, he was perusing a print copy of local real estate listings when, suddenly, a pair of hands descended over his eyes from behind.

Even without the metallic click of rings, he would've known it was Meredith.

#59: Because nobody else in the world would find this the least bit amusing.

"Get off," David growled, swatting his hands away. For a moment, he feared that Meredith would catch sight of his reading material, but a hasty attempt at concealment would only serve to draw attention. As it turned out, Meredith didn't so much as spare a glance at the pages; instead, he giggled and gave David a peck on the cheek before slipping into the seat opposite him. He seemed to have bounced back from the weekend's fit of melancholy and was right back to his usual insufferable self.

"Must you do that?"

"Oh, do you mind?" asked Meredith with a troubled look. "I didn't think—"

#60: He never thinks.

"It isn't—it's just—" David paused. It wasn't that he objected to affection from a—he balked at the word *friend*, but certainly a housemate of five years fell into that category for lack of a better term. It wasn't that he minded if anyone thought he was gay, either, since he *was* gay, even if people often didn't realize. He did, however, mind the idea of someone thinking that he and Meredith were together, but couldn't at the moment find a way to say so that wouldn't sound extraordinarily unkind. Instead, he settled on asking, "What are you doing here?"

"Well, you see, I just got back to town a bit ago and went to Two Way to see Kinley, only Luisa said—"

David tuned out the rambling story as he finished his lunch and refrained from expressing his disapproval of McKinley Hendricks. Eventually, his gaze traveled from his coffee cup to Meredith, who today wore an outfit of nondescript black beneath a men's tweed overcoat that would nearly have qualified as respectable had it not been two sizes too large and several decades out of fashion, and adorned with a haphazard collection of pins and brooches.

"—then I spotted you in the window here and thought I'd stop in for a cup of coffee."

"I see." David glanced at his watch. To his dismay, he still had another quarter of an hour before he had to return to his office. Then Meredith's half-heard words caught up with him. "Wait, what do you mean, back to town? Back from where?"

Perhaps David wasn't the only one engaging in some surreptitious house hunting. Of course it would be just like Meredith to go behind his back like that.

"Oh, didn't I say? Went to see *my* artist in Cleveland and got a new piece done. Really," he mused, "shame there's nobody around here as good as me, but Imani does come close."

#61: At times, his arrogance is staggering.

Still, David did have to admit, from his limited knowledge—as he had no tattoos himself, nor did he wish to—Meredith was quite good, and certainly in demand. As Bingham Junction's self-proclaimed leading practitioner of black-and-gray, it only made sense he'd have to go out of town to find someone else he deemed proficient in the same style. (Kinley specialized in traditional, as David had learned via a long and incoherent lecture after making the mistake of admitting his own ignorance as to the difference.)

"Do you want to see what I got done?" asked Meredith.

"Certainly not," said David. As Meredith already had both arms fully tattooed, decency precluded the public display of any other possibility, or would have, if he'd had the least sense of decency. "Anyway, I won't keep you from your coffee. I've got to be getting back," David added untruthfully.

Meredith rose up on his knees to peer over the back of the booth like a meerkat, surveying the front counter. "Never mind, the line's a mile long," he reported, sinking back into his seat. "I haven't got time for that."

Before David could reply, Meredith's phone chimed with a new notification, and he slumped forward onto his elbows in exaggerated defeat. "Oh, kill me *dead*, not another one."

"Another of what?"

Meredith sighed. "You remember Ed?"

"Who?"

"That guy last week I told you about."

"How should I remember what you told me last week?" asked David. "You tell me all sorts of things, all the time, whether I want you to or not."

"No, no, the guy—Ed—*he* was last week," said Meredith, "but I *told* you the other day. The one with the cover-up."

"Oh, yes. What about him?"

"Well, you see," said Meredith, taking up his coffee cup and gesturing with it in a dangerously careless fashion, "a few days ago he went and posted before and after photos online, and wrote this whole thing to go along with it about turning his life around." He took a sip of coffee and grimaced, at which point David realized that Meredith had never had a cup of his own to begin with and snatched it back from him.

"Do you *mind*?"

Taking no notice, Meredith went on, "Only, he tagged me in it, and now it seems the whole thing's gone a bit viral. I've had bookings pouring in left and right since yesterday. And a bit of hate mail, of course, but we're not bothered about that."

"So you've gotten some free advertising." David failed to see much of a drawback there. "Why not sit back and enjoy your fifteen minutes of fame?"

"My inbox is a disaster, look." Meredith held up his phone and scrolled through his messages. "Appointment, appointment, *die race traitor*—lovely—another appointment—oh, goodness, *that* isn't the sort of photo you send to someone you've never met." Nevertheless, his eyes lingered for a moment before he closed the image.

David drained what was left of his coffee. "That's hardly the—I'm sorry, did you say *race traitor*?"

Meredith sighed and dropped his phone to the table with a clatter. He tipped his head back to stare at the ceiling, and then, straightening up, he asked wearily, "You've not spent much time around neo-Nazis, have you, David?"

"What? Of course not!" said David in indignation. "What sort of question is that?"

"No, I mean, you don't know how these types think. Me doing what I did is a political statement whether I want it to be or not. I wasn't trying—I mean, I didn't want—oh, it doesn't matter." Meredith ran a hand through his hair, getting his rings caught as usual.

As he disentangled himself, David said slowly, "You didn't want attention from it."

"I expect my profile picture doesn't help, either," added Meredith.

David frowned in confusion. "But it's just that photo I took last summer of you and Kinley at—oh. *Oh.*"

Kinley sitting on a park bench, Meredith leaning in to wrap his arms around him from behind, chin resting on his shoulder. Meredith gazing at him in adoration, Kinley returning a sideways look of mock exasperation. A moment of affection between two best friends, who happened to be a few shades apart in skin color.

"Yeah," said Meredith. "And I ain't about to change it, either."

"No, of course not."

"Anyway, enough of that." Meredith managed a wan smile. "S'pose you've got to be getting back, but I'll walk over with you. Wouldn't mind doing a bit of shopping now that I'm here."

They crossed the lobby and emerged onto the sales floor proper, through which one had to pass in order to reach the back stairway to the upper offices. By the time they made it to the cosmetics counter, Meredith had brightened up again and was back to chattering away about nothing of consequence as they progressed into the men's department.

Perhaps, David thought, he could make his escape if he dodged past the pair of warlocks examining a selection of handkerchiefs, or perhaps if he managed to tunnel through that sale rack of winter coats—

No, the whole thing was likely to collapse on him if he tried that. He envisioned himself buried beneath an avalanche of outerwear, slowly suffocating under a heap of duffel coats and Alpine hats.

Then again, that might be the preferable alternative.

When Meredith abruptly fell silent, David first thought he'd missed his cue to reply—but no, Meredith's attention had merely drifted. David followed his wistful gaze to the mezzanine where ladies' formalwear was displayed—in particular, to the mannequin modeling a floor-length gown in emerald green.

"You can't be serious." While David took no issue with that particular aspect of his housemate's unconventional fashion sense, he had no intention of sanctioning his proclivity toward excess and impracticality; those, he considered fair game. "Where would you ever have the need to wear an evening gown?"

"Ah, well, s'pose you're right, it'd be a waste. Although," Meredith mused, "perhaps something more like that little number over there with the daring neckline in the back, what do you think?"

"Schwarzy!" Steve Corner's strident voice broke into the conversation as he hurried over to them. "Carew," he added with considerably less enthusiasm.

As glad as David was of the interruption, he couldn't find it in himself to be glad that it came courtesy of the store manager.

Steve Corner was a man of average height and average build, unremarkable in both features and manner aside from a grating voice and a tendency to talk in ad copy. There was something indefinably unpleasant about the glittering hardness of his eyes and the way they tended to linger—particularly on people such as Paulette from IT and Minh from the perfume counter. David couldn't stand him, and he suspected the feeling was mutual.

"Hi, Steve." Meredith air-kissed him, and David scowled.

"I didn't realize the two of you knew each other," he said. But of course Meredith knew everyone, and everyone knew him, if as nothing more than a local eccentric.

Meredith leaned back against a rack of parkas, draping one arm over it. The position lifted the hem of his shirt, and Corner's eyes drifted downward to the exposed sliver of pale skin. David suppressed the urge to reach over and adjust it for him.

"Actually," said Corner, "you are just the . . . thing I wanted to see."

Instead of taking offense, Meredith only giggled at that. "Oh, yeah?"

"I expect Carew's told you about our silent auction coming up?"

"No, not a word!"

#62: He has been told about it on no fewer than three separate occasions over the past week.

"You don't say." Corner narrowed his eyes at David, who glared right back. "Well, as it happens, our annual charity auction is the week after next, and since this is our centennial anniversary, we're going all out this year."

"Is that so?" asked Meredith politely.

Corner nodded. "The auction is the kickoff for a month of celebratory events commemorating the founding of the Corner Store by Josiah Corner a century ago. It's quite the exclusive affair."

David marveled at the man's ability to sound exactly like a promotional pamphlet. While it was true that the auction was invitation only, anyone who made a suitable donation *was* invited, whether said donation took the form of an outright monetary contribution or goods to be auctioned. David's attendance was already secured, but it occurred to him that if he could solicit a donation from Meredith, perhaps that would be sufficient to gain him admission to the VIP lounge. Clearly Corner was angling for the same thing (that and a fair bit more, David suspected, if those suggestive glances were anything to go by), but if he could beat Corner to it—well, surely the initiative had to count for something.

"Speaking of the auction," David began, "we are still accepting—"

"Yes, thank you, Carew," interrupted Corner. "That's just what I was getting at myself."

David forced a smile, but inwardly he was seething. This should have been *his* chance, and Meredith was *his* housemate. Still, David attempted to console himself, perhaps that association might be enough for Meredith's inevitable agreement to count as a point in his favor after all.

"We're seeking donations from local merchants and artists," Corner continued. "Paintings, pottery, gift vouchers, what have you. If you could see your way to offering, say, a free session—"

"I could—" Meredith paused, sending a searching glance at David. Apparently having taken to heart the recent scolding on the subject of his wanton philanthropy, Meredith amended, "I *couldn't*, but if you're looking for artwork, I've a handful of drawings I could part with, so long as you don't mind if they're not framed."

David tried not to grimace. Meredith's artwork was, charitably, something of an acquired taste, as Corner—and everyone else in attendance at the auction—would soon find out.

"Spectacular!" said Corner. "I knew you'd come through for us. Trust me, you won't regret it—our silent auction is northeast Ohio's event of the season."

"Course it is," said Meredith with an easy grin. "Can't wait."

Chapter Nine

By the time David arrived home a few hours later, Meredith's upbeat mood had undergonc another major reversal. David had no more than stepped through the door before his teary-eyed housemate threw himself into his arms.

"Good God, what's the matter now?" By this time, David had developed a good gauge for this sort of thing and was certain that these particular tears were frivolous rather than the result of anything dire.

"W-well, you see," said Meredith, thankfully releasing David so they could proceed into the living room, "I was doing a bit of cleaning, knickknacks and such since you said they was collecting dust, and I put on a film for a bit of background noise, one of yours that was on the shelf, but—oh, David, it was *awful*."

"What did you watch?" David strode toward the television to investigate.

Meredith pronounced, carefully and dreadfully, "*Les yeux sans visage*."

"Why would you do that? You know horror films always make you cry."

"Yes, but I thought—well, I mean, it's *French*, how frightening can it be?"

David wiped a hand over his face, at a loss for words.

"And Alida Valli's in it!" said Meredith. "But—but the poor dogs, and when they showed what he did to her *face*—"

“That’s—Schwarzy, that’s in the name,” David pointed out.

“Yeah, but I can’t read French,” Meredith wailed.

David sighed heavily and gave his shoulder a reassuring squeeze. “There, it’s all right,” he murmured. “You poor empty-headed little magpie. There’s just nothing going on up here”—he tapped him on the temple—“unless you catch sight of anything that sparkles, is there?”

Meredith giggled at that, then stepped back with his hands on his hips, frowning. “I’m not little.”

“That’s the part you object to, is it?” said David in disbelief.

“People only think so because they see me next to you, and you’re just so *big*.”

“Well, yes, but—”

“I’m quite medium-sized,” Meredith insisted. “I’m five ten.” Under David’s unwavering gaze, he crossed his arms and amended, “Five nine and a half.”

“Yes, well, *medium-sized magpie* doesn’t have quite the same ring, does it?”

“It’d be more accurate.”

“It was *meant* to be an endearment,” said David, then realized what he’d just said.

#63: It was meant to be an endearment.

So much for trying to comfort him. Distraction seemed to have had much the same effect, anyway.

“I’ll make some tea,” said David. “Why don’t you go and put on a Siouxsie Sioux record or something, that always cheers you right up.” He didn’t know how Meredith’s music was meant to cheer *anyone* up, but somehow it always seemed to do the trick.

The kettle boiled. The teapot was filled. A knock sounded at the front door.

As Meredith was now occupied reorganizing their combined record collection by some mysterious system that made sense only to him, David went to answer the door himself.

He opened it to find a young, dark-haired woman clad in a richly embroidered cloak of ultramarine silk.

"Good evening," she greeted him. "I'm here about the room."

"Ah, you must be the psychic. Do come in. I'm David, and this," he said, gesturing toward Meredith on the floor with Bianca at his side, "is the madman who lives in the upstairs closet."

David had hoped this would prompt Meredith to introduce himself properly.

It didn't.

"Yeah. Hi." He gave a little wave and got to his feet.

"Meredith," supplied David.

"Yeah?"

"*No*," said David, and led the way to the kitchen table, where he'd arranged the tea things. "I told you, you never introduce yourself properly."

Meredith ignored David and turned to their guest. "Lovely to meet you." After they'd gone through the usual business of embrace and cheek kiss, which she reciprocated, he asked, "What's your name, then?"

"I," she announced gravely, "am Sylvania Holland."

"That's a lovely name," said Meredith, dropping backward into a kitchen chair. "Quite perpendicular. Like a street corner," he elaborated.

Somehow, instead of slapping him, Sylvania Holland smiled. "Oh, I like you."

"I hate you," said David, pouring out two cups of tea. To Sylvania, he offered, "Sugar?"

In response, Meredith pulled a face at him and broke into giggles.

It took a second for Sylvania to react. "Oh! Me. Yes, thanks, just one."

"He wouldn't bother asking *me*," Meredith confided. "Not in a million years. David's terribly mean to me."

"I'm mean to you, am I?" repeated David, astonished at his utter audacity. "Just for that, you can pour your own tea, thank you very much."

"Well, I know how you take yours," said Meredith. "Just a pinch of sugar, and milk until it's the same color as that awful cardigan sweater of yours."

David bristled. "You'd better not mean the one I think you do. That's a traditional Cowichan design, I'll have you know, made for me by an artisan in British Columbia—Harriet's grandmother, in fact—and I won't have it insulted."

"I *know* what a Cowichan sweater is, David, and obviously I don't mean that one, seeing as how the one you've got is gray." Meredith shook his head at what he clearly considered David's hopelessness. "I mean the sort of camel-colored one, with the ugly toggle buttons."

Upon reflection, that was an accurate match to how David took his tea, even if he did disagree about the buttons. (Meredith preferred his black and very strong, and would sooner have coffee, not that David would admit to knowing it.)

"You keep your mouth shut about my sweaters." David splashed the remainder of the tea into a third cup and thumped it down unceremoniously in front of Meredith. "I'm sorry, Mrs. Holland. Did you say sugar, or no?"

Sylvania Holland stared at them. "Look, no offense, but I've seen enough, and I'm not getting into this. The upstairs bath doesn't work, those treacle wasps haven't gone for good, no matter what you think, and the two of you need to sort yourselves out."

"Yeah," said Meredith, sipping his tea. "That's fair. But you will stay and have cake, won't you?"

David was less shocked by this turn of events than he'd like to admit.

Of course the two of them did bicker on occasion, but he hadn't thought it so extreme as to drive away prospective tenants.

A new worry opened up. Naturally, David couldn't very well announce his impending departure yet, but what if they couldn't find a third housemate before he left? Although he was eager to make his escape, he hadn't intended to leave Meredith completely alone, or to stick him with the entirety of the rent.

Meredith, oblivious to this dilemma, was sharing the last of the Battenberg cake with Sylvania Holland and expressing at length his admiration for her jewelry, which consisted of numerous pieces of carved stone and hammered copper.

"That's a lovely jade ring you've got there," he said. "Don't suppose you'd trade for one of mine?"

She cast an appraising glance from her own hand to his. "But it'll never fit!"

"You'd be surprised," said Meredith, and lit up in the familiar dangerous way that he did whenever he got an idea. "Bet you a sugar cube it will!"

"I'm afraid I haven't any sugar cubes," Sylvania pointed out.

Meredith lifted the lid of the sugar bowl, removed three, and presented them to her. "Now you have!" he said brightly.

#64: He appears to have no concept of how gambling actually functions.

"Very well," she agreed. "One sugar cube that it won't fit."

Had David been a betting man, he would've put his money (or sugar cubes, as the case may be) on Meredith, who, in defiance of all artistic stereotypes, in fact had quite small and rather inelegant hands.

Sylvania removed the ring in question and offered it to Meredith, who slid it onto his third finger with no trouble.

"I stand corrected," she said, and presented him with one sugar cube, which caused him to laugh delightedly, and made David scowl all the harder.

"However," she went on, "I'm afraid I can't part with that one. It was made for me by my father. He does sell similar wares at the Night Market, if the style appeals."

With a final longing look, Meredith handed it back. "Wait, not Manuel Holland?" He raised his wrist to display an engraved silver bangle bracelet. "I got this off him ages ago."

Sylvania leaned in for a closer look. "Of course! I should have recognized it straightaway. You know," she said thoughtfully, "I can't give you this one, but I do have just the thing for you."

From the recesses of her cloak, she withdrew another ring, this one of intricately carved obsidian. Meredith removed one of his, a band of weathered bronze, and offered it to her in exchange, but she shook her head.

"Consider this a gift," she said, "in thanks for the tea and a wonderful evening. You must know, however, that I do not entrust this piece to you lightly. It bears an enchantment—the ability to reveal that which is concealed."

"Oh, yes?" asked Meredith, already admiring the ring on his finger as the lamplight played over the polished surface of the stone.

David was about to point out the danger of placing such a magical artifact in the hands of a man who was utterly hopeless at heeding directions, but Sylvania Holland's mysterious smile gave him pause. As a psychic, surely she knew what she was about.

"I trust it will clear up a few things for you," she said.

"Yeah," murmured Meredith. "Expect so." Then, finally tearing his attention away from his jewelry, he told Sylvania, "Thank you."

"Thank you," she returned, rising to her feet, "and good luck finding a roommate."

As soon as she'd gone, Meredith's accusatory gaze turned upon David. "She was lovely, David."

"She seemed quite pleasant, yes."

"Shame you frightened her off."

David stopped in his tracks carrying the empty teacups to the sink. "*I* frightened her off?"

"You did," said Meredith, "what with all that *I hate you, sugar* business."

"The sugar was for the tea!"

"Well, it's no use now. Anyway, I'm going to go have a shower before I go back out. Me and Kinley are going to the Rat Cellar," he added, "if you want to come with."

"When do I ever want to go to the Rat Cellar?" asked David.

"You do, though." Meredith turned in his seat to put his feet up on Sylvania's vacated chair. "I figure I've got about a two-thirds success rate getting you to go out."

"Well, consider tonight the other one-third," said David, returning from the kitchen. "Besides, the name alone is enough to drive any sensible person away."

"But it's brilliant! You see, it's a pun on *Ratskeller.*"

"Yes, you've explained before," said David.

#65: He attempts, in fact, to explain this every time.

"Besides, the place isn't a proper Ratskeller at all." It might have been at one point in the distant past, but for as long as David had known it, the graffiti-adorned bar had little to offer beyond cheap beer and a rotation of mediocre punk and goth bands.

"Oh, come on, you must admit it's a clever name."

Personally, David was inclined to admit nothing of the sort. "Yes, well, I suppose I fail to grasp the Germanic sense of humor."

Meredith considered that. "I don't think we've got much of one, really. Collectively speaking." Then he perked up again. "Oh, but they've got Desperation Pie playing tonight, they're quite good."

David gathered the empty cake plates and snatched Meredith's cup from his hand, ignoring his cry of indignation.

"Thank you, but no," said David firmly. "I do not wish to go to the Rat Cellar, and I certainly do not wish to go out anywhere with *you*. Two beers in and you're either abandoning me to go off chasing after anybody who catches your eye or making a spectacle of yourself shouting at the band to play 'Anglepoise Lamp.'"

Meredith narrowed his eyes but didn't bother denying it. "Yeah, well, I can think of a way for you to put a stop to both."

David picked up a stray dessert fork and gave up on attempting to parse that nonsensical statement. "What in the world are you on about?"

Meredith frowned. "What *am* I on about?" he echoed in apparent incomprehension of his own words, eyes traveling once more to the obsidian ring.

#66: Half the time he doesn't even make sense to himself.

Making the last trip to the kitchen sink, David didn't dignify the question with a reply.

"Well, as you like," said Meredith. "Your loss. I don't suppose the man's come about the washroom yet?"

"No, not until tomorrow," said David. "You'll have to use mine."

At last, as Meredith went to take a shower, David had a moment's peace. *Not much longer*, he told himself. As early as tomorrow, if all went well, he could be making an offer on a house. Still, there was no sense mentioning it to Bednarek—or Meredith, for that matter—until it was a sure thing.

The peace, as usual, was short-lived. David was just glancing at his email on the way to his own room when the crash sounded from the bathroom.

"All right?" he called, pocketing his phone.

Instead of a reply, there came a second crash, as of ceramic hitting the floor tiles, and, clearly audible from the other side of the door: "Oh, *hell*."

"Do you need help?"

The question was facetious. Naturally, Meredith took him up on it. "Would you?"

Cursing himself, David pushed open the door and stepped into the heady mixture of steam and heat and the scent of patchouli.

Though the two of them had shared a house for several years, neither was in the habit of appearing in common areas in a state of undress. Consequently, David found himself entirely unprepared for the sight of Meredith with nothing but a towel around his waist, for the jarring contrast of dark ink and pale skin before the initial overwhelming impression separated itself into details.

David had seen the tattoos on his arms many times. He had caught the occasional glimpse of the vaguely tribal, vaguely floral motif below his pierced navel, and the flock of Steadman bats along his collarbone. Though he hadn't been aware of the specifics, he was by no means surprised at two other previously unseen tattoos: a few lines of script over the ribs and, dead center of his chest, a black and spiky thing that David just recognized as a heavily stylized love heart, split open in places to reveal tiny, faceted slivers of deep ruby.

He had not known about the nipple piercings. He could have happily gone on not knowing.

#67: That is, unfortunately, no longer an option.

David cleared his throat. "What's the trouble?"

Meredith held out an open jar of an oily greenish substance—Mrs. Jupiter's healing salve. "Bit difficult at this angle," he said apologetically.

David didn't follow until Meredith turned, displaying his latest tattoo, a peacock feather trailing down his spine. It was the too-real bright black of fresh ink, with a few minuscule color details in the eye.

Perching on the edge of the vanity, Meredith swept his hair out of the way over his shoulder; though he hadn't washed it, the ends were wet from the shower. A single rivulet of water ran down his back.

David's eyes followed. Then, realizing, he tore his gaze away and blinked hard. The steam, he suspected, was slowly cooking his brain.

Best to get things over with. David scooped a large quantity of ointment onto his fingers and spread it between Meredith's shoulder blades; the surrounding skin was pink and warm to the touch. Despite David's efforts to be gentle, Meredith gave a hiss of pain.

David considered telling him that he ought to have known exactly what he was letting himself in for; similarly, he had no shortage of potential remarks on the subject of beggars and choosers.

What he ended up saying instead was, quietly, "All right?"

"Yeah," said Meredith. "It's just everybody says spine tattoos kill, and I mean, I believed it, only, knowing firsthand is something else."

With the lightest touch he could manage, David resumed his task. Before long, he found himself uncomfortably aware of Meredith's proximity, of his every little twitch and intake of breath. To break the silence, he asked, "This is good for tattoos, is it?"

"Like you wouldn't believe," said Meredith. "It'll be all healed by morning."

"Here, turn a bit, would you?"

As Meredith shifted position, David caught sight of the deep ugly bruise on his side. He reached out, fingers brushing over the spot. "What happened here?"

Meredith tensed at David's touch but didn't turn around. "Ah. That's from the other day."

"I didn't realize Brian actually hit you when he threw that jar." A sudden anger flared to life inside him.

"It's not—" Meredith began, but David cut him off.

"Believe me," he interrupted, "I'd have given him a bit more than a piece of my mind if I'd known." His gaze fell upon the jar in his hand. "Is this good for bruises as well?"

There was a long pause as Meredith considered. "Don't see why not," he said at last. "Never occurred to me to try it."

David gathered nearly the last of the salve from the bottom of the jar and carefully applied it over the area of the bruise. He could feel every rib beneath his fingers.

"Look," he said gruffly, "if you happen to see him around, or if—if anybody gives you any trouble—" David broke off, not quite sure himself what he was trying to articulate and already regretting the attempt. *The steam*, he told himself. He really must get out into cooler air. It was insufferable and probably unsafe, the way Meredith had practically turned the place into a sauna.

Meredith leaned back and rested his head against David's shoulder, heedless of the wet tips of his hair dampening his shirt collar. "I know," he said sincerely. "I'll be all right, so long as I've got you looking out for me."

#68: He just had to go and speak that cosmic temptation into existence.

Chapter Ten

The following morning, David slept late. Around eight, drawn by the scent of freshly brewed coffee, he pulled on his favorite tartan bathrobe and shuffled in the direction of the kitchen. He emerged from the hallway, only to be greeted by the unwelcome sight of Meredith dancing about the living room with Bianca in his arms, singing a song about—as far as he could make out—rabid dogs and monsters from space and other things David didn't care to know about.

David massaged his temples. "Would you stop *singing*."

#69: He is always going and singing to himself for no good reason.

In all fairness, though one would never guess it from Meredith's speaking voice, he was actually a rather good baritone. That annoyed David as well, even if he couldn't explain why.

Meredith, of course, paid no heed to David's admonition. Instead, he held up Bianca to face height, and when she nuzzled at his throat, he gave an exaggerated cry of distress and collapsed dramatically onto the sofa cushions. "You've done it, you've slain me!"

She celebrated her victory by licking his face, prompting him to break into laughter and kiss her atop the head.

"It's far too early for all this racket," grumbled David.

"But, David, it's Bianca's favorite song."

"Is it."

"Yeah! She loves acting it out—she's the mad dog, and I'm the blue-eyed heroine."

"Heroine?" David repeated, wiping a hand over his face. It was too early for Meredith in general, he decided, not that one ever did feel quite prepared for him at any hour of the day.

"It *is* in the lyrics, David." He released Bianca, who wasted no time making her escape.

"Some people change them to suit, you know."

"Yeah, well, that's where I've got an advantage, isn't it?" Meredith said brightly, taking up his coffee cup from its precarious position on the arm of the sofa. The earthenware mug, glazed in a gradient of sea green, had been a gift from Mrs. Jupiter that had somehow survived two years of Meredith's careless handling. (David suspected she'd had the foresight to add a charm against accidental breakage.) "I made coffee, by the way, if you want any."

"Tea it is, then." David made his way to the kitchen. He did indeed want coffee and wasn't going to waste time making tea when the percolator was still going on the stovetop, but that wouldn't stop him complaining about it.

#70: He makes the worst coffee in the world.

Meredith, unfortunately, followed. "Oh! You're so *mean* to me."

"I am, I'm hideously cruel," agreed David. He poured himself a cup of coffee and diluted it with a splash of hot water from the tap. "I don't know what else you expect when your coffee's like tar."

"You just don't know how to appreciate a bold cup."

David paused in the act of reaching for the sugar bowl. "A *bold cup*? You could pave the streets with this." He turned to find Meredith with his own empty cup in hand.

"You done, then? I'm having seconds."

After adding enough sugar and cream to make the beverage drinkable, if not palatable, David ventured a sip and sank into his seat at the table. "You're up early," he remarked. "For you, I mean."

Meredith took a drink of his undiluted coffee, appearing, against all probability, to enjoy it, and drifted past David into the living room. "Genevieve called a bit ago and I couldn't get back to sleep."

"Oh, yes? Any news?" He hoped there might be some new details on the wedding front, but he'd resolved to tread lightly on that topic.

"There's news." Meredith sounded put out. "She and Jayceon went away for the weekend, and it seems they're engaged now."

"Isn't that a good thing?"

He waved a hand. "Oh, for *them*, I suppose. Only now she expects me to be in her wedding, too." Taking up his usual spot in the window, he confided, "We'll see what Jayceon has to say about that. He doesn't like me, you know."

"No?" That, David had to admit, was a surprise. In his experience, nearly everybody liked Meredith, even if that did call their judgment into question. "You're quite sure?"

"Well, Genevieve says"—here Meredith slipped into an uncanny imitation of his cousin—"*You misunderstand. He's just quiet. You should get to know him better.*"

"Perhaps you *should* get to know him better," suggested David.

"Are you joking? The man doesn't speak, David. It's like talking to a—a microwave oven. Not even, because that at least lights up and goes *ding* every once in a while."

"I believe the usual comparison is talking to a brick wall."

"Well, that's daft, who'd go talking to a brick wall?"

"Who'd talk to a micro—" David gave up. "Never mind."

Meredith got to his feet and abandoned his coffee mug on the window seat, where it was likely to stay until he knocked it over or David picked it up.

#71: Dishes appear to wink out of existence in his mind the moment they leave his hands.

"Just as well, I suppose," mused Meredith.

"What, that Jayceon's a kitchen appliance?"

"No, that I couldn't get back to sleep." Meredith collected his sketchbook and pen from the coffee table. "I've got things to do before I go in to the shop."

"Oh, you're working?" At Meredith's quizzical look, David pointed out, "It is a federal holiday."

"Yeah, only I ain't a government entity, am I?"

"*Language.*"

Meredith flopped down onto the sofa and made an obscene gesture at him.

"Lovely," said David. "Truly, a man of refined and genteel nature."

"I am, thanks." Meredith flipped open his sketch pad to a fresh page and spent a moment in apparent thought, twirling his pen between his fingers. "Anyway, Thao said a couple guys came in asking after me for a consult yesterday. Of course I wasn't there, so she told them to come back today. Which, normally, I only see people by appointment, but I suppose one ought to accommodate if they've gone to the trouble."

"Is that so?" David tried, without much success, to ignore the rambling monologue. Ordinarily he'd reach for the morning paper and Meredith would get the hint, sooner or later, but of course he hadn't bothered to go out and fetch it from the mailbox.

"—and before *that*, I promised I'd help Kinley collect his last batch of signatures this morning. Did you know he's petitioning Senator Guzzledown to get the Midnight Wood on the National Register of Magical Places? Oh, you are coming to his party on Saturday, aren't you?"

A hint of unease crept into David's mind. "I thought you were going shopping with Adalynn on Saturday."

"In the morning, David. You can do more than one thing in a day, *honestly*. But you will come?"

"We'll see," said David, who did not approve of McKinley Hendricks and had no intention of doing any such thing.

At last they fell into a period of silence, punctuated only by the scratch of pen on paper, but it turned out to be all too brief.

"David?"

David sipped his coffee. "Hmm?"

"What if there was a porcupine made of forks?"

#72: This is the exact sort of nonsense he always comes out with if allowed to think too hard.

Unconcerned at the lack of response, Meredith turned his sketch pad toward David. "Lookit. I call him the Forkupine!"

By the time David emerged from the shower, Meredith was gone. The plumber came not long after, made short work of the necessary repairs upstairs, and sought out David where he sat at the kitchen table, absorbed in online house listings.

"Pretty bad buildup of timescale you had there," she told him. "No wonder the last guy was in over his head."

"Limescale?" echoed David absently, not looking up from his laptop screen.

"*Time*scale," she corrected. "Happens sometimes with exposure to temporal anomalies. Little bit of reverse rust, too. That's where your leak was coming from." She hefted a short length of corroded metal pipe for his inspection. "You're lucky you caught it before it spread."

At David's blank look, she launched into a highly technical explanation of metallurgy and alchemical processes that went well over his head. He nodded along, made vague sounds of dismay at what he hoped were the appropriate intervals, and accepted her invoice to pass on to Bednarek.

At one o'clock, David met Leonard Flood for the first of their scheduled house viewings.

It was an older farmhouse on the opposite side of town, just a bit too far to comfortably walk, which was a point against it. The house itself had been modernized in a utilitarian fashion, and an effort had been made at what David characterized as *rustic decor*. The flooring was easy to clean, he noted with approval, as the current homeowner trailed after Mr. Flood with a mop and a grim expression, wiping away the residue from his tentacles.

David had an hour to kill before the second showing, so he parked his van in the empty staff lot behind the Corner Store and took a slow stroll through downtown. The Corner Café, too, was closed today, so he made his way past Two Way Tattoo, Kinley's shop; past the Lost & Found directly across the street, where Meredith worked; past the trio of heavily tattooed, rough-looking types who were likely coming or going from one or the other, without paying them much mind.

There was Mr. Flood's office, in between the ice cream parlor and the pet shop. (*We carry exotics and familiars*, proclaimed the sign in the window.) Continuing down Main Street, he passed by the potions dispensary, the antiques shop (*Professor Cyrus Sandoval, Purveyor of Cursed Artifacts*), and the post office, closed for the holiday.

The furniture store, however, remained open, and the raven perched on the signpost out front cawed in greeting.

David nodded. "Afternoon, Ralph."

"You in need of any furniture, Mr. C? Home decor?" He waved a wing to indicate the window display. "We got your top-quality purple curtains, genuine antique busts of Pallas, whatever you're looking for to make your house a home."

David doubted whether anything sold here—or in any shop, for that matter—could make him feel truly at home in Midnight Cottage. "I think I'm all right for now, thanks."

"We're running a sale on office furniture," added Ralph with a touch of desperation. "Writing desks on clearance!"

"I'll keep it in mind."

David hastened down the sidewalk. He had no intention of joining the early crowd at any of the pubs, and though a newly opened Austrian bistro looked promising, he'd had the vague idea of keeping that one back for a special occasion. In the end, he went to the unimaginatively named Downtown Diner, where he took up residence in a corner booth, had a cup of mediocre tea, and sent photos of both houses pulled from their online listings to Harriet for her opinion.

You want me to be totally honest?

Please.

The first one is a little tacky

Like they went too far with the retro look

I haven't seen it in person yet. I think it might not be intentionally retro, just dated.

The second one is WAY too country

So not you

I'm inclined to agree.

Do you want me to keep an eye out for listings around here too?

David considered. It wouldn't be an unreasonable commute. In fact, the location would be all the more advantageous if he did get the job at

Cartier's headquarters. Not to mention he'd be closer to Harriet; he'd begun to keenly feel the dwindling frequency of their once-weekly coffee dates.

Yes, let me know if you come across anything suitable.

Will do

By the way, I finally managed to score an invite to the Corner Store auction this year

Congratulations.

What did Corner manage to get out of you?

I commissioned a couple pairs of mittens from my grandma

Which gives me an excuse to go visit next weekend

I don't suppose that was enough to make it onto the VIP list?

Me?

Not a chance

I'm sorry.

I'd get you in if I could.

I know

No luck on your end either, then?

Afraid not.

It's the least he could do when he's making you plan the whole thing

Any news on Contreras?

Nothing official yet

Just whispers

Heard she's been looking at retirement condos down south

Anyway, got to go

About to go meet up with my date

But I'll see you at the auction, okay?

And keep me posted on the house hunting!

As David took another sip of tea, a new message popped up on his screen. An afterthought from Harriet?

No. This one was from Meredith.

can we go to the rat cellar tonight

please

David sighed. He supposed he oughtn't to refuse two nights in a row.

Who's playing?

the estranged swedes

actually did a touch up on their bass player last time they were in town

wouldn't mind seeing how it healed

but mostly just really need a drink

just about had it with these mf nazis

#73: He makes even less sense in writing than he does in person.

What are you talking about? What happened?

nothing major

just had to throw some guys out of the shop

tell you about it later

at the rat cellar???

Yes, all right. What time?

I've got a long session booked that'll probably run late

let's say 9:30 and I'll let you know if it goes over

meet me at the shop?

All right.

thank you <3

David rolled his eyes at the heart.

That, unfortunately, was not the end of that. Meredith continued texting him whatever half-formed thoughts drifted through the barren landscape of his mind. At least David assumed it to be barren; he didn't want to spend much time contemplating exactly what the inside of Meredith's head looked like.

btw you think these are good for steve?

This was followed by photos of several drawings. David spared them no more than a cursory glance as he scrolled past, just enough to catch sight of the usual angular scribbles in black ink. In any case, Steve Corner was hardly a discerning patron of the arts; the important thing was to see that Meredith followed through on his promised donation.

Yes, those should be fine.

thought you'd be pleased

to see them go

David didn't know what he meant by that, either, and chose not to respond. It was nearly time for his second appointment. As he paid his bill, his phone buzzed yet again.

also, do we have any riesling at home?

a dry one

not a sweet one

think that's part of where I went wrong last year

David had reached his limit with the irritating notifications, and without replying, he set his phone to silent.

Chapter Eleven

The second house turned out to be much more to David's liking: a split-level in a residential area not far from downtown. Admittedly, some of the decor was dated, but the rooms were spacious, with good lighting. The fenced-in backyard, currently empty, was about the right size for a few trees, a shed, perhaps a small vegetable patch, without being so large as to make upkeep unmanageable. Inside, the appliances and carpets were new, and the living room boasted quite a nice fireplace. Yes, the quartz countertops were a bit garish, but he could live with that. The wood paneling, on the other hand, would definitely have to go. No matter; David liked a good home-improvement project. A proper one, that is—no nonsense about frescoes or decoupage.

After a thorough inspection of the premises, he thanked the owner and held a hushed conversation with Leonard Flood on the sidewalk outside. Though he did like the house, and the asking price was reasonable, he found himself held back by something he could not articulate, some sense that the property, though perfectly acceptable, was still somehow not quite *right*.

Flood seemed to sense his hesitation. "No need to make a decision right this minute," he reassured David. "Take a few days, think it over, look at some other listings. If it's meant to be, it'll still be here when you're ready, and if not, you'll find the right place."

Yes, David decided, that was the most sensible approach. He thanked Flood, shook his tentacle, and departed.

Back at Midnight Cottage, David poured himself a drink, a double shot of good bourbon. Briefly, he considered drinking it outside on the deck, or at the picnic table just down the path toward Mr. Bednarek's cottage, then thought better of it. He'd once taken his then-boyfriend to the latter spot for a picnic lunch, only for some wretched little creature to come darting out of the trees and make off with half of the deviled eggs. At the time, he'd taken it for an overgrown ferret, but now supposed it must have been the so-called Most Weasel.

Instead, he settled for the living room sofa, leaned back into the comfortable cushions, and slowly sipped the liquor. Thinking it over now, he felt foolish at having gotten cold feet. Purchasing a home was a major commitment, certainly, but it was high time he left Midnight Cottage, and there'd been nothing the matter with that house.

Perhaps a little positive visualization was in order. Closing his eyes, David tried to imagine his ideal life, or at least as ideal as was attainable in the near future. He envisioned himself, several weeks from now, sitting on the sofa—admittedly rather like this sofa—in the living room of his new house—also rather like this living room, but the point was, it didn't *have* to be.

Forget the living room, he decided, and instead imagined himself in the kitchen, gloriously alone, free of interruptions as he made his morning tea. Reading the newspaper alone in the back garden. Waking up alone in an airy bedroom with big east-facing windows.

Or perhaps *not* alone.

That thought came to him as a surprise. He hadn't allowed himself to seriously consider the possibility of dating in some time.

#74: As with most things, Meredith is to blame.

He ruined all of David's relationships: Eduardo had made eyes at him, and Omar had sneered at him, which had somehow been worse, and Jintao . . . well, all right, Meredith had had nothing to do with that one. Jintao had been nice enough, but there'd been a blandness and predictability in their interactions that had left David simply *bored*.

Then, of course, there had been the unpleasantness with Jean-Marc, which had caused him to officially give up on dating.

David was still a touch bitter about that. He didn't fall for anyone easily. Things going wrong with casual boyfriends had been more an annoyance than a heartbreak. But Jean-Marc was another matter altogether.

He'd been about as close to perfect as David could imagine, or at least perfect for him. He was David's exact type, tall and muscular, a former rugby player. In fact, Jean-Marc had briefly played lock for the Swiss national team. He was just a bit older, silver starting to show at his temples and in his beard, crow's-feet crinkling when he smiled. His dark eyes held a hint of bronze, and when he'd leaned in close behind David and spoken French to him . . .

Things had been going well, very well. David had finally invited him to spend a weekend at Midnight Cottage.

Then, after one drink too many, Jean-Marc had wandered into the kitchen while Meredith was in the midst of some late-night baking. From the next room, David had heard the surprised yelp, the distinct sound of someone being struck with a wooden spoon, the indignant cry from Jean-Marc, and Meredith's voice calling sharply: "*David!*"

He'd been in the kitchen in a flash, where he'd found a furious Jean-Marc pressing a hand to his face and backing away from an equally furious Meredith brandishing a mixing spoon at him.

"Tell your boyfriend," Meredith had hissed, not taking his eyes from Jean-Marc, "to keep his hands to *himself*."

David had physically thrown Jean-Marc out of the house and his overnight bag after him, and refused to speak to Meredith for the next three days.

Wiping a stray drop of bourbon from his moustache, David set his empty glass on the coffee table. That thought exercise had rather gotten away from him. Banishing any lingering memories of Jean-Marc from his mind, David resolved to revamp his online dating profile. Perhaps in a month or two, he *would* be waking up with someone in his bed. Perhaps next summer, a beach vacation to—well, he didn't much care where exactly, so long as there *was* a beach. Cool blue water, hot white sand, a suite in a luxurious seaside hotel where he and the as-yet-hazy vision of his future boyfriend (*Maitland Cartier's nephew?*) would return from a walk along the coastline and fall into bed together. A large bed, big enough for him to lie in comfortably, with crisp clean sheets.

He frowned. That was not quite the direction he'd meant to go in. Nor did he like the fact that even in this imaginary future, he still could not escape Meredith's presence, the idea of him buzzing at the edge of David's awareness like a persistent swarm of gnats. But he was sinking into the imaginary mattress, head resting on one of the enormous fluffy pillows . . .

David woke to Bianca whining and pawing at his side, and fumbled in the dark to turn on the nearest table lamp. He must have dozed off for a moment. Perhaps more than a moment—the sky outside the bay window was dark, the moon obscured by thin drifting clouds. Surely he couldn't have slept away the whole afternoon.

Uneasily, he recalled the warnings of the plumber that morning, now wishing he'd listened a bit more closely. But even if the time-twisting effects of the Wood could leak out at its edges, there was no way they could carry all the way to the cottage without undergoing some dilution. It was true, much to David's annoyance, that every clock in the place tended to run ahead or behind no matter how often one reset them (an endeavor he'd long since given up as futile), but only by a quarter of an hour, at most. No—he'd simply mistaken the time, or else his watch had gone wrong, that was all.

Still, something nagged at him, the feeling of something forgotten. Ah, yes, he'd neglected to leave the plumber's invoice in Bednarek's mailbox.

"I expect you want to go out, do you?" he asked Bianca distastefully. "Come on, then." He flipped on the exterior lights, took her outside, and reached for his phone to check the time.

It was after ten, and his screen was filled with missed calls and texts from Meredith.

Damn him. If he hadn't gone on rambling about drawings and dry wine and other such nonsense, David wouldn't have silenced his phone and forgotten. (Deep down, he was annoyed with himself as well. As reluctant as his agreement to their plans had been, he *had* agreed, and he didn't back out of commitments.)

David opened his messages.

> I'll be done a bit before ten
>
> you still coming?
>
> David?
>
> I'm locking up the shop now
>
> . . . see you at the rat cellar then?

He'd called three times; the last text had been only a few minutes ago.

On my way now, David responded hurriedly. He grabbed Bianca, rushed back inside, exchanged the Chihuahua for his car keys, and scrambled behind the wheel of his van. He had nearly reached the end of the lane when his headlights illuminated the silhouette of Mrs. Jupiter walking toward the main road.

David slowed and rolled down the window. "Evening, Mrs. Jupiter. Care for a ride into town?"

"Much obliged, Mr. C." She opened the door and heaved herself up into the passenger seat. Anticipating his next question, she said, "Drop me anywhere you like. I'm going to the Night Market, but I don't mind a bit of a walk."

The Night Market set up in an empty lot downtown where the city had razed a long-abandoned haunted schoolhouse, not far from the Rat Cellar. "The Night Market it is," said David, and then, for the sake of conversation, added, "Stocking up on herbs?"

Mrs. Jupiter straightened her large tapestry bag in her lap. "My regular shopping, and I intend to consult with a few colleagues as well." She lowered her voice. "There's something amiss in the Midnight Wood."

They'd reached the edge of town now, and David slowed as he turned at the first intersection.

"Oh?" he asked politely. In his opinion, there was quite a lot wrong with the Midnight Wood already, but he understood that to be the normal state of affairs.

"I fear something has been killing off the Midnight Mice," Mrs. Jupiter confided. "I found another of the poor creatures dead today." She turned and caught David's eye. "Has either of you been in the Wood again lately?"

"I haven't, no." David slowed to a stop at a red light. "Not since the weekend. I'm not sure about Meredith." It was impossible to guess what he got up to when he was out of sight, and David didn't care to speculate, especially knowing as he did now the probability of it involving sycamore dryads.

"Speaking of the Midnight Wood—" David began as he turned onto a downtown side street, then reconsidered. He himself still doubted what he'd seen. "Never mind."

Though he was indeed headed to the Night Market, he took a deliberate path that passed by both the Rat Cellar and the Lost & Found, keeping an eye out for Meredith on the chance of catching him en route.

"Are you sure?" pressed Mrs. Jupiter gently.

Still debating the answer to that question, David pulled up at a stop sign, cast a glance down the deserted street, and made another turn. Farther along, four figures gathered beneath a distant streetlamp.

One was unmistakably Meredith.

The other three David didn't recognize. Perhaps he'd run into a few friends, David told himself as the van rolled closer, but that did nothing to quiet the feeling of misgiving creeping down the back of his neck. Something about the way the three men crowded around Meredith, standing between him and the street—

Then David's already brittle conjecture shattered as Meredith cast a sharp glance toward the van and broke away from the trio—or tried to.

It all happened in an instant, yet David felt as if he were watching in slow motion: One man received a shove and a boot to the instep; another, an elbow to the ribs that knocked him off balance. As Meredith tried to dart past the third, a burly man with a shaved head, the stranger seized him and slammed him against the brick wall.

At that moment, the clouds passing over the moon thinned to mere shreds, providing a clear view of the scene, of the man flipping open a switchblade knife, of his tattooed knuckles shifting as he gripped its handle.

David braked hard, slammed the gearshift into park, and leapt out of the van, leaving it running. Dimly, he registered Mrs. Jupiter's footsteps behind him as he sprinted the last few yards toward the group, heart thudding in his chest.

The other two men had quickly recovered and taken up their positions on either side of their leader, blocking in Meredith against the wall. He shrank back against the bricks, head tipped back as he tried to avoid the point of the knife pressing in under his chin. A trickle of blood ran down the blade, nearly black in the moonlight.

"*No!*" David shouted, but he'd never get there in time.

The man's arm drew back, the raised blade glinting for an instant before it plunged.

Lungs burning, David surged forward, but he was too far away, too late—

Behind him, Mrs. Jupiter shouted an incantation, and the three men vanished, switchblade clattering to the concrete.

Rather, they appeared to vanish. In their place, three cockroaches skittered across the sidewalk to disappear into the dark alley.

Meredith staggered forward, both hands to his throat, wide blue eyes gone impossibly wider. "David," he choked out, "am I—"

"You're all right," said David firmly. Meredith *had* to be all right; that was simply the way the universe worked. He'd said so himself, in fact. At the time, David had been annoyed by it, but right now, it was the last thing he wanted to complain about. With as much reassurance as he could manage, he went on, "I'm right here. It's okay now."

Meredith took his hands away from his throat; no more than a few streaks of blood stained his palms. The only sound that escaped him was a wordless, panicked whimper.

"Christ," David breathed. "*Meredith.*"

Then, without warning, Meredith slumped against him, head falling onto his shoulder, leaving David to support his full weight as he reflexively caught hold of him.

"You're all right," David repeated, at a loss for any other words.

"Yeah, course I am," murmured Meredith. "Just—just gone a bit lightheaded, that's all."

David tried to work himself up to righteous fury at Meredith for putting himself in such a situation to begin with, even though he himself was still not entirely clear on what said situation actually was. When that failed, he tried for annoyance at the spots of blood now staining his shirtfront where Meredith clutched at him, and again came up short. He tried desperately to catch at any detail to take his mind off the spike of fear that hadn't faded from his heart—Meredith trembling in his arms, the tangles of brass-blond hair that David couldn't seem to get out of his face, the combined scent of patchouli and sweat and the antibacterial soap that Meredith always smelled of after work.

"Let's have a look." Though Mrs. Jupiter's eyes flashed with rage, her voice was gentler and more soothing than what David had managed. From her tapestry bag, she took a handkerchief and a small jar of healing ointment. "Look up for me, that's right, dear."

Mrs. Jupiter made quick work of wiping away the blood and applying ointment to the shallow cut. "There, that's all right now," she said briskly. "Go on home, have a cup of tea, and get some rest. That goes for the both of you."

Meredith straightened up and ran a hand through his hair, which did nothing to improve its appearance. In a subdued voice, he said, "Thanks, Mrs. J."

"Think nothing of it." She bent, retrieved the dropped switchblade, and examined it for a moment before wiping it clean and stowing it in her bag. "This one's a nasty bit of business."

"If you call when you're done at the Night Market—" David began, but she cut him off with a shake of the head.

"I'll walk." With a dangerous smile, Mrs. Jupiter added, "If there's any more of these types about—well, I'd just like to see them try."

"That's what I said," Meredith spoke up quietly. "To those three, earlier."

The pieces finally clicked together in David's mind. "Those were the men you threw out of the shop today? The ones who've been bothering you since the weekend?"

"I *told* you that." Meredith wrapped his arms around himself as though he were cold. "Or tried to, anyway. It was them who came looking for me yesterday, and the sort of things they were asking for—well, in this business, one gets to know the symbols. It was a deliberate provocation, David!"

David nodded. "What did you tell them?"

"What do you think? I told them to get the hell out, and they s-said I didn't want to get on the wrong side of them, and I said, *As far as I'm concerned, against you* is *the only right side*, and *they* said—" Meredith broke off with an uneasy look at Mrs. Jupiter.

"Do you think," she said, her voice hard, "that I have never heard the sort of things those people say? Go on."

Meredith was shivering in earnest now, so badly that David would have given him his coat this time, had he been wearing one. He suddenly regretted refusing to do so in the Midnight Wood, and was struck by a pang of guilt as he recalled how harshly he'd spoken to him that day.

"They had the nerve to say I ought to go in with them," Meredith went on, "and they said, *Down in your heart, you know we're right and you're just scared to admit it*, and I said, *I don't and I won't and you'll see me dead first*. And he said, *Yeah, perhaps we will*, and I said, *I—I'd like to see you try*."

"And they did." David felt ill. If he hadn't fallen asleep—if he hadn't silenced his phone—if he'd paid the least bit of attention to what had been going on the past few days—

"Oh, they tried," said Mrs. Jupiter, "and they failed. Remember that."

"Mrs. J?" Meredith glanced toward the dark mouth of the nearby alley. "Will they stay cockroaches forever?"

"That," she said, "depends entirely on them."

THEY MADE THE short drive to Midnight Cottage in silence. David gripped the steering wheel until his knuckles turned white in an effort to stop himself shaking. In the passenger seat, Meredith clasped and unclasped his hands in his lap, fiddled with his bracelets, appeared several times on the verge of speaking, only to remain silent.

It wasn't until David unlocked the front door that Meredith asked, sounding as if he hadn't a care in the world, "By the way, did the man ever come to see about the washroom?"

"The man was a lady," David corrected him, turning on the hall light.

"Oh, was he? I mean, was she? I didn't realize she'd changed."

Bianca came running to greet them, but Meredith drifted past her into the living room without a second glance.

"No, no, I mean the man's always been—the *plumber*," David amended, "was a lady to begin with. Different plumber this time."

#75: His brand of nonsensical speech seems to be catching.

In reality, David could barely string together a coherent thought, and couldn't imagine how Meredith was any better off. "Anyway, she's been and gone. It's all taken care of."

The plumber, of course, was of little importance, but in the absence of Mrs. Jupiter, neither of them seemed able to address the elephant in the room.

Meredith stood staring out the bay window without replying.

"Sorry to have ruined your plans," David said to his back. "I know you did want to see the, er—what band was it?"

"Estranged Swedes," said Meredith. "Yeah. 'S all right, though." He went to the sofa, sat down, and picked up the empty coffee mug left there from the morning. "They never play 'Anglepoise Lamp' for me anyway."

His voice caught on the last word, and the cup tumbled from his trembling fingers to land on the floor with a heavy *thunk*.

To David's surprise, it remained intact, and he gazed at it for a long moment before he spoke. "Meredith—"

"Oh, *don't*. I'm all right, really."

David had a hard time believing that, and because he couldn't bring himself to say *I'm not*, all his horror transmuted into wrath, which he directed at the only possible recipient.

"*But you almost weren't!*" David paced from one end of the room to the other, chasing down the necessary words to convey his outrage. "How could you be so irresponsible and go putting yourself in danger like that? What if we hadn't happened to find you? What if Mrs. Jupiter hadn't been there? What if—" He held himself back from saying: *What if I'd been able to do nothing but kneel over you helplessly as you bled to death in the street? What if I'd had to watch you die in my arms because I missed a phone call?*

He'd wanted to be rid of Meredith and all the accompanying annoyances, yes, but he hadn't actually wanted him to come to harm.

The response was infuriatingly nonchalant: "Yeah, but that's not what happened, is it?"

David spun on his heel to face him. "Meredith, they would have *killed* you."

Meredith stood, hands on his hips, and fixed him with a mutinous glare. "Yeah, well, I expect that'd be my problem, not yours."

"You," growled David, "are *always* my problem."

Acting independently of any rational thought, he strode one last step to close the distance between them, seized Meredith by the shoulders, and kissed him hard. Meredith kissed back frantically, hands scrabbling at David's back, drawing him closer. David lost himself in the warmth of it, the heavy lingering scent of herbal salve, Meredith making needy little sounds against his mouth as David kissed him deeply—

At which point he came to his senses, realized exactly what he was doing, and pushed Meredith away. There was little force behind it, only enough to make him take a single step back—a step onto the forgotten coffee mug, which rolled away beneath his foot and made him fall back onto the sofa with a surprised squeak.

For a long moment, the two of them stared at each other.

"I—that's not quite what I meant to do." David ran a hand over his face. "You all right?"

"I know," said Meredith, still frozen in place on the sofa, eyes enormous. "I'm okay."

"Good," snarled David, all his rage returning full force. "Then don't you ever in your life so much as *think* about kissing me like that again, or I swear to God it'll be the last time I ever speak to you."

He stormed out of the room, down the hallway, and into the doorway of his bedroom, where he stood motionless for a good half minute, hands pressed over his face. The kiss between them had felt alarmingly natural, but it was simply panic overriding his higher brain functions, panic and adrenaline and some residual effect of the single drink he'd had hours ago. A moment of temporary insanity. It had to be, because the last thing in the world that he actually wanted was to kiss Meredith Schwarzwelder.

#76: It is almost impossible to stay angry with him, even when he deserves it.

David turned around and stormed back into the living room. Meredith lay curled up on the sofa, clutching Bianca in his arms and not quite crying—not yet.

These, for once, were not frivolous tears.

"*Christ.*" David sank onto the cushion next to him. "Come here."

Even if he was still utterly mortified, even if he had no desire whatsoever for—anything of the nature that had happened a moment ago, in spite of that, in spite of everything, he couldn't find it in himself to leave Meredith alone like this.

"Come here," David repeated, softer, and scooped up Meredith and Bianca both, pulling them into his lap.

Meredith buried his face against David's shoulder, while Bianca, having reached the end of her patience, gave a discontented grumble and squirmed out of his grasp. Turning his attention now to David, Meredith curled his fingers into his shirt and murmured something unintelligible into his collarbone.

"Shh, you're all right now." David stroked his hair, mainly in an effort to keep it out of his own face, and tried not to think about how thoroughly embarrassed they were both going to be in the morning. "I'm here, I've got you. Everything's going to be all right."

For a long time, the two of them stayed like that, David whispering comforting nonsense and rubbing circles over Meredith's back until he stopped trembling and fell asleep against him.

Chapter Twelve

Just after six the next morning, David crept downstairs and through the still-dark living room. To his relief, Meredith was gone from the sofa where he'd left him the night before. David hoped that by leaving early and unobtrusively, he'd be able to avoid him for as long as possible after last night's fiasco. Slipping outside, he made his way down the dark and misty lane on foot. Though it was chilly this morning, he wouldn't risk the noise of starting the van.

The thought of facing Meredith again made David's insides burn with embarrassment, and perhaps a hint of—no. Purely embarrassment. He didn't know what he could have been thinking, going and—doing what he'd done. He *hadn't* been thinking, clearly.

His breath hung in the air, and frost muted the color of the grass, though the sun would soon make short work of restoring the green of spring. David shivered, drew his heavy coat closer around him—and nearly had a heart attack when a figure stepped into the path before him.

A wraith in the mist? (*The terrible dark figure that had pursued him through the Midnight Wood?*)

No—this particular wraith wore an oversized sweater and was accompanied by a Chihuahua.

David pressed a hand over his heart. "Oh, you wretched creature," he hissed. "You gave me such a turn creeping up on me like that."

#77: He has a talent for sneaking up on one out of nowhere.

Meredith giggled at that. "Sorry, David." He leaned in for his customary greeting, then froze halfway and instead gave David a tentative pat on the arm before drawing back.

Well, that was to be expected, he supposed. Things were bound to be a bit awkward for a time. Nothing for it but to move on; sooner or later, they'd get back to normal. And if it meant an end to Meredith's unnecessary gestures of affection, so much the better.

"What are you doing out here, anyway?" David demanded. "The sun's not yet up."

"Couldn't sleep, so I came down to get the paper. It hasn't come yet," Meredith said apologetically, "but I got yesterday's post. What are *you* doing?"

"Thought I'd get an early start at the office," David lied. "I've a great deal to do, what with the centennial auction coming up." It was true, though, that he did mean to speak to Steve Corner today to make one last attempt at securing a spot on the VIP list.

"You haven't had breakfast." It wasn't a question. The way Meredith said it, it wasn't even a statement so much as an accusation.

"I'll go to the Corner Café."

Meredith shook his head. "What, weak tea and tinned mandarins? That's no good, David." He spoke softly this morning, as soft as the creeping fog that surrounded them. "Come on back to the house, I'll do you some eggs and bacon."

"You're a vegetarian," David protested weakly.

"Yeah, but *you're* not. Brian left his groceries behind, and there's half a pound of bacon that needs used. Tossing it in the bin doesn't bring the pig back to life, does it?"

At a loss, David allowed himself to be led back up the hill to Midnight Cottage.

A STRANGE, GLOOMY silence descended over the breakfast table. Meredith only picked at his food, stared into the depths of his untouched tea, and soon retreated to his spot in the bay window. Even after David returned from washing up the dishes—glaring all the while at the bottle of hand lotion left on the kitchen windowsill, not at all a sensible place for it—the silence persisted.

No scratch of fountain pen, no jingle of bracelets, not a single one of the thousand little gestures that usually drove David up the wall: Meredith humming to himself or drumming his fingers against his sketch pad or clicking his rings together or tapping the nib of his pen against his teeth.

Just what David had wanted, of course. Proper peace and quiet at last. But Meredith did seem to stare awfully this morning: out the window, at the blank page of his sketch pad, down at his own stocking feet (one sock striped, one plain). At anywhere besides David, in fact. It made him uneasy.

He supposed he ought to say something, to tactfully inquire how Meredith was doing after the events of the previous evening. (The incident in the street, that is. David was quite sure they'd reached a mutual, if unspoken, understanding that anything that might have occurred afterward was best left forgotten.)

He was still trying to work out exactly what to say when his deliberations were ended by Mr. Bednarek's knock at the door.

"Good morning, good morning," effused the landlord. "So it seems we have lost another tenant, no? Such a pity that Mrs. Sylvania did not find the room to her liking."

"Yes, Mr. Bednarek," said David, "I've been meaning to speak with you about that."

Bednarek's cheery expression faded as his gaze landed on Meredith, who hadn't risen to greet him and instead sat with his chin on his knees, staring into the distance. "My dear Schwarzy, what has you looking so tragic this morning?"

David wished Bednarek hadn't asked that particular question.

Meredith heaved a sigh, then proceeded to astonish him by bursting out: "Everybody's getting married except for me!"

#78: It is impossible to ever guess what he will do or say next.

"Oh, come now," Bednarek attempted to console him. "The right person awaits you just around corner, no? I am certain you will make someone a lovely wife or husband someday."

Meredith brightened up a bit at that. "You think so?"

"Without a doubt!" proclaimed Bednarek.

"About the roommate situation," David broke in. "I did wonder if we mightn't perhaps have better luck in the long run if we were a bit more selective?" At Bednarek's puzzled look, he elaborated, "Making sure they're a good fit for the, er, household. Brian, for instance, turned out to be a bit volatile."

"And George-7 was simply awful to David," added Meredith, "even after we explained that accountants *here* don't do that business with the chickens."

"And Joanna," said David. Meredith shuddered.

"Ah, Mrs. Joanna," said Bednarek fondly. "A charming young lady."

"Charming? She went playing Charlie Parker records at all hours of the day and night," said David. "I tell you, she drove poor Schwarzy to tears."

"Oh, she did not."

"She did."

"I might've cried a *bit*," Meredith conceded.

"You wept for days and days."

"Well, I got her back in the end, didn't I?"

"I don't know how much of a victory I'd call that," David grumbled. "You played Gang of Four at her until she had a nervous breakdown, and we all had to suffer for it."

"It was Rip Rig and Panic, actually."

"God, you're a sadist."

Meredith grinned. "A bit, yeah."

#79: He admits to that a little too easily.

"Boys, boys," interrupted Bednarek. "I am landlord, not proprietor of record shop. I assure you, I take such preference into account. In fact, I have found for you already new roommate. He arrives this evening." The suspect cherub-grin had returned. "I tell you, we cannot keep them away from the Midnight Cottage!"

Not until Bednarek had gone did David remember he'd meant to press him for details about his meeting with Cartier. As usual, Meredith had gotten him badly off track.

It was a relief to finally leave for work, where his attention was occupied by preparations for the centennial gala and, during slower moments, sifting through house listings. Soon enough he'd find the right place and be able to wash his hands of Midnight Cottage for good—all the more urgent after last night.

Not, of course, that anything had happened. A moment of poor judgment, brought on by the adrenaline rush of a shared danger. Nothing more. They both understood that. Hardly worth mentioning again.

Still, David stayed late at the office. (Possibly it took him that long to work up the nerve to approach Steve Corner, only to find the manager's office dark and deserted when he finally did.)

Just as he stood outside the front door of Midnight Cottage, willing himself to actually step inside, tires crunched on gravel behind him. He turned in time to see a dilapidated sports car pull up next to his van.

From the driver's door emerged a small man with glasses, a septum piercing, and a wispy goatee, with curly dark hair piled up into a bun atop his head.

"Is this Midnight Cottage?" he asked.

"It is indeed," said David. "You're the new roommate, I take it?"

"Picked up my keys from Bednarek just now," the newcomer confirmed.

"Do come in."

As David led the way inside, the man said, "I'm Todd Billion, by the way."

David shook his hand. "David Carew. And this," he said, as they stepped into the living room, "is my pet magpie who's temporarily escaped from its cage."

He didn't know why he expected that to work any better than his last attempt at forcing Meredith to introduce himself, because it didn't.

In the bay window, Meredith looked up from painting his nails and gave a little wave. "Yeah. Hi."

After allowing himself to be embraced and air-kissed, Todd Billion cast an uneasy glance toward the window. "So, uh. Wow. I guess we are *really* up close to the Midnight Wood, huh?" He dropped his voice to a whisper. "Do the werewolves ever bother you at night?"

"There are no werewolves in the Midnight Wood," said David, then frowned. "Well. I suppose there was the one. And it *was* rather late when he came to the door."

"Oh, it was no bother, really," protested Meredith. "He only wanted to borrow a grammar book."

"Yes, which he never returned, by the way."

"Oh," said Todd, who didn't look the least bit reassured. "Right."

"Don't listen to David." Meredith held out one hand to watch his freshly painted nails shine in the setting sun. "There's nothing to worry about in the Midnight Wood."

David wished he himself could be so easily convinced.

He showed Todd to his room, returned to the kitchen to prepare his dinner, and murmured a noncommittal acknowledgment as Meredith passed by and announced that he was going for a walk. It was only some time later, after the sun had set and Bianca whined at the back door, that David realized he'd never returned.

"Didn't even bother taking you with him, did he?" David stepped outside after her. "All right, Bianca, you tell me. Where's your adoptive father gone?"

Surely Meredith had the good sense to stay out of the Midnight Wood after his luck had run out the night before.

#80: He has nothing of the sort.

David started off in the direction of the Wood, but paused just before the tree line. He'd gone into the Wood far more often than he liked of late, and wasn't keen to do it again if he could help it.

"Meredith?" he called, but received no answer.

Steeling himself for whatever horrors were in store for him this time, David stepped between two birches and into the darkness. He had to admit, it was not much darker inside the Wood than out, not now that it was really nighttime and the moon had risen.

He hadn't gone far when his guess was proven correct.

From the distance, carried on the cool night breeze, came Meredith's voice, deep and dark and melancholy as he sang:

"Ich weiß nicht, was soll es bedeuten,
Daß ich so traurig bin."

If he was singing, he was fine, David told himself firmly. There was no need for him to proceed any farther into the lurking dangers of the Midnight Wood—treacherous tree roots in the path, branches at just the right height to knock his head into, bloodthirsty creatures waiting just out of sight for the first opportunity to attack.

"Ein Märchen aus alten Zeiten,
Das kommt mir nicht aus dem Sinn."

David had meant to return to the house after ascertaining that Meredith hadn't wandered off into too much danger—possibly he might admit to just a touch of nerves after the night before—but found himself drawn in by the song. Though he didn't understand the meaning of the words, the sound of it opened up a quiet, aching sadness in him, an unfamiliar emptiness that made the thought of returning to sit alone in his room unbearable.

"Die Luft ist kühl, und es dunkelt,
Und ruhig fließt der Rhein."

There was a chill in the air, perhaps from the nearby brook that David could hear but not locate in the darkness. It occurred to him that if he turned back now, he'd be quite on his own when it came to finding his way back out of the Wood. (On his own aside from Bianca and that sinister shadowy figure that he hoped he'd only imagined and God knew what else that made its home in the Midnight Wood.)

In fact, David didn't have the least idea where he was now. (Was that the sound of footsteps in the underbrush mirroring his own, or the rattle of dry leaves in the wind? Catching sight of something from the corner of his eye, David whirled—no, of course it was nothing, only the fog rising among the gray willows on the banks of a distant pool.)

"Der Gipfel des Berges funkelt
Im Abendsonnenschein."

Nothing appeared familiar, panic threatened to set in—and then he recognized the ring of pines they'd come to before. He'd been sure this spot was much deeper in the Wood, but it sounded as though Meredith were just on the other side of the trees, and David wouldn't complain about the shifting topography if it meant he hadn't gotten himself lost in the Wood after all.

Bianca raced ahead, and David followed more slowly into the moonlit glade, picking up his pace only to avoid lingering too long by the towering black alder flanked by those vicious hawthorns.

"Die schönste Jungfrau—"

Meredith fell silent at David's approach. He didn't move from where he lay atop the flat stone at the edge of the clearing, arms folded beneath his head, staring up at the soft glow of the moon in the night sky.

In the continuing silence, David took a seat upon the rock at his side, while Bianca wandered a little distance away among the high grass.

"Working out how to get some moon cheese, are you?"

"Everybody knows the moon's made of meringue, *honestly*, David. How else do you think it stays afloat?"

"Oh, of course."

Meredith turned over and propped himself up on one elbow. "What's up?"

"Nothing. Er—well—" David floundered. "Bianca missed you."

Traitorously, the Chihuahua continued her explorations without so much as a glance in their direction.

"I'm sorry, precious," Meredith called to her. "I suppose I did lose track of time. Speaking of," he told David, lighting up with excitement, "I've come up with this wicked recipe to make for Kinley's party."

"Language," chided David.

#81: He collects regionalisms in the same way he collects shiny trinkets.

Every time the two artists spent time together, Kinley's Boston accent seeped into Meredith's speech the way all accents seemed to, and traces of it persisted for hours afterward. Apparently, the mere mention of his name was enough to induce the effect.

"Yeah, all right," said Meredith, "only I'm going to make a butter cake, right, with false prophet's balm *and* tincture of shrinking violet. You want to be sparing with that, of course—only a drop or two to open up your third eye just a bit, that's what Mrs. J says."

"Does she."

"You ought to try some," said Meredith. "It'd do you some good to relax."

David scowled. "You know exactly what happened the last time—and the only time, might I add—that you talked me into smoking prophet's balm with you."

Meredith giggled. "Yeah, you had a proper freak-out, didn't you?"

"It's *not* funny," said David. "It wasn't then, either. Not that it stopped you laughing at me."

Meredith's face fell. "I'm sorry, David." He reached out and brushed a stray lock of dark hair from David's eyes. (The unthinking, casual intimacy of the gesture brought back the same feeling provoked by the song, a feeling that threatened to careen out of control if left unchecked. David turned his face away, and made a mental note to have his hair cut soon.) "You're right, that was a dick move. Stoned Meri is a bit of an idiot. Well, so's the regular one, really," he admitted.

"Schwarzy—" David began with a frown.

"'S all right," said Meredith, reclining onto the rock once more. "I'm not smart, I know that."

"Look," said David, trying to get things back on track. He'd give it one last shot, and that was it. "I just thought you might want to talk about, er, whatever's bothering you."

Meredith held both hands above his face, turning his outspread fingers to watch his rings catch the moonlight, silver and jade and obsidian.

No, this was pointless. David started to stand, but was arrested by Meredith finally speaking. "Well, it's like I told Bednarek, isn't it? Everybody I know is getting married—"

"I'm not," interjected David. (Perhaps that fact did worry him, just a bit, if he allowed himself to dwell on it.)

"—and here's me, still single, and thirty-one this winter."

David choked. "*Thirty-one?*"

"Not yet," said Meredith. "I will be."

"You—but—you can't—*how?*"

#82: He neither looks nor acts his age.

"Bit sad, isn't it?" agreed Meredith, clearly misreading the reason for David's astonishment.

"But that's nonsense," protested David. "You know as well as I do, you can have nearly anybody. I've seen what happens every time we go out." Perhaps he ought to feel a hint of jealousy at that, but David had personally never found much appeal in the idea of going to bed with a stranger.

Meredith shook his head. "That's not the sort of thing I'm talking about. I mean, it's nice to be wanted like that, only it's not—well, not much chance of going anywhere, is it?" He looked up imploringly at David. "Not when I'm already in love with someone else."

For a second, David was almost taken in; then he laughed.

Meredith didn't.

"You're joking."

"I'm not," Meredith insisted. "Don't laugh. I'm sharing my deepest secret."

"I don't believe it."

"It's true, I've been in love with somebody for ages, but they'd never give me the time of day."

David remained skeptical. "You can't keep a secret to save your life, and now you're telling me you've been carrying a torch for somebody for, what, months? Without having breathed a word of it?"

"Years," said Meredith, and that fragile fog-soft quality had returned to his voice. "Only I don't think I quite realized it myself at first."

He really meant it. David had never imagined Meredith as the pining sort, not that he'd ever devoted much thought to the question, or wished to continue doing so now. He cast his mind back to the last person he could recall Meredith actually dating, a girlfriend of no more than a month, three years prior. "Don't tell me you're still hung up on Serafina?"

"*Serafina?*" Meredith laughed, then grew serious again. "No. I suppose I did fall for her a bit, but then she went and left us for Gerald Fuentes."

"Ah, yes, the encyclopedia salesman."

"Salesfrog," corrected Meredith.

"Sales*frog*," echoed David. "Right." At the time, Meredith had moped around for a bit, but had bounced back within the week, and soon after had come the first appearance of the cautionary speech.

"Who, then? Anyone I know?"

"Course not."

#83: On the rare occasion that he does attempt to lie, he is hopeless at it.

David had no desire to involve himself in his housemate's love life, no matter how indirectly, but he did have to admit to a certain curiosity. "Not Mrs. Jupiter?" he hazarded.

"Nah, me and Liz are just good friends." At David's look, Meredith admitted, "All right, maybe *especially* good friends after the other night, but it's not like that. She says we mustn't do that again, and she wouldn't've done in the first place if she'd known I was unavailable."

"Schwarzy, you're available to anyone who spares you a second glance." As the words left his mouth, David worried that in the present circumstances, this might cross the line from banter into mean-spiritedness, but Meredith only grinned.

"Yeah, I know, only she means, like, *emotionally*."

David ran through the short list of other possibilities. Bednarek, of course, was right out. Steve Corner, while a repulsive possibility, had made his interest all too clear. Then the answer hit David like a thunderbolt, stunningly obvious. He couldn't believe he'd never suspected before.

"You're in love with Kinley."

Meredith laughed himself near to choking at that, until he was forced to sit up and catch his breath. "David! You can't be serious. Me, in love with *Kinley*?"

That was not at all the reaction David had anticipated, and he couldn't help but feel a bit offended. It had been a perfectly logical conclusion to draw from the available facts. "Why not? You help him with all his petitions, you go around together holding hands, you spend all your time with him—"

"What are you talking about, I spend all my time with *you*," said Meredith, then went into another fit of giggles. "Me and Kinley! David, he's like a brother to me. *And* he's straight."

In any case, David acknowledged grudgingly, it seemed to have cheered up Meredith to no end. "Yes, well, if you're quite finished laughing at me, I'll be going."

"Hang on, wait for me." Meredith climbed down from the rock, and Bianca bounded out of the grass to join him. Growing more sober, he said, "I'm not actually sure why I went telling you all that—I know you don't care, really—but thanks for listening."

"That's all right," said David magnanimously. He, too, was unsure what had prompted the unexpected confession, but at least the awkwardness of the morning had faded. "Besides, it's just as you said the other day, isn't it? We tell each other all our secrets."

"Yeah," agreed Meredith with only the slightest hesitation, and added, "Nearly."

As they started out of the clearing, David ignored the sick feeling in his stomach and tried not to think about Leonard Flood and the house with the ugly wood paneling. "Are you sure this is the right way back?"

"What are you talking about, David, of course it is. It's the simplest thing, really, I don't know how you always go getting yourself—" Meredith broke off. "Do you hear that?"

"Hear what?" David hadn't heard anything at all, aside from Meredith's assessment of his apparently deficient navigational abilities.

Meredith shook his head. "Could've sworn I heard somebody calling my name just now. Oh, well, I suppose—you see, there it is again! Oh, you must hear it, all whispery and faraway." His step slowed, and he gazed off into the dense forest, which now seemed impossibly darker in spite of the moon above. "Perhaps I ought to just go and see—"

"It's the wind," said David firmly, and not least because he had no intention of allowing Meredith to wander off and leave him on his own again.

"Yeah," said Meredith with a soft laugh that might have been the tiniest bit forced. "Course it is. Who'd come calling for me, really, when you're already right here?"

"Perhaps Todd," suggested David weakly, notwithstanding the fact that he certainly did not yet know Meredith's first name. "We have been gone for some time, you know. And we ought to be getting back," he added. "It's bad enough in here without you imagining disembodied voices."

At the crack of a branch, David flinched. He was suddenly very aware of the darkness pressing in on all sides, of how little chance the two of them had if it turned out they *weren't* alone in the Wood.

David flinched again, this time at the unexpected touch of a hand coming to rest at his elbow, and turned to find Meredith studying him with an unnervingly perceptive look. Just for an instant, before he offered an apologetic half smile and took hold of David's arm. "It is quite cold out tonight."

It wasn't, but David couldn't bring himself to complain about Meredith clinging to him as they made their way through the last stretch of wood back toward Midnight Cottage, and if he happened, in fact, to be a bit glad of it, he had no intention of admitting any such thing.

Chapter Thirteen

The next few days passed uneventfully. Things were quiet at work as the centennial auction steadily approached, no further repair personnel were inflicted upon Midnight Cottage, and the household adjusted to its new occupant. Todd Billion worked the late shift bartending, and upon returning home was in the habit of pacing the back deck while holding long phone conversations in Ilocano. This latter detail was relayed to David with a great deal of admiration from Meredith, who likewise stayed up until all hours and appeared all too impressed by Todd's linguistic abilities. David decided it would be prudent to have a quiet word with him in the same way he had with Brian.

"Trust me," said Todd, "that won't be a problem. I've got no intention of stepping on your toes here."

"Stepping on—oh, no, no, no," said David hastily. "Whatever gave you that impression?"

Todd stared for a long moment. "You . . . you are fucking with me, right? You know what, never mind. Whatever situation you guys have going on, or don't have going on, none of my business. Besides, I'm ace anyway, so—" He shrugged.

"Right," said David, finding himself quite rattled. "Of course."

#84: However such a misapprehension came about, Meredith is certainly to blame.

On Saturday morning, David went out for an early house viewing. The ramshackle Victorian left him unimpressed, for reasons entirely unrelated to its outrageously high asking price, and he returned to Midnight Cottage to find Florian climbing back into his truck.

He raised a hand in greeting. "Hey, Dave."

"David, actually," he corrected automatically. "Er, good morning. I was just about to make some tea—coffee, I mean, if you'd care to stay a bit longer." Coffee, he was sure, would be Florian's drink of choice. Naturally, as the future son-in-law of Maitland Cartier, he was to be afforded every courtesy. Beyond that, though, David had to admit a certain fascination with Florian, and was curious to witness how an extended interaction between him and Meredith would play out.

"Thanks, but I gotta be on my way," said Florian through the open window. He flicked on his lighter, lit a cigarette, and, with it, gestured his farewell. "See you around."

Yes, David liked him. Florian seemed the sort of person he could become friends with, Adalynn or no Adalynn. Perhaps they *would* become friends. It was certainly far more plausible than David being friends with his polar-opposite brother, though he supposed he and Meredith *were* friends after a fashion.

Why, exactly, he couldn't say, especially as he entered the living room to find Meredith crouching in the corner with towel, broom, and dustpan, trying to clean up the remains of a coffee mug that had been quite full at the time of its demise, and making an awful mess of it.

"Good God, what have you done now?"

Meredith started at the sound of his voice, flinching and dropping a piece of broken ceramic glazed in dark sea green.

"That's your favorite cup, too," David observed.

"It *was*," he said mournfully.

"Though how you got pieces of it all the way back there, I can't imagine."

#85: He manages to destroy things in the unlikeliest of ways.

"Oh, you know me," said Meredith vaguely, "always making a mess of things. Like you said, not much going on up here, is there?" He punctuated the statement with a tap to his temple.

"Go on." David shooed him out of the way. "Let me." *Before you make it even worse*—but he refrained from saying that part aloud. He didn't quite like the way Meredith had spoken of himself the other night, or just now, for that matter.

By the time David returned with paper towels, Meredith was coaxing Bianca out from beneath the sofa. When she emerged, he promptly caught her up and cradled her against his chest, kissing the top of her head. "There, you're all right," he murmured. "The crash frightened you, didn't it, precious? But it's all over now."

David sighed and set to work wiping up the last of the spilled coffee.

"Sorry, David. I know I'm hopeless, really."

"Well, never mind that now." Again that little jab of unease made David seek a new topic. "I ran into your brother on his way out, by the way. What brought him around today?"

Meredith dropped onto the window seat and folded himself up in the corner, pulling his knees to his chest. "He wants me to do a portrait of Adalynn as his wedding gift to her."

"You're a surrealist."

"Yeah, I tried telling him that, only . . ." Meredith concluded with a shrug.

It was a nice idea, David supposed, for Florian to offer the chance, even if the style might leave something to be desired. As long as said portrait was unveiled to the recipient after the wedding, when David no longer had a stake in the proceedings.

"Only we're not to tell her he stopped by," said Meredith. "It's meant to be a surprise."

"By the way, when is—"

The knock at the door both interrupted and answered David's question. Genevieve entered, followed by a short, slender woman of about the same age with auburn hair in a tasteful upsweep. She wore a denim jacket over a ruffled floral sundress, and her handbag, though designer, was a smaller and less ostentatious affair than Genevieve's. Immediately, David decided he liked her.

"Hey, guys," said Genevieve. "This is Adalynn, Florian's fiancée." To Adalynn, she introduced, "My cousin Meredith and his friend Dave."

"David Carew," he said, offering his hand. "Wonderful to meet you." Not wanting to come on too strong at this juncture, he avoided mentioning his workplace.

Adalynn returned a surprisingly firm handshake. "Nice to meet you both."

"Might I offer you a cup of tea? Coffee? It's no trouble."

"Thanks, Dave, but we've got to get going," said Genevieve briskly. "We need to get this over with—no offense, Mere, but you've really been dragging your ass here—and find a new bridal shower venue ASAP."

"Oh?" David inquired. "You've not had it yet?" From his admittedly vague ideas of wedding proceedings, he'd had the impression that a bridal shower only a month before was cutting it a bit close.

"We had to push it back a few times," Adalynn explained, "but I want my grandmother there, and it's been difficult for her to get away until now. You know how it can be with diplomatic posts." At David's questioning look, she elaborated, "She's ambassador to Florida, you know."

"Oh, yes, of course." David cursed himself. Foolish, foolish, overlooking a crucial detail like that. (Behind him came the faintest clink of metal on ceramic, rather like someone surreptitiously secreting a handful of jewelry in the saucer beneath the nearby potted geranium.)

"I rented out the event center at the botanical garden," said Genevieve, "but there was a mishap at the Alchemists' Guild convention this week, and it seems the place has burned to the ground. And the worst part is that *nobody bothered notifying me* until this morning."

David would have hated to be the unfortunate employee responsible for making that phone call.

"It's not a big deal. In fact," Adalynn teased, "I think you're more invested in this shower than I am."

"It is a big deal!" said Genevieve. "I should've had Florian call them up. He really would've let them have it."

Adalynn frowned. "Oh, I hardly think that's necessary."

"Why not have it here?" suggested David.

Genevieve looked around doubtfully. "Here?"

"Why not?" Though he'd extended the offer without thinking, doing a favor for Adalynn Cartier was worth any inconvenience. (Surely it would warrant at least a casual mention to her father as well.) "There's plenty of space in the garden, we could rearrange the deck to make room for a few tables, and as long as the weather holds—"

"It is supposed to be nice out next Saturday," said Genevieve thoughtfully.

"I really couldn't impose," protested Adalynn. "We don't even know each other."

"Nonsense," said David. "You're my roommate's sister-in-law, or near enough. We're practically family."

"It would solve a lot of problems," said Genevieve. Already in planning mode, she continued, half to herself, "We'd have to bring in some chairs and a couple of extra tables, but between Jayceon and your brother—yeah, it could work."

Adalynn gazed around the room; already her face had lit up with a glowing smile. "This is such a cute little cottage, and I'm sure the garden is just as nice. If it's really all right with everyone . . ." She cast a glance toward Meredith, who'd been suspiciously silent for some time. In fact, David realized, he hadn't even given Adalynn his usual greeting.

"What do you say, Mere?" prompted Genevieve.

Meredith sat upright, hands folded in his lap and covered by his sleeves in a way that made him appear ludicrously childlike. "As you like."

"Great," said Genevieve, clapping her hands. "Now let's get a move on."

David had a mercifully quiet two hours to browse real estate listings and tidy up his room, at which point he took a break to make himself lunch. He was slicing tomatoes for a salad when Meredith came bounding in through the front door, causing Bianca to yap in excitement.

"How did it go?" asked David.

"Wonderful," said Meredith in a dreamy tone, retrieving his rings and bracelets from the potted geranium. (David decided it best not to inquire.) "Adalynn's lovely. Not sure what she sees in Florian, but I suppose there's no accounting for taste."

"Now don't you go saying anything of the sort to her," warned David, pointing his paring knife in Meredith's direction for emphasis—and then, as the memory of Tuesday night flashed in his mind, hastily lowered it. "We need this wedding to go off without a hitch, remember that."

Heedless, Meredith went on, "And she's picked out the most gorgeous bridesmaid dresses."

A terrible possibility occurred to David. "You didn't." He should have considered that this wedding business involved Meredith actually speaking to Adalynn, which posed a whole new set of dangers.

Meredith let his bracelets fall into place and gave his wrist a brief shake, sending them into a cacophonous jingle that seemed to please him. "Nah, what do you think? Florian'd skin me alive, and anyway, I am not trying to Make a Spectacle," he added conscientiously.

#86: He makes a spectacle of himself constantly whether he intends to or not.

Still, at least he was showing good sense on this particular occasion.

"She showed me photos of the dresses and the decor and everything," Meredith explained, taking up his usual perch in the window.

David returned to the kitchen, scooped the sliced tomato into his salad bowl, and reached for a red onion. It was not without suspicion that he pointed out, "You still sound awfully wistful."

"Course I am, who wouldn't want to wear a lovely ball gown—"

"I certainly wouldn't."

"—and dance to Edith Piaf?"

Without thinking, David scoffed, "Who'd dance with *you*?"

There was a little too long of a pause before Meredith replied, "Ah, well, nobody, I suppose. Just as well, then, isn't it?"

David paused in his slicing. This, too, was a deviation from the usual script. They insulted each other, yes, but then the other insulted right back. And in this case, the comeback should have been effortless: Meredith pointing out the obvious, that he had no shortage of willing partners for dancing and, in all likelihood, a good deal more.

Pushing aside his unease, David switched to the more important question. "And since when do you like Edith Piaf?"

"S'pose I've gotten to like her now since you play her so much."

David suspected Meredith couldn't tell the difference between her and any other chanteuse, but before he had the opportunity to question him further on the topic, there came a rap on the deck doors.

Mrs. Jupiter waved from the other side of the glass. David set down his knife and wiped his hands on a tea towel, but Meredith got to the door first. From behind him, Bianca growled at the black cat that sat at the witch's feet.

"Oh, hush, Bianca," said Meredith. "Morning, Mrs. J, won't you come in?"

Mrs. Jupiter graciously refrained from pointing out that it was past two in the afternoon, and instead said, "Thank you, but I've only got a moment. Left the cauldron simmering, you know, and I mean to go look in on the Mice here in a bit. However, you'll be pleased to know I've found an answer to your problem."

"Oh? Which problem was that?" David hadn't been aware of a problem, other than Meredith in general, but he didn't think she'd have any ideal solution for that.

"The two of you losing each other all the time, of course." From the folds of her voluminous shawl, she produced two bracelets. "Here you arc. I've enchanted these to track each other."

Meredith eagerly took the bracelet Mrs. Jupiter offered him, a wide bangle of embossed brass, and slipped it onto his wrist. "Thanks, Mrs. J. This is brilliant!"

David hesitated. She meant well, of course, and one oughtn't to refuse a gift, but he didn't wear jewelry as a rule, and he certainly had no intention of matching with Meredith.

Mrs. Jupiter presented him with his own bracelet—a cuff of braided leather, adorned with carved brass beads. "This seemed more your style."

That was true; it was understated and masculine, and if he had been of the inclination to wear jewelry, he would've chosen something like it.

"Thank you," he told her. "I appreciate it." He did appreciate the thought, if not the execution, and dutifully put it on. The moment he did, both he and Meredith exclaimed in surprise as each bracelet gave a faint but definite pull toward the other.

"Magnetism?" asked David.

"Magic," corrected Mrs. Jupiter. "A simple locator spell. It's effective at a distance as well, but both must be worn in order for it to work."

"How thoughtful of you," said David.

Afterward, he promptly shoved his into the back of his dresser drawer and put it out of his mind.

"Oh, David, come *on*, you can't show up to Kinley's like that," said Meredith. "You look like an accountant."

David lowered the newspaper to glare at him over the sports section. "I *am* an accountant."

"Yeah, I know, and so will anybody else who looks at you."

"Better this than parading myself around like a shameless strumpet." In David's opinion, his own outfit—dark slacks and a pin-striped button-down in soft gray—was perfectly presentable. Meredith, on the other hand, keeping to his usual black, had changed into skintight jeans so shredded that they consisted of more holes than denim, and a shirt cut low enough in front to expose a fair amount of ink and sparse dark-blond hair. Not, of course, that David was looking, but one could hardly help noticing. For some reason, Meredith had topped off the ensemble with a strand of black pearls, and—

"And what the hell have you done to your face?"

"It's triple-winged eyeliner! Do you like it?"

"No."

He also hadn't shaved in a few days, which made for quite the juxtaposition. Somehow it suited him, not that David was going to say so.

"Oh, come on," prodded Meredith. "Quit being such a dishcloth."

#87: He comes up with the most incomprehensible expressions.

David scowled. "Perhaps I won't go at all. I doubt you and Kinley would miss me."

Meredith's teasing grin fell away. "David," he said, "how come you don't like Kinley? He likes you."

"I just—he doesn't—" In all honesty, David's disapproval—he wouldn't go so far as *dislike*—was based on impressions he couldn't entirely articulate. It was something about the way Kinley and Meredith went around being obnoxiously affectionate with each other, laughing at their little in-jokes, slipping outside to huddle together smoking cigarettes, which Meredith never touched at any other time.

That seemed the one reason that wasn't too petty to say aloud, and David seized upon it. "You only smoke cigarettes when you're with him." To his chagrin, it sounded just as trivial outside of his head, but it was still preferable to admitting the truth—that David suspected the two of them really *wouldn't* miss him in his absence.

"That's not true," said Meredith indignantly. "We do lots of other things. We make *art*, David."

David took a deep breath and pinched the bridge of his nose. "I do not mean," he said, choosing his words precisely, "that you and he do *nothing but* smoke cigarettes, but rather that he is the only person *with whom* you smoke cigarettes."

"Oh, you should have said."

"Come on," growled David. "Let's go before I change my mind."

McKinley Hendricks was a tall, lanky man with snakebite piercings and a graduate degree in political science. He rarely smiled—in no small part, David suspected, due to the latter—and had a penchant for wearing black leather and anything that could be adorned with spikes. Tonight was no exception to either his expression or attire, though the bleach-blond streaks he'd sported in his Afro a few weeks before were now bright teal.

In his downtown apartment, located on the second floor above the antiques shop, the party was well underway. David recognized a few familiar faces from the Rat Cellar in the crowd, even if the corresponding names escaped him. False prophet's balm circulated in abundance, and fairy lights strung along the walls cast a hazy glow through its sweet heavy smoke. Currently, Kinley was occupied rolling a joint as he pointed out various party guests.

"You know Yvonne and Jalisa—my sister and her wife," he added, presumably for David's benefit, "and that's Spherical Jones over there talking to Ricardo—were you at the Rat Cellar the last time he came through town? And I *know* you've never met—hey, ladies," Kinley interrupted himself as two women approached side by side, one unsmiling and dark-haired, clad in full goth attire, the other cornsilk-blond in a long peasant dress of soft blue.

"Hi, Kinley," said the brunette.

"Hi, Meredith," said the blonde at the same time.

"Oh, good, I'd hoped you'd be here." After air-kissing them both, Meredith said, "David, this is Mary Alice and Corpseflower. David is my roommate," he explained to the pair.

"Hi, David," they said in unison, studying him with a frank appreciation that was admittedly rather flattering even if thoroughly misplaced.

"Oh, er—pleased to meet you, of course."

Meredith tutted at them. "Go on, can't you see you're embarrassing him? Don't mind them, David, they're harmless, really."

The two women exchanged a look; then the blonde turned her attention to Kinley as he patted down his pockets in search of a cigarette lighter, offering her own instead. The brunette, meanwhile, leaned in very close to whisper to Meredith—much closer than necessary, in David's opinion. Though he could excuse the whispering given the din of the crowd and the thumping bass emanating from the stereo, he was far less inclined to overlook the gross familiarity of her hand resting against Meredith's chest, her eyelashes brushing his cheek as she pulled back with an expectant expression.

He didn't seem to mind, however, so David confined himself to silent disapproval as he sipped his beer.

And now Meredith was *blushing*, which was somehow worse. His knuckles ghosted over her bare shoulder, and his voice dropped a little lower as he murmured something conciliatory and barely audible.

David turned away to give them privacy, but still caught a few words: "—no, no, last time was lovely . . . just not tonight, I don't think . . . wouldn't be fair to you, would it?"

The music had switched to something with screeching vocals, and more partygoers crowded themselves into the middle of the living room. A trio of vampires writhed against one another in a slow, sensual dance; one of them caught David's eye and raised their eyebrows in invitation, but he shook his head.

He wished he were back in his own room with a cup of tea and some suitable reading material. He'd much prefer a quiet night in and a sensible bedtime over this, and was not altogether sure why he'd allowed Meredith to talk him into coming.

A brief tap on the shoulder brought him back to the reality of his surroundings, and he turned to find Kinley taking a long drag of prophet's balm while Meredith, slowly exhaling smoke, leaned against him with a dreamy expression. Corpseflower and Mary Alice had departed in the meantime.

Kinley offered the joint to David. Against his better judgment, he accepted it.

"Only if you want to," said Meredith. He closed his eyes and snuggled contentedly against Kinley, who draped an arm around him and rested his chin atop his head.

David decided that he did.

Though smoking, as usual, sent him into a violent coughing fit that made his eyes water, a few hits were enough for the mild high to set in and dull the sharp edges of his surroundings. The overwhelming mixture of too-loud music and unintelligible conversation settled into a tolerable background noise, and David was content to lean against the wall and half listen to the conversation between Kinley and Meredith as it drifted in and out of his awareness.

"It's the principle, man," said Kinley. "What do I want to hang around a bunch of wealthy elitists for, huh?"

"But you'd be hanging out with *me*," protested Meredith. "It might be fun! Besides, it is for a good cause, and it would help David out."

David blinked at hearing his name and managed a vague sound of acknowledgment.

"Oh, please, won't you at least think about it?" Meredith fixed Kinley with that irresistible pleading look of his that David was all too familiar with.

"I'll *think* about it," said Kinley grudgingly.

Meredith rose up on his toes to give him a kiss on the cheek. "Thank you."

"Yeah, yeah," muttered Kinley, but wrapped an arm around Meredith's shoulders and gave him a brief squeeze.

David cleared his throat. "I think the young lady over there is trying to get your attention." He nodded in her direction.

One of the vampires who'd been trying to catch Meredith's eye gave a little wave and threw him a kiss, and he waved back.

"David, come dance with us," urged Meredith, tugging at his sleeve.

David pulled away from his grasp. "I don't dance." Then, feeling somehow responsible for Meredith's crestfallen expression, admitted, "I *can't* dance."

"Oh, neither can I, that don't matter."

"Language," chided David absently.

Something sharp and searching flashed to life in Kinley's eyes, some question that Meredith seemed to understand without words.

"'S all right," he said softly. "C'mon." He pulled Kinley after him to join the vampires, leaving David behind.

Alone, he drifted to the kitchen, conscientiously placed his empty beer bottle in the recycling bin, decided against a second drink, and helped himself to a handful of pretzels, avoiding both the prophet's balm brownies and the shrinking violet cake. The latter seemed to be a hit, though Meredith hadn't touched it himself, and David had no intention of doing so, either.

He commandeered a kitchen stool at one end of the counter and spent an indeterminate period of time scrolling aimlessly through house listings and home-design magazines until he'd ended up deep down a rabbit hole of virtual paint swatches and heated debates in online upholstery forums. Perhaps, David mused, he'd have to go and have a look at Ralph's wares after all. Though his own taste tended toward quiet neutrals, he had to admit there was something to be said for a touch of color here and there.

In the restroom, David splashed cool water on his face before venturing back out into the main room. The effects of the false prophet's balm had already faded considerably, as they tended to do. He half expected to be met with the unwelcome sight of Meredith still entangled with one or more of the vampires, but, in fact, he was nowhere to be found. David swore, if he'd gone home with someone and left him without so much as a word—

Kinley was sure to know where he'd run off to, but he, too, had vanished. Perhaps the two of them had stepped out for a cigarette—Kinley was oddly fastidious about not smoking tobacco indoors, even if everything else appeared to be permissible.

David was just reaching for his phone to text Meredith when he spotted Corpseflower and Mary Alice at the edge of the crowd. The blond woman knelt before the open window to converse on eye level with a group of pixies perched on the windowsill, while her black-clad companion who'd struck out with Meredith gazed around the room with evident boredom.

As she appeared otherwise unengaged, David approached her. "Pardon me, Mrs. . . . er, Corpseflower, was it? I wondered—"

"I'm Mary Alice," said the woman flatly, and jerked a thumb toward her friend. "*She's* Corpseflower."

". . . right," said David. "My mistake. I seem to have lost track of my roommate, I don't suppose you'd have any idea where he's ended up?"

He received only a wordless glare in response, and then, at last, she pointed toward the kitchen. David thanked her and started back in that direction.

Even before he reached the kitchen, he heard Meredith's voice from within.

"—asked him to ages ago, I swear it. I just don't want to s-sound, you know—" he faltered.

"I know," said Kinley. "Honestly, I'm glad I was misreading it. He seems like a decent dude, but I just wanted to make sure, you feel me?"

David paused, uncertain. Perhaps this was a private conversation—some oblique reference to Meredith's secret crush? Again, curiosity needled at him, but if Meredith didn't want to share, it was none of his business (even if Meredith had revealed their identity to Kinley and not to him).

"I know you can take care of yourself," Kinley went on, "but you know I've got your back if you need me, okay?" He glanced up as David strode into the kitchen. "Hey."

Meredith hopped down from his perch on the edge of the countertop and drifted over to wrap his arms around David; false prophet's balm always seemed to amplify his tendencies to seek affection. "*There* you are. I didn't know where you'd got to and was about to come looking."

"I think you were a cat in another life," grumbled David. "You'd be happy as anything among a litter of kittens all piled on top of each other, wouldn't you?"

Meredith giggled and nuzzled against David's shoulder. David scratched him gently between the shoulder blades, as he might do to a real cat, and admitted, "I was looking for you, too, as a matter of fact. Thought perhaps you'd gone out to smoke."

"I haven't been smoking," said Meredith. "Not cigarettes, I mean," he added quickly when David pulled back to look at him in disbelief. "Prophet's balm, *yes*, but you've no room to talk there."

David supposed he hadn't.

THE MOON HUNG full and silver in the sky by the time the two of them walked home along the dark road. David supposed, as far as parties went, he had no reason to complain—no more than usual, at any rate.

He might grudgingly admit—if only to himself—that perhaps it had done him some good to go out, to allow himself a little indulgence; there was no denying that he felt more relaxed. Perhaps that was why, as they made their way past the edge of town, David's mind wandered through snippets of conversation from the past week to Meredith gazing longingly at emerald-green satin *and the single frantic kiss between them, how desperately he'd returned it—*

David pushed aside that last thought. "Can I ask you something?"

Meredith, who'd been humming quietly to himself in the midst of his own contemplations, said, "Hmm?"

Ordinarily, it was a question serious enough for David to shy away from, but right now, it didn't seem so daunting. "Wouldn't want to bring on your, er, allergies, of course, but I realize I've never asked, about the dresses and so forth."

"But, David," said Meredith, "I'm not wearing a dress."

"Some of us, Meredith, are capable of thinking of a thing without it being directly in front of us."

They'd reached the foot of the hill now, not far from the low dark shadow of Mrs. Jupiter's cottage. David went on, trying to gather his thoughts as he spoke. "At first, I thought you were trying to be subversive or punk or something, but that's not it, is it?" He'd begun to realize it went beyond that—how far beyond was the question. "It's . . . important to you."

"That's not a question," objected Meredith placidly.

"I mean," David said with an inarticulate wave, "do you want me to call you differently, *they* or *she* or something?"

Meredith shook his head, no more concerned than if David had asked his plans for the weekend. "Nah, I don't think so. I mean, you can try if it'll make you feel better, I don't know that I'd *mind* really."

"How would it make *me* feel better?"

Meredith gave a soft laugh. "Come on, David, I know you. You like to go putting everybody in neat little boxes, with labels on."

"Meredith," said David sincerely, "nobody could ever fit you into a box. You're far too . . ." He gestured, seeking a word, and settled on "expansive."

"Thank you."

#88: It wasn't meant as a compliment.

The two of them walked in silence for a moment before Meredith said, "I just like what I like, is all. Don't see what's the big deal about it." He gave David a quick sideways glance. "Only if you're asking, what am I, in my head—if you want me to put a name to things—s'pose maybe I am a bit of this and a bit of that and a sprinkle of what-have-you, but I mean, in the end, I'm just me, aren't I?"

David thought about that for a long time and wasn't sure that he came any nearer to understanding, but ultimately there was nothing in that statement that he hadn't already known. "Yes, well, on the off chance that you ever find it does make any difference, you will tell me?"

"Course I will," said Meredith, and then, softer, "Thanks for asking."

He wrapped both arms around one of David's as they walked along.

"You're clinging."

"I'm cold."

Before David could point out that Meredith was always cold, and that it was entirely his own fault for not bothering to wear a proper coat, Meredith had stopped in his tracks, staring into the murky depths of the Midnight Wood. "Did you hear that?"

David hadn't heard anything and was about to say so when there came, very faintly, a distant sound that an imaginative person might take for a squeak of alarm, the cry of a Midnight Mouse in distress.

David was not an imaginative person. "I'm sure it's nothing. The wind in the trees, more likely than not."

Meredith shook his head. "There's something wrong, I know it."

Arguing that point would be fruitless, and in any case, Meredith did seem to have an instinct for this sort of thing. Still, David protested, without much conviction, "Anything that lives in the Midnight Wood can surely look after itself."

"They're my friends, David," said Meredith softly. Without waiting for an answer, he started off into the Midnight Wood, and David had no choice but to follow.

Chapter Fourteen

This time, it was no darker inside the Wood than outside, though that did little to alleviate David's sense of foreboding. Starlight illuminated the leaves of the trees, and bell-shaped purple blossoms scattered across the forest floor lit their surroundings with a dim glow.

"You see?" said David after they'd covered a little distance and found nothing amiss. "Everything is quite in order." As much as anything in the Midnight Wood ever was in order, anyway.

"S'pose so," Meredith conceded with evident reluctance. Then, brightening up, he went on, "Well, since we're here, we may as well go and see whether the sweet woodruff is out yet."

David groaned. "Can't it wait until morning? It's the middle of the night."

"Yeah, and it'll be the middle of the night then, too, in the Wood," Meredith pointed out. "Oh, come on, David, we're already right here."

For lack of any other option, David resigned himself to trailing after him as they made their way deeper into the Wood. Meredith resumed humming quietly to himself, which soon grew louder and then graduated to full-on singing, the same melancholy tune from a few nights before:

"Ihr goldnes Geschmeide blitzet,
Sie kämmt ihr goldenes Haar.
Sie kämmt es—"

"You leave off with that at once," David admonished. "You've no idea what might be in these woods, just waiting to come out and catch itself a stripey little songbird—excuse me, *medium-sized*."

"What are you on about? I'm not wearing stripes, eith—" Meredith stopped dead, and David crashed into him.

"What the hell are you—" He, too, broke off as he saw over Meredith's shoulder precisely what he was looking at.

From the shadow of the towering alder, flanked by hawthorn bushes, there stepped out the figure of a man, or something like one, clad in a hooded cloak of dark crimson. Though his face remained obscured, his hair and beard both flowed long and silver below his hood.

In a rasping whisper, he intoned, "*Come here, Meredith.*"

Meredith shrank back as the cloaked figure advanced slowly toward them. "David," he said urgently, tugging at his sleeve.

David was frozen. This was it, the same shadowy figure that had pursued him in the Wood the week before, the one he'd been trying and failing to banish from his memory ever since.

"Come with me," coaxed the stranger, his voice high and hoarse. "Come, darling child, and see what I can give you."

"I think I'm all right, actually." Meredith nudged David, but he could not move, could not tear his gaze away from the darkness beneath the crimson hood—*crimson like blood*—a darkness broken by the sudden flash of needle-sharp fangs in the moonlight.

"Just think what I can offer," the figure wheedled. "Flowers and finery the likes of which are beyond your imagination, delicacies to suit the most discerning of appetites, nightly dances in my court, music to soothe you into sleep more peaceful than you've ever known!"

"No, thank you," said Meredith firmly. Though David outweighed him by a fair bit, that didn't stop Meredith from seizing him by the arm and attempting with surprising strength to drag him from the spot. "David! *Move!*"

David snapped out of it, turned, and fled with Meredith back in the direction they'd come. The figure crashed through the brush behind them with a bone-chilling wail, ever closer as they dodged tree roots and jagged rocks and gnarled, grasping branches. He berated himself with every step. This was not how a sensible, capable man such as himself reacted in the face of danger.

They hadn't ventured far into the Wood, and already the trees thinned, the end of the forest in sight. In a new flash of terror, David questioned what exactly constituted the border of the Midnight Wood. Surely there was some line their pursuer couldn't cross. Running water? The cutoff between shadow and daylight, or at least where daylight normally fell? The last tree at the edge of the Wood? The footpath, at the farthest, and it was now in sight. Nearly there, just the other side of a few more silvery birches—

"*Come back*," howled the pursuing figure in rage.

Meredith stumbled.

Automatically, David threw an arm around his waist and dragged him along with enough force for them both to surge forward between the last few trees. They practically flew out of the Wood and across the path before both losing their balance and tumbling breathlessly onto the grass in a tangle of limbs beneath the clear moonlit sky.

At Meredith's muffled sound of protest, David scrambled off him, kneeling on the wet grass and gasping for breath. "What the hell was that?" he demanded. "*And how does it know your name?*"

Sitting up and brushing himself off, Meredith only shrugged helplessly. "Wish I knew."

#89: He is not nearly as concerned about this as he ought to be.

"Of course, perhaps it's nothing to worry about at all," he went on with a rather forced brightness. "Perhaps he's a friend of the Mice, and I've made an awful ass of myself, and we'll all have a laugh over it later."

He looked to David in a plea for confirmation. When David couldn't muster any, Meredith went on, words coming rapidly, "Or perhaps that was the Erlking. Did look a bit like him, and I have wondered—now you see, David, this is where you tell me—" Here Meredith dropped into his imitation of David: "*Now, Meri, the Erlking isn't real, and if he were, he'd not be in these woods.* Because you never believe in anything, do you? And then *I* say, *Course he's real, the Moon Calf told me so, and I have often thought, I wouldn't much like to run into* him *in the dark.* Although I'm not exactly his type, if you know what I mean," he confided in a low voice. Then, desperation cracking through, he exclaimed, "Oh, David, please, say something! I can only keep this up on my own for so long, you know."

David said nothing. He'd only halfway taken in the rush of words and couldn't tear his eyes away from the distant depths of the Midnight Wood, scrutinizing every shadow for a hint of that ghastly inhuman creature, even though it was the last thing he wanted to set eyes on now or ever again.

Inching closer, Meredith placed a tentative hand on David's arm. "You all right?"

He was not all right. He was not cut out for this, for living next to the Midnight Wood and encountering such beings, for living with a person who treated such things as run-of-the-mill. On top of that, he was still furious at himself for his own useless reaction in the Wood. What was the matter with him, freezing like a frightened child, needing yet again to be rescued by Meredith, of all people?

Meredith shifted to sit next to David and slid an arm around his shoulders. After a brief internal struggle, David leaned to the side to rest his temple against Meredith's cheek. Just for a moment, until he got his bearings again.

Meredith asked quietly, "Was that what you saw before? When we were in the Wood last week?"

"It was," David admitted, surprised at the hoarseness of his own voice.

"No wonder you didn't want to talk about it."

It had been a mistake to go back into the Midnight Wood, one that David didn't intend to repeat. At last he forced himself to his feet. "Right, enough of this foolishness. Let's go home."

Back in his room at Midnight Cottage, David paced. It was late. He ought to go to bed, but he was jittery, his mind racing. Of course his nerves were frayed after coming face-to-face once again with that . . . *thing* in the Wood. That would be enough to throw anyone off-balance.

He was not just off-balance but in a state of free fall, desperate for anything to catch hold of. *I want to go home*, he thought, and a manic urge to laugh bubbled up inside him, which he quickly suppressed, replacing it with annoyance at himself for entertaining such a nonsensical, childish thought. He *was* home, or at least what passed for it, for the time being. In fact, he was quite irritated by his own foolishness. He was a grown man, not a child who needed his parents to comfort him for the psychic equivalent of a scraped knee. Besides which, his father was across an ocean, and his mother—

David cut off that thought as though scything down garden weeds. Dwelling on it would hardly help matters.

He jumped when Meredith appeared in his open doorway, giving the doorframe a perfunctory rap before he stepped inside. "David? Can you help me off with this necklace? The clasp's a bit broken and I can never work this type anyway."

"Oh—yes, all right." David beckoned him inside.

Meredith turned his back, and David took a step nearer. He reached up and brushed Meredith's hair aside, shimmering the color of old brass in the lamplight. That was a mistake. They were standing too close, and David was all too aware of the heat radiating off him, heat and patchouli and the grounding familiarity he desperately needed.

Afterward, David was unable to provide himself with any satisfactory explanation for what he did next.

Perhaps it was the adrenaline once again. Perhaps it was the lateness of the hour, or the lingering effects of the false prophet's balm.

Perhaps it was Meredith's quiet shuddery little breath when David's thumb brushed over the back of his neck.

David angled his head down and kissed him in the same spot, and Meredith simply melted into his arms. The strand of pearls slipped from his fingers and tumbled forgotten to the floor.

When David's second, open-mouthed kiss turned into a bite, Meredith writhed against him, breathing out, "Oh, fuck, David, *please*—" His hand came up to cover David's, currently splayed across his chest, and urged it downward.

Though Todd wouldn't be home for some time, David still had the presence of mind to kick the door shut as he continued kissing his way lower toward Meredith's shoulder. David held him in place with one arm around his waist, Meredith's back to his chest. There was no question he must be aware of David's erection against his hip with the way he deliberately pressed himself back against him. David let his other hand drop lower, fingertips sweeping across the waistband of Meredith's jeans in wordless question.

"Yeah, please." Meredith tried to arch up into his touch, which made it no easier for David to get his fly undone one-handed.

#90: It does not occur to him to offer any assistance.

Instead, he tried to shift around in David's arms, accomplishing nothing except ending up in a ridiculous position with one arm twisted behind David's neck at an awkward angle and his face hidden against his throat.

"Would you keep *still*," David hissed. Meredith, of course, did not keep still, but kept squirming against him, attempting to caress his hair with one hand while the other made vague yet enthusiastic explorations everywhere within reach. David finally managed to get a hand down the front of Meredith's jeans, cupping his hard cock through his briefs, and found that his annoyance at being unable to properly remove his pants was quite mitigated by the way Meredith moaned obscene encouragements and thrust against his hand.

David buried his face against Meredith's neck, stubble scratching his cheek with a pleasant sting. His next kiss ended with his teeth grazing Meredith's earlobe, yielding him a mouthful of small silver hoops, and Meredith gasped out, "David, please—bite me—"

Seizing a handful of hair, David forced Meredith's head to one side, exposing his throat, and bit down hard enough to bruise while his other hand continued to grasp and stroke. Tried to, anyway, because he didn't even have hold of him properly, but that was all it took for Meredith to cry out and arch against him before slumping back into his arms.

When Meredith at last went completely still, David let go of him and stumbled back to sink onto the edge of the bed in disbelief. What the hell had he just done? What had come over him?

If Meredith had had any sense of decency, he would have been embarrassed, at least a little. As it was, he didn't even bother to do up his fly. Instead, with no apparent concern for the wet spot darkening the front of his briefs, he turned his rapturous gaze upon David.

"David? Can I suck your cock?"

That did absolutely nothing to help.

David passed a hand over his eyes. "You mustn't say things like that." Not least because he knew the correct answer was no. It *needed* to be no.

#91: It is not going to be no.

"Why mustn't I?" asked Meredith innocently. "I'd like to. Can I? Please?"

In a desperate bid for more familiar footing, David fell back on habit. "Language."

"*May* I?" asked Meredith.

David tried not to acknowledge the effect that hearing these words had on his already-hard cock. He was sure, somewhere in the back of his mind, that he disapproved of this. "Yes, all right, if it'll stop you talking."

The next thing David knew, Meredith had climbed into his lap, straddling him. He lost no time unbuttoning David's shirt and made a small disappointed sound at finding he had an undershirt beneath. David hadn't been with anyone in far too long, and even through the last layer of clothing, the sensation of Meredith's hands wandering over his chest and down his sides overwhelmed him.

David closed his eyes and sought a distraction by grabbing Meredith's ass. Gratified to hear the hitch in his breath, David couldn't help but roll his hips upward, seeking more friction.

When Meredith's fingers traced along his jaw, David's eyes snapped open at the unexpected touch. Their gazes met; Meredith's held something heavy and heated. (For an instant, David wondered what might be visible in his own, whether it betrayed how his heart was racing, how badly he ached for a far less innocent touch.)

Meredith leaned in as if for a kiss, but then, with a flash of expression that David couldn't read, quickly turned away.

"Hey," said David softly, "what's the matt–*oh*."

Because at that moment, Meredith slid out of David's lap and lowered himself to kneel before him on the bare wood floor, driving that thought–and any other–from David's mind entirely.

It did, however, occur to him to shift to a spot nearer the middle of the bed, beckoning Meredith to follow onto the softer surface of the rug. Soon David's trousers and boxers lay pooled around his ankles, and Meredith ran his hands up his muscular thighs, eyeing him in admiration as he edged closer between his legs.

Somehow David was still unprepared for Meredith's hand on his cock. It was a light touch at first, experimental, as though he were simply taking in the proportions of his thick shaft. Meredith gently rolled his foreskin the rest of the way back, and David's breath caught as the edge of one black-painted fingernail traced over his leaking slit. He gave a strangled cry as Meredith leaned in and flicked the tip of his tongue against the same spot.

"*God.* Do that again."

Meredith obliged, then sank down onto him, taking in as much of his length as he could. David groaned and tipped his head back, clutched fistfuls of the blankets in an effort to stop himself from trembling all over. His every muscle was strung taut, every nerve minutely attuned to the things Meredith was doing to him–and *God*, did he know what he was doing. The pure heat, the way he swallowed around him–

David was entirely at his mercy.

Meredith sat back to look up at him with mild reproach. "You're so *big*," he said. "I don't know if I can manage it all."

"I'd say you're doing all right," David panted. *All right* was an understatement. (Not to mention he'd be lying if he didn't acknowledge a certain forbidden allure in finally giving in after five years of staunch refusal to entertain the idea.)

Meredith took him into his mouth once more, and his eyes fell closed as, for once, he devoted his full attention to his task. Both his hands were on David now, one stroking the remainder of his length, the other cupping his balls, one finger pressing in just behind.

David let his hand fall to rest on Meredith's shoulder. "Yes," he breathed. "That's right, love, just like that."

At his touch, Meredith looked up. David didn't mean to make eye contact at all, and certainly not to hold it, but for an instant, he was captivated, fascinated by the way Meredith's eyes had gone more gray than blue, darkened to a shade reminiscent of storm clouds or winter rain, meeting his gaze so intensely that David had to look away.

Meredith gave a little moan around him, either in response to the praise or simply betraying his own enjoyment, and that was all David could take. The sensation made him shudder, the tension inside him winding tighter and tighter until it reached its breaking point.

He gripped Meredith's shoulder hard and just had time to stammer, "I—I'm coming." That was the last coherent thought he had as Meredith pulled back and stroked him through it, and blissful relaxation washed over him.

When David next became aware of his surroundings, Meredith was still in the same position, gazing up at him from where he rested his head against his knee.

Now finding himself imbued with a sense of indulgent goodwill, David reached down and let his knuckles brush over Meredith's cheek. He responded with a contented hum and leaned into the touch, and David stroked his hair.

That lasted only for a time. Soon, as his higher brain functions returned, David found his mind filled with questions such as *What have I done?* and *Oh, God, why him?* and, most pressing of all, *What now?* Taking a deep breath, he suppressed his impending panic and instead forced himself to consider the practicalities. His trousers lay crumpled on the floor, his shirt was stained embarrassingly with his own release, and, worst of all, Meredith was *still there*.

David had truly never been one for one-night stands and, in fact, had never had such an encounter with someone he wasn't at least casually dating. Surely there must be an etiquette to this sort of thing.

If only he knew what it was.

To defuse the increasingly awkward silence, David found himself saying, "That was—er—thank you." The words sounded quite wrong, and he suddenly feared that Meredith would laugh at him.

He didn't. Instead, he offered a smile that held an uncharacteristic hint of shyness and pressed a gentle kiss to the inside of David's knee. "Thanks for letting me."

David stood abruptly. "You forgot to give me the speech, you know," he remarked as he pulled his boxers back on.

Slowly, Meredith got to his feet. "David, I—"

"No, no, it's all right," David forestalled him. "I know it by heart: *I'm not in love with you, I've got no plans to fall in love with you and this isn't going to change that, and it's all right if that means you'd rather not do anything.*" Even if it was a bit late for that last part now.

Meredith frowned, and David couldn't help cringing at himself. All the times he'd heard Meredith say it, there'd been a soft earnestness to the words that David lacked. His own version sounded callous, a mere recitation.

"So you see, it's all right," David said brusquely. "I know all about it. No danger of any misunderstanding there."

"Yeah," echoed Meredith. "'S all right."

That was that. Of course it didn't mean anything. It had been bound to happen sooner or later. Such things were an inevitability where Meredith was concerned.

"Best that we've gone and got it out of the way, I expect." David managed a laugh. “I mean, really. As you said, the two of us together—could you even imagine? The very idea is absurd.”

Though Meredith had laughed when he’d said the same thing a week ago, he wasn’t laughing now. David supposed he, too, must be feeling quite unsettled by their mutual lapse in judgment.

After a silence that lasted a beat too long, Meredith gave a lopsided smile. “Yeah,” he said. “Of course it’d never work, would it? You and me, we’d be at each other’s throats every minute. S’pose you’ll be wanting the shower? You can go first, I’ll put the kettle on.”

“It’s twelve at night,” said David.

“Chamomile?” Meredith suggested weakly.

“Oh, all right, if you like.”

Meredith turned to go, then paused in the doorway. “David? Don’t freak out about this, okay?”

“Who’s freaking out?” demanded David. “Certainly not me.”

“David. I know you. But it’s like you said, yeah? Doesn’t mean anything.” At last the vacant grin had returned. “We’re just having fun, is all.”

“Right,” said David. “Of course. We’re on the same page there. Besides,” he pointed out, “you’re in love with somebody else, remember?”

Meredith bit his lip. “Yeah,” he said. “Course I am. Can’t forget that, can I?”

As David stood in the shower, he hid his face in his hands and let the hot water pour over him. It was just as Meredith had said. What had happened between them meant nothing. Just an impulsive moment of mutual stress relief, that was all.

Obviously they couldn’t do it again, but it had been, he had to admit, an experience. It assuaged any lingering curiosity, just on the chance that he might ever have wondered what it would be like.

David tried not to think about the fact that it was the best blow job he'd had in recent memory, or possibly ever.

Those storm-gray eyes staring up at him, burning into him—

He shook his head, determined to put it out of his mind. It was nothing. A minor dalliance. One more tally mark for Meredith, if he was counting.

Besides, David consoled himself, they hadn't even kissed.

Chapter Fifteen

"You should have come to me straightaway." Mrs. Jupiter regarded David and Meredith gravely from across her kitchen table. "An apparition of this nature is a serious matter indeed."

Over a pot of peppermint tea in the witch's kitchen, the two had recounted the events of the previous night—leaving out, of course, what had happened *after* their return to Midnight Cottage. Even between themselves, neither had made mention of Meredith's visit to David's room the night before, and David himself was doing his best to forget it had ever happened.

He ought to be relieved that Meredith appeared to be doing the same, yet he couldn't help but take slight offense. Surely it couldn't have been *that* forgettable.

#92: He is behaving quite as normal.

Normal for him, anyway: chattering on about nothing, stroking the ears of the tawny kitten rubbing against his ankles, watching Mrs. Jupiter's crystal jewelry sparkle in the morning sun.

"My apologies," said David. "I didn't get a good look the first time, and to be frank, I wasn't all that sure of what I was really seeing."

"I do not wish to alarm you unduly," said Mrs. Jupiter, "but the Midnight Wood is not so harmless as you like to believe. It is the site of an ancient magic more powerful than you or I can fathom, and a darkness, too—in more than the literal sense."

"Oh." Meredith's eyes were large and troubled over the top of his harlequin-patterned teacup, belying his nonchalant tone. "That's bad, is it?"

"Of itself, not necessarily, but in times past, the Wood has been host to forces far more dangerous than our friend the Moon Calf. The Midnight Mice keep meticulous records, and I have read, for instance, the most tragic account of a hundred years past when the dread Elephant Celebes stalked the Wood and decimated their population."

Mrs. Jupiter leaned across the table to place her hand over Meredith's and said, not unkindly, "If another such being has taken a personal interest in you, then I'm afraid, my dear, that may be cause for concern. You truly have no suspicion of why he has sought you out?"

Meredith shook his head. "None, I'm telling you."

Mrs. Jupiter swirled her cup and gazed into it with a thoughtful expression—consulting the tea leaves, perhaps. "Humor me and run through it one more time, exactly as it happened."

"Well, it's just as I told you," said Meredith. "Me and David were minding our own business looking for some sweet woodruff, and we came to that clearing, you know the one, with the great big alder and that rock that makes such a nice spot for lying under the stars—"

"Yes, I know it," said Mrs. Jupiter, adroitly averting this departure from the topic at hand. "And then?"

"Then, out of nowhere, here's this—this creepy Erlking type trying to make us go away with him—well, me, really," Meredith interrupted himself. "But I'm sure he meant the both of us. Of course there's no reason anybody *wouldn't* want to carry you off, too," he hastened to reassure David, which did not particularly make him feel better.

"Hold on," said Mrs. Jupiter. "What do you mean, *Erlking type*? Why do you call him that?"

"Well, I don't know that he was, really," Meredith conceded. "He just sort of looked like him."

Mrs. Jupiter paused to disentangle the claws of the kitten from her skirts as it now made a valiant but futile attempt to climb into her lap. There was perhaps a touch of skepticism in her voice as she asked, "Looked like him how, exactly?"

"He just *did*," insisted Meredith, "the way a teapot looks like a teapot. Oh, you know, you've seen the illustrations, you must have."

"I'm sorry," interrupted David, "but what—who—?" He was quite used to nodding along when he had no idea what nonsense Meredith was going on about, but perhaps he ought to have paid more attention the night before.

"The Erlking, David, he's—well, he's the Erlking. He's a sort of—" He turned helplessly to Mrs. Jupiter. "A forest spirit, a wicked fairy king, like the stories—like the poem. *Everybody* knows the poem."

David did not know the poem. Even if he had, the very idea stretched the bounds of credulity—yet there had undeniably been *something* that he'd seen with his own eyes, no matter how he might wish he hadn't.

"In any case," admitted Mrs. Jupiter, "there is certainly something strange afoot in the Wood."

Strange didn't begin to cover it. *Strange* might describe Meredith's fashion choices or the perpetual darkness of the Midnight Wood, but a mysterious figure come to life straight out of the pages of some sinister fairy tale was downright alarming.

Still, David didn't imagine it would help matters to quibble over the distinction. Instead, he asked, "So in practical terms—?"

"I must investigate further," said Mrs. Jupiter. "But in the meantime, I advise you both not to set foot in the Midnight Wood."

"Not go into the Wood!" repeated Meredith in dismay. "But—"

"Now, you had just better do as she says," admonished David. "If you go wandering about the Wood after you've been told not to, I certainly won't come to rescue you again like I did last night."

He hadn't, of course, done anything of the sort, last night or ever. It had been quite the other way around, not that he wanted to go advertising the fact, but giving Meredith the easy opportunity to hit back by setting the record straight might dissolve that worried look of his, which David didn't like at all.

"But—" Meredith stopped, and David swore a little more light went out of his eyes. "No, of course not. Couldn't expect you to, really."

That wasn't right at all. David had given him such an obvious setup. Not only had he failed to take it, but it seemed to have made things worse.

"Now, there's no need to worry yourself overmuch for the time being." Mrs. Jupiter gave Meredith's hand another pat, though her smile seemed to David slightly forced. "I shall consult with my coven, but in the meantime, I do implore you to be careful. You mean a great deal to me," she said with solemnity, "and I know I would not be the only one devastated should you come to harm." She cast a glance at David that he had to look away from. Of course he didn't want anything to happen to Meredith, but it was hardly the sort of sentiment that he needed to go voicing aloud. Besides, nothing *did* ever happen to him, so there was no need to go thinking about such things.

"Oh, I'll be all right," Meredith reassured her.

"The Night Horse stopped in this morning, by the way," said Mrs. Jupiter as she rose from the table. She removed a one-eyed calico cat from the top of a large steamer trunk, set it down, and shooed it toward the door before straightening the crocheted lace doily it had been resting upon. "Another of the Mice was killed in the Wood last night."

At that, Meredith's expression grew positively mournful.

"If things carry on at this rate," Mrs. Jupiter continued, "the temporal effects could be catastrophic."

"You don't suppose that sort of thing could spread beyond the borders of the Wood itself, do you?" asked David.

"It is possible," she said slowly. "That would indicate an even more serious state of affairs than I had imagined. Why? Have you observed such a phenomenon?"

"No, no," said David hastily. "Er. Well. Perhaps my watch might've gone a bit funny the other night, but all the same, it might've been only my imagination."

Mrs. Jupiter's shrewd gaze lingered on his face for a moment, but she allowed the matter to drop without further comment.

On the way out, she caught up with him in the doorway. "A word, David—if I may?"

"You may." They'd known each other quite long enough to be on first-name terms, even if he'd never dare reciprocate.

Glancing past him at Meredith leaning down to pet a gray tiger cat in the garden, she said in a low voice: "Be gentle with him."

For a second, David was horrified. Surely she couldn't know, unless by some witchy power? That was followed by indignation. He hadn't mistreated Meredith in any way, hadn't handled him roughly. Possibly he had left just one mark on him, but he'd been asked to—*urged* to. No one could find fault with that.

Quite against his will, David found himself given over to intense curiosity as to whether Meredith had left it or had allowed Mrs. Jupiter's healing ointment to work its effects. The idea of him walking around still bearing a hidden love bite made David's stomach flip in a way that was not altogether unpleasant. Nor was the idea of giving him a few more—

Mrs. Jupiter, however, continued, "I'll do what I can, but I fear this isn't going to be easy."

David relaxed. She was talking about something altogether different. She simply meant he ought to go out of his way to be nice to him, and he was doing that already. "Yes, Mrs. J," he said. "Of course."

As THE WEEK went on, David considered telling Harriet about what had happened, but was too embarrassed to admit he'd done precisely what he'd insisted he wouldn't. Besides, he had little to complain about. He'd had enjoyable, no-strings-attached sex that had required, in all honesty, little effort on his part. There was no danger of any misunderstanding or complication ensuing. Nothing had changed at all.

Except, perhaps, that Meredith was a bit quieter than usual. Then again, the discovery that a malevolent forest entity of indeterminate origin not only knew one's name but also sought an audience *was* the sort of thing to inspire some much-needed self-reflection. It was good for him, probably.

It was hardly cause for alarm, even if David's mind did keep drifting back to their tryst at inopportune moments (and perhaps a few opportune ones late at night, and in the shower). He hadn't been to bed with anyone in some time, and naturally his imagination was latching onto the details. Details like Meredith in his arms, reduced to a state of mindless desperation as he thrust against his palm. The undisguised admiration in the way he'd caressed him. That sweet little sound of contentment he'd made when David had stroked his face afterward.

It meant nothing, of course. The encounter had simply awakened urges David had been suppressing as best he could since his last relationship ended. Urges best acted upon with someone else, ideally a someone else with whom there was some chance of compatibility or a future together, a someone else who did not go rushing off on impulsive nighttime herb-foraging expeditions or inflicting acts of decoupage upon innocent surfaces.

Still, David kept Mrs. Jupiter's words in mind, and when Meredith invited him to join him and Kinley at the Rat Cellar on Thursday night, he agreed without protest.

"Oh, but, David, you must, Secondhand Orwell are playing and—wait." Meredith blinked as David's words caught up with him. "You said yes."

"I did," he confirmed.

Meredith narrowed his eyes in suspicion. "You never say yes, not on the first go."

#93: Which he takes as his cue to continue asking relentlessly.

"And you never allow me to decline," grumbled David.

"Oh, but that's our little game, isn't it? You like pretending you don't want to come with, but I think you'd miss it really if I gave up so easily."

David certainly would not, but he'd let him believe it for the time being. (Once again, he congratulated himself for doing just as Mrs. Jupiter had said.) Perhaps there was a grain of truth to Meredith's words, but it disconcerted him to have it laid bare like that when he'd never realized it himself. In any case, he wasn't going to admit it and encourage such behavior.

Kinley awaited them outside the Rat Cellar, leaning against the building's half-timbered facade and smoking a cigarette. He raised a hand in wordless greeting, and Meredith raced over to throw his arms around him.

#94: He acts as if an absence of hours or days has been years.

It was only when Meredith stood up on his toes to kiss Kinley's cheek that David realized he hadn't greeted *him* that way all week. Not that he wanted him to, of course. In fact, it was for the best that he'd stopped, especially after what had happened between the two of them. After all, where would they be if casual affection started to bleed into their everyday interactions?

Inside, once the three had obtained beers, Kinley made a beeline for one of the few remaining unoccupied tables in a dark corner, and David followed. Meredith, of course, was the last to arrive, taking his time to greet a number of the other regulars.

They, too, all received air-kisses, which caused David to scowl. Such excess was truly insufferable, and witnessing it brought on an unpleasant sensation as if someone were squeezing the air out of his lungs, crumpling something inside of him. Even if theirs was an unlikely friendship born of propinquity, he couldn't help but feel as though he'd been relegated to the scrap heap.

David instead devoted his attention to his pint of beer, which, as usual for the Rat Cellar, managed to be watery and sour at the same time.

Eventually Meredith drifted over to the table, taking the empty middle seat. His gaze wandered to the band, midway through their sound check onstage.

Kinley nudged him with an elbow and nodded in David's direction. "You tell him what we've got going this week?"

Meredith giggled. "I haven't! Oh, David, you'll love this—no, you tell him."

Kinley said, "We're making a collage of Cliff Richard—"

"Out of smaller pictures of Cliff Richard!" interrupted Meredith, unable to contain his excitement.

David considered this for a moment, then asked the only question he could. "Why?"

"It's *art*, man," said Kinley.

"But . . . does either of you even like Cliff Richard?"

"No!" exclaimed Meredith in delight. "It's a mockery!"

#95: Just like everything else he does.

Meredith, overcome with laughter, leaned over to hide his face against Kinley's shoulder. When he straightened up and tossed his hair back, David was captivated. Though exposed for only the briefest flash, the side of his neck still bore the faded but unmistakable mark of David's bite.

David forgot to breathe. An intangible force jerked at something deep in his belly, and he was seized by the urge to bury his face against Meredith's throat and do it again. *And again, and again, until he was quivering against him, begging for more—*

No. That was out of the question. It had been enjoyable enough, but it mustn't happen again. These little daydreams were really getting to be a problem.

He tuned back in to catch the tail end of Meredith's words. "—see the point, really."

"The point is to do it for yourself," said Kinley. "If you don't—" He broke off as he caught sight of the man hurrying through the crowd in their direction.

He was no one of David's acquaintance a chubby, balding, clean-shaven man whose cutoff T-shirt left his arms bare, revealing his freshly healed tattoos.

"One of yours?" Kinley asked. As if there were any question—the angular dark flowers interspersed with bits of swirling abstract blackwork were a dead giveaway. He added in approval, "That looks *sick*."

Judging by the man's dismayed expression, he had not come to discuss tattoos. "Schwarzy!" He seized Meredith by the hand before he could rise to greet him. "Jesus, I been looking all over for you. I'm so sorry, man."

"There, it's all right, Ed, take a breath." With his free hand, Meredith gave him a cautious pat on the arm. "What exactly—"

"It is so far from all right," lamented Ed. "I'm so fuckin' grateful to you, man, and the last thing I wanted was to cause you any trouble when I went and posted about what you did for me."

This, David surmised, must be the reformed neo-Nazi.

"I swear to God, I haven't had anything to do with those guys since I got out of that life years ago. I had no idea they were even gonna see, let alone come after you for it."

"What's he talking about?" demanded Kinley. "Who came after you?"

"Of course you didn't," Meredith soothed him, ignoring Kinley and extricating his hand from Ed's grip, forcing the poor man to begin wringing his own hands instead. "But how did you ever find out about that?"

That was the question. David hadn't mentioned the incident to anyone, and had assumed Meredith wanted it to be forgotten, as he'd never brought it up again himself. Strange, though, that he hadn't even told Kinley.

Ed darted a glance around the room and said in a low voice, "Jared turned back. Showed up on my doorstep this morning half out of his mind. Turns out a couple nights in the sewers can really make you reconsider your life choices."

David scanned the crowd, already rising to his feet. "Where is he?"

"No, man, he left town already," Ed hastened to reassure him. "Went to go stay with his mom and try to work some things out. He ain't gonna bother you again."

"He'd better not," said Kinley.

Ed went on, "He says he never thought Kevin was gonna take it that far. Says they were just gonna rough you up a little for mouthing off—not that that's cool, either!" he added hurriedly, palms raised in the face of David's murderous glare. "Only when you fought back, it got out of control and—I'm so sorry!" he interrupted himself yet again.

After further consolation and hand-patting, Ed finally departed. Kinley watched his retreating back with narrowed eyes, then turned to Meredith. "You want to tell me what that was about?"

Meredith did so, providing a condensed version of the story with surprisingly few embellishments—none, in fact, aside from depicting David as far more heroic than he had been.

"Dude, what the hell?" Kinley reproached him. "Why didn't you tell me any of that was going on? I would've handled those guys for you."

David had tried not to dwell on the memory of that night, but now the scene was fresh in his mind once more. All things considered, he thought Meredith had handled it pretty well himself, as far as anyone could be expected to. Three against one was hardly a fair fight.

"Because," said Meredith. "It was my problem to deal with. I didn't need to go dragging you into it. I—I suppose I never thought it'd go that far."

Kinley took a thoughtful swig of beer. David did the same and regretted it.

"You know what your problem is?" Kinley said at last. "You don't talk to anybody."

"I talk to everybody, all the time," protested Meredith. "Whether they want me to or not, really. Just ask David."

"I mean about anything heavy. You keep that shit to yourself and on the outside act like it's all smiles and sunshine—well, maybe not sunshine," Kinley backtracked. "You're a little too dark for that."

It was true—*sunshine* hardly fit a person who perpetually dressed in black, who preferred rain to shine and night to day.

"Starlight," interjected David, quite without meaning to.

Kinley started, as if he'd forgotten he was there, then gestured in David's direction. "Yeah. Starlight," he agreed. "But not everything is, not all the time. Trying to pretend isn't good for you, and it isn't good for the people around you, you feel me? Sometimes you have to tell somebody about these things before it turns into something you can't deal with on your own."

"Sorry, Kinley," said Meredith, chagrined.

"Hey. You're my little brother and I love you, okay?" Kinley threw an arm around his shoulders and pulled him into a rough embrace. "And that's why I will personally kick your ass if you ever pull something like that again."

"I know," said Meredith, resting his head against Kinley's shoulder.

"I love you, too." After a moment, he added, "But I do need another beer."

"I'll get it." David suddenly wanted nothing more than to get away from the table, from the two of them. "This round's on me. Another of the same for you?" he asked Kinley.

"Sure. Thanks," said Kinley in surprise. "I got the next one."

With a curt nod, David started off for the bar. It was as Meredith had said: the sentiment between him and Kinley was definitely familial rather than romantic. Though why the two of them felt the need to claim each other as siblings when Meredith already had a perfectly good brother of his own, David couldn't begin to understand. Then again, he and his sister, Ruth, had never had a close relationship, in large part due to their twelve-year age difference, so perhaps this sort of thing was beyond him.

Out of nowhere, he felt himself struck by a wistfulness, a false nostalgia for a closeness that had never been. He would not hesitate to say that he and Ruth loved each other, but they were by no means in the habit of making spontaneous declarations of it; on the whole, their family tended to share a quieter, more reserved sort of affection. Though David had never felt slighted by this, a small part of him now wondered whether things could have been different.

By the time he returned to the table, Meredith was alone.

"Kinley went out for another cigarette," he explained. "He says I stress him out."

"And you didn't go with him?"

"Nah, I'd best finish this beer before the band starts, otherwise I might not have the nerve to heckle them. Besides, you was saying just the other night how you don't like me to smoke cigarettes. *Were* saying." He winked at David as he took the glass from him. "See, didn't even need you to tell me that time."

All at once, it clicked into place: the wordless exchange in Kinley's living room that he hadn't understood, the tail end of the conversation he'd caught in the kitchen. That hadn't been about Meredith's one-sided infatuation at all, but about David himself.

Meredith *had* urged him long ago to point out when he slipped into nonstandard grammar, and it had become all too easy of a habit, so much so that he suspected the original request had been lost to memory for them both before Kinley brought it up.

And the way it must have looked—

David swallowed hard, and found that he couldn't bring himself to look up from the depths of his own glass. "Meredith?"

"Hmm?"

"Kinley is a good friend."

Meredith gave him a puzzled look. "I know."

"Yes," said David, "so do I, now."

Chapter Sixteen

Harriet.

Help.

What's the matter?

Do you remember that thing you said I should do that I said I wouldn't?

I did.

Doesn't seem very nice to call your roommate a "thing" ;)

THIS IS NOT FUNNY.

Ooh, bringing out capslock on me

I am SERIOUS.

Okay, okay

So what happened?

What do you think? I'm sure I don't have to spell it out.

So you got together with your roommate

No! It was a one-time thing.

Sorry, let me rephrase:

You fucked your roommate

No.

Sort of.

I swear you should have been a lawyer

You had some type of sexual encounter with your roommate

Yes.

So what's the problem?

I don't know.

Was it bad?

Not at all.

Is he being weird?

No more than usual.

Are YOU being weird?

Certainly not.

Yeah, I'll reserve judgment on that one

So what you're telling me is that there IS no problem beyond you majorly overthinking

Because it doesn't fit your ideas about how these things work

I am not overthinking.

In spite of everyone else insisting otherwise.

Couldn't imagine why

You're no help at all.

. . . coffee Sunday?

Can't

I'll be out of town

Oh, yes, you did say so.

How was your date last week, by the way?

Awful

I'll tell you about it next time we see each other

I'm spending all next weekend in town for the auction, so we'll catch up then, okay?

On Friday, David had another house viewing scheduled after work, and the failure of his past few attempts plagued his mind all day. This time, he was determined to see it through—so long as the house was suitable and the price within his means. In truth, the latter was more of a concern than he'd anticipated, particularly following his recent viewing of the overpriced Victorian. If he wanted to make his exit from Midnight Cottage—and he did, no doubt about that—it was imperative that he have the opportunity to meet with Cartier. With renewed determination, he went off in search of Steve Corner to demand his well-deserved place on the centennial auction's VIP list. He'd hired the auction staff, organized the catering, tracked the donations, overseen the expenses—it was only fair that he receive a few crumbs of recognition for it.

Corner was not in his office.

David found him instead leaning against one end of the sales counter in ladies' formalwear, taking no pains to disguise his enjoyment of the view from behind as Paulette, the resident IT specialist, crouched on all fours to prod at the impossible tangle of cords beneath the register.

David cleared his throat, and Corner eyed him with evident displeasure. "Yes, Carew?"

Before David could reply, Paulette emerged from beneath the counter and straightened up, sweeping their long locs out of their face. "Don't know how that managed to get disconnected, but it's fixed now," they reported.

"Excellent," said Corner. "If you happen to have a couple more minutes free, the printer in my office has some updates that need to be installed."

"Mx. Paulette," David broke in hastily, "actually I was just looking for you. I'm afraid the fax machine in the mail room might have gone wrong again." This was a lie, but he could not in good conscience walk away without giving them an out.

Paulette groaned. "I swear that thing hasn't been right since the Incident. Guess I'd better come take a look." To Corner, they added, "When

I have a chance to get back to my desk, I'll send you the tutorial I made for updating device drivers."

At Corner's icy glare, David decided the most prudent course of action was to retreat to his own office without further delay.

After work, David met Leonard Flood to view a cozy brick bungalow a few blocks from downtown. Neat box hedges flanked the front steps, potted houseplants filled the living room's bay window, and the warm low lighting gave the place a pleasant, lived-in feeling.

Yet there was still a hint of doubt in the back of David's mind—a whisper that something was not quite right, that something was missing. For just a moment, he thought of his own bay window at Midnight Cottage, the cluttered bookshelves, the scrabble of claws on hardwood, and was struck by a tiny pang of loss.

Nonsense, of course. He'd been dragging his feet long enough. He really needed to stop being so particular or he'd never make any headway. This was a perfectly nice house in a desirable location, only a fraction higher than his ideal asking price, and there was nothing whatsoever the matter with it.

Pushing aside any lingering reservations, David instructed Mr. Flood to make an offer on his behalf.

Upon his return to Midnight Cottage, he found the other occupants watching television in the living room—Todd Billion in an armchair, Meredith sprawled across the sofa, Bianca curled up atop a throw pillow.

"David! Come watch TV with us," urged Meredith. When David hesitated, he said, "Oh, come on, quit worrying about tomorrow. Bednarek came and mowed the lawn, and I already cleaned up the deck *and* the living room. And Bianca helped, of course."

#96: At times, it is as if he can read one's mind.

"Well . . ." It was true that everything within view was passably clean, if still disorganized. (The blue vinegar cruet on the bookshelf did not escape his notice, sandwiched as it was between a volume of poetry and an outdated Sorcerers' Almanac, the relic of another past housemate.) Nevertheless, David supposed he could allow himself to relax, and joined Meredith on the sofa. "All right, then. What are we watching?"

"Well, you've come too late for Karl Machine—he's got a new song that's just a recipe for vindaloo, it's brilliant!"

"*Mustard seed, that's what you need*," sang Todd.

"Wonderful," said David flatly. "What a pity I missed it."

"But now the Minnesang Carpenter is on," said Meredith.

David already regretted agreeing to this. "The what?"

"The Minnesang Carpenter! She lectures on medieval love ballads while refinishing cabinets."

"Ah. Of course. Don't see how I could've missed that from the name." Ignoring the show, David took out his phone to check the rugby scores and catch up on the business news, skimming an article about Cartier Property Investments scouting locations for a new housing development in Bingham Junction.

In the meantime, Meredith did what he always did every time he enticed David to join him in front of the TV, migrating closer and closer until the least annoying option was for David to rest his arm across the back of the sofa, which was slightly preferable to having it crushed against his side. Meredith, of course, took this as an opportunity to burrow one bony shoulder into the available warm spot until David resigned himself and draped his arm over him. In the back of his mind, he might admit, grudgingly, that there was something to be said for the contact, some degree of comfort in the way Meredith seemed to fit so easily into place against him.

Then again, David reflected as Todd raised his eyebrows, perhaps there wasn't. He glowered and moved away.

"Oh! But I'm cold," complained Meredith, though whether he'd caught on to the unspoken exchange, David couldn't guess.

Todd, however, wisely retreated to the kitchen to wash his teacup. When he returned with his sleeves rolled up, Meredith's gaze went straight to the long jagged scar running down his forearm.

David nudged him. "You're *staring*," he hissed.

"It's from a boating accident a couple years ago," said Todd. "Pretty brutal, huh?"

"Hmm? Oh, I am sorry," said Meredith. "I've done a few scar cover-ups lately and was thinking what I could do with one like that, but you're right, it was rude of me to stare."

"Hey, it's cool." With a grin, Todd suggested, "How about you guys both show me one of yours, and we'll call it even?"

This, David recognized, was an overture at friendship, or at least a degree of familiarity. Suddenly he felt a bit sorry for Todd, coming into the house like this where he was clearly the odd man out.

Perhaps that was why David acquiesced and pulled up the hem of one trouser leg.

Todd gave a low whistle at the sight of the wide shining scar that curved across his shin. "What's that from?"

"Rugby." The scar looked worse than the injury had been in reality, though it had weighed into David's decision to give up the sport toward the end of university.

"That's badass," said Todd, suitably impressed, and David couldn't help but feel a bit pleased. "What about you?" he asked Meredith, who was now staring off into space.

"Oh," he murmured, "none really."

Of course he didn't have any scars.

#97: He never gets hurt.

"Oh. Well, how'd you break your nose, then?" asked Todd.

"I didn't," said Meredith, with such an odd inflection that David turned to stare at him. Abruptly, Meredith rose. "I'm going to take Bianca out."

The Chihuahua trotted dutifully after him out the back doors.

Todd watched him go in dismay. "Jeez, I didn't mean to say the wrong thing. I didn't realize he'd be sensitive about it."

"He's had a difficult week. I wouldn't worry too much if I were you." David would have preferred Todd to avoid such personal remarks altogether, but then again, he'd only been trying to gloss over the situation Meredith had created himself. David sighed. "Excuse me."

Beneath the darkening twilight, he found Meredith perched atop the picnic table, a quantity of freshly gathered daisies spread across his yellow tartan skirt. Bianca chased fireflies in the tall grass nearby. He didn't look up at David's approach, but continued to gaze toward the last streaks of gold in the western sky as he plucked the petals from one of his daisies.

"*He loves me, he loves me not*?" inquired David.

Meredith blinked as if not really seeing him. "What?"

David nodded toward the flower in his hand. "That poor daisy. You may as well divine something if you're going to go ripping out all its petals."

"Oh. No, I've never won at that game."

"Are we . . . speaking metaphorically, or—?"

"Oh, *metaphors*," said Meredith in disgust. "Nah, I mean, my mind wanders and I always lose track of where I was at." He tossed away the denuded flower and took up three more, beginning to braid a daisy chain.

"Move over, would you?" Without waiting for an answer, David took a seat next to him upon the table and studied Meredith's face in the waning twilight. "Don't know what Todd's on about."

Meredith didn't look up. "Hmm?"

"Of course you haven't broken your nose."

"I didn't say I didn't," said Meredith. "I said, *I* didn't."

#98: He makes such incomprehensible distinctions.

Before David could follow that thought any further, Meredith said, "Anyway, you don't have to go trying to make me feel better."

"I wasn't, particularly."

"It's all right, I know I'm not much to look at."

David frowned, but before he could respond, Meredith added, "Not like you."

"I—what?"

"It's true," he insisted, finally looking up from his daisy chain. "Anyone can see how big and strong you are, you've got a good profile, and your eyes are that lovely color, like smoky amber."

Smoky amber. David was taken aback. He'd received his share of compliments, certainly, but never had anyone told him a thing quite like that. "I—er—really?"

Meredith nodded. "You're quite good-looking, David, aside from when you go around scowling at everything. Well, at me, usually, but I suppose I can't much blame you there." He returned his attention to his daisy chain and fell into a pensive silence.

David watched him for a long moment in growing concern, then said, more abruptly than he meant to, "Meri, are you all right?"

At that, Meredith looked up at him in surprise. "What?"

"I said, are you all right? These last few days you've seemed a bit off."

"Off?" he repeated.

This was unfamiliar ground, but David pressed on. "You've not been yourself lately."

"Oh, *I'm* all right," said Meredith. "Kinley's gone and put the idea into your head, hasn't he? Don't pay him any mind."

"I mean," David tried again, "one could hardly blame you if you weren't. The past couple of weeks have been . . . a lot." There was one other thing he needed to make sure of, but if he went about it the wrong way—no, it was best to be direct. "Are you all right after what we did the other night? I mean to say, I wouldn't like for you to feel as though I'd treated you badly. I mean I wouldn't like to have done. I mean—" David was floundering. "*Did* I?"

"Course not," said Meredith. "I've had much worse."

If ever anyone was damned by faint praise—

At David's expression, Meredith hurriedly amended, "Oh, no, I mean to say I had quite a nice time." He finished twisting the ends of the stems into place and held aloft his creation to admire it before setting the daisy crown upon David's head and looking quite pleased with himself. "There you are."

David found that he was not as exasperated with this as he might have been. Carefully, he removed the circlet of daisies and studied its construction, impressed in spite of himself.

"I think," he said gently, placing it on Meredith's head instead, "it suits you better." Then, struck by inspiration, he went on, "Besides, I could hardly usurp the throne from the rightful reigning monarch of the Midnight Wood. You'd have me executed for high treason in a heartbeat."

"Nah, what do you think? I'm a merciful king, I'd just throw you into the dungeons for a bit."

"Would you."

"Maybe let the Mice nibble your toes until you're properly remorseful."

"I see." David found himself holding back a smile. King of the

Midnight Wood indeed, in a tartan skirt and flower crown. He nudged Meredith and stood. "All right, Your Majesty, collect the royal hound and off to bed with you both. Tomorrow's going to be an early morning."

To his relief, Meredith giggled at that. He caught David by the arm for balance as he hopped down from the table. "C'mon, Bianca, did you hear that? You've gotten a promotion!"

Behind him, the darkness at the edge of the Midnight Wood seemed to have softened, speckled with the fuzzy green glow of fireflies; the sound of insects had faded from a menacing hum to the occasional reassuring chirp that felt almost friendly. It had become a forest at twilight, nothing more.

But looking down at Meredith's hand, David couldn't tear his eyes away from that carved obsidian ring.

"David, aren't you coming?"

"You go on," he said, reaching a decision. "I've got an errand to run."

"What have you done to my—my—" David gave up on trying to classify the relationship. "Meredith. What did you do to him?"

"Your what?" From across her table at the Night Market, Sylvania Holland regarded David with her infuriatingly serene smile. "Oh, yes. The charming Canadian."

"He isn't," said David, "but yes, that's the one. Whatever hex you've put on him, whatever you've done to him—undo it at once."

Sylvania rose with a swish of brocaded silks and beckoned David to walk with her along the row of stalls beneath garlands of greenery and the soft twinkle of stardust lanterns. "Whatever do you mean?"

"That ring," said David. "You said it reveals what's concealed, but it's defective or—or cursed or something. He's not been right since you gave it to him."

Surveying the offerings of a nearby booth whose wares appeared to consist primarily of live frogs, she inquired, "Oh, yes? What's the matter with him?"

David opened his mouth to reply, then closed it again. He'd come storming into the Night Market to confront her the moment he'd figured it out, but hadn't thought through the precise nature of his complaint. "Well. For instance. He doesn't insult me anymore."

"That hardly seems anything to complain about."

"No, no, I mean it's—" He waved a hand. "A sort of back-and-forth. It *was*. But it's no fun if he doesn't come back at me." David frowned. "Feels rather like kicking a puppy."

"Is that all?" she asked.

David found himself momentarily distracted by a stall offering artesian waters of oblivion, and nearly crashed into a bay centaur having his hooves polished, who flicked his tail in annoyance and gave David a look of disdain.

Hurrying to catch up to Sylvania, he said, "It is not. He has these moments where he seems so down and goes saying such awful things about himself." It was most disconcerting, and quite out of character. "Just put him back to how he was before, would you?"

Sylvania Holland picked up a jewel-encrusted amulet from the next table, examined it, and returned it to nestle in a swathe of rumpled velvet. "That ring does no more nor less than what I told you. If he says such things, then it's only because he already thought them."

"Nonsense," insisted David. "He doesn't think anything of the kind." Meredith was confident to the point of arrogance. She wasn't listening to him at all. "Now, you look here. I want my friend back. No more of this magical funny business, do you hear me?"

Her eyebrows rose. "Friend?"

David's face grew warm, and he had the distinctly unpleasant sensation that she was riffling through the contents of his mind like a stack of photographs, including his recollections of recent activities that were decidedly more than friendly in nature. "What do you mean by that?" he demanded.

Sylvania nodded to the proprietor of the next booth, who raised a tentacle in greeting. "Oh, nothing," she said. "Just that when I was there, you told him you hated him."

"That was just—" David stopped. "Of course I don't, not really."

"Does *he* know that?"

Of course Meredith knew.

Didn't he?

"Look, perhaps I get a bit fed up with him sometimes," admitted David, "but you don't understand. You and everybody else think he's so *charming* and *quirky*, but you don't realize what it's like to actually live with such a person all the time." Maybe that frustration manifested as the occasional barbed remark, but that was just a way of letting off steam. "But we *are* friends, and I won't stand by and see him hurt by you or those neo-Nazis or that wretched Erlking person."

"I see," said Sylvania solemnly, though David was not sure that she did. "Yes, that does complicate matters." They'd now passed the last row of market stalls and stood at the edge of the inky shadow cast by an ancient and towering oak in the adjacent lot. She turned to David. "Tell me, has he said anything out of the ordinary lately? Any startling confessions, for instance?"

"Well—" David hesitated. It felt almost too personal to share, but, he reasoned, a psychic was like a doctor: one must tell them the truth, no matter how embarrassing the ailment. "The other night, he was going on about being in love with someone, supposedly, but I couldn't get him to tell who."

"It would seem he's remarkably strong-willed." She darted an appraising glance at David, and murmured half to herself, "I wonder whether I didn't give it to the wrong one."

"I beg your pardon?"

Clapping him on the arm and ignoring his question entirely, she said, "Now, there's no need to lose hope. Just give it a bit more time, and it'll all work itself out."

"But—"

"If I were you," said Sylvania Holland, "I'd go home and get some rest. You're going to need it for tomorrow."

David was halfway back to Midnight Cottage before it sank in that she hadn't told him anything at all.

Chapter Seventeen

David slept poorly and rose early. Today's note on the kitchen table read:

Went down to see Mrs. J. Won't go in the Wood. Promise.

Meri

Just as the percolator was bubbling on the stove and David was taking a coffee mug from the cupboard, Meredith came bounding in from the deck, carrying a basket and followed closely by Bianca. Sliding into the kitchen, he spun a clumsy pirouette that made the skirt of his sundress billow out around him in a whirl of green and white chevron stripes. Atop his head, he wore a new daisy crown—no, upon closer inspection, it was, in fact, the one from the previous night, quite wilted, though he'd made an effort to revitalize it by adding in a number of fresh violets.

"Good morning, Your Majesty." It was a relief to see him in better spirits today. "You're up early."

Meredith shrugged. "Couldn't sleep." That seemed to be a common occurrence of late, but before David could remark on it, he went on,

"And the eggs was out. Got some more from Mrs. J, though. Oh, good, you've made coffee."

David should by now have been accustomed to these leaps from topic to topic, but he still found them dizzying—or perhaps it was only Meredith himself, setting down his basket of speckled eggs and slithering between David and the refrigerator, brushing against his side, resting a hand briefly on his arm and trailing with him the scent of violets and meadow grass and a hint of his usual patchouli underneath.

David was struck by the urge to take him into his arms and pin him against the refrigerator and kiss him senseless—which, of course, he wasn't going to do, he reminded himself firmly.

"All yours." Meredith replaced the percolator on the burner, then tilted his head in question. "You all right? You've just been staring off into space, and we both know that's my job."

"What? No, no, I mean yes, quite all right."

"Right," said Meredith, clearly unconvinced, but he retreated into the living room without further comment. As David fixed his own cup of coffee, the sound of vehicles pulling into the driveway sent Bianca into her usual frenzied yapping.

A moment later, the front door opened and the yapping dropped to a growl as heavy footsteps tramped into the room.

"Hey, Mere," Florian called out. "How about you get off your ass and come help—what the hell are you wearing?"

David found himself quite embarrassed at the prospect of facing Florian after what had happened between himself and Meredith, as if Florian would be able to tell from one look exactly what the two of them had done.

"It's a s-sundress, Florian," said Meredith, tripping on the *S* in spite of his nonchalant tone.

"Yeah, no shit it's a s-s-sundress," Florian mocked. "And you'd better—hey, Dave," he broke off as David finally steeled himself to step out from the kitchen.

He raised his coffee mug in greeting. "Morning. Everything all right?" He'd be the first to admit he knew nothing of the typical dynamic between the two of them. For all he knew, this was their usual sort of banter, and certainly it wasn't his place to interfere, but nevertheless the exchange didn't sit right with him.

"Yeah, we was just about to bring through these tables." With a glance down at Bianca, Florian added, "And you'd better watch out that little rat dog of yours don't get in the way, otherwise he's liable to get himself stomped on."

Meredith scooped up Bianca and clutched her protectively to his chest. "You leave her alone."

"Now, she does have a tendency to get underfoot," David mediated. "Actually, Florian, why don't you pull around into the yard? You could back right up to the deck and not have to carry anything through the house at all."

Florian nodded. "Good thinking. As long as you don't mind us driving in the grass."

Bednarek might, but David didn't. "Not at all, go right ahead."

"All right, thanks. Mere, let's you and me have a little chat while I bring the truck around. Dave, you want to give Genevieve a hand?"

Meredith set Bianca down on the window seat and cast a worried look back at her as he followed Florian out. No sooner had they exited than Genevieve came bustling in bearing an impossible volume of shopping bags.

She thrust a heavy grocery sack into David's arms. "I hope you've got room in the fridge."

"Er, some, but what—"

"Veggie tray," she said, hefting one of the remaining bags. "Backup veggie tray." She repeated the motion with the other. "And enough fruit for two fruit plates, but most of it needs cut up still."

"Wouldn't it have been simpler—" he hazarded before Genevieve cut him off.

"Oh, it would, Dave, it would. I *did*, in fact."

His patience had worn thin on that front. "Look, I'm sorry, but I don't like—"

"But those bozos," she barreled on, "they went and put pineapple on, even though I specifically ordered them without. Adalynn is allergic, you know."

"Yes," agreed David. "I mean, no, I didn't."

"You can bet I gave them a piece of my mind—and got a full refund, obviously. But I wasn't about to waste my time giving them a second chance to screw it up, so we're going to DIY it."

"I can take care of that," David offered.

Although he hadn't envisioned himself spending the morning playing sous chef, he hardly intended to pass up any chance at getting himself further into Adalynn Cartier's good graces. If she were sufficiently impressed, she might even mention him to her father. And Cartier, in a show of gratitude, would—well, perhaps he wouldn't offer him the VP position outright, not just for that, but surely it would make a favorable impression.

"That'd be a big help," said Genevieve, already starting for the kitchen. "But for now, can you see if the boys need any help with the furniture? I need to get the tables and chafing dishes set up by the time Sophie and Aurora get here with the hot food." At his blank look, she explained, "That's the other bridesmaids."

"Yes," said David. "Of course."

Outside, it was a touch more overcast than David liked, but in a pinch, they could always move the proceedings indoors, even if it might be a bit cramped. To the left of the deck were parked a pair of pickup trucks, and from the right came Bednarek up the path, casting a pained look in the direction of the tire tracks in the grass.

"Good morning, good morning," proclaimed the landlord. His expression brightened at once when he caught sight of Genevieve. "My! Who is this vision?"

"Ah. Mr. Bednarek, our landlord," David introduced, and did his best to ignore the spectacle playing out in the background. A heavyset, bearded man who must be Jayceon stoically advanced toward the deck, carrying several folding chairs under each arm, while Florian found himself in the unenviable position of directing Meredith—now sans flower crown—as the two of them maneuvered a large folding table down from the bed of his truck. (David had long since learned his lesson about attempting anything of the sort, ever since he'd made the mistake of offering to help carry a set of shelves down from the second floor, even if Meredith had subsequently insisted the damage was barely visible.)

"And this is Genevieve Schwarzwelder, Meredith's cousin."

("Other left, dumbass.")

"Zwiebelbauer," she corrected. "Not Schwarzwelder. We're cousins on our mothers' side."

"Oh, yes, he did say."

("For fuck's sake, would you watch where the hell you're going?")

"Delighted to meet you, young lady," said Bednarek, keeping hold of her hand for far too long. "Absolutely delighted."

("God, you're useless.")

"Thank you, Mr. Bednarek," said David. "So kind of you to stop by." When Bednarek still failed to detach himself from Genevieve, he added, "Or did you mean to help set up? That's most generous of you."

The threat of physical labor did the trick.

"Lamentably no, in fact, I must be going," Bednarek excused himself, already backing away. "I did have one or two small matters to discuss, but I return later. I have, you see, a business matter most urgent to attend to."

"Ah. Do you know," said David, "I thought you just might."

Once Bednarek had departed with one last wistful look over his shoulder, the group made short work of arranging the furniture to Genevieve's satisfaction, and David allowed himself to be shooed back into the house. He was topping off his half-finished coffee when Meredith returned as well, but he bypassed the kitchen and vanished down the hall.

"David?" he called. "Don't s-suppose you'd let me borrow one of your shirts from the dryer?"

David was puzzled. In all the time they'd lived together, he'd never known Meredith to stammer like that, nor to have any interest in David's clothing, beyond insulting it.

Misunderstanding his silence, Meredith elaborated, "I mean a proper one, with a collar and buttons and all."

#99: He thinks this is the time to go and entirely change his look.

David entered the laundry room to find him rummaging in the clothes dryer. "Mine would surely be too big on you. Can't you borrow one of Todd's?"

"He's still asleep." Meredith tossed aside a bath towel, which David managed to catch before it hit the floor. "And anyway, have you seen him? His would never fit." He straightened up holding one of David's shirts, an understated windowpane check in blue and white. "Really, we're just like the three little bears, aren't we?"

"I think you've gotten a bit mixed up there," said David. "If all the bears were—" He gave up. "Never mind. Go on, then, but I expect that back in acceptable condition."

"Thanks. Be right down."

He was not, of course, right down. Though David had no objection to

Meredith embracing a more conventional style, it was hardly the most convenient moment for him to reach that decision.

David occupied himself slicing and arranging a selection of fresh fruits on one of the serving platters Genevieve had brought, though doubtless she would adjust them to her own exacting standards. Outside, engines started, then receded down the lane, signaling the departure of Florian and Jayceon. David started a fresh pot of coffee, then peered outside to check the progress of the decorations: pastel yellow bunting draped the deck rail, and matching tablecloths and centerpieces of tulips adorned the tables.

As the hands of the clock crept closer to ten thirty, new vehicles began to arrive. As no one knocked on the front door, David surmised that Genevieve had waylaid the guests and ushered them around back through the yard.

He went to the bay window for another peek outside, and as he took in the transformation of the deck and back garden, uncertainty began to creep in. What was he playing at, insisting upon hosting a bridal shower for a woman he barely knew? If one took an uncharitable view of the matter, why, he'd practically forced her to go along with it in spite of her protests. Perhaps he was no better than Steve Corner, with his obscene lingering glances, always just within the bounds of plausible deniability.

Ordinarily, David tried to devote as little thought as possible to the repugnant general manager, but upon contemplating Corner now, a new and dreadful vision of the future opened up before him. This particular future involved neither a Cartier nephew in a seaside hotel nor a new house with a wide bay window and hedges along the walkway. In this one, David saw plainly the course his life would take if he continued down the same path he was on—though, at times, it felt as if he were standing stationary, not moving along any path at all. Never leaving Midnight Cottage or the Corner Store, drifting still further away from everyone in his life, chasing fruitlessly after those who did not want him. Ending up a pathetic and grotesque figure like Steve Corner, who at nearly forty was unmarried and still taking a room in the boarding-house on Rutherford Street, who stank of expensive cologne and cheap vodka, who dyed his hair to hide the gray at the temples. (Some people, of course, were perfectly content to remain single all their lives, but David could not count himself among them. He supposed there was nothing all that wrong with dyeing one's hair, either, except when Steve Corner did it, because it was him.)

If that was where David was destined to end up in ten years' time—well, it didn't bear thinking about.

He tore his gaze away from the window, turned around, and nearly had a heart attack at finding that Meredith had crept up on him yet again. Then, when David got a proper look at him, he could only stare in disbelief.

"Better?" asked Meredith.

David opened his mouth and closed it again. *Not at all*, he wanted to say, but that would hardly help matters.

Meredith had changed into a loose pair of threadbare, paint-spattered blue jeans he must have dug up from somewhere, along with David's borrowed button-down worn open over a white undershirt. (It came as no surprise that he'd had to fold over the cuffs of the sleeves more than once.) It was clear at once why Meredith avoided light colors—he looked terrible and washed out in them, and David couldn't understand why he'd chosen to dress that way on purpose. He'd even removed his ubiquitous black nail polish, and still carried with him a faint whiff of acetone.

No, this was all wrong. Meredith didn't look himself at all. No nail polish, no black, no clashing patterns, no foolish grin, no visible jewelry—

Correction: no visible jewelry aside from the single brass bangle on his wrist, the locating bracelet given him by Mrs. Jupiter.

David gestured toward it. "Just the one?"

Meredith glanced down and adjusted his shirtsleeve to conceal the bracelet. "That one's important."

"Is it." David didn't follow his logic at all.

"Yeah. Supposing you needed me for something—"

"What are you talking about?"

"Which you wouldn't, of course," said Meredith meekly. "You never do. S'pose I'd just like to think so, just on the chance of it."

Before David could try to make any sense of that, the door to the deck slid open. Adalynn stepped inside to greet him with a hug, while Meredith shrank back behind him.

"It's so good to see you both!" she said. "And thank you so much, again, for letting us have this here."

"Oh, it's no problem," David reassured her. "No problem at all."

Genevieve joined them in the open doorway. "All right, guys, here's the plan. We're still waiting on a few more—" She broke off as she caught sight of Meredith and gave a quizzical tilt of the head. "Why'd you change? I thought that dress you had on before was cute." Without waiting for an answer, she went on, "Anyhow, I've got a game to start things off in about ten minutes, and then we'll give everybody some time to help themselves and mingle. We'll do gifts at the end, and then I figure the guests will all be out by two or so. Sound good?"

Adalynn nodded, and Genevieve turned her attention to David. "I've been trying to get everybody to come around through the yard, but if you don't mind, we'll leave these doors open so it's easier to restock the buffet. Speaking of, Dave, you got those fruit plates ready yet?"

"One, yes. I'll get started on the other right away."

"You've done plenty. Hey, Mere, how about you try doing your fair share for once, huh?"

"It's really not—" David began, but Genevieve was already gone, pulling Adalynn along with her like a moon in orbit.

After carrying said fruit plate outdoors and helping to set up the last of the chafing dishes, David returned to find Meredith not in the kitchen, but crouched down to eye level with Bianca, where she lay on the window seat, apparently trying to reason with her.

"Of course not, precious, you know I'd never let anybody step on you, but this is a different matter altogether."

Bianca gave a whine and sank down to rest her head on her outstretched forelegs.

"Yes, I *know* it's your favorite collar. I'm only asking you to take it off for a bit, you can have it right back after."

When he reached for the Chihuahua, she shied away from him with a growl of disapproval. Meredith heaved a sigh and ran a hand through his hair, disarranging it even worse than usual. He looked suddenly very tired. "Yeah, I feel the same, only you've got to be reasonable, don't you?"

David quietly collected Meredith's untouched cup of cold coffee from the end table and emptied it down the kitchen sink. By the time he returned with a fresh cup, Bianca had retreated to her hiding spot behind the sofa, and Meredith stood gazing out the window, idly rubbing at one wrist.

David nudged him and held out the cup in offering. When faced with Meredith's blank stare, he explained, "Thought you might want this since you never drank your first one."

"Oh. Yes, thanks." He took a sip and turned back to the window as a pair of young women came through the yard carrying a number of shopping bags.

These, David guessed, must be the other bridesmaids. "You'll have to tell me who everybody is. More cousins?" He nodded toward the pair outside, a tall redhead in a blue dress and a muscular brunette with box braids and gossamer-delicate wings in the palest shade of lavender.

"Not of mine," said Meredith. "The one in blue is Adalynn's cousin Aurora, and the other is her friend S-Sonia. I think."

"Sophie?" asked David.

"Oh, yes, that's right."

"And those?" Now a blond woman with a pair of small girls rounded the corner of the house.

"That's Genevieve's older sister, Lucille, and her twins, forget their names, and that coming up behind them's my cousin Jana, and—oh, kill me *dead*."

David craned his neck to get a glimpse of what had provoked this reaction. "What's the matter?"

"Auntie Lisl," whispered Meredith. "And my mom."

"I expect you'll want to go see them, then."

Meredith's hand flew to his one remaining bracelet. "Yeah, I will. In a bit."

Genevieve, however, had other ideas. "Mere!" she called from outside. "Get out here and say hi to your mom!"

Meredith froze, and then, with the look of a prisoner about to face a firing squad, drifted out onto the deck. David hung back, watching from the doorway. He couldn't deny a certain degree of curiosity as to what sort of parents had produced the two wildly different siblings.

"Meredith." His mother was, at a guess, in her fifties, with sensible tortoiseshell glasses and short ash-blond hair beginning to go silver. One glance at her face was enough to remove any doubt of her relation to both Meredith and Genevieve—and to the woman who stood next to her, presumably Auntie Lisl.

"Hi, Mom."

It was an oddly lukewarm greeting from both sides. Neither seemed to know quite what to do with the other, and eventually, she pulled him into a sideways one-armed hug. Meredith tensed his shoulders at the embrace but voiced no protest.

Mrs. Schwarzwelder released him and said distantly, "We really must catch up sometime."

"Yeah," echoed Meredith. "S-sometime."

Then, catching sight of Adalynn, she lit up and swept off to greet her, calling, "Adalynn, dear!"

"Well," said Lisl, casting a critical glance over Meredith, "I haven't seen you around in a while."

"No."

"You get yourself a real job yet, or are you still a hairdresser?"

"I'm not a hairdresser, Auntie Lisl," said Meredith patiently. "I'm a tattoo artist."

"Guess that explains this mess." She reached up to swat a lock of wavy hair away from his face. "Letting it get long enough, aren't you?"

"Yeah," said Meredith, leaning back out of her reach. "I have been."

Lisl's eyes narrowed in disapproval. "What's this?"

Too late, David noticed that Meredith's unbuttoned shirt had slipped aside, leaving one edge of a tattooed bat wing just visible at his collarbone—and so had Lisl. She tugged his collar aside as he tried to back away.

"More tattoos, huh?"

"Oh, st-st—*don't*." He brushed her hand away, and her expression darkened with such suddenness it was as though a switch had been flipped.

"You just watch it," she said, jabbing a finger at him, and Meredith flinched.

"Mere, quit being a brat," scolded Genevieve. To David, she added, with fond exasperation, "He's the baby of the family, you know."

Meredith smiled then, a jagged smile filled with broken glass. No, David told himself, it contained nothing of the sort, nothing but slightly crooked and coffee-stained teeth. The two of them really were spending too much time together lately, with the way Meredith's flights of fancy had begun to creep into his own thoughts.

"Oh, dear me," said Meredith, and the brightness in his voice rang false. "I've left the sugar out. Best go put it away before it goes off." He turned and hurried past David into the house.

David wasn't sure he understood the interaction he'd just witnessed, but still glanced around to assure himself that it hadn't attracted undue attention from Adalynn or any of her relatives.

When Genevieve caught his eye, he felt himself compelled to offer an apology. "Sorry about that. I think he's just a bit—er—"

"Oh, trust me, I know," she said. "Me and him and Florian grew up together, and we're more siblings than cousins, but I'll be the first to admit the cupboard is a few teacups short there."

Privately, David agreed, even if it would be disloyal to say so aloud, then gave himself pause. It felt, in fact, rather disloyal to have thought it to begin with, and he was not so sure that he *did* think it anymore. Swallowing down his guilt, he said, "Well, I'll just be getting back to that other fruit plate, shall I?"

This time, he did find Meredith in the kitchen, slicing strawberries at a rather manic pace.

"Perhaps you ought—" David began.

"I can *handle* it, David."

He took a step back, palms raised. "As you like, then." Far be it from him to take over if Meredith felt the need to get involved in the proceedings after all.

At that moment, Todd Billion entered the room, yawning. "Morning, guys. Guess the party's already started, huh?"

He wound his way between David, Meredith, and the kitchen cabinets, and poured himself a cup of coffee. Circling back to the opposite side of the kitchen island, he leaned against it and took a long drink.

Outside, Genevieve had taken on the role of emcee, and directed Adalynn to a ribbon-adorned chair at one end of the deck. "Okay! Everybody knows the Newlywed Game, right? Florian couldn't be here today, so it's going to be a little one-sided, but I have his answers right here." She held up a stack of index cards. "So, let's see how well you know your future husband."

There was a smattering of applause and giggles from the seated guests.

"First off, an easy one: What is Florian's favorite color?"

"Red," said Adalynn confidently.

The audience looked raptly to Genevieve.

"Right!" She held up her index card in confirmation. "Okay, now that we're warmed up, let's make it tougher. How did you and Florian first meet?"

Adalynn smiled. "When we both went to your birthday party at Put-in-Bay the summer before last."

"Hey," said Todd, bringing David's attention back to his immediate surroundings. "You guys have lived together like twice that long, right?"

David shot him a glare across the counter. He'd had quite enough of Todd's insinuating looks ever since having had to correct his initial misconception, and didn't like where he seemed to be going with this.

Todd raised his free hand in a gesture of concession as he took another drink of coffee. "Nah, I just mean, I bet you two know all the same stuff about each other, right? Only I barely know anything about you guys." Jerking a thumb in Meredith's direction, he asked David, "What's *his* favorite color?"

David retrieved the spare serving platter from where Genevieve had left it on the kitchen table and set it next to the cutting board. "That's easy," he said. "Black, of course."

"It's green," said Meredith quietly, not looking up as he continued to rapidly quarter strawberries.

Outside, Genevieve boomed, "Okay, let's try a harder one. Who's his favorite music artist?"

Adalynn's answer was drowned out as Todd spoke up again, this time addressing Meredith. "Who's *his*?"

David breathed a sigh of relief. Meredith was going to go for the obvious, just as he had done, and say Edith Piaf. He'd be wrong, and then it would be all right again, because they'd be even.

"Nina Simone."

Heart sinking, David nodded in confirmation. No matter, he could redeem himself. Before Todd could throw another question at him, he said, "Yours is—it's the Damned, isn't it? No, wait," he interrupted himself. "Sisters of Mercy? One of those old ones."

"The Soft Boys," said Meredith, quieter still.

"Oh, yes. That song you always try getting everyone to play at the Rat Cellar."

Meredith was silent.

"Give me another," demanded David.

Todd hesitated. "Hey, chill, I just thought—"

"*Another*," David insisted.

Todd's eyes darted uneasily between the two of them. "Okay, uh, when's his birthday?"

"It's in, er—November. No, December." Damn Todd and damn his questions. Why couldn't he have picked something easier? "Isn't it?"

At that, Meredith finally looked up, glaring at David with raw fury as he chopped the strawberries into tiny bits. "Your favorite color's gray, your birthday's January the twenty-third, you drink your bourbon straight but only like rye in an old-fashioned, your left ankle aches when the weather's bad even though you pretend it doesn't, and *I don't like this game anymore*."

"Look, I'm—" began David.

"And what's more—oh!" Meredith's erratic chopping finally caught up with him, and the knife clattered to the countertop as blood flowed from the cut across his index finger.

David tried again. “Meredith—”

“Don’t bother,” he snapped, and stormed past David, out of the kitchen, and up the stairs.

Chapter Eighteen

Todd stared after Meredith in dismay. "I'm sorry, man. I was just having fun. Thought this'd be a way to get to know you guys a little better."

David sighed and ran a hand through his hair (once again making a mental note to have it cut soon). "It's all right." It wasn't, but he could hardly blame Todd. In fact, it felt about a hundred times worse than all David's unreciprocated insults combined, even though he'd not uttered a single word in malice. "He's just a bit on edge at having a houseful of his relatives, I think."

"Should I go talk to him?" asked Todd.

Somehow David couldn't imagine that improving matters. "No, no. I'll go sort it out. If you could keep an eye on things down here for a moment?"

He started toward the staircase, then, on second thought, made a brief detour down the hall. After retrieving the nearly empty jar of Mrs. Jupiter's healing salve, he climbed the stairs and tapped on the door of the second-floor bathroom. "Meredith?"

Silence.

"I know you're in there."

"No, I'm not."

"I'm opening the door." David found Meredith sitting in the empty bathtub, injured hand pressed to his mouth as he glared up at him. The way he held his arm cradled against his chest put David in mind of a bird with a broken wing.

He held up the jar. "Looking for this? You left it downstairs last week."

When Meredith refused to answer, David took a seat at the edge of the bathtub, opened the jar, and gathered every last bit of remaining ointment before taking hold of Meredith's wrist. He didn't resist, and let David lift his hand.

"You poor silly little bird." David tried his best to be gentle in both tone and touch as he applied ointment to the cut. The wound was deep, and the bleeding had lessened but not stopped. "Of course I know all about you. I know you call yourself a surrealist, but you take just as much influence from expressionism, and you adore Ralph Steadman. I know you can't do math to save your life, and you can't discriminate between good and bad beer. I know you've got a remarkable memory for verse, you sing beautifully, and you make the best shortcrust pastry I've ever had."

At Meredith's look of suspicion, David said, "Cross my heart. I'd never lie about pastry." He'd finished with the ointment but didn't let go, and found he didn't want to yet. As he went on, he studied Meredith's hand, soft and pale with remnants of black nail polish around the cuticles and bands of even paler skin in place of his absent rings.

"Your handwriting is dreadful, but you can do lovely calligraphy because you think of it as drawing and not writing. You love thunderstorms, but blizzards make you uneasy. If I were to ask your favorite flower, you'd say you could never choose, but," he went on quickly, curtailing Meredith's protest of exactly that, "I know that really you like common wood violets best."

David did release his hand then, and Meredith tipped his head back against the tiled wall. In the subdued daylight filtering through the small high window above the bathtub, the dark circles beneath his eyes were more evident than ever.

"I do still like all them things you said before," he admitted wearily, "even if they're not my *most* favorite. Only—I mean it's not *your* fault, only I s'pose I sort of wished—you see, Florian's found s-somebody who cares enough to know all that about him, and it all just reminded me that I haven't."

Once again, David found himself struck by that awful breathless, crumpled feeling as though his lungs, or something thereabouts, were being crushed by some invisible force. To buy himself time to formulate a response, he rose and went to the sink to wash the traces of blood and healing salve from his hands.

When he couldn't put it off any longer, he turned back around and dried his hands. "I hadn't realized." That much was true; he hadn't imagined sibling rivalry to be at the root of the matter, but it fit with the picture becoming increasingly clear in his mind, like a developing Polaroid photo or a jigsaw puzzle beginning to take shape. "I'm sorry I got it wrong."

Meredith shook his head. "Nah, it was a stupid game. I'm sorry, too. I know sometimes I can be a bit high-st-st-*strung*," he finished, forcing out the word.

#100: Sometimes—

David paused. Even if it was true that *sometimes* was the understatement of the year, he couldn't bring himself to hold it against him, not right now.

"And I can't even sp-speak properly."

Frowning, David returned to sit at the edge of the tub. "Hey," he said, softening his voice. "Hey, now, none of that. Although if you'll forgive me asking—I mean to say, I've never heard you speak with a stutter before. Not so that I've noticed."

"I don't. I mean, I haven't, not in years. It used to be pretty bad when I was a kid, but now it's only when I get st-st-*st*—" Meredith closed his eyes, and made a rolling *go on* motion that conveyed far more resignation than words ever could.

David waited.

"Stressed," Meredith concluded in a small voice.

David would have been stressed himself if half of his extended family descended upon Midnight Cottage, and he actually got on with his relatives. He was not so sure that was the case here.

"Come now," David said encouragingly. "It can't be as bad as all that." True, there seemed a degree of unspoken tension between Meredith and his mother. Neither did Lisl impress him as an especially pleasant woman, brief as their interaction had been. As for Florian—David still didn't know what to make of him. He couldn't say he *liked* the remarks he'd overheard earlier, but, he reasoned, anyone could become abrasive in the face of sufficient frustration, and surely Florian couldn't be that bad if Adalynn Cartier had chosen to marry him. In all likelihood, it was simply an off moment. In any case, the whole lot of them would be gone in a few hours more.

"David?"

"Hmm?"

"Thanks for not laughing at me. About—" Meredith made a vague gesture toward himself, but David understood exactly what he meant, and it sent a hot stab of rage through him. No matter how ridiculous Meredith might be, something like that was absolutely off limits.

"Don't you *dare*—"

Misunderstanding, Meredith interrupted, "No, no, I didn't mean to s-s—" He gave up and amended, "Imply that *you* would, only—"

"No," said David, "don't you dare thank me for showing you the most basic decency."

"Oh," said Meredith. It was a sad little sound, as though he'd been chastised—which he had, David supposed, though he hadn't meant it that way.

"December the twelfth," he said suddenly. "Your birthday, it's December the twelfth."

Meredith stared.

"Oh, come on, don't go making those big saucer eyes at me. Of course I knew it all along," said David, with more confidence than perhaps was warranted. But it *had* been there in his memory, somewhere or other, buried beneath a heap of petty grievances. "It just threw me, being put on the spot like that."

Feeling much better, he gave Meredith's shoulder a reassuring pat and got to his feet. He'd left Todd in charge for far longer than he'd meant to. "I'd best be getting back. Come down when you're ready, okay?"

"Yeah," said Meredith, and offered a weak smile. "Be right down."

By the time David returned to the living room, Todd had dozed off on the sofa, and Genevieve was showing Lisl and Mrs. Schwarzwelder in from the deck. As David hastened to descend the last few steps, Todd jerked awake. Mumbling a bleary apology—something about werewolves, as far as David could make out—Todd slipped past him to make his escape to the second floor.

"*There* you are," said Genevieve. "I wondered where you two disappeared to. I was just going to help Mom and Aunt Lotte find the restroom."

"My apologies," said David. "Meredith went upstairs for a moment to, er . . ." He couldn't imagine that Lotte Schwarzwelder, or anyone else for that matter, would want to hear, *Your son has just stepped away to have a crisis in the bathtub.* He was not, in fact, sure any longer whether *son* was the correct term. Nor was he sure he ought to share—besides which, the situation had been resolved. Everything was perfectly all right *now*.

"Throw a tantrum," supplied Lisl. "Of course he did."

"Oh, I'd hardly call it that. It was—" David stopped. He also didn't want to admit that Meredith had fled upstairs because of something he himself had said.

Lotte exchanged a look with her sister. "Look," she said with an air of resignation, "I love my son, but I'm not blind. He can't stand not being the center of attention."

David frowned. Though he would be the first to concede that Meredith's relatives surely knew him best, the two of them had lived together for a considerable period, and David was confident in his assessment of him. Meredith was scatterbrained, mercurial, arrogant at times, a bit self-absorbed—but not particularly attention-seeking, and certainly not calculating or malicious.

Lisl scoffed. "If you ask me, you should've—"

"Mom," interrupted Genevieve with a pointed look. "Come on, Aunt Lotte, let me show you where the bathroom is."

"Down the hall to the left," supplied David, and Genevieve nodded. He wasn't sure whether he imagined it or whether she threw him an apologetic glance as they passed by.

Left alone with Lisl, David racked his brain for some light topic of conversation. When she folded her arms and scowled, he decided he oughtn't to press his luck after all.

Then she caught sight of Bianca, and her face twisted in disgust. "Rhinestones!"

"I beg your pardon?"

(Bianca, perhaps sensing the hostility, took refuge behind the sofa.)

"Rhinestones, he's put on that little ankle biter. Just has to go prancing around shoving it in everybody's face that—"

"*Mom.*" Genevieve's voice held a definite note of warning as she returned from the hallway.

Despite the interruption, David understood perfectly well what Lisl was getting at. No, he decided, he didn't like her one bit, but he was capable of biting his tongue for a few hours for Adalynn's sake, so long as Genevieve continued to run interference.

Meredith, of course, chose that moment to descend the staircase.

"Done sulking?" asked Lisl.

"I'm not s-s-s—" Meredith gave up. "I'm *not*."

Lisl barked out a laugh. "I'll believe it when you can say it."

When Lisl *smirked*, David thought he might be sick. Then the nausea was followed by a return of that same white-hot rage. *Nobody* deserved to be treated like that, no matter how they might get on his nerves.

David took a deep breath and composed himself. He could not make a scene at Adalynn Cartier's bridal shower. He could not throw out a relative of the groom.

He could not abide Meredith's utterly crushed expression—all of David's careful reassurances undone by a single cruel remark.

#100: He has the worst—

No. Meredith could not be blamed for his relatives, regardless of how awful they were turning out to be. Not when David himself had been the one to invite them in.

"Hey!" Adalynn popped into the open doorway. "You two should come out and make yourselves a plate."

"Oh, we wouldn't want to intrude," protested David.

"Not at all! It is your house, after all," she pointed out. "And, Meredith, I'd like you to meet a few people, now that we're going to be related."

He blinked at her for a little too long before replying, with an effort, "Oh. Yes, if you'd like."

With a last uneasy glance at Lisl, David followed Meredith and Genevieve outside.

There were perhaps two dozen women milling around the deck and yard, chatting over paper plates of food from the buffet table, heedless of the clouds hanging low and dense in the sky. Though an occasional breeze swept through bearing the scent of heated grass, it did nothing to dissipate the oppressive humidity in the air.

David had intended to tag along closely enough to overhear a few introductions, but lost his nerve. Instead, he turned his attention to the buffet table and found himself gazing down without much enthusiasm at trays of cream horns and underbaked miniature strudels as he tried to banish wistful thoughts of misshapen Battenberg cake.

Deciding to forgo the desserts, David sipped a cup of weak punch and tried to make himself unobtrusive leaning against the deck rail. The breeze itself seemed listless, the drone of insects in the heavy air mingling with the indistinct conversation all around.

At the opposite edge of the deck, Meredith had fallen into conversation with Sophie, one of the bridesmaids. The two of them appeared to get on well—perhaps *too* well, judging by the way she traced a fingertip along the inky swirls of his filigreed wrist as they spoke, the tips of her wings giving the occasional flutter. David scowled. He'd have to have a word with Meredith about that. It simply wouldn't do to have him go seducing other members of the bridal party.

In the far corner stood a table heaped with a small mountain of wrapped gifts, and with a start, David realized he'd forgotten to add his own, a set of linen tea towels in a tasteful sage-green stripe. He fetched the wrapped package and made his way stealthily toward the gift table. Adalynn's attention was occupied as she spoke with an older woman, presumably the grandmother she'd mentioned. Near the buffet, Lotte Schwarzwelder approached Meredith—now that the initial awkwardness had faded, a reconciliation appeared to be underway. Lisl was safely off in the yard with the two twin girls. A few more steps and David could slip his gift into the pile—

"Hey, Dave, what you got there?" asked Genevieve behind him.

("Here," said Lotte, handing Meredith a paper plate. "I put together a plate for you.")

"Oh, er, just a small gift I picked up for Adalynn."

("It's creamed chicken," said Lotte, as Meredith lifted the top bun of the sandwich in suspicion.)

"It's been so kind of her, after all," said David, "including us like this."

("But I c-can't—"

Lotte sighed. "You know, I really thought you would've grown out of being such a picky eater by now.")

"I hope that's all right?" inquired David anxiously. "I wouldn't want to overstep, of course."

("I'm not *picky*," said Meredith with an edge to his voice. "I've been a vegetarian for ten years.")

"Not at all," said Genevieve. "Go ahead and stick it over there with the others."

("Oh, just eat it. No wonder you're so skinny." Lotte gave Meredith a poke to the ribs, which he flinched away from. "You need to get some meat on your bones.")

"We're about to get started with those in a couple minutes," Genevieve added.

(Patting Meredith on the arm, Lotte departed to join Lisl with Genevieve's two nieces in the yard, leaving him gazing down morosely at the sandwich in his hand.)

"Thank you, I'll do that." David added his gift to the designated table and made his way over to Meredith. He dropped his voice low enough not to be overheard. "Don't you dare."

"Oh, what's it matter?" Meredith asked hopelessly.

"Remember when George-7 fried those potatoes in bacon grease and didn't tell you? You were ill for days."

"Yeah, only I suppose perhaps she's got a point, I could st-stand to—oh!"

At his wit's end, David snatched the sandwich from him and flung it into the flower bed.

"Oh! But the garden," protested Meredith.

"*Fuck* the garden," growled David. "I won't have you bullied into making yourself sick."

Meredith ran a hand over his face. "She means well, it's just that she doesn't *listen*."

David was struck by a sudden memory of his own mother changing the recipe for her Christmas stuffing upon learning that Ruth's then-husband had a nut allergy, even though nobody aside from Ruth herself had particularly liked him. The thought filled him with a longing so intense that it nearly brought tears to his eyes. Surreptitiously clearing his throat, he resolved to call his father and sister both sometime that week, if not later that day.

"David?" asked Meredith. "You all right? Only you had this awfully funny look just now."

"Fine," said David. "Perfectly all right." He busied himself straightening Meredith's shirt collar, which had wilted considerably in the heat. "You ought to have ironed this properly, you know."

"Oh, would you st-st—*quit* it?" Meredith made a feeble effort to bat his hands away and gave up halfway through. "You're always *at* me with your big paws, you and everybody else."

"Okay, everybody!" called Genevieve. "It's time for what you've all been waiting for—gifts!"

It was, admittedly, not the most thrilling entertainment, but David did want to see Adalynn's reaction to his gift. Not that he expected anyone to get terribly excited over tea towels, but there was still a certain gratification in the acknowledgment. His impatience grew as he watched her open an electric kettle, a set of bed linens, a cake stand, and a fondue pot, which he could not picture Florian Schwarzwelder happily enjoying.

The mental image forced David to stifle a laugh, and he turned to whisper to Meredith—only to find that he'd vanished.

Irrational as it was, a sudden fear seized David that Meredith had slipped away unseen to the Midnight Wood, but he quashed that thought at once. Of course he hadn't. He'd simply gone back inside. He must have, David told himself as he ducked through the curtained doorway—and found the kitchen and main room entirely deserted.

Suddenly, the tea towels didn't matter anymore.

David stole out the front door so as not to disturb the bridal shower and started down the hill toward the Midnight Wood at as brisk of a pace as one could still rightfully designate walking rather than running; belatedly, he became aware of Bianca hurrying along by his side. He soon spotted Meredith a short distance from the picnic table, his back to the cottage.

As David reached him, slightly out of breath, Meredith gave no acknowledgment, but continued to stand staring into the distant depths of the Wood. David was used to his bright stare of inspiration (often followed by an incoherent but enthusiastic explanation of a new and usually ill-conceived art project); he was accustomed as well to the vacant gaze indicating that Meredith was lost in thought (which had occurred with increasing frequency over the past weeks). This was something altogether different, and far worse. It was a dead blank stare, as if something were missing, as if he'd retreated entirely within himself.

And now, daring a glimpse into the Wood himself, David had the awful feeling that something might be staring back.

With a whine, Bianca pawed at Meredith's ankle, but he took no notice.

"Hey." David nudged Meredith's shoulder, to no effect. He tried again. "Meri, where've you gone? Come back."

Another, harder nudge did the trick: Meredith started, blinking at David with wide, disoriented eyes.

"*There* you are," said David, feigning more cheer than he felt. "Bianca was terribly worried about you, you know."

"Was she," murmured Meredith distantly.

"Of course she was. You just vanished and—what are you doing down here, anyway?" David interrupted himself. "You know Mrs. Jupiter told you to stay away from the Wood."

"I don't . . . what *am* I doing here?" Meredith looked around in bewilderment as though only now becoming aware of his surroundings. He ran a hand over his face and looked so distraught that David started to reach out toward him—to do what, exactly, he was not certain, beyond attempting to offer some measure of comfort. But in his fractional hesitation, Meredith turned away and ducked down to take Bianca into his arms, and David lost his chance.

"Well," he said, "let's head back, shall we?"

Though Meredith cradled the Chihuahua to him as they started back up the hill, that awful blankness threatened to take over again.

To stave it off, David asked the first thing that came to mind: "They're twins, aren't they? Your mother and Lisl."

"Oh. Yes. Runs in the family."

"Not you and Florian, though."

"No, no. God, could you imagine?" Meredith shook his head. "He's three years older, then Genevieve, then me."

Talking seemed to be helping; perhaps giving him some other task to focus on would keep him grounded.

"Why don't we clean up the kitchen a bit?" suggested David. He'd led them toward the front side of the house, but peeked around the corner toward the back deck. "It looks as if Adalynn's just about finished with the gifts."

Back in the kitchen, Meredith set about washing the dishes that had accumulated in the sink while David consolidated the unused fruit and pastries into a few discarded shopping bags and kept up a steady stream of inconsequential remarks.

"By the way," he inquired, "did you ever take those drawings to Steve Corner for the auction?"

Meredith's face fell as he dried a paring knife. "Oh! No," he said in dismay. "I forgot. I'm s-sorry, David."

"No, no, that's quite all right. Perhaps once everyone's gone, we'll take them into town and then stop in somewhere for a drink. Goodness knows I could use one myself after all this."

When Meredith only rinsed a plate with a pensive expression, David pressed on, "We could go to the Rat Cellar, if you like. Who's playing tonight?"

"The Ultraviolence Committee," said Meredith, now scrubbing the cutting board, "but that's—" He broke off as Lisl came through the open doorway, faltering as she navigated the threshold.

With a scrabble of claws on hardwood, Bianca rose to her feet and emerged from beneath the kitchen table, giving a tiny grumble at the disturbance.

Lisl wavered, and then her contemptuous gaze settled on Bianca. "I ought to rip those goddamn rhinestones right off the little rat."

"You st-st-st—*keep* away from my dog," said Meredith, but in the time it took him to drop the dish sponge and turn off the tap, Lisl was already leaning down to make a grab for Bianca. The Chihuahua backed away, growling.

"Don't you growl at me or I'll kick you into next week."

In the blink of an eye, Meredith stepped between Lisl and Bianca, holding out an arresting hand. "*Don't.*"

Disoriented at the sudden movement, Lisl stumbled back a step and clutched at the edge of the table. Her cheeks took on a deeper flush. "Don't you put your hands on me."

"I'm n-not, I'm only—"

"I don't care how high and mighty you think you are just because you ran off to school and England and God knows where else, you're not too grown for me to still give you a good smack when you deserve it. It's what your parents should've done a sight more often, if you ask me."

"Yeah," said Meredith, and smiled his broken-glass smile once more. "You're p-probably right."

David didn't know which was worse, that sharp unnerving smile or the lifeless stare. There flashed into his mind a sudden image of Meredith as a child, in the care of these people he'd met today. It wasn't a happy picture, and David had the desperate, absurd wish that he could have been around then to do something, anything at all.

He edged toward the two of them, keeping a wary eye on Lisl, and picked up Bianca just in case. Though there was no love lost between him and the Chihuahua, she still ranked far above Lisl in his book.

"I've had about enough of your smart mouth." Lisl swayed slightly, and her pointing finger jabbed Meredith in the chest. "You know, it's your mother I feel bad for. She thinks it's her fault you turned out to be a queer."

"*Mrs.* Zwiebelbauer." David only just managed to keep his tone one step this side of civil. He ought to have gone with his first instinct and thrown her out straightaway, repercussions be damned. How *dare* she come here, into their house, and behave in such a fashion? "I think that's quite enough."

Before Lisl could turn her ire upon David, Genevieve stepped inside. "Mom! There you are." This time, there was no mistaking the silent apology written on her face. "Come on, you're riding home with Aunt Lotte, aren't you? She's waiting on you."

With one last sneer at them both, Lisl allowed herself to be led outside.

Meredith slumped into the nearest chair and pushed up his sleeves, scrubbing his knuckles over both forearms. This time, it was impossible to deny that his skin was covered in hives.

Bianca kicked against David's chest in protest, and he started to return her to the floor, then, on second thought, set her gingerly in Meredith's lap. David pulled aside the curtain; outside, the last few guests bid Adalynn farewell as the bridesmaids cleared the tables.

"Meredith—"

"Don't. It d-doesn't matter. She's drunk."

"I didn't realize they were serving alcohol."

"Oh, they weren't, but that don't make any difference." At David's questioning look, Meredith elaborated, "It's an open s-secret at this point, Auntie Lisl is s-s-*seldom* without a flask of Kirschwasser."

"Not that awful cherry brandy you keep up in the cupboard? Of all the things to—would you leave off with that?" David interrupted himself as Meredith continued to scratch miserably at his inflamed skin. "You'll have yourself bleeding in a moment, and we're out of salve until we next see Mrs. Jupiter."

"I'm s-sorry."

"You needn't be sorry."

"No," said Meredith, "I'm sorry you had to hear that."

"You needn't be sorry for that, either."

The faraway look had begun to creep back into his eyes, and David caught hold of his wrist as he absently began scratching again. "Isn't there anything that'll help with that?"

"What?" Meredith shook himself out of the fog. "Oh, it usually goes away on its own, but I think I've got some allergy pills upst-st-st—in my room."

In the gentlest tone he could manage, David suggested, "Why don't you go take one, and while you're up there, you can get those drawings together for me, all right? And Bianca can help, of course." At this point, it was simply damage control to keep them both out of harm's way until everyone had departed, and if anyone took issue, David would answer for it.

As Meredith started up the stairs with Bianca at his heels, David called, "And, Meri? Take your time."

Alone in the kitchen, David took a deep breath. After the events of the past hour, he was not at all sure whether he could consider the bridal shower a success, or whether he hadn't, in fact, made things worse for himself than they would've been if he'd stayed out of it altogether.

He was not sure how much that mattered to him any longer.

OUTSIDE, THE FINAL guests had taken their leave. As Genevieve helped Adalynn stow the last of the gifts in the trunk of her late-model hybrid sedan, two trucks pulled into the driveway—Florian's, followed by that of the taciturn Jayceon. The two women shared a final embrace before Genevieve climbed into her own SUV and drove off, and Florian took her place at his fiancée's side.

David caught just the tail end of their conversation as he approached.

"—kidding me? She couldn't have sprung for something better than a freaking *blender* with the kind of money she has?"

"It's the thought that counts, Florian," said Adalynn. "Besides, we do need a blender."

"If you ask me—" Florian broke off. "No, okay. You're right, honey. Me and Jay are gonna grab these chairs now, okay?" He kissed her on the cheek, then started toward the deck, nodding to David as he passed by.

After offering her profuse thanks once more, Adalynn departed, and David assisted the other two men in loading the furniture into their trucks.

Florian slammed his tailgate into place. "I gotta hand it to you, you must have the patience of a saint."

"Oh, not at all," David assured him. "Hosting was no bother, and really Genevieve handled most of the work."

"I didn't mean the party," said Florian as he lit a cigarette, "although I do appreciate that, believe me. I was talking about putting up with—" He tilted his head in the direction of the house.

David's stomach simmered with a mixture of guilt and resentment. Even if he would have agreed with the sentiment not long ago, it was a different thing entirely to hear it from someone else. Truth be told, he was beginning to dislike Florian, and he was going to make him say it straight-out, Cartier or no Cartier. "What do you mean?"

Florian took a drag on his cigarette and exhaled a cloud of smoke. "Listen, Dave, you're a nice enough guy, but let's not beat around the bush. My brother is kind of a retard."

"*Excuse me?*" David had expected something unkind or distasteful, yes, but that was going much too far. "I'm sorry, but that's—that's—" He was too astounded to formulate a reply.

"Sorry if my choice of words isn't PC enough for you," said Florian with a wave of his cigarette, and his voice held a trace of that same mocking tone he'd directed at Meredith that morning. "Sugarcoat it all you want with some fancy psychology bullshit if that makes you feel better, but that's what it comes down to, and me and you both know it."

All decency dictated that such a remark must not be allowed to stand, yet David could envision the disastrous personal consequences of telling off Maitland Cartier's son-in-law. As he wrestled with his indecision, Florian clapped him on the shoulder. "Anyhow, I've got to be going. See you around, Dave."

At last David stood alone outside Midnight Cottage and walked slowly around the house to inspect the damage. Physically, there was almost none. Genevieve and the bridesmaids had cleaned up thoroughly. The only indications an event had taken place were the lightest tire tracks in the grass and a few last bits of shredded chicken among the rhododendrons.

And, at one edge of the driveway, a discarded flower crown, wilted and trodden into the dirt.

David stared down at it for a long time.

WHEN HE RETURNED to the living room, Meredith had ventured out to peer over the railing of the upstairs landing.

"They've gone," said David.

Wordlessly, Meredith came down the stairs and presented David with a folder of drawings.

"Meredith," said David. He ought to say something more, but his throat had gone dry, and every word out of his mouth that day had only made things worse. The situation called for a delicate touch that David lacked. Eventually, he managed, "Come on, then. Let's take these down to the Corner Store, and then we'll go out someplace, wherever you like."

"I think," said Meredith quietly, "maybe I hadn't better go. You can take them."

"But they're *your* drawings," David protested. "Why in the world not?"

Eyes downcast, Meredith hugged himself, and when David thought he wouldn't answer at all, he looked up at him, wearing a hurt, bewildered expression like a lost child. "David? Do I embarrass you?"

Any other time, he would have replied, *Only every waking moment*, but these were no ordinary circumstances. Meredith really meant it, and to David's own surprise, he found himself *furious*.

"Of course you don't," he said briskly. "And if anyone has told you so, they haven't the least idea what they're talking about. Now, go and put your dress back on. We're going out."

Chapter Nineteen

In a surprisingly short time, Meredith returned, hopping down over the last few steps to land at the bottom of the staircase in a flurry of stripes and jingle of bracelets. A surreptitious glance at his now-bare arms assured David the hives were beginning to fade already.

"Shall I drive us?" he offered. "It looks like rain."

"What, in your k-kidnapping van? No, thank you," said Meredith. "I'd just as soon walk."

"It is not a *kidnapping van*, I'll have you know," protested David, beckoning Meredith out the door, but secretly he was relieved.

"You bought it at police auction."

"Yes, after it was seized from a business whose owner had been convicted of tax fraud. It was a Sound Financial Decision."

"*It was a Sound Financial Decision*," mimicked Meredith, and David nearly laughed as he shut the door behind them. (Still, he could not understand how Meredith, with his unsettling knack for impersonations, always went so far afield with David's.)

They fell into silence as they started down the hill, no sound but the crunch of gravel beneath their feet and the plaintive birdsong in the distance. By the time they reached the foot of the hill, the silence weighed on David, but he still didn't trust himself not to make a worse mess of things. Like the clouds above, it grew heavier and heavier, and when they reached the first stoplight at the edge of town, he couldn't take it any longer.

As they waited for the light to turn, David leaned into Meredith's space to lightly knock their shoulders together, a tentative gesture of affection. To his relief, Meredith returned the gesture and offered the faintest attempt at a smile. Although they continued their walk in silence, the tension had broken, and the discomfort bled away.

Thankfully, Steve Corner was absent from the Corner Store—David didn't think he could abide the sight of Meredith giving Corner a kiss on the cheek, not today. (In fact, David realized, he hadn't done so to anyone all day, hadn't been his usual overaffectionate self at all.) It was the work of a few moments to fill out the necessary paperwork and add the folder of drawings to the hoard of donated goods accumulating in a disused conference room, and then the two of them found themselves back on the sidewalk.

"So," said David, "where to?" It would inevitably be the Rat Cellar, but he'd spend the rest of the afternoon there without complaint if it prevented Meredith from looking so unbearably tragic again.

When he received only a shrug in response, David said, "Rat Cellar it is, then."

Meredith hesitated. "To tell the truth, I'm not really feeling it."

That was a surprise, and a worrying one at that. David considered. "How about that new bistro down the street? I've not been there yet."

"The Austrian place?" Another shrug. "If you like."

Within minutes, they were seated at the outdoor patio of the nearly deserted restaurant, and David offered the wine list to Meredith. "I suspect you're the authority here. I'm a bit out of my wheelhouse when it comes to wine."

"You'll want s-something on the drier side, I expect." He perused the list with a thoughtful expression, then pointed to two entries. "Them two you might like. *Those* two," he corrected. "Blauer Zweigelt, that's a red, and Grüner Veltliner is a white."

David glanced at the indicated listings. "So the blue is red and green is white, is it?"

That got him a small smile. "Yeah, bit confusing, isn't it?"

"Which would you prefer?"

"Don't make a difference to me." Then, as his words caught up to him, Meredith groaned and hid his face in his hands. "Oh, David, please, you're supposed to tell me when I go sounding ignorant like that." He turned wide imploring eyes on him. "I *want* you to."

"Er, yes, but—" As much of a habit as it had become—not that it had ever seemed to make much difference—today David couldn't quite bring himself to do so.

He was spared having to reply when the waiter arrived, and his attention went to floundering his way through the pronunciations as he ordered.

"And sparkling water for me as well, thanks," Meredith added.

Once the waiter had departed and David had had a moment to compose his thoughts, he said, "You're not ignorant. You just speak—"

"I know," interrupted Meredith. "I sound like I'm from where I'm from."

#100: He does not sound—

No. It was true that he did not, in fact, sound like anyone from anywhere that David had ever encountered, but he'd come to find an odd charm in it.

Meredith dropped his gaze and fiddled with his bracelets. "Only I wish I didn't."

David suspected this had far less to do with the place itself than with the people—a few particular people—and couldn't help but feel he'd just prodded at a psychic wound that was still raw in spite of its age. (He also couldn't help but notice the marked decrease in the frequency of Meredith's stutter since his relatives had departed, but he wasn't about to bring that up.)

David was still searching for the right words when the waiter returned to deliver a bottle of white wine and something along the lines of a charcuterie board that contained rather more pâté and sausages than were necessary for a table with only one carnivore. He poured a glass of wine and ventured a sip—dry, as promised, with a pleasantly bright citrus quality. As Meredith mixed himself a spritzer, David considered how, at last, to address the elephant in the room. He'd meant to take a roundabout approach and lead in gently, perhaps by thanking him for rearranging his schedule to be present that morning, or asking what came next in terms of wedding activities.

Instead, he found himself saying, "I'm sorry."

"Hmm?" Over his wineglass, Meredith returned a puzzled look. "Sorry for what?"

"For today, for—" David made an all-encompassing gesture. "All of it. Offering up our place for this bridal shower without really asking you, and insisting—"

"What are you on about? You didn't do anything."

David stared. "But your family—they're *awful*." Perhaps he shouldn't have said it straight-out, but he couldn't keep the thought to himself any longer.

For a time, Meredith was silent, save for the clink of his rings as he drummed his fingers against his wineglass. Then, with a quiet, startling defiance: "They're not my family."

David's heart broke. Had they not been sitting on opposite sides of the table, he would have hugged him, wrong impressions be damned. "Meredith—"

"'S all right, really," he interrupted. "I've got my own family now, I've got you and Kinley and Mrs. J and Bianca and Bednarek—not necessarily in that order." Then, with a glance around and a lowered voice, he added, "Only don't tell Bianca she wasn't first."

"Wouldn't dream of it," said David. He was not altogether sure how he felt about being claimed as a part of Meredith's patchwork family, but he'd still gladly accept that over leaving him to the collection of people they'd spent the morning with, who were hardly deserving of the title. Besides, he realized, it was true in a sense. They'd lived together for years; they'd merged their record collections; they shared meals and in-jokes and, as of today, clothing; they each knew exactly how the other took his tea. What other word was there?

Returning to the matter at hand, David said, "But Bednarek doesn't count. One's landlord is hardly one's friend."

"We are friends," Meredith insisted. "Who do you think I spend Christmas with?"

"*What?*" That was too sad for words, and guilt washed over David once more. He always traveled at Christmas to visit his father, but he'd never made more than the most superficial inquiries into Meredith's plans. After what David had witnessed that morning, he couldn't fault him for finding it preferable to spend holidays with his landlord rather than his blood relations.

With a shrug, Meredith picked up a slice of dark bread, turning it over absently in his hands. "Kinley always invites me to his parents', and I did go once. They were all very kind, of course, but I couldn't help but feel I was intruding. And to be fair to Genevieve, *she's* not all bad. She tries getting me to come around every year, too, but it seems better for everyone involved if I don't. So now me and Bednarek get together and I make Glühwein and he puts on these old spy films he's terribly nostalgic about. I don't understand the Polish, of course, but he explains enough to follow."

For a time, David occupied himself heaping a slice of bread with soft cheese and plum preserves, then finally voiced the question that had plagued the back of his mind ever since he'd found the remains of Meredith's daisy crown. "What did Florian say to you earlier?"

Meredith spent a moment tearing off bits of his bread. "Nothing really, just reminded me of all I've forgotten after so long away."

After which he'd immediately come in and changed—it wasn't difficult to put the pieces together there. "I take it some of them have a problem with you being, er . . . unlabeled?" David inquired cautiously.

"It's not exactly—" Meredith faltered. He looked away, took a sip of his drink, and then took another before continuing, "I don't think they would, if I were more like you. It's just, you know, the rhinestones and such." He rolled the foot of his wineglass along the table, tilting it from one side to the other. "S'pose if I really made up my mind to it—"

"No." David reached out to place an arresting hand atop his and stop him before he tipped his glass too far and spilled it everywhere. "Some people need to—" He made a vague gesture toward Meredith, searching for a descriptor. "To sparkle. I don't, but you do. Don't let anyone take that away from you."

Meredith only gave David a long, unfathomable look at that, at which point he hastily took his hand away and finished off his own glass of wine.

"Let's not talk about them anymore," said Meredith. "You've got a sister, haven't you? What's she like?"

David recognized the deliberate change in topic, abrupt as it was. "She—well, we don't see each other all that much anymore. Her name's Ruth, she's a pharmacist. Er, divorced, lives in Cardiff—"

"No, no, not like that," said Meredith. "That's just a list of facts. I mean, what's she like as a person?"

Such a simple question, yet difficult to answer. "Well, you see, that's just it. She went off to university when I was still in primary school, and then we moved, and we've not ever spent much time together," David explained. "She's nice enough, I suppose."

Meredith did not appear satisfied with this answer, nibbling bits of bread and looking at David in expectation.

"She likes animals," he offered. "Cats in particular. She used to have a brown tabby called . . ." His brow knit with the effort of recollection. "It was called Leticia."

Meredith gave a solemn nod, buttering the remainder of his bread slice. "Cats is good."

Slowly, David found further details coaxed from him: His father, a chemistry professor, a kind but undemonstrative man. His mother, a journalist and avid gardener who'd always kept a vase of daffodils in the house when they were in season. A move from one ocean to the other, with weekend trips to the beach remaining constant before and after.

David found that the longer he talked, however haltingly, the more Meredith seemed to brighten up and to show more enthusiasm toward the food, taking a bit of cheese here, a sliced radish there, so he kept at it in spite of how awkward it felt. In truth, there was nothing all that interesting about his own life, yet Meredith acted as though it were the most fascinating subject in the world.

David spoke of traveling at holidays as various relatives rotated hosting each year; of his parents' mild surprise and easy acceptance when he'd come out at sixteen; of playing rugby at university until his comparatively minor injury had laid him up for a few weeks and led to the decision to focus on his studies. He admitted to having chosen accounting as he often felt more at home with numbers than with people, though the latter had come more easily over the years. He told at last, stumbling over his words a bit, of his mother's late cancer diagnosis in his final year of university, of her death a few months before graduation—the first time he'd spoken of it in years. It had not been a deliberate choice, but there was only so much he could bear of Harriet's sincere sympathy, of his father's quiet grief, of the way his boyfriend at the time had turned away uncomfortably upon seeing David shed tears.

When he and said boyfriend had broken up just as David was sitting his CPA exams—

"Was it very awful?" Meredith broke in sympathetically.

"No, no," David reassured him. "It was quite amicable. Simply a case of realizing we weren't compatible long-term."

"Well, I'm glad of that, at least." Meredith took a sip of his drink. "Wouldn't like to think of anyone being horrible to you that way."

"Who, Charles?" David couldn't suppress a laugh at that. If Meredith had ever met him, he'd certainly know better. "He was as harmless as a kitten. I think the worst thing he ever managed to say to me was that I was entirely unremarkable."

"But that's awful!"

"Is it?" asked David in surprise. "I don't see what's all that bad about being ordinary." It had been meant as an insult, yes, but as insults went, it was rather mild, and his feelings had not been hurt particularly. (Perhaps it had gotten to him just a bit, though, if it had stuck with him all these years since.) Still, he recognized the distraught quaver in Meredith's voice and patted his hand. "Come now, it's all right. I'm all right, I promise you."

Meredith didn't look convinced. In an effort to distract him, David hastened to resume his tale:

After the breakup, he'd found himself at a loss, and followed his father's advice to seek a change of scenery. It had seemed as good a time as any to take up Harriet's oft-repeated invitation to visit. His intended stay of a few days stretched into a few weeks, and soon enough he'd accepted a position at the Corner Store. After a few months in a cheap sublease in town, he'd moved into Midnight Cottage, and from there, of course, Meredith knew the rest.

David was unaccustomed to talking about such things, and to the intensity of receiving Meredith's full attention without the usual distractions and interruptions. It left him feeling strange and exposed, as though his previous understanding of himself had been peeled back to reveal something soft and fragile underneath, like the petals of a new-blossomed flower.

By that time, they'd finished the bottle between them and set out for home beneath the darkened sky. It was only early evening, but the gathering storm clouds hung low and heavy, and thunder rumbled in the distance. David could no longer ignore the twinges in his left ankle and gave up trying to conceal how he favored it as they walked along.

"So that's why you were so gloomy when you moved in," said Meredith.

"I suppose I was, wasn't I?" admitted David.

A cool wind swept past, turning up the pale undersides of the leaves on the trees lining the road, and the first drops of rain dotted the pavement. Meredith gave a little shiver, and David had to resist the urge to wrap an arm around his shoulders.

"If you'd ever said—I mean, I'd just lost someone, too, back then."

"Your grandfather."

"Yeah."

David was tempted to ask for further details, but though it seemed a safer topic, he didn't quite dare.

Meredith, however, leaned down to pick a ragged daisy from the roadside and took up the subject unprompted. "Me and Florian never got along, so I was off by myself in the woods more often than not—s'pose that shows, don't it?" he interrupted himself with a rueful laugh. He plucked one petal, then another. "By myself, or else they'd send me to him—Grandpa, I mean. Being that I was the difficult one, not Florian."

Another pause, another two petals gone. "Our grandmother died when we were quite young, and he never remarried, so it was just him on his own. He'd have me read aloud to him, poetry and such. Probably where it comes from—the remembering, like you said." Two more petals were discarded in the breeze. "He caught me trying on one of my grandma's dresses once."

David tensed. Perhaps this wasn't a safe topic after all. "And what did he say?"

"*White don't suit you.*" Meredith broke into a grin, and David huffed out a soft laugh of relief. Still plucking petals from his now worse-for-wear daisy, Meredith continued, "It was him who taught me how to make May wine. And bought me my first set of proper drawing pens. Never gave me a hard time when I dropped out of college, either. Only, you see, I was offered an apprenticeship, and I figured, well, I am a bit stupid anyway, so—" He broke off with a shrug.

"You're not," said David. They had neared the top of the hill now, and Midnight Cottage was in sight. Todd's space in the driveway had been vacated—it was well past time for him to be at work.

"Kinley was telling me I ought to go back, but I don't see much—oh!"

"Oh?"

Meredith held up the daisy, now with only one petal remaining. "I won," he said in wonderment.

At that moment, the storm broke in earnest, and they both took off at a sprint toward the front door as the rain came pouring down. Meredith caught David by the wrist and pulled him along and stumbled against him breathless and giggling as they ducked beneath the eaves.

"Told you it was going to rain," muttered David as he fumbled with his keys, but he couldn't bring himself to complain, not when Meredith was finally smiling again without a trace of broken glass. Not when he was standing so close, skin shimmering with rainwater, chest heaving, eyes bright with exhilaration.

"Yeah, but you were right," said Meredith, stepping out from beneath the overhang and turning his face upward. "I do love storms."

Chapter Twenty

Inside, David wiped his face dry with his shirtsleeve and tried to ignore Meredith misappropriating a tea towel from the kitchen for the same purpose. Instead, he found himself struck by the urge to do it for him, to dry his face and pull him close and lose himself in rainwater and wildflowers and starlight.

He knew then what he wanted—what he'd wanted for the past week, or perhaps even longer—despite having spent the intervening time trying to convince himself otherwise.

With a tingle of anticipation and, yes, a bit of fear coursing through him, David went to the record cabinet and, without much debate, made a selection. As the scratchy strains of old piano music came over the speaker, a melancholy ache filled him.

He turned to Meredith, just emerging from the kitchen, and beckoned to him. Meredith tilted his head in question but made his way over to join him in front of the window.

A new song began, a single piano chord followed at once by a woman's voice, low and yearning, and David beckoned again. "Meri. Dance with me?"

Meredith giggled, but David did not think he was laughing at him. It was a nervous laugh, as if he didn't know what to make of it. As if he wasn't quite sure whether the invitation was serious. "What?"

"You said before, you wanted to dance. So I'm asking you."

"I said—oh!" Recognition dawned in his eyes. "But this isn't Edith Piaf," he murmured, though he took a step nearer and rested a tentative hand at David's waist.

David was about to protest that he wasn't meant to lead, but of course, with Meredith, all the rules went out the window.

"No." David moved Meredith's hand to his shoulder. "But you haven't got on a ball gown, either."

"Nina Simone," he identified.

"Yes. Thought she was a bit more the speed for this sort of thing. And, of course, you don't understand French."

David had never been much for dancing, and now faced a moment of temporary panic. He had little idea what he was doing, but Meredith didn't seem to mind, and they swayed gently to the slow sad music as lightning flashed outside and water streamed down the windowpanes.

For once, Meredith didn't fill the silence with his usual chatter, and before long, he rested his head on David's shoulder. Gradually, one of David's hands left his waist and traveled up his back, stroking his damp disheveled hair and brushing it aside to trace over the fine bones of his neck. At Meredith's quiet gasp, David gave a gentle squeeze, a kind of acknowledgment in the lightest application of pressure.

They were so close together that David was sure Meredith must hear his heart pounding in his chest. The last time—both times—had been impulsive, thoughtless, but now something had changed. David ought to apologize for those times. He ought, in fact, to say a great many things, but he did not know how to say them, so he simply let go and took a step back, just far enough to draw a soft sound of disappointment from Meredith.

More importantly, just far enough to make him look up.

When he did, David kissed him.

At first, Meredith didn't quite seem to know how to respond, but then he kissed back with as much enthusiasm as he had before. He caught David's lower lip between his teeth and darted his tongue along it before biting down with a surprisingly pleasurable sting. They kissed deeply, hungrily. David couldn't get enough of Meredith's delicious little pleading noises, or the way he clutched at David as if afraid to let go, one hand at the back of his head urging him closer.

When David finally broke away, he distantly registered Meredith breathing something that sounded like *sorry*.

But he still didn't let go.

David leaned down and kissed along his throat from jawline to shoulder. He couldn't resist returning to the point where he could feel Meredith's pulse thrumming beneath his skin, letting his tongue drag over the spot.

"*Yes*—oh, David, please—"

"Anything," he rasped out, face buried against Meredith's neck, and found that he meant it wholeheartedly. "Anything you want."

Meredith pulled back and cupped David's face in both hands. "What do *you* want?"

"You." David didn't even have to think about it. "I want you properly this time."

At first, Meredith only managed a wordless sound of assent, then, pulling himself together, suggested, "Upstairs?"

"Yes." David straightened up and kissed him again, timing it wrong and just catching the corner of his mouth as he turned away. "After all, I've got to redeem myself if the best you could say last time was that you've had worse."

At the top of the stairs, Meredith paused. "Go on, I'll be right in. Had to make a few adjustments with the dress." He started through the bathroom doorway, then leaned back out to say, "Top drawer."

"Top—oh! Yes," said David. "Right." Though he'd never been one to shy away from the necessary conversations around safe sex, Meredith's easy matter-of-factness left him unexpectedly flustered.

"Second drawer, too, if you're feeling adventurous," he added with a wink, and disappeared behind the door.

Half of the bedroom had been repurposed into a makeshift studio, and the entire space was as bohemian as David had expected from the few brief glimpses he'd had—beaded lampshades, mismatched throw pillows, odd trinkets scattered over every available surface. He turned on the nearest lamp and tried not to look too hard at the artwork lining the walls. Some pieces were Meredith's own work and others were prints of the classics; everywhere David looked, there were stark angular lines and melting objects and creeping substances and missing faces.

No wonder Meredith had trouble sleeping.

As promised, in the top drawer of the bedside cabinet David found condoms and lube, which he set out neatly atop it. He did not quite dare to look in the second drawer.

After a moment of debate, David began to unbutton his shirt. He reached the last button as Meredith entered, now in a kimono robe tied loosely at the waist.

"I thought the idea was to take your clothes *off*," David remarked.

"Yeah, only I thought you might want to undress me. People often do. I mean, not me in particular—well, also me in particular—I mean to say, I wouldn't want to deprive you, if you like that sort of thing," Meredith concluded.

David supposed he was glad Meredith had taken off the dress, as he'd never particularly wanted to have sex with someone wearing one—or someone wearing a ladies' dressing gown, for that matter, yet here he was.

Perhaps it was best if he didn't think about it too hard.

David loosened the sash of Meredith's robe and slid it from his shoulders, letting it slip to the floor. Meredith shivered at his touch as David traced down his side, over the script tattoo on his ribs and a few raised scars above his hip that he could feel but not see. "What are these from?"

"Falling into those thornbushes like I told you about."

David leaned in and, mistiming it again, ended up kissing him on the cheek. He kept at it, trailing open-mouthed kisses down his neck until he pulled back to glance down and trace over the lines of script once more. "And what's this say?"

"I—what?"

David liked the way his voice had gone all breathy. He ran his thumb over the spot again, along his ribs. "This tattoo."

"*Hast du nicht alles selbst vollendet, heilig glühend Herz?*"

"I can *see*—never mind."

"It's *Goethe*," said Meredith with a hint of reproach.

"Mm-hm." David leaned in and kissed the hollow of his collarbone. "I didn't come here to discuss Goethe with you."

"Well, you wouldn't know it, the way you're still dressed like you belong in a history lecture, and—*oh!*"

David's fingers had found their way to one of his nipple rings, and his gentle tug at the jewelry was enough to curtail the complaint.

"Good?" he asked.

"Oh, *fuck*—oh, David, *please*, you've got to take off some clothes, it isn't fair." Eager hands scrabbled at the hem of his undershirt, and in no time David found himself stripped to the waist. Meredith was somehow touching him all over at once, stroking his back and running his fingers through his chest hair and leaning in to nip at his shoulder.

"Hey, now," warned David, "you just watch those sharp little teeth of yours."

"Oh, do you mind? 'M sorry," murmured Meredith without lifting his head, every word burning against David's skin, and pressed an apologetic kiss to the same spot.

"Well . . . no, I can't say I do," admitted David. In truth, there was something unexpectedly arousing about that little spark of pain.

Meredith did look up at him then, a wild stormy light in his eyes. This time, the sharpness in his smile made David's heart race with anticipation. "Good. Because I wasn't joking when I said I was a bit of a sadist."

In order to get a handle on himself, David ran a hand up Meredith's naked back, tracing along his spine. "But last time you wanted me to bite you."

"Yeah," said Meredith, as though he'd pointed out the stunningly obvious. "I like that, too. Haven't you caught on yet, I like just about everything?"

"In that case—" David made short work of discarding his own pants and boxers, pushed Meredith down onto the bed, and lazily traced a fingertip along the winding paths of ink below his navel. Only the erratic sparkle of his rhinestone belly ring in the lamplight betrayed how wrecked his breathing was, and he gave a little groan of frustration as David's hand bypassed his cock and traveled down his thigh (adorned from knee to hip with a Dalí elephant).

"David," Meredith panted, propping himself up on his elbows. "*Please.*"

Relenting, David wrapped a hand loosely around him, causing Meredith to whine in the back of his throat and arch up into his touch. David stroked his cock—a bit smaller than his own, dark and straining, with a tempting bead of precome collecting at the tip—and discovered that he wanted, very badly, to have it in his mouth.

And there was nothing stopping him.

He lowered himself to the bed and kissed the inside of Meredith's thigh. "All right?" he asked, although he was already quite sure of the answer.

"Yeah—*God*, yeah, go on."

David licked up the underside of his cock, which made Meredith immediately begin squirming under him. "Keep *still*," David ordered, and pinned his hips down.

It was hopeless, of course. The moment David took him fully into his mouth, Meredith writhed and cursed and generally made a nuisance of himself—which David, to his dismay, found an unbearable turn-on.

Yes, it had been far too long since he'd done this with anyone, and he could have continued indefinitely, listening to him moan and knowing himself to be the cause. David was tempted to take his own cock in hand and get off to Meredith's reactions alone, but before much longer, Meredith nudged him in the shoulder with his knee. "Hang on, give me a moment."

David raised his head to look up at him. "What's the matter?"

"Nothing." Meredith sat up and stretched like a cat. "Only you said you wanted me properly, yeah? Come here."

David obliged, making his way up the bed to join him. Meredith pulled him into his lap so David straddled his hips, and ran a hand down his back with a light scrape of fingernails.

Briefly, their cocks brushed together, making David shudder. To distract himself, he reached out and traced the spiky, distorted outline of Meredith's heart tattoo.

"I designed that one myself, you know," said Meredith as he leaned in to nuzzle against David.

"Did you."

"Course I did. 'S not everyone who knows what their own heart looks like."

"Quite accurate, I'm sure," said David absently. He sucked in his breath with a hiss as Meredith bit down on his shoulder.

He rested one hand at David's hip, and the other trailed over the small of his back with just enough scratch to make it interesting. Then David gave an embarrassing yelp that was more surprise than objection as exploring fingers continued lower, tracing between his ass cheeks.

Meredith stopped and took his hand away. "No?"

"I, er—" David's face was burning. He was not sure if it was a *no* or not. "I mean, I had rather thought—that is to say I usually—which is not to say *never*—" What was *happening* to him? Never before had he had a problem stating plainly what he wanted or didn't want—only now he was not sure what he *did* want, now that he'd found himself in bed with the most unpredictable person he'd ever met.

"Oh, you'd rather have me?" said Meredith, unconcerned. "That's all right, I don't mind. Although . . ." He cast a dubious glance downward.

"What's the matter?"

"Looks a bit much, is all. I ain't a size queen, David, and to tell the truth, I haven't gone this far in a while, one way or the other. But," he went on, "for you, I will."

David sat back, putting a little distance between them. "Hey. I don't want you to do anything you don't like. Er . . . what *do* you like? I mean, what do you usually prefer?"

"I told you, I like it all, but I mean, that's not really the end goal for me." Meredith glanced away, and that sudden shyness came back into his expression. "I just like being touched, is all, and—" He broke off and reached over to trail his fingers down David's chest once more.

"And what?"

Meredith gave a soft laugh. "David. It's *fine*. Don't go getting all serious on me. You can fuck me if you want to. I'd *like* you to."

Hearing those words caused David's brain to short out, but at last he managed, "Yes, I—I'd like that as well."

Meredith reached toward the bedside table. "Just give me a moment, and I'll—"

"No, no, let me—"

Several minutes later, they were in much the same position, though David now knelt between Meredith's legs with one arm around his shoulders and two fingers inside him. Meredith squirmed against his hand, and David rather suspected he was making a show of enjoying it.

"David, *more*," he insisted. "God, do you know how many times I've imagined this?"

"This in particular?" said David dryly.

"Yeah," breathed Meredith, "just thinking what you could do to me with those big strong hands of yours." He slumped back against the headboard with a groan as David eased another finger into him.

The full meaning of Meredith's words finally caught up to him. "Wait, you've thought of me?" It was flattering, but David wasn't sure whether he should believe it. Meredith was good at charming his way into bed, and while he wouldn't outright lie to get there, David wasn't sure it would go against his bizarre little moral code to exaggerate once he was if he thought the other person would enjoy it.

"Course I have—*fuck*, do that again—haven't you?"

"Perhaps on occasion," David admitted, "but you're entirely to blame there. You're not always as quiet as you might be when you bring someone upstairs, you know." It was hardly David's fault if that led to certain wanderings of the imagination. Right now, for instance, he couldn't stop himself imagining exactly what further reactions he himself might provoke from Meredith once he finally got his aching, neglected cock inside him.

"David, *please*, it's—" Meredith broke off with a gasp. "Enough, I'm ready, I swear."

"How do you want to do this?" asked David, and the next thing he knew, Meredith had reversed their positions and was rolling a condom onto him and drizzling more lube and—

This time it was David's turn to say, "*Oh.*" He bit the inside of his cheek as Meredith sank down onto him, willing himself not to lose it right then. When he began to move, it was all David could do to hold on.

It became clear to him at once that no matter who was doing what to whom, Meredith was in charge of the proceedings. He braced one arm against the wall and held tight to David with the other, leaning down so their foreheads touched.

"That's right," breathed Meredith, "that's it, precious, give it to me."

#100: He has only one—

Even if Meredith did seem to have only one term of endearment in his vocabulary, even if David did object to being addressed with the same pet name he used for his dog, he could not fault him for being incapable of deep thought at the moment.

This time, when David went for a kiss and failed yet again, he caught on: Meredith was deliberately turning away.

"Hey." Frowning, David reached up to brush Meredith's bangs from his eyes. "Don't you want me to kiss you?"

Meredith drew in a ragged breath and let his eyes fall closed. "More than anything," he whispered.

"Then quit being weird and *let* me." David seized a handful of hair, holding him in place, and kissed him hard. It was all so much, Meredith shuddering in his arms and surrounding him with unbearable heat and moaning shamelessly into his kiss. "*Fuck*—Meri, I can't—it won't be much longer."

"Touch me," ordered Meredith.

David got a hand between them and stroked Meredith's cock as he thrust up into him. His rhythm was a bit clumsier than he would've liked, but judging by the way Meredith swore and gripped his shoulder hard enough to hurt, it was getting the job done.

When David pulled him into another kiss, Meredith came with a muffled shout, and that pushed David over the edge right after him. They collapsed in each other's arms, trembling with the aftershocks, and for a time, the world dissolved into a pleasant haze.

Some time later, David returned after a brief interlude cleaning himself up in the adjacent bathroom and hesitated in the doorway. He had not thought things through this far.

Doesn't mean anything. We're just having fun, is all.

That's what Meredith had said last time, and it still held true.

I've been in love with somebody for ages, but they'd never give me the time of day.

Which was why there would not and could not be anything serious between them. Not, of course, that David was entertaining any such idea. Nor was there any reason in the world why reminding himself of that fact should feel like a plunge into an icy lake, knocking the breath from him and leaving him unmoored, splashing and grasping for any point of reference.

The sensible thing to do would be to return to his own room, get his thoughts in order, and, if necessary, give himself a stern talking-to. Certainly he could not sleep here, not when Todd would return by morning.

David would not, however, leave without saying good night.

Meredith lay sprawled out on the far side of the bed, naked, and either asleep or near enough to it. Sitting down at the edge of the mattress, David ran a hand over his side.

"Meri? Are you awake?"

When the only response was a noncommittal hum, David drew the bedsheets over him, taking care not to disturb him more than necessary. "I'll let you sleep now, okay?"

"Don't go," he murmured sleepily. "Not yet."

"I—well—" David gave in. "Just for a bit." He slipped under the covers next to Meredith, who promptly snuggled against him, resting his head against his shoulder and making that little contented sound that caused David, against all his better judgment, to wrap an arm around him and draw him in close.

He would stay, he told himself, just for a bit.

Chapter Twenty-One

The twisting black branches of the bare trees trembled, and the earth shook with each heavy footfall as the cloaked figure approached, no more than a dark silhouette. David stood frozen in fear.

This time, he was entirely alone.

This time, there was no one to break the spell or drag him away.

"One more!" The voice was an unwanted caress, sweeping over him with the whisper of dry leaves.

The man came nearer, still in shadow, though David could just make out the outlines of spiky protrusions upon his head through the material of his cloak—a pair of horns? The sharp points of a crown?

"One more," he rasped again.

At last David forced himself to move, scrambling backward. Rather, trying to, as the ground had become gelatinous and, for some reason, chartreuse.

The figure lowered its hood.

"One more, and he is mine."

DAVID JERKED AWAKE with a deep shuddering breath. For a moment, he was disoriented by the unfamiliar angles of the shadows, by moonlight streaming in from a window on the wrong side of the room.

"Shh," whispered Meredith, and draped an arm over him. "'S all right."

David shook his head, unable to properly articulate what he'd just seen or precisely why it was not in the least all right, and when he tried, to his own embarrassment, all he managed was a piteous, broken sound devoid of any words.

"There, it's just a nightmare, isn't it? I have them all the time," Meredith reassured him, and drew David closer against him. "It can't get you, I won't let it. Promise."

In his embrace, David drifted back to sleep, and the dream faded from memory.

By the time he woke again, the early-morning sky, still overcast, spilled a cool watery light into the room. The first semi-coherent thought to register in David's mind was an awareness of how astonishingly comfortable he was in his cocoon of blankets, in spite of the rather pointy elbow jabbing into his ribs.

That caused a number of new thoughts to spring into existence and compete for attention, but he swept them firmly beneath the metaphorical rug to be dealt with later. (It was a tasteful rug, with an orderly geometric pattern in subtle earth tones.)

Meredith stirred beside him, causing the blankets to slip down and expose his back. David couldn't resist running a hand over the expanse of pale skin, softer than it had any right to be—perhaps there was something to be said for moisturizer after all. He slowed when he reached the scars he'd felt the night before. Upon closer inspection, they were just visible in the daylight, a group of irregular puncture wounds faded silvery white.

With a sudden protective impulse, David pressed himself against Meredith's back and pulled him close. At his sleepy hum of protest, David leaned in to nuzzle at his jaw. "Hey there, little bird," he said softly. "You awake?"

"Am now," murmured Meredith, then added, "'M not little."

The words had quite bypassed David's brain on the way to his mouth, but he was not awake enough to feel much embarrassment. "Little medium-sized bird," he corrected, words half lost as he buried his face in a tangle of unruly brass-blond waves.

"That don't make any sense."

"You simply don't understand endearments." David kissed the nape of his neck. With a soft laugh, Meredith swatted lazily backward at him and missed. "Oh, that's funny, is it?"

"Your moustache tickles."

That registered as a kind of challenge, and David seized him around the waist and peppered his neck and shoulder with kisses until Meredith was giggling uncontrollably and struggling to escape. Finally, he managed to turn over and wore such a joyous expression that David once again felt as though the air were being forced from his lungs. This time, however, the sensation was not an unpleasant one.

"God, David, I—" Meredith cut himself off and hid his face against David's shoulder as his laughter subsided.

"You what?"

"Nothing," said Meredith, "just—" He met David's eyes with startling earnestness. "Thanks for last night. Meant the world to me."

That sent a tingling warmth all through him, entirely different from that of the night before. David's inconvenient thoughts threatened to come crawling out from beneath the rug, and he firmly stamped down the edges. "Well, I know I'm good," he said lightly, "but I wouldn't claim to be *that* good."

"You're *pretty* good—"

"Just pretty good?"

"—but that's not the part I meant."

There were many things David wanted to say in response: *You deserve nothing less. I'd do it all over in a heartbeat. I'd have done anything to make you smile again.* (The inconvenient thoughts had not only escaped from beneath the rug; they had set fire to it and now frolicked amidst the flames.) But he mustn't think such things, and certainly mustn't go saying them aloud. That would be crossing a line. After all, as Meredith had said—as they'd both agreed—nothing more could come of this, nothing beyond the physical.

To prevent himself from saying anything foolish, David instead reached over to brush Meredith's bangs out of his eyes—and then, giving in to his long-held curiosity, back from his forehead.

Meredith shied away. "Oh, don't, don't look," he protested. "I don't like when you can see my face."

David frowned. "Is that what you're up to, trying to hide under all that hair? Come here," he coaxed. "Let me see."

"Told you, I've got a scar there." Though Meredith kept his eyes cast down, he didn't turn away when David brushed his bangs aside once more.

"*Where?*" After much scrutiny, David finally spotted it at his hairline, small and very faint, and ran a fingertip over the spot. "What, this? You can hardly see it." Studying Meredith's profile, he traced his thumb along the bridge of his nose, and now finally felt where the line of the gentle curve was interrupted by the tiniest bump.

Meredith twisted away from him. "Ah, don't."

"You can't even tell," insisted David.

"No," said Meredith reproachfully, "but if you touch there, it goes all funny and I get a bit of a headache."

David nearly asked how it had happened, but thought better of it. Judging by Meredith's reaction when Todd had inquired, the topic wasn't up for discussion.

So instead, he just said, "Sorry," and kissed him gently between the eyes.

David tiptoed past Todd's closed door, descended the stairs, and took refuge in the shower. The hot water, as usual, brought him a sense of clarity.

What the hell did he think he was doing?

He had kissed Meredith again.

He had slept with him.

He had stayed the night in his bed.

Those were undeniable facts.

Undeniable, too, that he'd enjoyed it. Quite a lot, in fact. To claim otherwise would be the most brazen of lies.

David couldn't stop replaying it all in his mind: Dancing badly to Nina Simone. Holding each other close as the rain poured down outside. Every touch, every exquisite sting, igniting something within him and turning all his expectations upside down.

He wanted to do it again. He wanted to fall asleep with Meredith in his arms and wake up next to him, to watch him light up at something as inconsequential as getting caught in the rain or winning at Loves-Me-Not, to hear him give that wordless little sigh at being held tight or having his hair stroked that cracked open something in David's heart every time.

Amidst the steam and cascading water, David was experiencing a revelation. An unveiling, much like brushing aside a layer of fine snow from one's windshield on a winter morning or finally locating the error that had upset the total of a running balance.

He hadn't realized—perhaps hadn't allowed himself to admit—how much Meredith actually meant to him, all his little quirks included. Not until yesterday.

Not until Florian and Lisl had tried to force him to be something he wasn't, until David had watched his sparkle fade before his eyes, until—

worst of all—Meredith had tried to make himself *less*, for the sake of appeasing people who didn't appreciate him at all.

Not until the two of them had, after all this time, truly listened to each other, and David had felt the quiet thrill of something finally clicking into place. Despite his initial hesitation, once he'd gotten started, sharing the private details of his life had come with surprising ease, and he found that he rather liked having someone to share them *with*.

David couldn't pretend anymore. He felt something for Meredith, and that terrified him.

There was no way they could be together; in fact, they were already in agreement that it would never work out. Meredith was the exact opposite of David's type in every respect, although he wasn't sure if the inverse were true. (In fact, he rather doubted whether Meredith *had* a type.) Their lives were already so intertwined that if things went wrong, as they were bound to do, it would upend everything for them both. It was simply too great a risk.

And anyway, none of that mattered because the simple fact was that Meredith didn't want *him*. David was just a convenient distraction as he continued to pine for the mysterious object of his unrequited affections. Perhaps there was a sliver of hope that the option of someone both interested and immediately available might outweigh the longing for someone who wasn't, but David didn't like the idea of being anybody's second choice.

Viciously twisting the shower knob to the off position, he yanked aside the curtain and seized the nearest towel.

There he had it. A perfectly sensible reason to take all those troublesome impulses toward affection and sentimentality and kick them right back under the charred remains of the rug where they belonged. He would not waste time devoting any more thought to the matter.

After roughly towel-drying his hair, David reached for a comb and scowled at the sight of himself in the mirror. Somehow he could not quite bear to look at his own reflection just now.

Well, no matter. It was the weekend. The world would hardly end if he broke from habit and skipped shaving for one day.

In the kitchen, David put the percolator on, sautéed vegetables for a frittata, and did his best to put the previous night out of his mind despite Bianca's judgmental gaze following his every move from beneath the kitchen table.

With a lurch, David recalled the other matter that he'd put out of his mind with rather more success—the house offer he'd placed on Friday afternoon. Of course he would not derail his plans on the basis of what had happened last night. That would be rash in the extreme. But—

In the past day and a half, something had changed, something that had shifted his view of the world, a subtle alteration—a correction?—of perspective. David was no longer certain what he wanted. He needed time to think, to catch his breath and reassess before entering into any major commitment, on the home-buying front or otherwise. As for the former, he'd been hesitant to begin with, and it would be equally foolhardy to rush into such a significant financial obligation if he wasn't absolutely sure—especially when the possibility of a promotion, and the accompanying increase in salary, had begun to seem no more than a pipe dream.

Very well. He would call Leonard Flood and instruct him to withdraw his offer. There would be other houses. David took up his phone and began to swipe away the accumulation of email notifications—until he caught sight of the one from Maitland Cartier.

Hands trembling, he opened the message.

Dennis,

I know Adalynn has already thanked you, but I wanted to express my gratitude as well for the way you stepped up to host her bridal shower. I look forward to speaking with you this week at the Corner Store's centennial auction—I've taken the liberty of adding you to the VIP guest list in the hope that our paths might cross in the lounge.

Yours,
Maitland Cartier

David's phone clattered to the countertop.

Maitland Cartier had sent him an email. Possibly he had made a small error in the name, but that was of little importance. What mattered was that Maitland Cartier had personally added him to the VIP guest list. *Maitland Cartier wanted to speak with him.*

Taking a deep breath, David straightened up. Right. Perhaps it wasn't necessary to call Mr. Flood quite yet after all. In any case, little could be done before the start of business hours Monday, so there was no point getting ahead of himself. He'd give it until the morning and call Flood then if he still felt the same.

The ding of the oven timer brought David back to the present. Just as he was sliding the hot pan from the oven, Meredith appeared in the kitchen doorway. He was wearing David's borrowed shirt, open over the usual black.

They had slept together, and now he was *wearing David's shirt*.

David fumbled with the pan, and only just managed to avoid dropping it on his bare feet. Of course, in all likelihood, it had been the first item at hand, worn for no more than a few hours the previous day. A simple matter of convenience, David reasoned.

Not that reason did anything to calm the multitude of butterflies that he appeared to have swallowed sometime in the past ten seconds.

The last remaining bits of the rug crumbled to ash.

"I THINK," SAID Meredith a short time later as he sipped scalding coffee, "I've really got to go out and pick some sweet woodruff for the May wine this morning. I've left it far too late."

"Not in the Midnight Wood?" It came out more of a question than David meant it to. "You know Mrs. Jupiter told you to stay away."

"Oh, but it'd be just for a bit. I know right where it's at, and if you go with me," he coaxed, eyes bright and hopeful above his coffee cup, "then of course everything will be all right."

David was not actually sure how his presence would have any effect one way or the other, but it was flattering if Meredith thought so. Perhaps that was why he hesitated instead of shooting down the idea at once.

Meredith took the opportunity to go on, "Really, straight there and back again, I swear it."

"Are you sure that's a good idea after what happened last time?"

"But nothing even *did* happen last time," Meredith protested. "And nothing's happened since, either."

When he put it like that, it was hard to deny that he had a point, but David was well aware that Meredith was very good at making very bad ideas sound seductively reasonable.

As David continued to wrestle with his better judgment, Meredith finished his coffee and rose from the table. "That's all right, David, don't worry about it. I'll be quite all right on my own."

That option didn't sound any better—in fact, it sounded even worse. But if there was really no talking him out of it—

"Oh, all *right*," agreed David, "but Bianca had best stay behind, just in case."

To his surprise, Meredith offered no argument to that, and before long, the two of them made their way down the hill toward the edge of the Midnight Wood. As they passed between two leafy maples and crossed the border, the overcast sky shifted to an expanse of opaque black. All around them hung the scent of dank vegetation. The oppressive humidity had drawn a blanket of silence over the Wood, broken only by the occasional unanswered birdcall from above and worrying skitterings in the underbrush.

As David walked along just behind Meredith, he fought the urge to rest a hand at the small of his back. He was not certain of where things stood between them, of what he wanted—what either of them wanted—and his own feelings were all a chaotic jumble.

With a start, he realized that Meredith had been speaking to him while he was lost in his own thoughts.

"—tried making it with woodruff syrup one year, but that turned out much too sweet. He never did write down the recipe, you see, and I've never managed to get it quite the same." Meredith slipped one arm through David's and rested his head against his shoulder. "But it'll turn out right this year, I'm sure of it."

"Oh, get off," grumbled David, shrugging him away. "It's warm enough in here already without your incessant clinging." It was, but he didn't really mind any more than usual. In fact, he found that he was rather anticipating Meredith's familiar protest, and his own inevitable surrender. After all, it was, as Meredith had pointed out, one of the little games they played.

But the protest didn't come. Instead, Meredith murmured, "Sorry," and let go of David, moving ahead of him to sidestep a fallen branch leaning against a tree trunk and partially obstructing the path. A forlorn wind swept through the trees with a most unsettling wail, and the sky grew darker—drifting clouds, or the canopy of treetops drawing in to block out the light and make them lose their way?

Unable to banish his nerves entirely, David inquired, as they reached a dense copse of pines, "Where exactly are we going?"

"Down by the sycamores," said Meredith. "We're nearly there. Once we get back home, I'll get it started infusing, and—oh!" Emerging from the trees, he stopped short, causing David to crash into him and nearly bowl him over.

Before them on the other side of the clearing stood the man in the crimson cloak.

In the bony fingers—*talons?*—of one hand, he held aloft a struggling white mouse, dangling by its tail; in the other, a tiny cordial glass that seemed to fill of its own accord with a cloudy lavender liquid. At that instant, the mouse went limp.

The figure threw back its head and drank, tossing away the lifeless creature to land with a sad, soft thump among the underbrush. With a gesture of his other hand that David could not quite follow, the glass vanished into thin air.

"Oh! How *could* you!"

At Meredith's outburst, the man turned toward them. At long last, he lowered the hood of his cloak, and at the sight, David's forgotten dream came rushing back.

Above a gaunt face, a crown of alder twigs rested upon his head, surrounding a pair of short, spiked antlers. His silver hair and beard shone in the light of the stars, his skin held a livid tint, and his pale, pale eyes were no color David knew the name for.

"Can't abide Mice," he said in a papery whisper as he started toward them across the clearing, paying no heed to the surrounding firs as their needles caught at his cloak. "Always sneaking up in the night to gnaw at one's toes, and you can't get but a thimbleful of despair out of the wretched little things before they expire."

"Meredith," hissed David. "We ought to go." Easier said than done, as he found himself frozen to the spot, ice creeping down his spine.

Meredith stood his ground. "No. I'm sick to death of the whole business. We may as well find out what he wants."

"Yes indeed," agreed the apparition, "now that we find ourselves face-to-face once more."

"Yeah, and who are you, exactly?" asked Meredith.

"Who am I?" said the man in mock disbelief. "Why, don't you know me? I am the Erlking!"

Though the words individually registered, David could not make sense of them in any meaningful way, not seized by terror as he was. Perhaps that was why he found himself stammering, "But—but you're not real."

"I am the Erlking," repeated the man, "he who sustains himself by man's destruction of man, who imbibes the delicacy of utter hopelessness. This is my domain, and he who dares enter, who dares come riding so late in the night and wind—"

"Yes, yes," said Meredith dismissively. "Erlking with your crown and train, et cetera. We can recite poetry at one another all night, but where's that going to get us?"

Somehow Meredith treating it as a normal conversation allowed David to do the same. He took a deep breath and steeled himself to think of it as nothing more than an adversarial work meeting. "Yes, what is your business, precisely?"

"I've no business with *you*," said the Erlking, "save that you would deprive me of your tantalizing companion."

Meredith stared in bewilderment. "Me?"

"You indeed, my dear boy," said the Erlking with a mirthless grin that bared sharp, inhuman fangs. "In truth, I have had my eye upon you for some time. By all rights, you should have belonged to me ages ago, but you're stubborn, oh, yes."

With a crackling of dead leaves underfoot, the Erlking ventured a step nearer. David took a step back, bumping against the broad mossy trunk of an oak. "You won't let me win, won't allow me inside your mind, so I've had to resort to more drastic measures. Most are easy enough to bend to my will. But *you*."

The Erlking came nearer still, his cruel colorless gaze never leaving Meredith's face as he extended a hand toward him, beckoning. David, in back of him, could only guess at his expression, but Meredith stood where he was. "You fascinate me, the way you fight against it. Such a tease, you are, always just out of my reach and carrying all that exquisite despair so deep it's in your very bones."

"Nonsense," David interjected. Supernatural entity or not, the Erlking hadn't the least idea what he was talking about. A person brimming with despair did not go around braiding daisy chains and singing to his dog and cheerfully frescoing the ceilings in the face of all good sense. Besides which, if it were true, David surely would have noticed.

Ignoring David, the Erlking went on, "Now that your blood has been spilled in my territory, sooner or later your defenses will weaken until you have no choice but to succumb."

"Blood?" repeated Meredith, mystified. "What are you talking about?"

The Erlking stamped his foot. "Do not insult me with your feeble trickery! You cannot imagine such a thing would truly escape my attention, not when it took place practically upon my altar—or alder, if you will," he added with a mirthless chuckle.

The thornbush, David realized. That day two weeks ago, Meredith had pricked his finger on a hawthorn bush next to the alder tree—and he had bled.

"I had still thought to bide my time now that I have claim to your blood, but after yesterday—" He broke off with a lascivious shudder that made Meredith recoil.

David rested a hand at Meredith's waist in what he hoped passed for a comforting gesture. He ought to say something, to voice an objection, but his mind had gone utterly blank.

"Oh, *yesterday* it was so strong, so tempting. You were practically begging for it—for me to come claim you and all your misery. No longer can I wait to possess you! To taste you!"

"I *beg* your pardon," said Meredith. "I won't be spoken to like that, it's indecent."

"You little fool," said the Erlking. "I desire not your body, but to indulge at last in the rare ambrosia of such singular despair! A particularly fine vintage, if you will. Though I daresay," he added, casting an appraising glance over Meredith, "you would make a lovely little pet, wouldn't you?"

"He's speaking in metaphors, isn't he?" whispered Meredith over his shoulder. "Can't you make him talk sense?"

"*Make* him?" repeated David in astonishment. "Why would you ever think I can make him do anything?"

"But you can." Meredith turned to him at last with wide imploring eyes. "You can do anything, David, you always make sure things turn out all right."

That wasn't true by any stretch of the imagination, and it certainly wasn't true right now.

"Oh, he's done plenty, believe you me," said the Erlking. "Though I can't say I'm not a touch disappointed. Just one more would've been enough to break you entirely, blood or no blood, and I could've taken you just like that." He punctuated the sentence with a snap of the fingers. "Ah, well, it may be near enough anyway."

"One more what?" demanded David. Whatever it was, he certainly had no intention of providing any such thing. They needed to leave this place at once, but just as before—just as in his dream—David was paralyzed with fear.

"Why, one more reason, of course! You'd given me nearly enough. I tell you, stand any man before me to face a hundred reasons why nobody wants him around, and it's guaranteed to drive him irretrievably into despair, without fail!"

"What are you talking about?" Meredith turned to David again, no less imploring, but this time, with an added hint of panic. "David, what does he mean?"

David couldn't bear to answer, couldn't bear to meet his eyes, and only shook his head. Impossible as it was, somehow the Erlking had read his private thoughts, and from a distance at that.

"No? You haven't the nerve to say it to him yourself?" mocked the Erlking. "You think you're so clever, so *sensible* and *sophisticated*. Do you think he can't feel it, the disdain that seeps out in your words, your voice, your little snide remarks? Do you think he doesn't see it in your eyes?" In a grotesque mimicry, he recited: "*He's an irredeemable eccentric. He flirts with everyone in his path. He clings. He drives everyone away. He's impossible to live with. He talks to mice. He makes the worst coffee in the world.*"

"Oh!" said Meredith in dismay. "Who says all that?"

"Oh, that denial does impart something special to the bouquet." A smirk holding equal parts malice and triumph flitted across the Erlking's face, and he pointed one spindly, clawed finger straight at David. "*He* does! He's got it all tallied up in his head, every single little thing he can't stand about you."

That pointing finger was more than an indictment; it might as well have been an execution. Seeing Meredith's expression of absolute heartbreak was more than David could bear, knowing himself to be the cause of it.

"Oh," repeated Meredith in a small, crushed voice. He wrapped his arms around himself, eyes downcast. "I s-see."

David couldn't speak. He couldn't even breathe.

There was something obscene in the way the Erlking wet his lips in anticipation, in the eagerness so obvious in those uncanny eyes. "Doesn't that upset you? Doesn't it *hurt*?"

Then Meredith smiled his broken-glass smile. "Course it does, hearing it like that," he said, "but it's like you said, isn't it? Did you think I couldn't already tell? Did you think," he went on, voice steel-sharp, something dark and previously unseen surfacing in his eyes, "that it doesn't already hurt *all the time*, just being me?"

David was drowning, plunged into a deep black ocean of his own making, unable to break the surface. On sheer instinct, he reached out for Meredith, who jerked away from him.

Undaunted by his failure, the Erlking tried a new angle of attack. "I know who you've been pining for, boy, but don't you know there's no point? Don't you know it's *hopeless*? *He* doesn't love *you*."

Meredith went still and closed his eyes. In a flat, unreadable voice, he said, "I know."

The Erlking slunk nearer. "Nobody does."

"I know."

"Nobody *could*."

"*I know!*" shouted Meredith, startling the birds from the nearby trees in a flurry of beating wings. The darkness seemed somehow to thicken around them as the wind howled through the Wood, and tendrils of fog began to creep in at the edges of the clearing.

The thought registered, in a distant, fleeting way, that David ought to intervene, but it was drowned out by the immediate, ironclad certainty that there was nothing he could possibly hope to achieve. His thoughts were only half his own, only halfway formed before being reshaped by a flat empty hopelessness too strong to resist.

In truth, he had little recourse beyond his standard strategy of intimidation via looming with nothing to back it up, and that was useless here. Though the Erlking stood just shorter than Meredith, his very presence seemed to tower over them both. David was small and weak and worthless, and there was nothing he could say or do to stop him.

There was no aid he could offer in Meredith's quest for this mystery man who did not return his feelings—even if he'd wanted to, which he didn't. At that realization, David's heart plummeted even lower. Not long ago, not far from this very spot, he'd called Meredith selfish, but in reality, he was far more so himself.

David was powerless to fight. They both were. The situation was hopeless.

"That's right," coaxed the Erlking. "Go on, give in, just like your so-called friend is doing. It'll be easier for the both of us." Once more he reached out, gnarled fingers stroking the air in a dreadful shadow play of an intimate caress. "It wouldn't be so bad, being my plaything. All you'd have to do is surrender yourself to my every whim, and every so often, I'll just siphon off a bit of that delicious sorrow. It'll hardly hurt any *worse*."

There was something to that, David thought. It would be a relief, really, to let him take away this crushing hopelessness, this suffocating feeling of self-loathing. It would be so easy to *just give in*.

Meredith faltered. "I—I don't think—"

"All that pain, deep down in your heart—wouldn't you like me to put an end to it? Aren't you *tired*?"

"Don't know what you're talking about," said Meredith, and then, in a whisper tinged with what might have been hope: "Could you really?"

"After a fashion." The clouds parted again, and the twinkling light of the stars shone on the short sharp points of the Erlking's antlers, on the jagged leaves of his alder crown. "Why, I'll even let you bring along your little doggie."

With that fatal mistake, the thrall was broken.

"What? No!" Meredith stumbled back a step and clutched at a nearby birch for balance. "You can't have Bianca, never in a million years, and you can't have me, either."

"Is that so?" hissed the Erlking. "You've always got to be difficult, don't you? No matter. *If thou art unwilling, then force I'll employ!*" With outstretched hands, he started the last few paces toward Meredith, but the moment the Erlking made to seize hold of his arm, he recoiled with a cry as though he'd been burned.

It took David a moment to realize that Meredith was speaking, low and toneless, eyes squeezed shut, fists clenched at his sides. No, not speaking—reciting. David could make out only some of the words: "*Wer half mir . . . wer rettete vom Tode mich . . . Hast du nicht alles selbst vollendet, heilig glühend Herz?*"

Though David did not understand their meaning, he recognized the last line as the same one Meredith had recited under quite different circumstances as he'd stood before him naked the night before. The same words David had traced with his fingertips, the words Meredith had etched into his very skin—and which, through some mechanism David could not guess, appeared to prevent the Erlking from laying hands on him now.

"Enough!" snarled the Erlking even as he fell back a pace. "Perhaps you elude my grasp for the moment, but it's only a matter of time until you give in. And *you*!" He swiveled to face David. "Always chasing after the next thing you pretend will make you happy—a promotion, a raise in pay, a new house, your darling *Cartier*. But you know the truth, don't you? You know you'll *never* be happy. It'll never be enough for you because you don't care a damn for what you've already got."

"I—but—" David faltered.

"You think you've got it all figured out with your bloody numbers and spreadsheets and everything totaled up in neat little columns, don't you? But you don't understand people at all. You don't even understand yourself."

David could only nod as cold despair filled him from head to toe. It was true. Meredith had told him nearly the same thing, and hadn't even meant it as an insult.

You like to go putting everybody in neat little boxes.

He really doesn't know how to switch off business mode.

It's sad, isn't it?

"You pretend you can't stand that boss of yours, but do you think you're really any different? You know exactly what your future holds, and it won't be long until you become just as much of a disgrace as he is. As it stands now, you're merely *tolerated*, and when it really comes down to it, what have you got to offer? You're nothing special. You're nobody's favorite. Nobody likes you best, and could you honestly expect them to?" The Erlking's harsh cackle rang through the clearing. "Perhaps *you're* the one who's not real."

"Stop it," whispered Meredith.

"You know I speak the truth," said the Erlking to David. "You're blind to what's right in front of you, and you go hurting everybody you claim to care about. No wonder all your lovers have left you. No wonder—"

Meredith stepped between them. "You leave him alone! This is between me and you, and I won't have you dragging him into it. Come on," he told David. "We're leaving."

He grabbed David by the wrist and dragged him along back the way they'd come.

"Don't you walk away from me," roared the Erlking. "You're bound to me by blood. I'll have you yet, you'll see."

Meredith turned back. "Will you," he said, his vicious sneer coming out full force. "I'd like to see you try. But you can't, can you? You can't even touch us."

As Meredith stormed through the underbrush, it was all David could do to keep up in spite of his longer stride. He felt disoriented and numb, the movements of his own body distant and unfamiliar to him. It didn't matter, anyway. Nothing mattered, not when the things the Erlking had told him were all true.

For a moment, David wondered distantly whether he oughtn't to be concerned about the Erlking catching up—but no. It seemed that he couldn't do any harm to Meredith, not now, even if David didn't entirely understand why. Perhaps it had been something in his words, or the conviction he'd had in speaking them, in his certainty that the Erlking could do them no physical harm—David was not sure whether it was strictly truthful to say he'd done them no harm at all. He also doubted that Meredith's apparent immunity extended to him, though he had no desire to test this theory. Not that it made any difference since even the Erlking didn't want David. *Nobody* did, and he couldn't blame them.

"Come *on*." Meredith shoved aside a low pine branch with far less care than usual and trampled straight through the carpet of glossy green leaves and white blossoms spread out before them.

"But—but—" David groped around his mind for a coherent thought, and settled for the first that he could put into words: "Aren't you furious with me?"

"Yeah," said Meredith, finally releasing his hold on him, "only I'm not leaving you with *him*, am I? You can never find your way about the Wood, and even if you c-can't stand me, I—" His voice broke.

"Meredith—"

"*Shut up.*"

It was the first and only time Meredith had ever told him in all seriousness to shut up, and that stung worse than anything the Erlking had said.

David shut up.

Meredith, however, was only getting started. "Do you think, David, that I don't know how impossible I am to be around? Do you think I don't realize I'm—I'm"—he whirled on the bank of the creek to face him, flapping his arms in frustration—"an insufferable fuckup?"

Astonished, David stopped in his tracks. "Whoa, whoa, where is that coming from?"

"Do you know why Kinley and I don't live together?" Meredith continued across the creek without waiting for him, and David hurried to catch up. "Haven't you ever wondered?"

"I have, actually, but—" He offered a steadying hand as Meredith slipped off a moss-covered stepping stone to land in the streambed up to the ankles in clear dark water.

Meredith batted his hand away and splashed his way to the opposite bank. "We tried, did you know? Lasted about a month before he said, *I'm sorry, I love you, but I can't live with you or we won't be friends anymore.*"

It took David a moment to register what was off—and when he did, his blood ran cold. Meredith hadn't even bothered with an imitation.

"So I moved out and came to Midnight Cottage. And it's all right, between him and me, but do you know what it's like when even your best friend can't stand to live with you because you are *Too Much*? And everybody else has left, too, every single one, except you. I'd thought—I'd thought maybe—" He broke off.

The edge of the Wood was in sight now, the light of day bleeding in between the distant trees. With it came reason. Of course there was nothing in what the Erlking had said, no more than the barest shade of reality, amplified and distorted into an ugly half-truth. David could see that now; surely Meredith must realize it as well.

"Now, look," David began. "Don't you think you're taking this a bit—"

"Do I have to spell it out for you?" Meredith exploded again. "That speech ain't about setting expectations for anybody else. It's for *me*, so I don't forget myself and go thinking anybody will ever care enough to stay."

They passed through the last row of trees and out of the Midnight Wood. Before David could say a word—not that he had the least idea what *to* say—Meredith took off at a brisk pace down the hill without so much as a single look back.

David watched him go. As much as he wanted to follow, perhaps it was just as well if he stayed behind. Really, he told himself as he started back toward Midnight Cottage, the space was much needed; the two of them had scarcely had a moment apart since yesterday morning.

Meredith seldom got truly angry, and when he did, it never lasted long. Of course the real object of his wrath was the Erlking; David had just been a convenient target. The Erlking had touched a nerve, obviously, but once Meredith had had time to clear his head, he'd come to the same conclusion and dismiss his remarks for the hateful rubbish they were.

Except in Meredith's case, it wasn't entirely rubbish, was it?

David *had* thought those things, even if he'd never had any intention of saying them aloud, even if he didn't mean most of them, or even remember them once the momentary frustration had passed. But how could he possibly explain any of that to Meredith?

And if that much was true, did that mean he believed everything the Erlking had put in his head?

Did that mean Meredith really was filled with the despair the Erlking so craved? Could David really have overlooked such a thing?

As he crested the hill, he was met with the commotion of Todd on the back deck, attempting to fend off a trio of enormous vultures with a rolled-up newspaper.

"Fuck *off*!" he shrieked at them, and soundly whacked the nearest bird with the paper. With an indignant squawk, it took to the air.

Abandoning his ruminations, David hurried over and helped to shoo away the other vultures, then went to fetch the broom. When he returned, Todd had sunk into a deck chair, face in his hands.

David set about sweeping up the remnants of Todd's breakfast dishes that lay scattered over the floorboards, along with the odd stray feather. "All right?" he asked.

With a violent jerk, Todd looked up, disheveled ringlets falling into his face. "Huh? Oh, yeah, yeah, I'm all good." He leaned down to pick up an overlooked shard of coffee cup with a trembling hand and rose to his feet. "Schwarzy did try to tell me, but I didn't really think . . . I didn't think he meant it." He trailed off, gazing toward the dark and foreboding treetops in the distance.

"No," said David, his mind on a different track entirely, "neither did I."

Chapter Twenty-Two

Trying to gather his thoughts, David went to wash up the breakfast dishes, but found himself instead staring at the bottle of hand lotion Meredith had left on the windowsill above the sink. No matter how viciously David scrubbed the skillet in front of him, the images haunted his mind: misshapen shadows among the trees, the Erlking with those grasping claws and colorless leering eyes—and Meredith's look of utter devastation.

But surely there was no way that awful creature could get to them here, was there? As far as the Erlking was concerned, Meredith was untouchable. He'd simply walked away, and someone who could do that was hardly drowning in despair. Clearly the Erlking's assessment was not to be trusted. As for David himself—he, too, had bled in the Wood, though not upon the cursed altar of the Erlking. So that meant he was safe, didn't it? In any case, he grimly reminded himself once more, the Erlking had no use for *him*.

Abandoning the dishes, David retreated to his room, where he flung himself down onto the bed and pressed his hands over his face.

The unfathomable hopelessness he'd fallen into back in the Midnight Wood had sprung from the tiniest seeds of self-doubt, amplified by whatever evil magic was possessed by the creature in the Wood. Tiny, but not unreal. Not entirely baseless.

If there had been some truth in what the Erlking had said to Meredith, was David brushing aside his words too easily? Was he in the habit of rejecting any criticism out of hand?

You don't understand people at all.

Perhaps that was a weakness, but it was not insurmountable. He had friends, even if he was no social butterfly like Meredith. He and his family got on well enough, even if they rarely met in person; it didn't mean they cared for one another any less. He was on good terms with his work colleagues, with the exception of Steve Corner, who didn't count.

You know exactly what your future holds.

No. He was *not* going to end up like Steve Corner. He would not allow that to happen, end of discussion.

You're nothing special. Nobody likes you best.

Well, perhaps not, but he stood by what he'd said the night before: he found nothing wrong with being ordinary. Still, it *would* be nice to have a few people who thought a bit more highly of him than that. The realization came with more of a sting than David expected, but he pushed the thought aside for later.

No wonder all your lovers have left you.

Now that, David could say with confidence, was pure nonsense. For one, in most cases, he'd been the one to break things off himself. David's self-respect wouldn't allow him to tolerate Eduardo blatantly checking out someone else right in front of him, and the way Omar had turned that contemptuous look upon Meredith—no, anyone who did that wasn't worth his time. David had taken pains to let Jintao down gently; he'd done nothing wrong aside from being so nice and agreeable all the time that he bored David out of his mind.

But Jean-Marc—that was where he'd really botched things.

Right now was not the time to think about Jean-Marc.

You go hurting everybody you claim to care about.

Did he? He'd had quite a nice time with Ruth and his father when he'd visited at Christmas, and had thought the feeling was mutual. To his knowledge, there were no problems between him and Harriet; his last interaction with Mrs. Jupiter, too, had been perfectly amicable. He'd done nothing to offend Todd, though neither had he gone out of his way to include him.

As for Meredith—

Meredith always was the problem, wasn't he?

Leaving aside the revelation of the list, had David actually been hurting him? Had he blamed Sylvania Holland for the consequences of his own behavior? In reality, those unsettling *off* moments had preceded the appearance of the obsidian ring. The day Genevieve had arrived to announce Florian's wedding—the day David had forced Meredith into it despite his protests—that was when things had really started to go wrong.

You know you'll never *be happy.*

David didn't believe that, but he had to admit that at this very moment, he wasn't happy at all—and for reasons that were nearly all his own doing.

With a groan, he turned over onto his side and caught sight of an unexpected gleam beneath the dresser. Upon closer inspection, he recognized the strand of black pearls Meredith had dropped and apparently forgotten the night he'd been in David's room. Had that been only a week ago?

It was as good an excuse as any to go seek him out.

David retrieved the necklace, started out the door, and paused. Though it hardly required any brilliant detective work to make a round of the likely spots, there was a more efficient option. He returned to the dresser, dug through the bottom drawer, and located the bracelet Mrs. Jupiter had given him. The moment he slid it onto his wrist, he felt the same faint pull as before—not uncomfortable, but nonetheless jarring.

Todd must have returned upstairs; the living room was empty save for Bianca, who waited by the front door with a look of expectation.

"Yes, all right, you can come along," David told her. He couldn't help adding, "You wouldn't have enjoyed our last walk at all, I'll have you know."

They slipped out the front door and hadn't gone more than a few paces down the driveway before the magical force controlling David's bracelet nudged him in the opposite direction.

Following the gentle pull, he and Bianca started down the hill toward Bednarek's. Meredith soon came into view, perched atop the weather-beaten picnic table, his back to Midnight Cottage. David caught the faint song, quieter than usual:

"Ich weiß nicht, was soll es bedeuten,
Daß ich so traurig bin—"

Meredith faltered, and repeated the last line, quieter still and strained:

"Daß ich so traurig bin . . ."

He trailed off at David's approach but didn't turn to face him.

"Meredith."

For a moment, David thought he was being ignored. Then, still with his back to him, Meredith asked, "What?"

David circled around the table to stand facing him, though Meredith wouldn't meet his eyes. "Bianca was worried about you." Then, more truthfully: "*I* was worried about you."

Bianca hopped up onto the bench to sit at Meredith's feet, and he reached down to pet her without answering.

"Look," began David. He hadn't considered what he meant to say. Perhaps that was for the best—the outcome was too important to risk his usual overthinking. "Even if you never want to speak to me again, I'd like you to hear me out. Please. And then—then I'll leave you alone, if you want."

Meredith voiced neither objection nor encouragement, but tilted his head to one side: he was listening.

"What he said, back there in the Wood—yes, a few weeks back, the day Brian left, I was particularly annoyed with you. I started off that list in my head, and it sort of . . . took on a life of its own. Most of it was stupid. A little bit was true. I won't lie to you and say you're not difficult to live with sometimes." He ought to come clean all the way, to admit that he'd considered moving out, that he'd gone so far as to look at other places, but he could picture Meredith's exact look of hurt surprise at that, and he couldn't bear it, not now.

"A hundred reasons, David?" Meredith's voice was faint.

Only ninety-nine, David wanted to protest, and then, ashamed of himself, let the words die unspoken. "Yes. *But*," he said significantly, "you need to know there's a hell of a lot to outweigh all of them. And I'm sorry for keeping all that in my head instead of telling you properly, and pushing you to talk to your brother, and—I know we give each other a hard time, but sometimes I don't quite catch on when I'm taking it too far, and I'm sorry for that, too. That's—er, that's it, really."

That wasn't it, not nearly, but it was as far as David could go just then. As far as he could be sure of, without making things worse.

Meredith allowed David's conclusion to hang in the air as he lifted Bianca into his lap.

As usual, David never could have anticipated his reply.

"You came to find me."

"What—*that's* what you're—of course I did! I would've come sooner, but I thought you might need some time to cool down."

"I think I did," agreed Meredith, and finally looked up at David. "I'm sorry, too. Went a bit mad back there, shouting at you and all. It—" He paused, biting his lip. "It didn't feel very nice, hearing some of that, but the way I see it, you can't fault anybody just for what's in their mind, only what they do with it. Everyone's a bit evil inside their own head, I think. I know I am."

David frowned. "Meri, you don't—you don't really believe all those things the Erlking said, do you?"

"What? No, no, course not." He lifted Bianca to press a kiss between her ears, then regarded David over the top of her head. "It was all a bunch of nonsense, just like what he said to you."

"Oh—yes. Quite," said David. "Of course it was."

Lowering the Chihuahua back to his lap, Meredith took on a pensive expression. "But, David?"

"Yes?"

Very seriously, he asked, "Do you really think my coffee's all that bad?"

David sank down to half sit, half lean at the edge of the tabletop. "Honestly?"

Meredith nodded, eyes wide and earnest and brimming with uncertainty. "Cross-your-heart-and-hope-to-die honest."

"I've had worse."

That, at last, got a rueful laugh from him. "S'pose I deserved that, didn't I?"

David extended an arm in invitation. "Still friends?"

Meredith leaned against him, into the embrace. "Course we are," he said. "Always."

Mrs. Jupiter thumped her teacup onto the table. "You went into the Midnight Wood, against my explicit instructions." Her voice held none of its usual warmth.

"Yes, Mrs. J." Meredith hunched in the chair opposite her, voice small and contrite. "Sorry, Mrs. J."

Standing behind him, David rested a hand on his shoulder without thinking. "I'm partly to blame. I ought to have discouraged the idea to begin with instead of going along with it." He *had* discouraged it, but he had also found it all too easy to give in, and in light of the disastrous results, he was not so sure that that he deserved any credit for the attempt.

"Yes," she said, "you ought. Frankly, Mr. Carew, I expected better judgment from you." With a shake of her head, she rose and went to the bookshelf along the far wall, from which she withdrew a scarred leather-bound tome.

"But I only wanted to pick some sweet woodruff!"

Mrs. Jupiter didn't look up from leafing through the pages. "And how did that work out for you?"

Meredith hung his head. "It was awful," he whispered.

David squeezed his shoulder, and then, to his surprise, Meredith reached up to take his hand.

"Yes," said Mrs. Jupiter. "I expect it was." Then she relented, her tone softening as she admitted, "It pains me to watch you place yourself so recklessly in danger. And I will not lie to you—you face a fearsome enemy in the Erlking, and the danger has not passed simply because you managed to elude him this time."

"I'm sorry," said David, "but I'm still not sure I understand. I mean to say, surely there's not much he can do if he's in the Wood and we're out here." As he spoke the words, he realized that he was not sure of any such thing. "Is there?"

Mrs. Jupiter was silent for a moment, drumming her fingers against the yellowed pages of the volume in her hands. At last she said slowly, "Your account of this most recent encounter troubles me. You are absolutely certain he made no attempt to give pursuit?"

Meredith shook his head. "No, he just let us go after I told him off." He paused to consider. "Do you suppose I ought not to have done that?"

Her expression grew still more perturbed. "He did nothing whatsoever to stop you?"

"Well, he did try, a bit, but it seemed as if he couldn't touch me without hurting himself somehow. Then he just went on shouting after us about blood and whatnot, like I told you, and how he'd get us in the end, you know, the usual sort of thing, but I didn't really follow."

"The hawthorns," said David, his heart sinking. He'd pieced it together, back in the Wood, but Meredith evidently hadn't. "Don't you remember, the weekend before last when we went hunting for herbs and you pricked your finger on that hawthorn bush?"

"*That?* But that was just such a little bit of blood," Meredith protested, "and Mrs. J fixed me right up afterwards."

"I'm afraid that blood is blood, my dear," said Mrs. Jupiter. "In this case, the quantity makes no difference. The single drop you've given him is all he needed to stake his claim."

"Oh." Meredith looked once again as though he were about to cry. "I am sorry, Mrs. J, I didn't mean to."

"So to answer your question, Mr. Carew, I would not discount the ability of the Erlking to enact his will at a distance and find some way to do you an injury yet. I fear you are in grave danger indeed."

Meredith shrank back against David, who rubbed his shoulder and hoped he could somehow convey his reassurance through touch.

Then again, he was not so sure he had any reassurance to offer.

Frowning, Mrs. Jupiter paged further into her book. "Tell me," she said, "what exactly do *you* know about this Erlking? I admit he is somewhat outside the scope of my own knowledge, and there is only so much to be found in the literature of magical research."

Meredith considered. "Well, there's all different stories—I found that out later on—but the one I always knew was the poem, the Goethe one."

He traced over the scarred wood of the table, running a fingertip along the joint between two boards. "In the story, it's this man, and he has a child, you see, and the Erlking wants to take him away—the child, not the father—and he tries to, and—well, in the end, he dies."

"The child," said Mrs. Jupiter.

"Yeah. My grandfather read it to me once when I was little. I was quite terrified," said Meredith with a laugh. "Didn't sleep all night after, just cried and cried. My dad was furious, of course."

"At him? For frightening you?" asked David quietly.

"Well, that, too, I suppose," agreed Meredith, "but mainly at me, for crying."

David's heart splintered once more, but he suppressed the urge to pull Meredith into his arms and instead gripped his shoulder just a little tighter.

Unconcerned, Meredith went on, "Florian would always tease me about it after that, you know, saying the Erlking would come and carry me off."

David exchanged an uneasy look with Mrs. Jupiter.

"Meredith," she began, then appeared at a loss for words.

"Oh, it was just childish nonsense and that," said Meredith dismissively. "Like being scared of monsters in the cellar. Anyway, Grandpa came to hear about the whole thing, and he said I oughtn't to be frightened because if you know yourself, if you believe in yourself, the Erlking can't hurt you at all. Of course that was probably nonsense, too," he conceded, "but I did believe it then."

For a few moments, there was silence save for the sound of Mrs. Jupiter turning pages. At last she said, "I would surmise, then, that at this stage the Erlking cannot make away with you unless you should submit willingly, but—"

"Of course I won't!" interrupted Meredith in indignation.

With a pointed look, Mrs. Jupiter continued, "True, his initial efforts to drive you both to despair have come to naught, but given sufficient time, a blood connection such as he has established seldom fails. Now, behold."

She pushed aside the sugar bowl to set the open book on the table in front of them, though David could make little sense of the crabbed writing and strange symbols on its pages.

"The good news is that I can, in fact, counteract the Erlking's claim on you. The bad news is that the spell requires elderflower blossoms and ratbonnet gathered at the new moon, which is more than a week away, and I'll have to hunt down some extract of ragged tiger lily as well. In the meantime—"

"I won't so much as look in the direction of the Midnight Wood," promised Meredith.

"If you venture into his territory again, I can make you no promises about what may happen," she warned.

"I won't, I swear it! That awful man—the Erlking—he said he'd take Bianca, *and* he spoke to David in the most appalling way."

"The worse news," Mrs. Jupiter went on, "is that this spell will cancel only the blood debt itself. Any underlying factors that attracted his attention in the first place shall remain to be dealt with."

Meredith waved away this information. "Oh, *that's* all right. I don't have any underlying factors."

Mrs. Jupiter raised a skeptical eyebrow.

"I don't!" he insisted. "He's got it all wrong about me."

Mrs. Jupiter caught David's eye, and he had to look away. No, he didn't believe it, either, but he was in no position to press Meredith further, not when they'd only just smoothed things over. Not with his own unwitting aid to the Erlking still fresh in his mind.

Mrs. Jupiter clapped the book shut with a bang that made them both jump. "Very well, I'll leave that for you to sort out. And if you'll excuse me, I really must be on my way. I'm quite late as it is for my appointment with the Moon Calf."

"Sorry to have put you to the trouble, Mrs. J," said Meredith meekly as she shepherded the two of them out the door.

"Yes, well, if the two of you could avoid placing yourselves in mortal peril while I'm out, I'm sure I'd be much obliged." Gathering her shawl about her, she said in an icy tone, "Good afternoon, Meredith."

David supposed he was being snubbed, not that he could blame her, but as he crossed the threshold, she caught his attention with a clearing of the throat. "*Mr.* Carew. A word, if you please."

He turned back, guilt surely written all over his face. Though they'd again been sparing with the details, he didn't doubt she'd filled in some of the blanks. "Yes, Mrs. J?"

Checking that Meredith's attention was suitably occupied by a striped kitten amidst the flowering sage, she hissed, "I *told* you to be gentle."

"I was! I—I thought I was," David faltered.

"Clearly not. You know how he adores you—"

"Now, that's overstating it a bit, I think."

"—and you've hurt him immeasurably, even if he won't admit it."

"He did," said David. "Admit it, I mean. Sort of. And I did apologize."

Mrs. Jupiter plucked a bright pink azalea blossom and tucked it behind her ear, but her expression remained grim. "Well," she said, casting one last glance around the garden, "perhaps that's a start."

Chapter Twenty-Three

As they walked up the hill, David couldn't help but replay the Erlking's words in his mind once again. Perhaps he'd been quite mistaken about Mrs. Jupiter, presumptuous in considering her a friend. Perhaps he'd been mistaken about *everyone*.

"S'pose that could've gone worse," remarked Meredith, who seemed to have brightened up.

"Could it?" muttered David. "I didn't hear you being demoted to *Mister*."

"Oh, she's never called *me* that," said Meredith.

"Of course she hasn't." David might admit to a touch of jealousy at the way Meredith could immediately talk to everybody as though they were his best friend.

"Well, she did the one time, actually," Meredith corrected, "when we first met. Must've made a face at that because she took one look at me and said"—here he slipped into quite a good impression of Mrs. Jupiter—"*No, you're not, are you?* and I said, *No, I don't think I am*, and she said, *Well, we'll dispense with that, then.*"

David thought this over as Bianca stopped several paces ahead to look back at them, whining in impatience. "So *he* is all right, but *Mister* isn't?"

Meredith gave a crooked smile. "Yeah, doesn't make much sense, does it? I mean, I'm not about to go crying over it, just feels a bit . . . wrong somehow."

David refrained from pointing out that Meredith had, in fact, cried over much smaller matters, and instead asked, "Is there a different title you like? If I were making introductions, for instance." The scenario was likely to come up at the centennial auction on Saturday, with the higher-ups from both the Corner Store and Cartier's offices in attendance. (Recalling Cartier's words gave David a warm glow of pride, but it soon faded, replaced by the image of Steve Corner. For a moment, the whole thing seemed rather a sham, an ostentatious and self-aggrandizing pantomime of generosity.)

"Nah. Don't want one, really."

Now that David had gotten a glimpse into Meredith's logic, it made a certain sense. "Because it's another kind of label?"

"Exactly." Meredith beamed. "Besides, the last time you introduced me to someone, you called me your pet magpie."

"I never—oh. Yes. I, er—sorry about that."

"Oh, I don't mind. Maybe—" Meredith gave him that sideways searching look of his that David had come to recognize. "Maybe I like being your pet magpie."

Of all the ridiculous statements to make him go red—

David was spared having to answer as they reached the top of the hill and Bianca ran ahead, yapping in excitement.

In the driveway was parked a dusty station wagon, and waiting for them on the back deck was Maurice Wolkowitz, reclining in an Adirondack chair with his paws behind his head. At their approach, he rose, pushed up his sunglasses to rest against his pointed ears, and raised a paw in greeting. "Schwarzy, hey! I was hoping I'd catch you."

"Maurice!" Meredith rushed over to embrace the wolf, managing to gracefully carry out the usual air-kiss in spite of his friend's unwieldy snout. "I haven't seen you in ages."

"Been a while," Maurice agreed. At his side, Bianca rose up on her hind legs, and he leaned down to return her high five. "Yeah, missed you, too, cousin."

"Come in and stay for tea," said Meredith. "David was just about to put the kettle on."

"Oh, I was, was I?" grumbled David. (He had been, not that Meredith needed to know that.)

Straightening up, Maurice retrieved his bag from the floor and rummaged inside. "Nah, man, I just stopped by to return this book my buddy Phil borrowed from you a while back." He produced a dog-eared German grammar book and presented it to Meredith. (It had certainly taken long enough, but David kept that thought to himself, as it hadn't been his book to begin with.)

"Besides," Maurice added, "I think I kinda freaked out your other roommate. Looked like he was about to have a heart attack when he answered the door, so I told him I'd wait for you out here."

"Oh dear." Meredith glanced toward the house. "That won't do at all. I'm sure if the two of you met properly—"

Maurice waved a dismissive paw. "It's cool. I have to get going anyway. Got a bunch to do—car needs washed, and errands and that, but we'll catch up sometime soon." He clapped Meredith on the shoulder, nodded his farewell to David and Bianca, and departed.

Inside, Meredith immediately abandoned his book on the coffee table, retrieved a bottle of nail polish from the bookshelf, started toward the window seat, and then stopped in the middle of the room—directly in David's path to the kitchen.

Suppressing a sigh, David gently nudged him aside. "Do you mind?"

"I think perhaps I'd better have a word with Todd."

"I wouldn't be too hard on him," said David. "He's just had a bit of trouble with the—" He broke off as Todd himself appeared at the top of the stairs, eyes wild and face ashen, dragging an overstuffed suitcase. "Everything all right?"

"No. No, man, it's not all right at all." Todd descended the staircase unsteadily, suitcase thumping after him on every step. "I don't know how the hell you guys do it, but I cannot *deal* with this anymore. Not with—" He made a distraught gesture in the general direction of the Midnight Wood. "Witches and werewolves and vultures and—and—" He broke off, hands trembling.

"Maurice isn't a *were*wolf," protested Meredith, "and you'd really quite like him if you got to know him." He paused. "Wait, vultures?"

"You missed the vultures," David told him. "Now, Todd, why don't you just sit down for a moment? I'm sure once you've had a cup of tea—"

"Tea isn't gonna cut it." Todd dragged his suitcase toward the door; when he paused, Bianca ventured forward to inspect the floral-patterned luggage. "Look, I'm real sorry. You guys are cool and all, even if you do have some shit to work out, but I'm not staying here another second. I'll be back to get my stuff tomorrow."

The front door fell shut behind him, and for a time, there was no sound save for that of a car engine receding down the lane.

"Oh dear," said Meredith. "He didn't last two weeks." After only the slightest pause, he added, "I think I'll paint my nails."

As he took up his usual spot in the window, David went to the kitchen, made a pot of chamomile tea, and took a quick inventory of the fridge and cupboards.

By the time he returned to the living room with two cups of tea (one lightly sweetened, the other oversteeped to the point of bitterness), Meredith was collecting stray pens and paintbrushes from around the room.

At David's footsteps, he turned. "Thought the place could use some ridding up," Meredith said quickly. "I know how it gets on your nerves when I leave things lying about, and, well—s'pose I haven't been pulling my weight lately."

"You don't need—" David paused. "Yes, I would appreciate that, actually. Thank you. And here." He handed Meredith his cup.

Meredith nodded his thanks. As the two of them drank in silence, an unspoken tension hung over them once more. David had to say something, had to address what Meredith had said in the Midnight Wood.

David cleared his throat. "Look. About earlier. With the—in the Wood, I mean." For a moment, his focus narrowed to the juxtaposition of freshly painted black nails against blue-and-white china; then he forced himself to go on. "What he said—and what you said—I mean to say, if there's anything on your mind—"

"Course there isn't." Meredith developed a sudden intense interest in his teacup before admitting, "S'pose it did get to me, just a bit, same as it did to you." He looked up quickly. "Unless you—I mean, because he did say to you as well—"

"No, no, I'm quite all right." There, David had made the effort and checked in. If Meredith said he was fine, then of course he was. There was no need to go pressing the issue. No need to say a single word more on the subject, in fact.

David said, "You're not an insufferable fuckup."

Meredith stared at him over his teacup. For once, he seemed to be taken totally by surprise. Just for a second, before his usual grin crept back onto his face. "Course I'm not, David." He took a sip of his tea. "I am a *delight*."

David was about to say, *Let's not overcorrect*, but confined himself to making a vague sound of agreement as he raised his own teacup. "By the way, if you don't mind me asking—what exactly was it that you said to him back there? I know it was this"—he briefly touched a hand to Meredith's side—"but I thought you said you didn't know any prayers."

"Oh, that was hardly a prayer."

"I suppose I'd thought—that is to say, you spoke it as though it were."

Meredith shook his head. "No, but I suppose one must have *something* to believe in. That one has always—meant something to me. It's Goethe, too," he elaborated. "I did tell you last night."

"Yes, well, you'll forgive me for having been a bit distracted at the time," said David. "What does it say?" Then, recalling the last time he'd asked, he forestalled Meredith's response: "In the English, please."

Meredith looked down, fiddled with the shirttails of David's too-large button-down that he still wore. Without raising his eyes, he recited, "*Did you not achieve it all yourself, sacred glowing heart?*"

Tentatively, David reached out and pressed two fingertips to the center of his chest. "They go together, these two."

"Yes," said Meredith. "Something like that. Though perhaps not quite so sacred." He gave David a crooked little smile. "You're the first who's ever put that together, you know."

Now, in a total reversal of their conversation from the day before, David felt as though he'd just been entrusted with something fragile, eminently breakable, with nowhere near a secure enough hiding spot to lock it safely away.

He blinked hard to chase the unexpected sting from his eyes. He wanted to hold Meredith to him, to stroke his face, anything to show that he understood what he'd just been given.

Instead, he found himself saying, "I'm afraid the time's rather gotten away from us, but how would you feel about chana masala for a late lunch?"

"I'm not hungry."

"But if I made some."

Meredith shrugged. "Yeah, I'd have a bit."

"Right," said David, yet he was reluctant to leave the room. "Well. I suppose I ought to get on that. Perhaps you might put some music on."

He returned to the kitchen, retrieved a cooking pot, set out the tinned tomatoes and chickpeas, fished out the necessary spices from the disastrously overcrowded cupboard, finally locating the turmeric in the very back—and still the silence prevailed.

Peering into the living room to investigate, he found Meredith crouched in front of the record cabinet in apparent indecision. At David's footsteps, he turned and rose.

"Everything all right?"

"Yeah, only I was just thinking." Meredith took up his cup again, swirling the dregs of tea and avoiding David's eyes.

When he didn't elaborate, David prompted: "Yes?"

"That song you played for me last night, about the lilac tree?"

David's heart beat faster. "Yes?"

"I quite liked it. I mean—" Meredith looked up at him with another flash of uncharacteristic shyness. "If you ever wanted to, you know, listen to it again . . ."

It was the perfect opportunity for a clever teasing remark—for David to point out that Meredith understood metaphors perfectly well after all.

Instead, he kissed him.

THIS TIME, THEY ended up in David's bed, and soon enough had divested each other of their clothing. David couldn't even muster an acerbic remark about the amount of time it took Meredith to struggle out of his ridiculous skinny jeans—after all, it would hardly be fair when David wouldn't stop kissing him long enough to give him a chance.

As David kissed his way downward, Meredith couldn't seem to keep his hands off his face, quite impeding his progress. "You're all prickly."

"Yes, I know." David lowered his head to nibble a bit farther along his collarbone. "I need to shave."

"Nah, I like it."

"Do you."

"I do. Like to feel it here . . ." Meredith straightened up and traced his fingertips over his own face. "And here . . ." The touch descended along his throat. "And here." He swept a hand up the inside of his thigh with a wicked grin.

David raised an eyebrow. "Would you like to feel it there now?"

"Oh, *God*—" Meredith fell back onto the pillows.

Taking that for a yes, David pushed his legs apart and began to make his way in a new direction. He took his time, nuzzling at Meredith's thighs and deliberately letting his stubble scrape over soft skin as he moved upward. Already Meredith twitched under him, and David preemptively pinned him to the mattress, thumbs pressing into his hip bones.

When David took him deeply into his mouth in a single motion, Meredith cried out, and both his hands descended upon David, stroking his hair and the back of his neck. Not pushing him down or holding him in place, just petting him with a frantic, desperate affection.

David eased back to tease the head of his cock, working his tongue lazily around the ridge as Meredith did his best to thrash out of his grip.

"You know," David reproached him, "it would make things a great deal easier for us both if you didn't go all squirmy every time I touch you."

"Can't help it," panted Meredith, arching up and lifting his hips off the bed in a wordless plea. David took mercy on him and gave his cock a few slow strokes while he mouthed at his balls, making him shudder and resume his too-eager petting. "Oh, David, please, let me do something for you."

David rubbed soothing circles into Meredith's thigh. "Just lie back and relax, love, plenty of time for that later." Hoping to give them both a moment to cool off, David rose up to press a kiss to the scar at Meredith's hip.

"No, I want to now," insisted Meredith, a manic brightness in his eyes. "My mind's wandering and I don't want to think about anything else—just you, just what we're doing."

David's resolve was crumbling. "What did you have in mind?"

"Come up here?" suggested Meredith hopefully. "Or turn around for me—just so I can get at you, too."

"And that'll help, will it?"

"Course it will. Can't think about much else when I've got your cock in my mouth, can I?"

David wasn't able to come up with any rational argument against that.

Afterward, David found himself curled up next to Meredith, resting his head on his chest. Somewhere in the back of his mind, a vague objection tried to make itself known, a whisper that this was not the way things were meant to be done. That, however, was easy enough to ignore in favor of the warm comforting scent of patchouli and Meredith's steady heartbeat and his fingers tracing slow abstract patterns over David's back.

"Good idea you had there," murmured David. Meredith gave a hum of acknowledgment and rested his cheek against the top of David's head.

Then, surprising himself, David asked, "What's that song you're always going around singing?"

"Which?"

"The German one." He hesitated, then softly hummed a couple bars, not trusting himself to attempt any of the few words he did recognize.

"Oh, the 'Lorelei'! Had to learn that one by heart for the school choir." The hand on David's back went still. "Do you know," said Meredith in realization, "I've never once heard you sing."

"I assure you, you're not missing anything." David didn't need to look to confirm Meredith's pouting expression at that, but he did anyway. "Really. I can't sing."

"Anybody can sing, David."

"You'd soon reconsider if you heard me."

"I wouldn't," said Meredith softly, combing his fingers through David's hair. A few locks near his temples were beginning to curl with the dampness of sweat. "I think it'd be wonderful, because it's you."

David was too embarrassed to reply to that, and instead occupied himself tracing the now-familiar outline of Meredith's heart tattoo. He stayed like that longer than he'd like to admit, until drowsiness began to creep in—until Meredith's phone chimed on the bedside table and he slipped out of David's embrace to turn over and retrieve it.

Fully awake now, David took advantage of the opportunity to run a hand over Meredith's now-exposed back (and, he hoped, to discourage him from leaving the bed or getting dressed anytime soon).

As Meredith tapped out a reply, David traced teasing fingertips down his spine, along the tattooed peacock feather. He followed the same path with his mouth, trailing kisses from the nape of his neck down between his shoulder blades, taking in the feel and taste of his skin the way he'd wanted to ever since he'd first seen him shirtless in the steam-filled bathroom.

Meredith gave one of those intoxicating little sighs that David could never get enough of. "'S nice," he murmured. "Really nice, actually, even if you *are* making it quite difficult to concentrate."

David shifted to a sitting position, nudged Meredith until he lay on his stomach, and resumed stroking his back, pressing his knuckles in gently to work out spots of tension. "Anything important?"

"Nah, just progress pics of some flash art Kinley's been working on." Meredith finished sending his reply, then said, apropos of nothing, "Florian's having his bachelor party on Saturday."

In all honesty, anything to do with Florian Schwarzwelder or his upcoming marriage had escaped David's mind entirely. "Are you going?"

"I'm expected to."

"I don't want you to go." Hearing the words leave his mouth, David was taken aback by his own bluntness. It was true, though. He didn't want Meredith to go, not when he thought back to Florian's disparaging remarks, that hateful mocking tone, the sight of daisies trampled into the dirt. Not now that bits of scattered information gathered from offhand comments and evaded questions had begun to come together in his mind. Yesterday's jigsaw puzzle rearranged itself, revealing a new image David didn't like at all—a picture that went far beyond childish rivalry. No, this was a deeper contempt, a cruelty that had persisted well into adulthood.

He didn't realize he'd ceased his back rub until Meredith moved away and sat up. Unsure whether he'd overstepped, David amended, "I mean, I wish you wouldn't. I don't think it's good for you, being around him."

Meredith gave a mirthless laugh. "Course it isn't."

Another piece of the puzzle fell into place. David reached out and cupped Meredith's chin. In return, he got a look of puzzled apprehension, but he kept his touch light, and Meredith didn't flinch away. Slowly, David turned his face until he found the angle at which, if one were looking, it was just possible to guess that his nose had been broken after all.

I didn't say I didn't, Meredith had said. *I said,* I *didn't.*

"*You* didn't," said David, "but Florian did." His voice came out harder than he intended.

"Oh, go on." Meredith swatted his hand away in annoyance. "Don't go getting all het up over it, that was ages ago." He pulled away and rose from the bed. "Siblings fight, you know how it is."

"I'm not sure that I do." In fact, David could not recollect a single instance of himself and Ruth striking each other, but perhaps things would have been different if they'd been closer in age. He, too, got to his feet, but found himself standing awkwardly at the side of the bed as Meredith prowled the room in search of his haphazardly discarded clothing.

"Besides, he's always had a temper, same as me."

"Same as—" David stared in disbelief. "Meri, your version of *having a temper* is telling me you don't like my moustache."

To his surprise, Meredith cringed. "I am sorry about that. I didn't mean it. That is," he amended, "I did *mean* it, but it wasn't true."

"I don't follow."

Meredith turned away and picked up his—or, rather, David's—rumpled shirt from the back of the desk chair, gazed at it in indecision for a time, and then set it back down, his shoulders drooping. "I'm ashamed of it now, of course, but I was just trying to say the worst thing I could think of, to hurt your feelings so you felt as bad as I did."

"That's—" David stopped himself from saying, *That's all right*, because it wasn't, and, after consideration, settled on, "I forgive you. And I seem to recall that coming right on the heels of me saying a lot of things to you that I shouldn't have, either."

Meredith waved a dismissing hand. "'S fine."

"It isn't," David persisted. "It wasn't right for me to speak to you like that."

"Well, it doesn't matter now, anyway."

The next few moments were spent in silence as the two of them dressed, not looking at each other. At least David took care to keep his eyes off Meredith, and thus was taken by surprise when he asked thoughtfully, "David? You don't suppose—I mean, he wouldn't be unkind to *her*, would he?"

Despite the vague question, David knew exactly who he was talking about.

"No," he said slowly. "No, of course not. She'd hardly stick around long enough to marry him if he did, would she?" Though he'd met Adalynn only a few times, she projected confidence and self-assurance, and she was a successful businesswoman in her own right. David knew, of course, if in an abstract sort of way, that anyone could be mistreated by a partner, but he truly hadn't gathered that impression.

"Course not," agreed Meredith. He leaned in close to the mirror to finger-comb his bangs. "All the same—nah, what am I on about? What would one even say, really? *Oh, lovely centerpieces you've picked out, and by the way, do you mind that your fiancé is a bit of a dick?*"

David huffed out a laugh in spite of himself, but sobered when he met Meredith's eyes in the mirror.

"Hey," he said softly. "I know I made a fuss about going to this wedding, but if you'd rather wash your hands of the whole thing right now—"

"I said I was in, didn't I?" When Meredith turned to face him, his vacant grin had become quite unreadable. "Best not back out now. Besides," he added with a philosophical shrug, "it'll all be over soon."

Chapter Twenty-Four

On Monday morning, David studied his reflection in the mirror and neatened up the edges of his beard, which was coming in nicely. He left the house early, though he did not take pains to conceal his departure, and went to the Corner Café for breakfast.

By midmorning, reality had violently set in; although he'd spent the entire weekend ignoring the outside world, it had nevertheless continued to turn. Already he was inundated with emails and paperwork about the Corner Store's centennial kickoff, and when he finally returned to the Corner Café for a late lunch and checked his neglected personal phone, he found a series of missed calls from both Bednarek and Leonard Flood.

Bednarek hadn't left a voicemail, doubtless having reached the conclusion that David already knew of Todd's departure. Flood had, confirming that he'd withdrawn David's offer as instructed by his late-night text message. Upon hearing that, relief washed over David, as though a dark cloud hanging over him had cleared away.

Maybe he couldn't stay at Midnight Cottage forever, but there was no urgent need to flee, no reason he couldn't stay put for just a little longer, until he'd had time to think things through.

Besides, he hadn't liked that oppressively cramped little bungalow anyway.

THOUGH HE REALLY ought to cut his lunch break short and return to the growing mountain of paperwork in his office, David instead placed his long-overdue phone call to his father, who answered after the first ring.

"David?" he said in surprise. "Is anything the matter?"

David winced. Of course that would be his first thought, given how rarely he phoned. "No, no, everything's quite all right. I was calling just to call, I suppose. I . . . I missed you," he admitted.

"I've missed you, too."

At the familiar warmth of his father's voice, something inside of David seemed to settle into place, and part of the ache that had resided in his chest since Saturday receded. He was content to listen as his father recounted the latest about Ruth and her two boys, and the neighbors, and the article he was writing at present—and was not in the least prepared for him to shift topics and delicately inquire whether he should expect to accommodate one or two at Christmas this year.

"Oh—well, I hadn't really . . ." David trailed off. He had not allowed himself to consider such a thing. A week ago, the idea of him taking Meredith home for Christmas would have seemed ludicrous. It ought to still. But now that the idea was in his head, God help him, it was exactly what he wanted. In fact, the thought of going without him left David feeling hollow.

At the same time, a new possibility flashed into his mind, really no more than a passing fancy: staying at Midnight Cottage for Christmas and inviting his father to come to him—to them both. Swirls of frost on the windows, mulled wine steaming on the stovetop, Bianca resigned to wearing the tiny sweater Mrs. Jupiter had knitted for her,

Meredith curled up against him on the sofa while snowflakes fell softly outside.

"Sensitive subject?" ventured his father when David didn't continue.

"No, no. Well—" David hesitated. Saying it aloud felt like something he couldn't take back, but he forged ahead anyway. "There is someone, but things are a bit, er . . . undefined at the moment."

"No pressure, then, eh?" His father laughed. "Really, I'm sure it'll work itself out in time. In all seriousness, if there's someone you'd like to bring by the time Christmas rolls around, I'd be delighted to have him, and if not, I'll just be happy to see you."

Once David had ended the call, he found himself gazing into the depths of his half-drunk coffee and trying very hard to avoid entertaining his wildly improbable holiday daydream any further.

When David finally arrived home, it was so dark that he nearly trod upon the bouquet of flowers left on the doorstep. (In spite of his annoyance, he could not place blame on Meredith for not leaving the light on, not when David himself had failed to anticipate his own late departure from work.) Heart sinking, he scooped up the bouquet and trudged inside. Tucked in among the wrapping was a card from the local florist's shop, unsigned. Grumbling to himself, he plunked the daffodils into a vase and dutifully texted Meredith:

Someone has sent flowers.

oh yes???

Reasonable or not, the idea of Meredith receiving anonymous flowers ignited a tiny spark of jealousy, and try as he might, David couldn't snuff it out.

Any idea who they're from?

a secret admirer <3

Even over text, David was sure Meredith was not being truthful. He had no shortage of admirers, though rarely secret, and rarer still that they sent gifts. Still, David was certain: Meredith knew exactly who was responsible, and he wasn't telling.

After spending far too long glaring down at the daffodils, David roused himself and snatched up his phone again. He needed an outside perspective, someone to talk sense into him.

He dialed Harriet, but she didn't pick up.

The rest of the week passed by in a blur. David found himself working long hours in preparation for the upcoming auction, and Meredith seemed to spend every spare moment at the Lost & Found, so they never caught each other at home.

Finally, on Thursday, David slipped out of the office a bit early. Any final tasks that remained to be done before the auction could wait until the following morning. His mind would be fresher then, anyway. It had, of course, nothing to do with the fact that Meredith didn't work Thursday evenings.

Except for today, apparently.

The note on the table read:

Working tonight.

No signature, no ridiculous closing, no needless postscript.

Well, that was fine. Having some time alone to unwind was just what David needed. He fed Bianca, changed, and went for a run. Before he'd taken a break for the winter, part of his usual route had been along the edge of the Midnight Wood, but today he went down the main road and all the way to the far side of town. His thoughts had been swept into an uncharacteristic disorder, and the rhythmic pounding of his footfalls on the pavement helped to drive the swirling miasma of invoices and line-item approvals and the cost of cocktail napkins per gross from his mind. Even the burning of his lungs felt good, a much-needed catharsis after too many hours spent behind a desk. (There was another small matter, too: he could no longer ignore the extra weight he'd put on about the middle. The realization left him a bit self-conscious, although Meredith certainly hadn't seemed to mind.)

Before he knew it, David had reached the spot past the edge of town where Main Street forked into two county roads. As he turned back toward home, a new realization struck him with an unpleasant jolt. In reality, the thought had been lurking in the back of his mind ever since Maurice Wolkowitz had stopped by: Meredith *still* hadn't returned to inflicting his overaffectionate greetings on him. No air-kiss, not even an embrace, and suddenly David missed it, missed *him,* terribly. It had been days—no, weeks, ever since the night when David had first kissed him, furious and frightened half out of his mind in the living room of Midnight Cottage.

Which he very much wanted to keep doing.

It wasn't about sex—not *just* sex, anyway. It was affection and companionship and the way the scent of patchouli now made him go weak in the knees. David no longer cared whether he was Meredith's first choice or hundredth choice, so long as he was on the list somewhere, and that terrified him.

Never before had he longed for someone with such intensity, and he didn't know how to make sense of that. He didn't know what it meant to love someone who constantly went upending everything David thought he'd understood about himself and the world.

David stopped dead in the lane.

Love?

Was it love?

He'd had a handful of past relationships, a few quite serious. Certainly he'd cared for his exes, cared deeply. With a couple of them, he would have said at the time that he'd been in love—*had* said so, in fact. He didn't disavow that now, even though things had not worked out.

But this—this was something that went far beyond that, something that had spent the past five years stealing up behind him in the metaphorical night before bludgeoning him over the head with the realization at long last.

He still couldn't dismiss the thought that had sprung into existence at his father's invitation. He wanted to take Meredith home with him, and spend holidays with him, and wake up next to him for the foreseeable future. David couldn't imagine returning to a state of existence in which he *didn't* want that, and, in fact, couldn't imagine how he'd gone so long believing he didn't. The idea of having that future snatched away from him just when he'd caught a glimpse of the possibility was more than he could bear.

But he still had no idea how Meredith felt about *him*. He was free with his affection and casual in his choice of bedmates and had outright said that was the case here. Well. Technically he had neglected to give his usual speech, but he'd said it meant nothing. He'd said he was in love with someone else.

No, David realized with a start. He'd said he was in love with *someone*. Surely he couldn't have meant—no, no. That would be too much to ask. Meredith rarely held back from doing exactly as he pleased. If, by some minuscule chance, David were the object of his affections, he would've made some attempt, given some indication.

Besides, David thought, his spirits sinking, he himself was entirely unremarkable, just as Charles had told him. *Nothing special*, in the words of the Erlking. This had never bothered him before, true, but a person like Meredith would hardly settle for someone ordinary.

Then, too, there was the matter of the daffodils. Perhaps the mysterious individual Meredith was pining after returned his feelings after all. He'd certainly been cagey enough when asked about it. In person, David might have chanced pressing him further, but as it was—

Of course it was always possible that he knew who had sent the flowers and it was a different person entirely, one whose interest flattered him but remained unreciprocated. (Steve Corner came to mind, but a man like Steve Corner would not send a gift anonymously.) So there remained at least a glimmer of hope.

Wiping sweat from his brow, David let himself back into the house and trudged to the shower. There was no reason to panic, he told himself severely. He was a sensible and rational man. He need not go making any grand declarations, but only to raise the perfectly reasonable question of their respective intentions if he and Meredith continued sleeping together, daffodils or no daffodils. David just needed to frame it carefully so he could get an idea of Meredith's inclination without making things too awkward. Besides, if he could forgive the list, surely a degree of misplaced affection was nothing in comparison.

Simple enough, then. David would do exactly that, as soon as things settled down a bit, as soon as he'd had time to calm his nerves and get his thoughts in order and work out what to say. He wouldn't hold out until the wedding, but just until the auction had concluded. That gave him twenty-four hours, and then no excuses.

Satisfied with this plan, David changed into a soft T-shirt and pajama trousers, intending to go to bed. It was early, but he was tired and needed the sleep.

Instead, he went to the living room, silent and empty save for Bianca on the center cushion of the sofa.

"Think you could spare some room for me?"

Bianca deflated with a sigh and rested her head on her forelegs.

"I know the feeling."

David paused. Now here *he* was, holding a conversation with a Chihuahua. He sat up to reach for the television remote, but on second thought picked up the grammar book that had remained on the coffee table all week in spite of the bookshelves being only a few feet away.

He paged through it idly; there were a handful of words he recognized from the few weeks of a German course he'd attended long ago in university, before the complexities of grammar had scared him off and he'd switched to French. To his surprise, this book appeared quite advanced, and the more technical portions were interspersed with a selection of footnoted literary texts. On a hunch, he checked the index and turned to "Die Lorelei," with its familiar opening lines:

Ich weiß nicht, was soll es bedeuten,
Daß ich so traurig bin.

Between the footnotes, the glossary, and his own memory, he was able to piece together a rough translation. *Ich weiß nicht*, he remembered: *I don't know.* A consultation of the glossary yielded him the next few words. "*I don't know what it means*," he recited aloud, "*that I am so—*" He broke off with a frown. *Traurig* had escaped his memory. Since Bianca failed to volunteer an answer, he began to turn back to the glossary when it came back to him:

"*That I am so sad.*"

David slammed the book shut. It was only a poem. A bit of imagination, no more accurate than Bianca's supposed favorite song casting her in the role of the mad dog.

All the same, it would do no harm if he waited up for Meredith to come home.

DAVID AWOKE ON the sofa with Bianca snuggled into the crook of his arm and a crocheted blanket draped over him. The table lamp next to him had been turned on, and subdued sounds of activity came from the kitchen, where he found Meredith rolling out pastry for a piecrust.

He started toward David as though to embrace him, but stopped short, glanced down at his own flour-covered hands, and turned back to the counter to take up his rolling pin once more.

David should have been glad of the consideration, as he did not particularly wish to be dusted with flour, but his heart sank in disappointment. Nonsense, of course, but now that the idea had been put into his head, after a solitary and stressful week, the prospect of being hugged by someone—and by Meredith, in particular—was something he wanted badly.

Pushing away the thought, David grasped for something to say, and came out with the inane observation "You're later than usual."

Meredith lifted the pastry with care and draped it over the pie tin. "Yeah, I rearranged a few appointments, what with everything coming up this weekend, and now the whole bridal party is doing brunch on Saturday morning, and I've got to redo that portrait as well. Really, I've been rescheduling far too often anymore," he confided. "People are going to start thinking I'm unreliable."

"I'm sure they won't," said David. Meredith gave him a strange look, and David kicked himself. That had been the perfect setup for a playful jab, and now he was the one who'd missed his cue. "Wait, Adalynn's portrait? How come?"

Meredith heaved a sigh and left off crimping the edges of his piecrust. "I was nearly finished, and Florian wanted to have a look, so I sent him a photo."

"And?"

"Well, he wasn't pleased." At David's expectant look, he elaborated, "Might have been a *bit* Magritte-influenced."

"But you're a surrealist," David pointed out. "You told him that."

"Yeah, well—" Meredith shrugged and wiped his hands on a tea towel. "The beard suits you, by the way."

Disoriented by both the leap between topics and the compliment itself, David didn't reply. Instead, he leaned in to peer over Meredith's shoulder as he spooned a yellowy-green substance into the pie shell. "What's this?"

Without waiting for an answer, David reached around him and swiped a finger through the filling, narrowly avoiding Meredith's attempt to rap his knuckles with his wooden mixing spoon.

"You just keep your big brutish paws out of my gooseberry tart."

"*You're* a gooseberry tart," muttered David. Ignoring Meredith's sound of indignation at that, he tasted the dollop of stolen pie filling. "Not bad. But gooseberries aren't in season yet, are they?"

"Nah, this is preserves. I got a jar off of Mrs. J earlier. Told me she was glad enough to part with it if I'd go make a pie and keep myself out of trouble. *And* she said she'll bring us more of her healing salve once the next batch is ready. Oh!" He lit up with excitement. "I almost forgot the best part."

"About Mrs. Jupiter?"

"No. Well, not exactly." From the refrigerator, Meredith retrieved a small covered container, which he opened and presented in a conspiratorial manner. "She gave me bit of moon meringue to go with it." In response to David's raised eyebrows, he explained, "The Night Horse brings her some every week. It's the real thing, you ever tried it?"

David shook his head. Meredith, in spite of his own admonition of only a few moments earlier, collected a quantity of meringue on his fingertips and offered it to David. "Go on, then."

David leaned in to have a taste of meringue from his hand and tried to banish the ludicrous feeling that he was being treated as a tamed animal in a petting zoo. Though the texture was what one would expect for meringue, the flavor was strong, and not as sweet as he would have imagined. "Bit sharp, isn't it?"

"Yeah, thought it'd be a nice contrast." Meredith licked the rest of the meringue from his fingers, leaving a spot of it on his lower lip. Whether deliberate or not, David couldn't tell, but he wasn't going to pass up the opportunity, and kissed him.

Meredith broke away far too soon. "Now, you just leave off with that till I've got this in the oven, or—or—" He brandished his mixing spoon at David.

"Or feel the wrath of your spoon?"

"Yeah," said Meredith. "You will."

"Your weapon of choice, is it."

"It is, thank you. You've seen the damage I can inflict."

Though the remark was lighthearted, David's thoughts traveled in a darker direction. As Meredith turned to pick up the pie tin, David said abruptly, "I'm sorry about Jean-Marc."

"Not your fault," said Meredith, but David could read the tension in the line of his shoulders.

"It was, a bit. I shouldn't have brought somebody like that into the house."

Meredith occupied himself making unnecessary adjustments to the edges of his piecrust. "Yeah, well, how were you to know he'd try it on with me the moment your back was turned?"

"But the way I reacted, it was awful." David had wanted somewhere to lay the blame, other than upon himself for misjudging someone he'd liked very much. (Jean-Marc himself would have been the logical option, David now reflected, but at the time, he hadn't wanted to go there.) "You weren't to blame, and I behaved as if you were, and it was—wrong of me."

At last Meredith faced David. "But you still came running when I needed you, and you still threw him out. You still believed me."

"That," said David, "was never in question." No other option had ever crossed his mind, even as he'd stormed away and slammed his door and left Meredith alone in the kitchen without ever bothering to check on him. The pit of David's stomach dropped. "I hope he didn't—I mean to say—I never even asked what he did, or if you were all right."

Meredith shrugged. "Yeah, well, could've been worse. It's hardly the first time somebody has grabbed my ass without permission."

"I should think that's bad enough."

With a faraway look, Meredith went on, "It wasn't that that had me so shaken up." He turned away and picked up the unbaked pie, then set it back down. "Only I turned around and there was no way to get past him, the way he was standing over me and just so—so *big*. Frightened me a bit," he admitted softly.

David went still. "Do I? Ever frighten you like that?" It wasn't a thing he'd ever much worried about himself, but someone who wasn't as physically imposing, someone who was seen as more effeminate regardless of what terms he did or didn't choose to refer to himself—in short, someone like Meredith—must have an entirely different experience.

"You? Never. With you, I can just . . ." Meredith sank back against him, and David wrapped him in his arms. "Feels . . . safe."

David held him close, resting his chin on his shoulder. "Meri," he began, "I've been meaning to—"

A knock at the door interrupted.

David took a deep breath. Surely that was for the best. He had nearly blurted out an impulsive confession, not at all the way he'd meant to go about things.

"Who could that be at this hour?" asked Meredith and then, to David's disappointment, slipped from his grasp to go answer the door.

"Mr. David! My dear Schwarzy!" Bednarek beamed as he stepped through the front door. "At last I catch you at home."

"Ah. You've found a replacement for Todd?" That had been inevitable, but David couldn't avoid a twinge of disappointment. He'd rather enjoyed the two of them having the place to themselves.

"Regrettably, no," said Bednarek, still beaming. "Truthwise, I must admit, with recent goings-on, new tenant has not been priority."

This was it, then. Just as David had suspected. "I suppose there's no more need to dance around it, Mr. Bednarek. You're selling the cottage, aren't you?"

Meredith looked from David to Bednarek in dismay. "Selling the cottage?" he repeated.

"But no!" protested Bednarek. "It is not the cottage I sell, but the Wood. Thanks to Mr. Cartier, soon we shall have lovely new condominium development where the Midnight Wood now stands."

"*What?* But you can't—you can't just get rid of the Midnight Wood!" said Meredith, horrified. "What will become of the Mice? Where will the Moon Calf and the Night Horse go? Where will *any* of them go?"

Bednarek patted him on the arm. "There, now. I assure you, all will be quite all right. If your friends need new place to stay, you give them my card, tell them come see me."

When Meredith did not appear to take any consolation from this, Bednarek added magnanimously, "Special offer, as you are my dear friend: with referral from you, I do not even charge application fee."

Meredith turned helplessly to David, who'd been struck speechless by the whole thing. He'd thought he'd known what was coming, yet somehow the rug had still been yanked from beneath his feet.

"Incidentally," Bednarek went on, "my true purpose in stopping by: Mr. David, I require still the bill from plumber."

Wordlessly, David went to the end table, removed an empty teacup from a stack of mail, shuffled through it, and presented the only slightly coffee-stained invoice to the landlord.

"Wonderful! Now, then." Bednarek clapped his pudgy hands together. "It is late, I intrude upon you no longer. Good night, boys!"

The door fell closed behind him. After a silence that lasted an eternity, Meredith asked, sounding quite lost, "David, what are we going to do?"

"Well, it's hardly the end of the world," said David with far more conviction than he felt. He was not sure how the Midnight Mice, or any of the other purported inhabitants of the Midnight Wood, would fare when displaced from their natural habitat. "I'm sure Mr. Bednarek will see to it that they have someplace to go."

"What, you think the Moon Calf and the Night Horse will just take an apartment over on Chavez Street? Can you imagine, the Mice in that triplex across from the butcher's shop? God, I can't believe Bednarek," Meredith fumed. "What's next, he sells this place out from under us, too?"

"If it were to come to that—" began David.

"We'd just move into the boardinghouse behind the cinema where Steve Corner lives, is that it?" Meredith's question held a stinging sarcasm. "Oh, yes, won't that be lovely? I'll smuggle in Bianca in a suitcase, and perhaps we could all live down the hall from one another and play pinochle on the weekends."

"You don't play pinochle," David pointed out. "You can never make sense of the scoring. And why are you angry with *me*?" It hurt more than he liked to admit, even if he himself knew he'd done nothing to warrant it.

At that, Meredith seemed to deflate. "I'm sorry, David, I'm not really. I'm just—it's not—" He gestured in frustration, bracelets jingling. "It's not fair! It's not s-supposed to be like this."

David started to reach out for him, but arrested the motion as Meredith turned away to pace the length of the room. He searched desperately for something to say, but all he could come up with was "I'm sorry." It felt inadequate—it *was* inadequate, and he tried again. "I know the Midnight Wood means a great deal to you."

"Wait." Meredith whirled to face him. "Cartier's going to be at the auction tomorrow night. You're going to talk to him then, aren't you? You can ask him not to tear down the Midnight Wood."

David sympathized, but how could he make such a demand of Cartier upon their first proper conversation? It would hardly make a favorable impression. Besides which, the Midnight Wood appeared to have become rather a dangerous place of late—perhaps it would be better for all concerned if its current residents sought a new home. "We'll see how it goes," he offered, and even to him it sounded like an evasion.

"David, *please*," begged Meredith. "If anybody can change his mind, it's you."

David had to look away from the pleading intensity of his gaze. "I don't think that's true," he said gently. "I mean to say, I wouldn't like for you to get your hopes up."

"But you will try, won't you?"

David didn't know how to answer, and eventually settled for repeating, "Let's just see how things go." At Meredith's look of disappointment, he added, "I promise you, one way or another, it'll turn out all right."

But as David retired to bed—alone, not having dared to ask Meredith to join him, no matter how he longed for his presence—he was not sure it would turn out all right at all.

Chapter Twenty-Five

When David arrived home after work Friday, Bianca greeted him at the front door, tail wagging. A record played in the background, deep male vocals over dark and foreboding music, but Meredith was nowhere in sight—not in the living room, kitchen, or laundry room.

"Meredith?"

Not a sound from upstairs.

The gingham curtains billowing in the open back door gave David his answer. Pushing them aside, he stepped out onto the deck. At the far corner, Meredith leaned against the railing, staring off in the direction of the Midnight Wood.

"Meredith," David repeated, and laid a hand on his arm. "What are you *doing*?"

Meredith turned, blinking in confusion. "I was just—" He broke off uncertainly, brow furrowed. "I don't know. I can't remember why I came out here."

"Well, come on, then," said David. "We need to be back at the Corner Store by seven, and you take forever to change."

He expected Meredith to counter that he himself was free to be as fashionably late as he liked, but he only turned away to look toward the Wood again.

"David?"

He checked his watch. "Hmm?"

"If—if anything were to happen to me, you'd see that someone looks after Bianca, won't you?"

It was six already, and Meredith *did* spend far too long getting ready, and of course traffic must be taken into account, and—

"What?" Of all the nonsensical things to worry about at a time like this. "Of course nothing's going to happen to you. Mrs. Jupiter has the situation under control, so long as you do as she says. Now come *on*."

This time, Meredith made no protest at being ushered back inside.

Trying to ignore the unease prickling at the back of his mind, David combed his hair, changed into a dark suit, and debated over his choice of necktie. His favorite, a diagonal stripe in a silver gradient, would be a touch too monochrome, so he selected a blue paisley print instead (given to him by Harriet at Christmas one year, though in the past he'd always found it too whimsical for his taste).

There was nothing left to do but wait on Meredith. David found himself pacing the living room and resisting the urge to begin returning items to their proper places. Except, to his bewilderment, he found that everything *was* in its proper place, and had been recently dusted to boot. He'd resorted to straightening the sugar bowl on the kitchen table when footsteps sounded on the stairs at last.

"What do you think?" Reaching the bottom of the staircase, Meredith gave a slow twirl, showing off his black cocktail dress, cut very low in the back and exposing most of the feather tattoo down his spine.

"You really went and bought it," said David in astonishment.

"Course I did," said Meredith. "What do you think, are the heels too much?" He extended one foot to display a high-heeled sandal in bottle green, doubtless from the women's section, though after the past five years, David found that such distinctions had ceased to hold much meaning.

"No, no, you want a spot of color," he said. "I'm just surprised you found them in your size."

"Do you know, I only wear a ladies' size eleven?" asked Meredith cheerfully.

"I actually didn't need to, thanks."

He gave another twirl, then made a face at his faint reflection in the window glass. "Feel I'm missing something, though. Need a bit more sparkle."

"You sparkle enough all on your own." It was meant to be a mild insult, but somehow sounded like anything but when David spoke the words aloud.

"Do I really?"

The question was so earnest David couldn't stop himself from answering, "Like starlight." Then, remembering, he cleared his throat and added, "Hold on, I've got just the thing."

He hurried down the hall to his room and returned with Meredith's strand of black pearls. "Meant to give this back to you the other day and it slipped my mind entirely."

Meredith turned away, then ventured an expectant look over his shoulder, and David understood what he wanted. He nearly made a comment about not having signed on to play lady's maid, but it wasn't particularly witty, and in any case, it was much more interesting to make a pretense of having difficulty with the clasp of the necklace and watch Meredith shiver at his touch.

"Oh, you do like that," murmured David, and leaned in to press a kiss to the nape of his neck. "I've found your weak spot."

The next thing David knew, he found himself spun around and pushed over the kitchen table, its edge biting into his thighs as he braced himself to avoid falling flat atop it.

Meredith pressed himself close against David's back, there was the threat of teeth at his earlobe, and then the harsh growling whisper: "I ought to fuck you over this table right now so you can still feel me all night while you're trying to impress all them business people you care so much about. Bet you'd like that, wouldn't you?"

To his own surprise, David found that he would like that very much indeed.

Instead, Meredith released him. "But," he said innocently, "I'm afraid we haven't time. Wouldn't want to make you late, after all."

"A man is allowed the occasional poor decision." A feeble protest, but it was the best David could come up with.

"Perhaps after."

"Right." David took a deep breath and tried to redirect the inconvenient blood flow by sheer force of will. (The new discovery that being manhandled in such a fashion had made him instantly hard was pushed aside for later consideration.) "Let's go, then."

By the end of their short drive to the Corner Store, thanks to an intensive mental review of tax regulations surrounding charitable donations, David had managed to put Meredith's words out of his mind and was no longer at risk of public indecency. The two of them joined the other attendees filing into the lobby. At the registration tables, each guest was given a glossy pamphlet about the Corner Store and the beneficiaries of the auction's proceeds, and assigned a randomized number for bidding.

"To make it more interesting," Steve Corner explained. David nodded and pretended not to notice the eye-watering scent of vodka on his breath. "I have to hand it to you, Carew, it was a good idea of yours to hire professional staff for this."

In all honesty, it was because David had wanted to avoid being roped into handling the finances of the auction himself—but as the whole event was a tax write-off, the more expensive, the better. He simply nodded again, signed the registration sheet, wished Corner luck, and hurried away to catch up with Meredith.

Though it was early, the first level of the Corner Store was already crowded. It appeared Corner had made heavy solicitations in the local arts scene, judging by the dazzling mix of avant-garde and traditional formal attire on display.

The sales floor had been rearranged, racks and merchandise carted away and concealed behind partitions. At the far end of the room near the mezzanine stood a buffet table, and waitstaff circulated distributing champagne cocktails. Much of the space, however, was taken up by a labyrinth of display tables draped in expanses of sumptuous textiles. A description card and bid sheet accompanied each lot—gift baskets, luxury clothing items, intricate beadwork, service vouchers displayed in picture frames, and all manner of pottery, paintings, and jewelry. David recognized the work of Harriet's grandmother (two sets of mittens knitted in thick natural wool with geometric motifs), a collage of Cliff Richard bearing Kinley's illegible signature, and, even before Meredith pointed them out, a few pieces of jewelry by Manuel Holland.

Only a few tables down, they found Meredith's series of now-framed drawings.

"*Damaged Scribblings Nos. 1 through 5*," David read aloud from the card. He ought to have looked at the donation form when Meredith had filled it out. "Not a very encouraging name."

"It was *supposed* to say *Deranged*," complained Meredith. "That's what I wrote."

"That's even worse." David held back the obvious remark on the difficulty of deciphering Meredith's handwriting.

"But you're the one who said it."

"I never did."

"You did, that day I drew Siouxsie Sioux riding into battle on a vampire bat, remember? *And* you said I was trying too hard to imitate Ralph Steadman, and then I stomped around and cried a bit?"

"Oh, yes." David did now recall saying something of the kind, and his cheeks warmed with guilt. "Sorry about that."

"Nah, you had a point." Meredith offered a sheepish smile. "Actually helped me make some progress once I got over my wounded pride."

David glanced over the pictures. A knight upon his faithful steed in armor made of broken crockery. A drunken giraffe twisting its neck into an impossible corkscrew as it leaned down to sip a martini through a crazy straw (from an equally twisted glass garnished with tiny skulls on a skewer). What appeared at first glance to be a collection of abstract swirls and jagged angles that resolved itself into a landscape of towering, leering wildflowers and brambles with grasping thorny tentacles. And—

"You've given away the Forkupine?" he asked in dismay. "I thought you liked him."

"Yeah, but you didn't."

David frowned, but before he could reply, his attention was caught by the final drawing. "What the hell is this nightmare creation?"

"Oh, do you like it? It's stargazy pie with rats instead of fish."

At a total loss, and mouthing rather like a fish himself, David could only ask, "Why?"

"It just made *sense*, David."

Before David could question precisely what kind of sense it made, Meredith shivered. "Cold in here."

"Yes, well, it is spring still," David pointed out. "Perhaps you ought to have considered that before wearing a backless dress."

"Perhaps *you*—oh!" Meredith darted past David to throw his arms around Kinley, who had not bothered to swap out his leather jacket for anything more suited to the occasion.

"Hey," said Kinley. David raised a hand in greeting.

"You came!" said Meredith. "I thought you'd never go for this sort of thing."

Kinley shrugged. "I don't, but hey, I figure I gotta show up for my little brother"—he leaned back to take in Meredith's outfit—"or sister today, whatever. Maybe start a bidding war for a couple of your pictures and see how much the fat cats are willing to shell out."

Meredith giggled and linked an arm through Kinley's. "Let's go mingle with the aristocracy, and you can tell me all about your meeting with the senator."

"It's called *networking, darling,*" drawled Kinley in very proper British. Switching back to his normal voice, he added, "This is a capitalist event first and foremost, don't forget that."

"Yeah," said Meredith, "and speaking of, I spotted this jade bracelet of Manuel Holland's and I mean to have it. Come on." As he and Kinley departed, he called to David, "Good luck."

Then David was left alone. His gaze traveled over the *Deranged Scribblings* again. With a sudden impulse and a furtive glance around, he placed a bid on the Forkupine, then made haste for the VIP lounge.

It turned out to be a small area partitioned off between the mezzanine and the back staircase. David had expected someone to check his presence against the guest list, perhaps even to question it so that he might have to mention being invited by Cartier personally, and was rather let down to find the door open and unattended.

No matter. He was here now, and lawfully so. After taking one last moment to compose himself, he stepped inside.

Maitland Cartier wasn't there.

Adalynn was, speaking to a woman David didn't recognize, while

Florian poured himself a drink at the makeshift bar. David did not think he could bring himself to hold a civil conversation with Florian Schwarzwelder. In a stroke of good fortune, however, his back was turned, so David gave Adalynn a quick nod and ducked back through the doorway.

Returning to the auction floor, he tried to quell his bitter disappointment—not only at Cartier's absence, but at the betrayal of the unguarded room. Nobody would have stopped him from walking right in, not that it mattered any longer.

No. Cartier *would* be there, David insisted to himself. He'd said so. Perhaps he was simply late to arrive, held up by other matters. He was, after all, an important and busy man. David could wait, and resolved to relax and enjoy the auction in the meantime.

He had several canapés from the buffet table, made polite small talk with the few coworkers who had sufficient clout to receive an invitation, and waved to Harriet across the room in a brilliant red dress. She was deep in conversation with a group of women in conservative formalwear—definite finance types. Best not to interrupt, David decided. At one point, he thought he caught a brief glimpse of Sylvania Holland in her brocaded silks, but soon lost track of her in the crowded room.

Detaching himself from his colleagues, he prowled through the throng of auction-goers alone. He kept an eye out for Maitland Cartier, did his best to avoid Steve Corner, and tried to quash the mix of frustration and longing that arose within him every time he caught sight of Meredith in the crowd. He was in his element, sparkling and effortlessly charming and going around air-kissing everyone who wasn't David.

Tearing his gaze away, he turned to the nearest table and found himself standing before Manuel Holland's jewelry. Even if it hadn't been obvious which piece Meredith liked—a bangle bracelet in pale green jade, carved with a dragon motif—he'd know his handwriting anywhere. His was the only bid so far, a modest but respectable offer.

David smirked to himself. Perhaps a bit of petty mischief was in order, payback for Meredith's whispered words before they'd left the house. He entered a bid for one dollar more, and tried not to think about Meredith bending him over the kitchen table.

I ought to fuck you over this table right now so you can still feel me all night.

Perhaps when they got home, he could convince Meredith to make good on his . . . threat? Offer? Or perhaps they'd venture upstairs again so that David might acquaint himself with the contents of the second drawer.

Not the time or place, he admonished himself. Even if that was rather the point—Meredith hadn't even had to go through with it to ensure that the idea stayed in his head all night.

He straightened his tie and mentally reviewed all the line items he remembered from the caterers' invoice, which was burned into his brain nearly as vividly as the words he was trying to forget.

"David!"

Startled, he whirled around, and Harriet seized him in an embrace. David hugged her tight, lifting her off her feet. Another measure of tension left him; though he'd gotten caught up in his work, he'd been more worried than he realized about his unreturned phone call.

When he released her, she gave him an appraising once-over. "Hey, nice tie." Then, taking in his expression, she tilted her head to one side. "You okay?"

"I was starting to think perhaps I'd offended you," he confessed, then paused. "*Have* I offended you?"

"What? Oh!" She punched him lightly in the arm. "No, you big dummy. I went up to Vancouver Island to visit my grandparents this weekend, remember? I was flying back when you called. Sorry I dropped the ball on getting back to you, though. I've been playing catch-up all week since I got back."

"That's all right," said David, and meant it.

Retrieving her glass from the nearest table, Harriet asked, "How are you? How's the house-hunting going?"

"It isn't," said David. "It was, but I've stopped, but—" He shook his head. "It's a long story."

Her eyebrows rose as she took a sip of her drink. "Is everything all right?"

Of course it is, he meant to say. *Why wouldn't it be?*

"Everything," said David, "has gotten quite complicated."

Harriet nodded. "Walk with me."

He filled her in on it all—Meredith, the Erlking, and the impending sale of the Midnight Wood—over the course of several circuits around the room, punctuated by numerous stops for each of them to check their respective bids. Harriet was determined to acquire a hand-painted silk scarf and a blown-glass figurine of a swan. Meanwhile, David raised his bid on the Forkupine twice, and was secretly impressed at how Meredith managed to outbid him on the bracelet every time it left his sight.

Though David glossed over the more salacious details, he gave Harriet the main points. A small worry that he ought to be properly networking still gnawed at the back of his mind—no matter how disparaging Kinley's pronunciation of the word—but David felt much better talking to Harriet and getting it all off his chest.

"This is a mess," said Harriet. David nodded morosely. "A *mess*," she repeated. "A train wreck."

"Yes."

"Tomorrow," she said. "I'm staying at the Bingham Inn tonight and

I've got a business brunch in the morning, but before I leave town tomorrow night, you can take me to dinner and we'll figure this out. As for right now?"

"Yes?"

"Right now," said Harriet, "you're going to talk to Maitland Cartier."

"What?" At Harriet's nudge, he turned, and she gave him a little push right into Cartier's path.

"You've got this," she whispered, and then she was gone.

Chapter Twenty-Six

David froze. Somehow he'd imagined that Cartier would sequester himself in the VIP lounge all night, and was not in the least prepared to encounter him roaming freely among the other guests. Now his disappointment increased tenfold. Not only had his efforts over the past weeks—months—been a foolish waste of time, but now he was about to humiliate himself further still.

Then again, perhaps not. The unexpected thought flashed into David's mind as he recalled their first meeting at the edge of the Midnight Wood, and the way Meredith had waltzed right up to Cartier and air-kissed him without batting an eye. If David himself could channel even a fraction of that confidence—well, perhaps Cartier was not quite so untouchable as David had built him up to be.

Summoning all his courage, David extended a hand. "Mr. Cartier, good to see you again."

"Nice to see you again as well, Douglas," agreed Cartier, shaking his hand. "I hear you were one of the major players in putting this event together."

"Thank you, sir. And, er, it's David, actually."

"So it is, so it is. But no more of that *sir* stuff," said Cartier, wagging a finger at him.

"No, si—no. As you say." Then, with a boldness that surprised himself, David said, "I hear you've bought up the Midnight Wood."

"I certainly do hope to, once Mr. Bednarek and I iron out the last few details," said Cartier. "By the way, son, I know I've already said so, but I can't tell you how much I appreciate you helping out Adalynn by hosting her bridal shower."

David ought to redirect the conversation back to the fate of the Midnight Wood, but this was exactly the recognition he'd been waiting for. (He tried to ignore the sick sinking feeling that invaded his stomach at the thought of Adalynn Cartier marrying Florian Schwarzwelder. Either she knew his true character and had no objection to it, or she didn't, in which case—well, that was too awful to think about, but how could David possibly interfere? How could he possibly know the difference?)

"No trouble at all," said David. "Genevieve organized it all, but I'm glad to have helped in any way."

"I'm looking forward to having a chat with your roommate soon, Ada's brother-in-law—what was it? Vivian or Evelyn or something? The funny little fella with the tattoos."

"Meredith, actually," supplied David, and added conscientiously, "He's not little. He just looks like it next to me."

Cartier waved a hand. "Oh, yes, I knew it was one of those old-fashioned names. Those drawings of his are making quite the stir."

"Are they really?"

"I don't mind telling you, I've been bidding on a couple of them myself. Brilliant stuff."

"Oh, yes," said David. "Absolutely." As he said it, he realized he wasn't just agreeing with Cartier—he meant it. When it came to art, Meredith *was* brilliant, even if his style might not be to David's personal taste.

David turned to search for him in the crowd and soon spotted him and Kinley in conversation with Belinda Fairfax (she of the argyle sweater) and Rick Pangolin, the head of HR.

"Actually, he's right over there, if you'd like to—" David stopped, his heart sinking. Cartier had seen Meredith, too, and his affable expression had morphed into hard disapproval. But the day they'd met at the edge of the Midnight Wood, hadn't Meredith been wearing a skirt then, too?

No—David followed his line of sight. He was watching Steve Corner, who stood a short distance away, champagne flute in hand, gaze sweeping down Meredith's bare back with undisguised lust as obscene as if he were raking his hands over him.

As though he could feel it, Meredith shivered, shot an uneasy glance over his shoulder, and inched closer to Kinley.

"Excuse me," said David, already turning away before Cartier's absent nod registered. He made his way through the crowd, slipped past the partitions, and hurried up the back staircase to his office, where he retrieved the cardigan sweater he'd left draped over the back of his desk chair.

By the time he returned downstairs, Kinley was nowhere in sight, Harriet had fallen into conversation with Sylvania Holland, of all people, Florian and Adalynn were perusing the lots at the far end of the room, and Cartier was chatting with Rick Pangolin by the buffet table.

"I wondered where you'd got to." Meredith's voice at David's shoulder made him jump.

"You mustn't come creeping up on me like that."

"Oh! But I wasn't trying to. Only, Kinley took off, and I was staying away till you'd had your chance with Cartier so I wouldn't mess it up like last time, but I saw you talking to him a bit ago, so I thought it'd be all right now." Meredith hesitated, then went on, "Did you ask him about the Midnight Wood?"

David's insides twisted with guilt. "I—er, well, not exactly. I mean to say, I did try, but he didn't quite take to the idea." This was not a lie, he told himself. He *had* brought it up, and the conversation had rather gotten away from him.

"Oh," said Meredith quietly. (Did David imagine it, or was there a momentary flicker of hurt in his eyes?)

He hastened to change the subject. "Actually, I was looking for you." David offered his sweater. "I know it doesn't really go, but I thought—it looked as if you were still cold."

Meredith eyed it doubtfully. "That's your favorite sweater."

"Yes, and you can borrow it, if you'd like."

"You told me once if I ever so much as thought about touching that sweater, you'd lock me in the cellar and throw away the key."

"I—well—"

"I don't want to live in the cellar, David. Although"—Meredith tilted his head in consideration—"I suppose ours isn't so bad. Could be quite cozy with a bit of redecorating."

"Nobody is going to put you in the cellar," said David in exasperation.

"Florian used to."

David stared, then ran a hand over his face. "*Christ*, Meredith."

Meredith shook off the faraway look that had crept over him. "Sorry," he said. "Don't know why I said that. 'S true, though. But you were saying?"

The urge to hug Meredith competed with the urge to go give Florian a good punch to the face, though David did not punch people as a rule.

Instead, he held out the sweater once more in silent offering.

Carefully, as though he were handling something as delicate as cobwebs, Meredith took it from him and slipped it on. The combination of a Cowichan sweater with a cocktail dress and pearls looked ridiculous—but no more ridiculous than usual. It suited him.

David's breath hitched, and something in his chest fluttered. The sight of Meredith wrapped in his too-big, incongruous sweater made David want to sweep him into his arms and press close against him in a way that was entirely divorced from any kitchen table–related fantasies.

"Thank you," said Meredith. Something in his delivery of the words seemed off in a way David could not quite put his finger on. Perhaps he had caught sight of Florian across the room. But just in case he hadn't—

"Your brother's here, by the way," said David. "With Adalynn. I wasn't sure if you knew."

"Oh, yes," said Meredith vaguely, "we've been playing at cat and mouse all evening."

An inexplicable heaviness seemed to have settled over them. In hopes of dispelling it, David remarked, "You make rather an outsize mouse, I'm afraid."

"S'pose so." Meredith made an effort at a smile, but even that last bit of cheer faded as he looked down at the sweater he wore, at the cuffs of the sleeves slipping down over his hands. "Oh. Is that why?"

David didn't follow. "Is what why?"

"Five minutes!" bellowed Steve Corner from the mezzanine. "Five minutes left on the bidding!"

The auction floor erupted in a frenzy of activity.

"I'd best go check mine one last time," said Meredith, and disappeared into the crowd.

David managed to keep him in the periphery of his vision while pretending to be interested in a nearby earthenware jug; as soon as Meredith was safely out of the way, he dashed over to Manuel Holland's table. Meredith's final bid had been underlined for emphasis, and David smiled to himself as he pictured his expression of mock indignation.

He bid another dollar.

How to court a magpie—David snorted as the absurd phrase popped into his head. But wasn't that what he was doing after all as the two of them bid dollar by dollar, playing a pretend game of tug-of-war over the nearest shiny object?

"One minute!" announced Steve Corner.

David just had time to place a final bid on the Forkupine, where he had some more serious competition. It was a little higher than he ordinarily would have been happy with, but winning this one mattered a great deal.

"Time's up!" shouted Corner. "All right, folks, relax and enjoy the refreshments for the next little while as we process the bid sheets. You'll receive a text message to your registered mobile number to notify you of any winning bids, and a complete, anonymized list of the winners for each lot will be sent out shortly."

David stole a glance at the sheets for the other *Scribblings* before they were collected by one of the auction staff, and was astounded at the numbers they'd risen to, particularly the rat pie. He'd gotten off lightly with the Forkupine.

This time, it took him longer to locate Meredith among the milling guests, and by the time he did, phones were beginning to buzz with notifications.

"Did you win anything?" David asked casually.

"I think so, but I haven't got a text yet." Meredith checked his screen again as Corner called everyone to attention and launched into a long and boring speech about the history of the Corner Store. In that time, David received notifications that he'd won both the Forkupine and the jade bracelet. Finally, Corner began to wrap things up, expressing his gratitude toward Cartier, the donors, and the attendees. Just when David thought he had to be finished, he added, "And I want to give an extra-special thanks to a few of our donors who were instrumental in our success tonight—Omega Stevenson, Lydia Morton-Bentley, and Meredith Schwarzwelder, whose *Damaged Scribblings* series brought in more than any other single donor."

The crowd applauded; cameras flashed.

"*What*," whispered Meredith, eyes wide. "But it's nothing, I just gave away a few stupid sketches that nobody liked, and they didn't even get the name right."

"Mr. Cartier liked them." David also suspected Kinley hadn't been joking about instigating a bidding war, which he'd no doubt dropped out of when the stakes became high enough.

"If I could have the three of you join me up here, please!" called Corner.

Meredith hid his face against David's shoulder. "Oh, I can't."

It was strangely endearing seeing him turn shy in front of a crowd, and it went a long way toward making up for his arrogance at other times.

"You can." David rubbed his knuckles gently between his shoulders. "Go on."

Looking like a deer in headlights, Meredith joined the other two in making the trek to the front of the room. Corner, under the guise of ostensibly thanking the three donors, spent the next several minutes congratulating himself for having had the foresight to make the request of them.

At last he concluded his speech. "If you've received confirmation of a winning bid, please proceed to one of the registers to collect your items, and thank you again for coming."

The audience broke into deafening applause—no doubt at the fact that he'd finally stopped speaking—and the journalists from the local and regional papers descended upon the quartet.

By the time Meredith escaped the publicity, David had already paid for and received his items, wrapped in tissue paper and concealed inside a large shopping bag. He waited at the bottom of the mezzanine as Meredith descended, checking his phone. After he spent a moment scrolling, his face fell.

"What's the matter?"

"I didn't get it," he said in disbelief, still staring at his screen.

A tiny seed of guilt sprouted in David's mind. "You mean you didn't win anything at all?"

Meredith shook his head. "I was only after the one thing, but *somebody* must have gone and outbid me at the last second."

His tone gave David pause. Had he misjudged the whole thing? "Look, I—"

"Mr. Carew!"

David turned to find Leonard Flood hailing him with one upraised tentacle as he oozed toward them across the auction floor.

"Ah, Mr. Flood, I hadn't realized you were here." He made an effort to keep his tone polite, but inwardly he cursed the man's timing.

"Yes, it's a bit difficult getting around in this crowd," said Flood. "Hadn't heard from you in a bit, so I just thought I'd touch base to see where things stood. Been a busy week on your end, of course, I quite understand." Catching sight of Meredith, Flood slapped a tentacle to his forehead. "Forgive me for not introducing myself. Leonard Flood, real estate agent. If you're ever in the market for a place yourself, do give me a call," he said, and presented him with a rather soggy business card.

"Oh . . . thank you . . ." Meredith accepted it delicately between two fingertips.

"Not the time to talk business, of course," Flood told David, "but I did want to check that everything was all right after you withdrew your offer so suddenly."

"You made an offer," said Meredith quietly. It was not a question. "You made an offer on a house." His voice trembled. "You're going to leave."

"No, I—I did, yes." David admitted. "I mean, I thought about it, for a bit, but it wasn't—I mean to say—" He turned from Meredith to Leonard Flood and back again, unsure which of them he was actually addressing. "You see, I was doubting myself the whole time, and I couldn't go through with it, and—and—" Every word out of his mouth was making the entire situation worse.

"Finding the right place can take some time," Flood barreled on, "so don't let that discourage you. Give me a call when you're ready to schedule another viewing—no rush, of course."

"No, in fact, Mr. Flood, I don't think that'll be necessary." David looked desperately to Meredith, who had gone faraway again, his expression quite unreadable. "Actually I've realized I'm quite content with where I'm at, for the time being."

"Understood, understood. Do keep me in mind if you reconsider." Flood gave David a jovial and somewhat damp clap on the shoulder and took his leave.

"Meredith—"

"No, no," Meredith interrupted, "no need." He pressed both hands to his face, exhaled a slow, shaky breath, then lowered them and turned a sad, tired smile on David. "Bit of a shock, that's all."

"I'm sorry," said David. "It was sort of on impulse, and when I really thought about it, that wasn't what I wanted at all, and—I'm sorry," he repeated uselessly.

"Ah, well, no harm done."

David wasn't convinced, but Meredith reached out to rest a hand on his arm. "'S all right, David, really. Can't blame you, all things considered."

Moving aside to clear a path for two women making their way toward the exit, David said, "Perhaps you should."

"Nah, what do you think? Course you never c-could've gone through with it, you'd miss Bianca too much."

I'd miss you *too much*, David wanted to say, but before he could—

"I'm going home," said Meredith. There was a weariness in his voice, and as they followed the departing throng out through the lobby, he looked startlingly haggard beneath the fluorescent lights.

David wanted to ask when he'd last slept properly, but didn't imagine either of them would take any comfort from the answer. Instead, he said, "All right. Come on, then."

Meredith shook his head. "You don't have to. I know you probably want to stay and . . ." He trailed off with a gesture that encompassed the surrounding crowd. "I can walk."

"In those heels?"

David's tone was light, but Meredith's empty, distant look didn't lift. "I'll manage."

"I mean it," insisted David. "I've just about had my fill of all this as well. Let's go home."

Meredith made no reply to that, and as soon as they were in the van, he curled up in the passenger seat, resting his cheek against the window.

As they drove back to Midnight Cottage, David's unease grew. This hadn't turned out the way he'd intended at all, and he didn't for one moment believe Meredith's insistence that everything was fine. As soon as they got back, he decided, he'd give Meredith the bracelet, apologize again, make sure he understood that David really meant what he'd said to Flood, and, from there, somehow lead into the conversation the two of them desperately needed to have.

It wasn't until David turned on the living room lights that he saw the shine of tears on Meredith's lower lashes. "You really are upset," said David quietly.

Bianca climbed up onto the arm of the sofa, wagging her tail and demanding attention. Meredith listlessly stroked her fur. "I wanted that bracelet, David."

It was by no means the answer David had expected, but *that* at least he could do something about. He set down his shopping bag and reached into its depths, grappling for the flat square box. "I'm sorry. I didn't realize it mattered to you that much."

"It ain't about the thing itself, 's just how Kinley s-said I ought to do something for myself seeing as how—you know, lately things have been—oh, *I* don't know." Meredith made a gesture of futility. "And then he was giving me some lecture about the *Protestant work ethic*, which I didn't really underst-st-st—follow, but in the end, I really just wanted—" He stopped, too near tears to continue.

David was dying inside. He had to be the lowest person on earth. He'd thought they were playing a game—he'd only meant to tease him a bit and make him laugh, but he'd accomplished the exact opposite.

Wretchedly, he presented the box to Meredith.

He opened it, and his eyes darted between its contents and David in disbelief. "*You* were number 108?"

David was floored. Meredith really hadn't known he was the one bidding against him all along?

"Oh, you poor silly little bird." His voice came out huskier than he'd expected. "Do you mean to tell me after all this time, you still don't know my handwriting?"

Sinking down to sit at one edge of the sofa, Meredith lifted the bracelet from its nest of cotton wool and regarded it for a long moment. Then he returned it to the box, slid it onto the coffee table, and said, tonelessly, "Thank you."

Taking a seat next to him, David wrapped an arm around his shoulders and pulled him into a sideways hug. "Meri, sweetheart, I'm sorry. I thought you were just playing along, pretending you didn't know it was me," he confessed. "I never meant to make you sad, not about that or about—any of it."

Meredith gave a tired laugh and inclined his head to rest against David's shoulder. "'S all right. Sorry I ruined everything being a bit of an idiot."

"You're not." David brushed a stray lock of brass-blond hair from his face. "I'm always going and pushing you a bit too far, aren't I? Sticking my big paws in where they don't belong."

“Nah, normally I’d get a kick out of a thing like that.” Meredith sagged against David, winding up halfway in his lap and slumping down further so his face was hidden against his chest. “Don’t know what’s the matter with me lately.”

“You’ve been having a hard time.”

With a sigh, Meredith admitted, “S’pose you could say that.”

“And I haven’t made it any easier on you.” Especially not with his clandestine attempt to move out.

David stroked his hair, and in that moment, he had a crushing realization. He was no good for Meredith. He wanted to be with him, more than he’d ever wanted anything in his life, but he’d only go on hurting him. All this time, he’d been blundering along, his attempts at showing his affection rough and clumsy—a child grasping at a butterfly, heedless of its fragile wings.

For a time, David had seen the possibility of something between the two of them, something with enough momentum to carry him out of the inertia of his present life and into some kind of future, whatever that future might be. But perhaps it was just the opposite. Perhaps Cartier had the right idea, and the only way to move forward was to raze his current life to the ground and for them both to walk out of the rubble—in separate directions.

“Meri?”

“Hmm?”

David focused on the sliver of night sky visible between the curtains, pinprick diamonds on black velvet.

Perhaps only rhinestones, but in the end, it didn’t make a difference.

“Whoever it is you’re in love with—” David hesitated. No matter how he might hope, there was no chance that Meredith could return his feelings. How could he possibly love someone who was so dull by comparison, who went hurting him at every turn, who surely could not compare to the unknown admirer who’d sent him those hated daffodils? (Even in their wilted state, they mocked David from their place on the coffee table.) He shouldn't finish the sentence. It was terribly selfish of him. It would give everything away, yet he couldn't stop himself continuing, "If you ever decide to tell them, I hope they realize how lucky they are."

Meredith pulled away and sat up, leaving David bereft of his warmth. It had been the wrong thing to say—either an unwanted revelation or a reminder of Meredith's own unrequited feelings.

Meredith's eyes darted over toward David in that sideways searching look of his. "Actually, I think . . ."

David closed his eyes. This was it. Now that he'd gone and raised the subject, he was about to be let down gently, and that was even worse than a short sharp rejection.

"I think I've just about got up the nerve to tell him. Soon. Quite soon, actually."

"Oh." David had been wrong. *This* was worse. He blinked against the sting in his eyes. Meredith not only didn't care for him, but he'd been about to put a stop to things between them anyway.

"David, I—"

"Don't."

The single word came out with a harshness he hadn't intended, and Meredith recoiled as though David had slapped him.

"What?"

David couldn't look at him. It was all he could do to make a pretense of studying the window, but his eyes couldn't take in the stars anymore. All he could see was a smudge on the glass, the unraveling hem of the curtain, his own reflection pale and wavering.

"I know what you're going to say," said David hollowly, "but I can't bear to hear it. So if you have the least shred of care for—for me, for our friendship, you won't say it."

Meredith went still, barely breathing. "Oh," he said. "I—I hadn't realized. I mean—I thought—"

There was no longer any point in trying to save face through denial. "I'm afraid so."

After a long pause, Meredith said simply, "I see." Coming from him, that terseness was shockingly cold.

David made an effort to keep his tone brisk, to show that he wasn't hurt, not at all. He'd known all along what he'd been walking into. "Yes, well, it should have been clear from the beginning. As you said, we were just having fun."

"Yeah," said Meredith, blinking hard. "S'pose it had to come to an end s-sometime." He shrugged out of David's sweater, rose to his feet, picked up Bianca, and turned to go. Then, turning back: "I'm sorry."

"No need," said David.

Meredith ascended the staircase, and David could only sit frozen, watching his retreating back, left with nothing but a crumpled heap of wool that held the faintest scent of patchouli.

Chapter Twenty-Seven

David had cried. Alone in his room in the dark, he had really, genuinely cried for the first time in years, for the first time since moving to Midnight Cottage, pressing his face to a pillow to muffle his uneven breathing and the occasional hiccuping sob. It wasn't that he believed crying to be humiliating or unmanly; he simply wasn't the crying type, or the emotional type in general.

He hadn't believed himself to be, anyway, but now he couldn't seem to hold back. Everything he'd been pushing aside for so long came flooding back at once: The death of his mother. The distance he'd allowed to develop between himself and his father. The relationship with his sister that had never had the chance to be. Admitting to himself that he missed the closeness he'd once had with Harriet; that Charles's words *had* hurt him; that he was furious at himself for allowing his infatuation with Jean-Marc to cloud his judgment, for allowing him even the chance to put his hands on Meredith, for remaining oblivious to dangers to which he himself was largely immune.

How lost he felt now, unable to see a clear path forward in life, and the one he'd begun to imagine abruptly cut off.

He must at some point have fallen asleep because he woke at three in the morning to Bianca whining and pawing at his door—quite out of the ordinary for her.

David tried to muster enough annoyance to drown out his misery, failed to do so, and kicked off the covers and opened the door.

"Fine," he muttered, "I'll let you out." Really, it was unconscionable of Meredith to sulk to the point of neglecting his dog.

But when they reached the end of the hallway, Bianca ran not to the door but up the stairs.

"Absolutely not. I'm not going up there." David did not like to imagine that Bianca had the mental capacity to stage an attempt at reconciliation, but even if she did, he wasn't going to fall for it. Meredith had given him his answer, and there was nothing else but to accept it. David *did* accept it, but that didn't mean he wanted to be around him just now.

Bianca whined insistently.

"No, thank you. I'm going straight back to bed." And he meant to, but he hesitated. If something was really wrong, he'd never forgive himself for ignoring it.

With a grudging sigh, he started up the stairs. "This had better be important."

Meredith's door stood open, his room empty. The bedsheets were rumpled, but as David doubted he actually ever made the bed, that told him nothing.

"So what, he went for one of his walks and didn't take you with him?" It was more to reassure himself than Bianca, and it didn't work.

Meredith's shoes lay where they'd been kicked off; all his jewelry was scattered over the nightstand, including the pearls he'd had on tonight. David found his gaze drawn toward the obsidian ring and slowly picked it out from amidst the small treasure hoard. He rubbed at the carved surface of the stone as he glanced into the other second-floor rooms—empty—and made his way back down the stairs, the nape of his neck prickling.

"Meredith?" he called.

No answer.

Absently slipping on the ring, which just barely fit his little finger, David checked the downstairs rooms, and even glanced into the cellar. All were silent and empty.

In the open sliding doors to the deck, the gingham curtains rippled in the night breeze, and upon the table lay a note. David rushed to it, only to find that it was no note at all but a blank sheet of paper.

His heart plummeted. Flying to his room, he couldn't get Mrs. Jupiter's bracelet onto his wrist fast enough. He only prayed Meredith hadn't removed his own—David didn't think he'd spotted the brass bangle among the others upstairs.

Because no matter where things stood between them, no matter whether Meredith loved him, David wasn't about to let anything happen to him.

The bracelet pulled him sharply and with no room for doubt in the direction of the Midnight Wood.

Fuck.

It shouldn't have come as a surprise, but still he'd held out hope.

David's heart raced, but he forced himself to take a breath. There was no time to lose, but neither could he afford to rush into things unprepared. He shoved his feet into his boots and fumbled with the laces, fingers made clumsy by panic. Bianca cried all the while.

"You can't go," he told her. "Look, I'm sorry, I know you want to help, but you'll—" He didn't have the heart to say, *You'll only get in the way.*

"I'd be afraid of losing you," he said gently. "You know he'd never forgive me. Besides," he added, inspired, "you'd be derelict in your duties. The royal hound must stay behind to guard the castle."

That appeared to placate her, and he took a few final seconds to scribble a note of his own, *Gone to the Midnight Wood*, which he stuck on the glass sliding door. Should anything go wrong—a possibility that

David was not going to think about—Mrs. Jupiter would find it sooner or later.

He stepped outside, closed the door behind him to prevent Bianca following, and took off at a sprint down the hill. He didn't stop or slow, not even when he crossed through the trees and plunged into the humid pitch-black darkness of the Midnight Wood.

The pull of the bracelet was stronger than ever. David didn't think proximity had anything to do with it, since it had been quite weak when he and Meredith had stood in the same room.

Urgency, on the other hand, seemed a likely possibility.

He said aloud, as if it would do any good, "I'm coming for you. Just hang on."

David kept running. Shadows and rustlings in the darkness terrified him at every turn, and so did the knowledge of precisely whom he was about to confront, but still he didn't stop. Vainly he sought something to distract his mind, a poem or song to recite, but couldn't come up with anything aside from the multiplication tables.

Was that why Meredith went around singing all the time? But that was nonsense. *He* was never scared. He'd stood up to a gang of neo-Nazis and kept his head when confronted by the Erlking and hadn't even shied away from asking David uncomfortable questions. David had never seen him intimidated by anything—at least not until his relatives had shown up.

"I'm sorry," whispered David. "Meri, this should be the other way around. You're the brave one. You're the strong one. Not me."

David was weak and cowardly, no matter how he might pretend. He'd hurt someone he cared about for the sake of a half-baked plan to impress Maitland Cartier, who couldn't care less about his existence. He hadn't been able to shake off a few put-downs from the Erlking. He hadn't put a stop to Florian's hateful remarks or told off Lisl for her abominable behavior. He hadn't even been able to get Genevieve to call him by his proper name.

He hadn't had the courage to ask Cartier for the one thing that really mattered, to spare the Midnight Wood—as much Meredith's home as the cottage itself.

In the end, I really just wanted—

David had thought he'd understood, that Meredith's losing bid had been the final straw after a particularly trying few weeks, but it wasn't that, either. It was David's failure—his refusal—to do the one truly important thing Meredith had asked of him, and his own shameful attempt to flee in the night without so much as a word of warning.

Moonlight broke through the clouds, and the obsidian ring shone on David's hand.

It bears an enchantment, Sylvania Holland had said, *the ability to reveal that which is concealed.*

That which was concealed—even from oneself. David understood now.

He was forced to slow as he picked his way through the brush, and replayed his last painful conversation with Meredith in his mind once more.

Whoever it is you're in love with—if you ever decide to tell them, I hope they realize how lucky they are.

I think I've just about got up the nerve to tell him. Soon. Quite soon, actually.

David kicked himself. It was all so clear now, how they'd been talking at cross-purposes all this time. There had never been anyone else. Meredith had been trying to confess to *him*, and David had misread it entirely.

And when he'd said, *Don't*, when he'd said, *I can't bear it*, Meredith had thought—

"*Fuck*," David said again, this time out loud. He followed it with every other curse word he knew and invented a few new ones. It failed to lessen the sting of the realization, of knowing he'd inflicted the same pain on Meredith that he'd felt himself, and needlessly at that.

And now, because of him, because he hadn't been willing to admit even to himself how he felt until it was much too late, Meredith was about to lose himself to the Erlking—forever.

"*No*," said David. The possibility was too awful to contemplate, and therefore, he could not allow it to happen. A world without Meredith Schwarzwelder did not seem quite worth living in.

Fighting his way through the briars, David picked up speed.

I'm sorry. I'll find you. Hang on for me.

He only hoped it wasn't too late.

He ran and ran, and then, all at once, the ground gave way beneath his feet as he slid and stumbled along the soft bank of a pool of black stagnant water. To avoid falling into its depths, David flung himself in the opposite direction and tumbled to the ground, landing heavily and scraping his arm on a fallen log.

Despair came over him again. If he even managed to find them, what could he possibly do against the Erlking? Every time they'd run afoul of him before, David had had to rely on Meredith to get them out of it, but now it was his turn, and he was at a total loss.

Then there came a strange metallic tinkling, rather like the babbling of a brook, if instead of water it were filled with ball bearings and bits of sheet metal. A small spiky creature scurried into view, glinting in the moonlight.

"Hello," it greeted him in a scratchy, tinny voice.

David instinctively scrambled back. "What the hell are you?"

"I'm not a what," said the creature in indignation, "I'm a who."

"What?" repeated David. "Er, I mean, who?"

"I'm the Forkupine!"

"You're—real?"

"I am now," said the Forkupine. "*He* made me real."

He made all of you real, David realized, *and he has no idea.* He understood now. As absurd as it might be, there was a kind of logic at work here in Meredith's unerring ability to find his way through the Wood in the dead of night, in the way the landscape shifted to clear paths forged with will alone. Even the Erlking, a nightmare conjured up from childhood fairy tales and warded off by the words Meredith believed in so deeply that he'd inscribed them on his skin.

David took a deep breath and let it out. He was out of his element here, and he knew it. But he supposed it made as much sense as anything else in the Midnight Wood—as much sense as anything else where Meredith was concerned. "Okay," he said. "Right. Pleased to meet you."

"Come on, come on, up on your feet, no time to lose," urged the Forkupine. "We must rescue the king of the Midnight Wood! Onward!"

With renewed determination, David rose to his feet and hurried to keep up with the Forkupine.

They raced deeper and deeper into the Wood, dodging between trees and crashing through thickets of brambles, heedless of the thorns and branches tearing at them. The Forkupine ducked beneath another fallen log. Following close behind, David vaulted over it, and then halted abruptly as the pull of the bracelet led him straight toward the face of a massive rock outcropping.

David swore. Of course the thing didn't function like a proper GPS. It only urged him along the shortest route in the right direction, but he couldn't move through solid rock.

"This way! This way!" came a chorus of tiny voices. There was a flash of white, then another, and another, and a trio of white mice had assembled next to the Forkupine.

"We," they said in unison, "are the Midnight Mice."

This time, David took it in stride. "And I'm very pleased to meet you," he said. "In fact, I owe you my thanks. I believe one of you tried to help me when I was in these woods before."

That cast a pall over the Mice, but the leader of the trio spoke up. "That was Hyacinth." She solemnly bowed her head. "She met her end at the hand of the Erlking."

"I'm sorry to hear it," said David.

"But you will banish him from our forest and restore our queen to the throne. Come, we will show you the way."

"Matriarchal society and all," explained the Forkupine in a low voice. "Only title they recognize."

David nodded, though he didn't imagine Meredith would mind either way.

The group pressed on. The bracelet tugged harder and harder at David's arm, and every time a new obstacle blocked their path, the Mice led them to an alternate route. As they stumbled through a sycamore grove carpeted with sweet woodruff, they were joined by a pair of dryads—extraordinarily beautiful women with mottled silver skin and luxuriant green curls.

Their band continued to gain new followers, leaving David with mere impressions as they rushed on—the large luminous eyes of the Moon Calf, the flowing inky mane of the Night Horse, the rapid patter of the Most Weasel's paws.

At last they slowed at the outskirts of the fir grove. The trees were in poor condition, their needles brown and brittle.

"The lair of the Erlking," said the Forkupine in a hushed tone. "He's made the trees too sad to live."

"We can accompany you no further," said the Moon Calf. "Banish the Erlking and return to us the rightful ruler of the Midnight Wood."

David didn't know whether there was going to be a Midnight Wood for much longer if Maitland Cartier had his way, but one thing at a time.

"May fortune be with you, valiant knight!" called the leader of the Mice, and the rest of the group cheered in a cacophony of agreement.

"Right," said David. "Here I go, then."

Squaring his shoulders, he crossed into the ring of pines. Some knight he was—trembling with fear, clad in his pajamas, and without the first clue what he was going to do when he came face-to-face with the Erlking. Then again, Meredith was hardly the standard golden-haired fairy-tale princess, either, so perhaps it didn't matter. Perhaps it was enough for David to have shown up as he was.

In the center of the empty clearing, he called out, "Erlking! I demand an audience!"

In a blink, the man himself appeared before David, and it took everything he had not to jump back in the most ignominious fashion.

"Well, well, you've shown up after all," the Erlking greeted him. "I'm surprised you made it this far."

It was hardly any of the Erlking's business, David decided, if he had happened to have a little help on that front.

"I have," he said, his voice hard. "Now, what have you done with my—my—" To his shame, he faltered once again, this time out of fear. What if, in spite of all he thought he'd understood, Meredith still didn't want him?

"With your *what*?" mocked the Erlking. "What's he to you?"

But this time, David knew the answer. "*Everything*."

A sickening smile sliced across the Erlking's face, a flash of pointed teeth in his silver beard. "Oh, I do find that hard to believe. Why, if that were true, you never would've shattered his heart so thoroughly that I could get into his head and take over without ever leaving my domain."

David's glare was icy. "A simple misunderstanding."

"Is that so?" The Erlking's wheezing laughter faded as quickly as it had begun. Collecting himself, he said with a pretense of solemnity,

"But where is my hospitality? Are you thirsty, boy? His despair is simply unparalleled."

At a loss, David followed the Erlking to the far side of the clearing and beneath the overhang of the towering, moss-covered rock formation.

There in the shadows, surrounded by the glowing white blossoms of dozens of candleflowers, Meredith lay upon the flat stone. He appeared to be asleep, hands folded over his chest, tangled hair splayed out around him. His dress was torn, his arms and face bore the telltale scratches of thorns, and his bare feet were black with grime.

David hurried to him and seized hold of his hand. "Meri, wake up."

He remained still and silent, save for the rise and fall of his chest. Dread washed over David, but he channeled it into rage and turned to the Erlking. "What have you done to him?"

"Me? Oh, no, no. *He's* the one who let despair into his heart. I simply called, and this time—this time, he came to me." The Erlking extended a hand, summoning a wineglass into existence. From nowhere, it began to fill itself with a pale green liquid. "You're sure I can't tempt you with just a little sip?"

Upon the stone table, Meredith gasped as though in pain, but still he did not wake.

"Stop it," said David.

The Erlking paid him no heed, and the glass continued to fill. Meredith twitched and turned his face to one side. Though his eyes remained closed, tear tracks glistened on his cheeks.

"*Stop it!*" shouted David. "You're hurting him."

"Now, that is rich, coming from you," said the Erlking, a hideous amusement twinkling in his colorless eyes. "You go hurting him all the time."

He drank deeply, and Meredith threw back his head, a whimper escaping his throat.

David knelt beside him and placed a hand to his cheek. "Hush, little bird," he whispered. "I'm here now, it's going to be all right. I always make everything all right, don't I?"

He still didn't know how he possibly could, but Meredith believed it. He'd said as much, and judging by the way his breathing evened out, the reassurance seemed to work.

Meredith believed it, and David had to make it true.

Chapter Twenty-Eight

"Pretty easy on the eyes, this one," said the Erlking conversationally. "Is that why you've gone and changed your mind?"

"Changed my mind?" repeated David. It was hardly the most intelligent remark, but it was the best he could do as he tried desperately to come up with a plan. Certainly the Erlking wasn't going to let the two of them go without a fight—besides which, Meredith appeared to be in a kind of enchanted sleep. If the Erlking refused to break the spell, perhaps Mrs. Jupiter could, but who knew whether she'd be willing to help them this time?

The Erlking shook his head in facetious sympathy. "First you turn him down, and now you want him back. His poor little heart can't take it—and all the better for me."

"I didn't mean to," said David, talking more to Meredith than to the Erlking. "I was trying to tell you something quite different, but neither of us ever can say a thing straight-out, can we?"

"You mortal men are such hopeless fools," cackled the Erlking, and drank another long draught of despair, drawing a cry of pain from Meredith.

Fury surged up inside David. "You can't do this. You can't have him," he said. "I won't allow it."

"Oh? You would challenge me for his hand?"

"No," said David, standing up to his full height. "He's his own person. But I challenge you in his place, since you've prevented him being able to do it himself."

After a moment of apparent consideration, the Erlking shrugged. "I'll tell you what. If you want to try sorting out his strange little brain cave, then by all means, have at it. I've had a peek in there and it's an utter disaster."

David didn't follow. "In his . . . ?"

The Erlking threw out an arm with a swish of his crimson cloak, and their surroundings shimmered and changed. They stood now inside a long, twisting corridor, the walls tilted at sharp and unexpected angles, patterned in a dizzying combination of clashing swirls and stripes of black and white. Much of their surface was taken up by mirrors, many of them shattered. Splinters of silver glass stuck into the walls and littered the floor.

Over walls and glass both were scrawled words, some barely legible, others painfully clear.

Following the Erlking through the maze, David tried to take it all in, feeling rather as though he'd entered a horror-film fun house. In the openings of connecting passageways, sinister shadows darted by, though David could not properly catch sight of them no matter how quickly he turned. Every so often, a wind swept past, carrying whispers that he could not make out. Upon closer inspection, the words on the walls appeared in a variety of different handwritings. Meredith's appeared frequently, and in some spots, David recognized his own (even if Meredith didn't).

He leaned down to retrieve a sliver of glass from the chevron-striped floor. Its surface bore the words *God, you're useless.*

That wasn't true at all, but David remembered Florian saying it.

He remembered himself ignoring it in favor of continuing his own conversation with Genevieve and Bednarek.

You're not, thought David, *and I'm sorry.*

The glass in his hand dissolved in a puff of silver glitter that dissipated into the air.

A bit farther on, David caught hold of a larger shard of glass and gave it a tug, dislodging it from the oddly soft and pliable wall. It left behind a deep and jagged hole. The sight of the wound distressed him, and he placed a hand over it, as if he could somehow wipe it away. To his surprise, the surface of the wall shifted beneath his palm, healing over—but not entirely. There still remained a depression where the glass had been, a kind of scar.

The Erlking hadn't slowed, and David hurried on, afraid to lose sight of him in the broken labyrinth; he did not like to imagine what might happen if he lost his way here. He wondered whether the inside of his own mind looked anything like this, and suspected that it contained nowhere near as much shattered glass.

The shard he'd taken from the wall read, in a different handwriting, *She thinks it's her fault you turned out to be a queer.*

But it isn't, thought David. Phrasing aside, such a thing was nobody's fault. It was nothing that required a casting of blame. It wasn't even a problem. It simply *was*.

This time, the glass exploded into a small shower of rhinestones that sparkled at his feet for a moment before dissolving into the floor.

Okay, thought David, *there might be something to this.*

Before he could speculate any further, however, the hall of mirrors ended. He and the Erlking entered a large open chamber, similar in appearance to the space they'd just come through, save for the multitude of angular arched doorways leading to what he guessed must be more corridors.

In the middle of the room, at the center point of the floor's spiraling stripes, there stood a twisted pedestal of opaque black glass. Atop it rested a massive glittering ruby, deep dark red and bigger than David could have held in both hands.

It was faceted into the shape of a heart.

Rather, it had been. Now it was cracked throughout into so many pieces he feared it would collapse into a heap at the slightest breeze, and impaled dead center with an enormous, wickedly sharp piece of mirror glass.

David swallowed hard and tried to ignore the sting that pricked at the corners of his eyes. "I thought you said this was his brain." That should be the least of his problems; he ought to know by now not to seek logical consistency in the Midnight Wood, not in a place where time ran backward and anything could happen.

The Erlking waved an unconcerned hand. "Brain, heart, he doesn't know how to make the distinction." Then those unnerving pale eyes settled on David, and the Erlking's mouth cracked into a sly smile. "Now, here's an idea. You're a sporting sort of gentleman. Supposing you and I make ourselves a little wager, eh?"

David had a suspicion as to where this was heading, and he didn't like it one bit. "What sort of wager?"

"I'll give you one hour. You fix that"—one blackened claw pointed at the shattered ruby—"and he's yours. *And* I'll take my leave of the Midnight Wood for good. If you should fail—"

"Now look here," David interrupted, his fury rising once more. "You can't go betting with—with *people* as though they were so many poker chips."

"Or sugar cubes?" suggested the Erlking.

It was a calculated strike. David could not help but recall the night of Sylvania Holland's visit and Meredith's sheer joy at his inconsequential winnings—at finding someone to join in the game—in spite of all David's grumblings. In that moment, he knew that no matter the stakes, no matter what the Erlking said next, he would do anything to get Meredith back.

"If you should fail," the Erlking repeated, "then you and he both shall be forfeit to me."

Taking a bet with those terms would be dangerous and foolhardy to the extreme, against all good sense.

"I accept," said David without hesitation.

With a smirk, the Erlking went on, "Or perhaps better to say *when* you fail, because there's no way you'll ever manage it, not if I gave you all the time in the world. You've no hope of doing anything but making it worse, and my libations shall be all the sweeter!"

"You don't know that." David tried to quell the hopelessness rising up in him. "You don't."

"Are you joking?" The Erlking made a sweeping gesture. "Look around you! Nobody could fix this. He's broken beyond repair, which suits my purposes just fine." He reached out to caress the nearest wall, tracing along a zigzagging black stripe.

"Stop that," said David sharply. "And you're wrong. It's not true."

"Good luck," said the Erlking, "not that it'll help." With a final cackle, he faded away.

One hour.

David hadn't the least idea how to go about fixing anything. He'd made a few pieces of glass vanish, and he thought he understood how, but there were far, far too many for him to ever have any hope of clearing them away entirely.

He pulled another glass shard from the wall and smoothed over the gash it left behind. On it were the words *You, on the other hand, are the most selfish person I have ever met.*

The handwriting was his own.

"I'm sorry," breathed David. "God, I'm sorry."

This piece, too, disappeared in a puff of glittering smoke.

Selfish, selfish, selfish, echoed Meredith's handwriting on a trio of tiny shards, as if he hadn't been able to banish the words from his mind.

As if he believed it himself.

No, no, no, thought David, and the three fragments simultaneously vanished.

Eyes stinging, David continued his exploration of the room. Some of the smallest bits of glass bore single words like *freak* and *retard* and *faggot*, but those, too, faded away the moment he thought a simple *no* at them. He pulled out glass splinters that had penetrated deep into the wall, doing what he could to heal the resulting lacerations and dispel the cutting words.

One handwriting in particular appeared frequently, saying terrible, insidious things, and David knew exactly whose it was:

Take off those fucking daisies.

You're a goddamn embarrassment.

Can you pretend to be normal for a few hours, or are you too fucking stupid to handle that, too?

I feel bad for your roommate—can't you tell how ashamed he is to be seen with you?

"I'm not," he said fiercely. "Meredith, I'm not, you've got to know that."

For the second time that night, David found himself truly in tears. At the idea of anyone having said such things to Meredith, at him taking the words to heart. David cried at knowing he had been responsible for some of the damage himself, at looking around the room and seeing what little difference his efforts had made. His time must be nearly at an end by now, and he was still too frightened to touch the heart ruby for fear of destroying it completely.

But as David wiped his eyes and gazed around the room once more, he realized that not all the mirrors were shattered. Some remained intact, and others were spiderwebbed with cracks but seemed to be held together by the words scrawled over them.

In Kinley's unmistakable slanting all-caps: *You're my little brother and I love you, okay?*

In Bednarek's surprisingly graceful calligraphy: *I am certain you will make someone a lovely wife or husband someday.*

In Mrs. Jupiter's looping hand: *You mean a great deal to me, and I know I would not be the only one devastated should you come to harm.*

In David's own neat script: *You sparkle enough all on your own.*

Dotting the walls throughout was the odd pawprint he recognized as Bianca's (all too well, after the incident with the India ink).

And, freshly painted, with a weak glow around the words: *Hush, little bird.*

That brought a smile to his face, albeit a bittersweet one. So Meredith liked to be called that after all, even if he did protest.

Wait.

Wait.

David had said that only a short time ago, here in the Wood.

"Meredith," he said aloud, "can you hear me? You can, can't you?" He didn't know what sort of response he expected, but he had an idea of how to get one. In fact, he knew exactly what he had to say, no matter how the words seemed to stick in his throat, weighted by remorse. "I know now just how badly I let you down tonight when I didn't talk to Cartier, and I'm sorry. I was afraid of what he'd think, but I shouldn't have been, because it doesn't matter—not nearly as much as you do."

Nothing. Perhaps he was approaching this all wrong—or perhaps it wasn't enough, not yet, and Meredith was waiting for him to continue.

"It can't have been easy to find out that I'd been looking at other places, either, and I wish you hadn't found out the way you did. I wish I hadn't set about it without telling you to begin with, and if I could take it back, I would. Deep down, I knew all along something was wrong with all those houses, and now I understand what it was. Not a single one of them was right because no place feels like home without you there."

Did David imagine it, or was there a faint indefinable sensation just beyond the edges of his perception?

"And I hope you know, when I offered you my sweater, it wasn't because I was trying to make you cover up in front of Cartier or your brother or anybody else. There's nothing the matter with you just as you are. You just seemed so uncomfortable with the way Steve Corner was looking at you, and I couldn't stand the thought of anyone making you feel that way, and to tell the truth, I—I like it when you wear my things," he confessed, in spite of his own embarrassment. "Makes me go quite wobbly inside."

At that, there was a dull but unmistakable glow deep within the mass of ruby fragments.

"You *can* hear me."

There were so many things that needed to be said. David hadn't managed to say them properly before, and he still didn't know if he could now. But that was how they'd wound up in their current predicament, and if there was to be any hope of them getting out of it, he had to try.

"Meredith, I'm sorry, for so many things. I'm sorry for the awful things I've said, and for not making sure you knew I didn't mean them. Right now I'm especially sorry that we've misunderstood each other so badly. Neither of us has been saying what we really mean, and I suppose that went about as well as one might expect. Earlier tonight, I wasn't turning you down. I was trying to tell you—" He took a deep breath and forced himself to say it. "I was trying to tell you that I love you. I had hoped you might feel the same."

This time, there was a definite pulse of dark red light that lasted for a full second.

"You do?"

The cracked ruby pulsed again, throbbing so intensely he could practically feel its affirmation.

"I know, love, I got it all wrong. We both did. You were trying to tell me exactly that—you've been trying to tell me all along, only I've been such a fool, I never realized it was me you were talking about." David scrubbed a hand across his eyes, but his voice grew steadier. "I've loved you for a long time, I think, only I was too caught up in my own head to realize how I felt or what it meant. But the truth is, I can't imagine what I'd do without you. That frightens me like you wouldn't believe, and I've been trying to convince myself I didn't need you, but I do."

Saying it aloud brought him a certain relief, but he'd expected something more to happen, something to signify his success.

But of course, how could he have succeeded when Meredith's heart still lay in pieces before him?

David had to take the chance, or they were never going to get anywhere. He pressed both palms to the mound of ruby fragments and hoped his idea would work.

"Meri, I love you so much. I love your innocence, and how you want to hold hands and kiss everybody without a second thought because that's just how you think the world should be. I love that you never match your socks, I love that you make coffee so strong nobody else can stand to drink it, I love that I never know what you're going to do the next day or the next hour or the next five seconds. I love that I have to know dozens of obscure singles by bands nobody remembers just to have the least idea what you're talking about half the time, and that you cry every time Peter Gabriel comes on the radio, and that you never let anybody else define you because you know who you are. I wish I had your confidence, and I wish I'd understood how I really felt instead of blundering around for so long and hurting us both."

At his words, the light continued to pulse with increasing speed. At each heartbeat, the cracks in the gem seemed to heal themselves, until it was whole and shimmering—whole, aside from the single piece of glass still lodged in its center.

David took another chance. He took hold of the glass shard, sharp and jagged and bigger than his palm, and, with all his strength, managed to pull it free. It bore the single word he'd already known it would: *Don't.*

He rested his hand over the single deep crack that remained. "You poor silly bird. You *are* just like one, you know, going and throwing yourself against windowpanes because you can't see what's right in front of you. But I didn't, either, did I?" he admitted. "But you're *my* little bird, my glittering magpie. My starlight," he whispered.

David pressed a kiss to his fingertips, and his fingertips to the spot where the glass had lodged.

It filled in, solidified, and light emanated from the jewel, no longer dark but blindingly bright.

David gripped the glass tight, heedless of the blood on his fingers, a fierce joy in his own heart.

The chamber of mirrors faded away, and he stood in the Erlking's dark lair, surrounded by dying pines.

"It's impossible," growled the Erlking, fumbling with his half-full wineglass. "You were supposed to be stuck in there forever."

So that had been his plan. "Yet here I am," said David. "Will you keep your word or not?"

"You impudent wretch!" The Erlking took a step toward him, reaching out, grasping—and then stopped short, looking sharply past him.

"He has defeated you fairly, according to your own terms," said the Moon Calf, now entering the clearing to join David. He hoped that was a sign of the Erlking's power waning.

"Go and seek your sustenance elsewhere," added the Night Horse, stepping up to stand at the Moon Calf's side. "You are not welcome here."

The Erlking glowered.

In the tense silence, the Night Horse tossed his mane. The Moon Calf pawed the ground. The Forkupine's tines glinted in the moonlight. The stance of the dryads shifted subtly in preparation. The Most Weasel rose up on its hind legs. Even the Mice bared their tiny teeth.

The Erlking charged, razor-sharp claws outstretched.

David was frozen. He had no time to think, no time to do anything except close his eyes and clutch the only weapon he had at hand, the final shard of mirror glass. On sheer instinct, he thrust it forward as the Erlking lunged at him—surely a futile gesture.

The Erlking skidded to a halt, howling in rage. The glass broke apart and fell to pieces, leaving David holding one last remnant, half its original size.

The Erlking drew a long, rasping breath. David forced one eye open, then the other, and took in the truth: it was neither the threat of the jagged glass nor the sight of his own reflection that had stopped him in his tracks, but rather the glowing ruby light that emanated from the remaining mirror shard.

Unable to repress a shudder, the Erlking backed away, one arm shielding his face. "Stop!" he cried. "Take it away! I cannot bear it!"

David still could not find his voice, but the Moon Calf spoke in his stead.

"Begone from here," it ordered, "and do not return to darken this forest with your foul deeds."

"Do not imagine you have seen the last of me," hissed the Erlking, and with as much dignity as he could muster, he turned away and stalked off into the darkness, cloak swirling about him.

David was ready to collapse with relief, but he couldn't, not yet. He returned to Meredith, who still lay peacefully upon the stone table, and nudged his shoulder. “Come on, then, Your Majesty. Your loyal subjects await.”

When he didn’t stir, David tried again, giving him a firmer shake. “Meri, love, wake up. We’re going home.”

But Meredith didn’t open his eyes.

Chapter Twenty-Nine

"You're never going to wake him up that way," the Forkupine piped up.

"How, then?" demanded David. "A potion? A spell? Whatever it is, I'll do it, or find it, or get someone who can." He didn't care if he had to go hunting for the rarest herbs or throw himself upon the mercy of someone with a more withering look of disappointment than Mrs. Jupiter; he'd do whatever it took.

The Forkupine laughed, the sound of a million forks tinkling against a million drinking glasses. "No, silly, it's nothing that complicated—just the standard method." When David only stared in incomprehension, the Forkupine elaborated, "True love's kiss, of course!"

"Oh," said David. "Right. Of course." He looked down at Meredith, then at the assembled residents of the Midnight Wood. Though it would hardly be the first time they'd shared a kiss, the idea of an audience left him self-conscious. "I don't suppose you'd mind—"

"Say no more," said the Forkupine with a knowing wink, and gave David a rather spiky nudge to the ankle. "We'll be waiting just the other side of those trees." To the others, he called, "Clear out, you lot! This is an intimate moment deserving of privacy!"

Only after the group had vacated the clearing did David realize he still held the last piece of splintered mirror glass. Absently, he slipped it into his pocket, then brushed Meredith's bangs aside, leaned down, and kissed his forehead.

Even before David had straightened back up, Meredith's eyelids fluttered, and a bit of color returned to his cheeks. Then his eyes opened wide, and in the next instant, he launched himself upright and threw his arms around David in an embrace that knocked the breath out of him.

"Oh, David, I was so frightened," he whispered, and hid his face against his shoulder.

David held him just as tight and leaned down to kiss the top of his head. "Of course you must have been. But it's all right now." He stroked Meredith's back, trying to return some warmth to the exposed skin that still held a chill from his long repose upon the damp rock. "I'm here, love."

"I know." Meredith looked up at him, eyes the color of the sky after a heavy rain. "I knew all the time my big strong bear would come for me."

"Your—" David was too astonished to echo him; Meredith never ceased to find ways to make him blush.

"You heard me, precious."

It left David just as breathless as the crushing embrace of a moment before. Then, anxiously, he stepped back, holding Meredith at arm's length to look him over. "Are you all right? He didn't hurt you?"

Meredith paused to take stock, then shook his head. "Nah, I don't think so. Just feels as though I've slept for ages. But you're bleeding," he said in dismay, catching hold of David's wrist.

Only now did the sting across his palm register. "Must've been from this." David produced the last shard of mirror glass.

"What's *that*?"

"I pulled it out of your heart." At Meredith's look of alarm, David hastened to add, "Or, rather, a symbolic representation of it on a metaphysical plane."

"Oh." Meredith nodded placidly. "That's all right, then."

David sank down next to him upon the stone. "You weren't quite right, you know. About how your heart looks. It hasn't got all the black spiky bits on."

Meredith plucked the nearest candleflower within reach, turning it slowly as he watched its light fade. Without looking at David, he said, "It feels as though it does, sometimes."

Wrapping an arm around his shoulders, David pulled him close again. "I know. But really it's an enormous jewel, huge and sparkling and filled with light so bright you can scarcely bear to look at it. It was—God, I wish you could have seen it yourself. It was beautiful." He hesitated but decided to press on. "And I think I understand some things about you now that I didn't before."

Meredith tensed against his side and appeared to remain intensely interested in his wilting flower. His voice held a deliberate unconcern as he asked, "Oh, yes? Like what?"

"Mainly that you've been hurt a lot, more than I ever knew."

When that got no reply, David shifted to angle himself toward Meredith, who was now shredding the white petals to bits. He kept his eyes downcast, and David touched a finger to his chin, tilting his face upward until their eyes met.

"Listen. Whatever has happened in the past, whatever you've been going through now, you don't have to deal with it alone." David's heart ached knowing that he'd been trying to, but that wasn't going to be the case any longer. "I can't put everything right, not by myself. I think you're going to need someone more qualified than I am for that, but I'll still be here with you all the way. And not just me—you've got so many people who care about you." People who wouldn't hesitate to show him a bit of extra kindness if only they knew he needed it. "But—"

"But they can't help if they don't know anything's wrong, is that it?" asked Meredith, once again practically reading his mind. He gave David that quick sideways look that he understood at last—the look that meant Meredith was apprehensive of his reaction. "Because there is. A lot that's wrong. I don't know how to talk about these things, David, only after everything you told me trying to wake me up, I can't go letting you down now." He took a deep breath. "I really haven't been all right. For a while. I mean, sometimes I am, but other times there's things I can't get out of my head, even if they happened years ago. These past few weeks, I haven't been able to stop thinking of that night—those men—if you and Mrs. J hadn't shown up when you did. And s-sometimes—sometimes I just feel so sad for no reason at all."

With that confession, he hung his head as though awaiting judgment.

David reached over and took his hand. "Sweetheart, it's all right. No matter what anybody's told you, there's no shame in feeling that way. Nobody is going to hurt you or stop liking you just for admitting that you're not okay or asking for help. Not now. Not anybody who matters. It won't make me love you any less. And I do love you." Though he couldn't help wishing the circumstances were different, David still couldn't stop himself breaking into a smile. "It's nice to be able to say it to you when you're awake."

"I love you, too," said Meredith. Tossing away the remains of his flower, he curled his fingers around David's wrist and rested his head on his shoulder. "God, I do. I'm sorry I made you think I didn't, all because I was too scared to come out and say what I was really getting at."

"I'm no less to blame there," said David. "I should've known better than to believe that's how you'd react if we'd truly understood each other."

"But you do, though. Ordinarily, anyway. You understand me like nobody else ever has."

David hugged Meredith to him, too warm in the humid forest, one bony elbow digging into his ribs, tangled hair catching in his beard—and completely perfect in his arms. "I could hold you like this forever."

"You couldn't," objected Meredith. "Not really forever. You'd have to stop sometime and make tea, and I'd need to look after Bianca, and I hope you'd want to do, you know, *other* things."

"You don't do so well with hyperbole, either, do you, love?"

"Nah, never could get the hang of triangles."

David buried his face in Meredith's hair until he managed to stop laughing. "Okay," he said at last, releasing him and wiping his eyes. "How about I say I'd *like* to do it forever, if I could, allowing appropriate breaks for tea and what-have-you. Is that better?"

Apparently that was no good, either, because Meredith drew back, wrapping his arms around himself and gnawing at his lower lip. After a worrying length of time, he looked up at David with troubled, searching eyes. "Do you mean it? That you could see a *forever* with me? Only—you know I've never been serious with anyone for any length of time to speak of, and I'm not at all sure I know what I'm doing."

"Nonsense," said David. "We've stuck by one another for years now. This is hardly much different, just adding in a few things that we ought to have done long ago." He reached out and took his hand. "When you ask if I see a *forever* with you—" David's voice caught in his throat, but he wasn't going to hold back, not anymore. "Meri, the truth is, I can't imagine one without."

The brightness of his smile—his real smile, not the sharp false one—caught at something in David's heart, caught and squeezed so that he thought he might not be able to bear it. But bear it he did, because Meredith sat up on his knees and reached out to cup David's face with both hands, stroking his beard, tucking a strand of too-long dark hair behind his ear.

"Good," said Meredith. "Because I might need that long to tell you all the reasons I love *you*, after all them things you went and said to me. 'S only fair, after all." He traced a thumb below David's eye, wiping away a tear he hadn't realized he'd shed. "Like how I always feel safe with you, because I know you're always looking out for me even if you pretend you're not. I adore the way you can never quite manage to intimidate anybody until it's actually important, and how you get so embarrassed over the least little things. And you aren't afraid to talk some sense into me sometimes, even if I don't always like it."

"I think you might be overestimating me there," said David, but everything inside him was positively melting into a puddle.

"Well, for instance, you might have convinced me perhaps there *are* some surfaces that just don't need decoupaged."

David never thought he'd see the day when Meredith would admit a thing like that.

"And," he went on in a rush, "I know we tease each other, but you never go after me for anything that really matters, and I've been a bit in love with you ever since I realized how you always make my tea just right, and no matter what you think, you *are* brave and you *are* good enough for me—oh, David, I'm no good with words the way you are."

David had no time to be embarrassed at Meredith having heard those thoughts, too, because right now he was in David's arms and leaning in and—hesitating in uncertainty?

"David? When you said—" Meredith broke off, but whether it was thanks to the obsidian ring, or whether David had figured it out himself, the source of his doubt had become clear.

"You do realize," said David, "when I told you never to kiss me again, that went right out the fucking window the minute I broke my own rule?"

"Oh," said Meredith. "I—I wasn't quite sure."

"You are allowed to kiss me whenever you like, I mean it. In fact, right now, I'd like nothing more."

This time, Meredith didn't hesitate. He pressed the softest, gentlest kiss to David's lips—gentle for about two seconds until he deepened it and tangled a hand into David's hair and didn't let up until they both had to stop for breath.

Afterward, Meredith closed his eyes and rested his forehead against David's. "Can we go home now?"

"Of course." David stood and offered a hand to help him to his feet. "Although you ought to address your subjects first. I'd never have made it here without them, and they were quite adamant about getting their king back. Or queen, in the case of the Mice," he added.

Meredith grinned. "That's all right, I can be both. Or maybe something in between." Then, sobering, he asked, "But, David? Is that—I mean, I know you only like one sort of thing, but I'm a bit more than just one thing. Do you mind that?"

Had David been asked in the abstract, he honestly would not have been sure of his answer. But in this particular case, there was no question. "Well, it's as you said, isn't it?" He reached out and brushed a stray lock of hair from Meredith's face. "In the end, you're still just you."

At the edge of the clearing, the dry brown needles had dropped away from the fir trees, replaced by the sharp green spikes of new ones emerging—the work, David suspected, of the sycamore dryads.

When he and Meredith stepped through the trees, hand in hand, the leader of the Mice bowed low. "Welcome back, Your Majesty."

"Oh, now, none of that," said Meredith. "You know I don't hold with such things. But thank you all the same. I'm glad to be back, too."

"Pleased to meet you at last," said the Forkupine, giving a little bow.

"Oh, *hello*, you're new." Meredith knelt down to greet him, and it was difficult for David to guess which of them was more delighted as Meredith cooed over the Forkupine and stroked his tines. The Mice scurried up to perch on his shoulder, and the Most Weasel, taking a liking to David, came and sat up expectantly in front of him until he consented to give it a few pats between the ears.

"You will come back and play with us again soon, won't you?" asked the Moon Calf in low, mellow tones.

"Course I will, if you'll have me." Meredith carefully returned the

Midnight Mice to the forest floor, and as he rose to his feet, the dryads swept in to place a circlet of sweet woodruff upon his head.

"Much better," said the Forkupine with a nod of approval.

"Oh, thank you," said Meredith. "I'd been meaning to come and find some for ages."

The Night Horse whinnied, and the group fell silent. "The time has come for you both to depart. You have business to attend to beyond our borders."

Meredith nodded. "I expect you're right." Turning to his assembled subjects, he said, "Weasel, you can be king while I'm gone—or queen, if you'd rather—but do let the Forkupine have a turn, too."

The Most Weasel clapped its paws joyfully and scampered over to Meredith, who stroked it behind the ears.

"If you're ready," said the Night Horse, "I shall carry you to the edge of the Wood."

The journey was a quick one. David held tight to Meredith as the scenery rushed by. Though it would have been easy to hide his face against his shoulder, this time David found he had no desire to block out the sights around him. Undeniably, the Midnight Wood was an eerie and dangerous place, but it likewise held beauty and magic and creatures who had banded together to come to their aid, and it no longer frightened him the way it once had.

Before he knew it, the Night Horse was graciously lowering himself to allow them to dismount.

"Thank you," said David.

"Yeah, thanks," echoed Meredith, adjusting the ragged hem of his skirt as he stood.

"The Moon Calf and I shall expect you to tea this week," said the Night Horse.

"I'll bring along some Battenberg cake," Meredith promised, "so long as I can get it to turn out right this time."

David cleared his throat. "Er, pardon me, Mr. Night Horse, but I thought perhaps if you didn't mind—if you all didn't mind," he ventured, turning to Meredith, "it might be all right if I came along, too?"

Meredith's eyes lit up. "David, of course you're invited! I never thought you'd want to."

"The consort of our queen is always welcome in the Midnight Wood," added the Night Horse.

David inclined his head. "Much obliged."

"But now I must be getting back," said the Night Horse, "and the two of you must be getting on."

OUTSIDE THE MIDNIGHT Wood, the sun was high in the cloudless sky—certainly well past daybreak. The grass was warm and fragrant in the gentle breeze, and Meredith took David's hand as the two of them started up the hill.

"It must be past noon," said David in surprise. Of course the passage of time in the Wood did not correspond to that of the outside world, but he couldn't help but wonder whether the Mice hadn't adjusted the clock to give him a bit of extra help meeting the Erlking's one-hour deadline. "I'd wager you've missed your brunch appointment."

"S'pose so," mused Meredith. "Well, no great loss there. I will give Florian a call here in a bit, though. To tell him I won't go to his bachelor party tonight, *or* his wedding." With a note of defiance, he went on, "I—I don't have to, just because he says so."

"You don't have to do anything just because I say so, either."

Meredith rolled his eyes. "David, I have never in my life done a single thing just because you told me to. Mostly I don't do what you want at all."

"That's true enough," said David, but he still couldn't escape the nagging tendrils of guilt at the back of his mind. "But you agreed to be in this wedding because of me."

"That was never because I thought I *had* to, even if you were a bit pushy about it. But that day you seemed so miserable, and I *was* partly to blame, and I just . . . I wanted to make you happy," Meredith said softly.

When the squeeze in David's chest let up enough for him to speak again, he said, "I ought to have stepped in when I saw how he and the rest of them spoke to you. I had half convinced myself that I must be misunderstanding, but I was wrong, and I'm sorry I didn't."

Meredith shook his head. "'S all right. You was just giving me the chance to stand up for myself, is all. I *wanted* to, only I didn't quite manage it. Didn't think it'd hit me so hard seeing everyone again at once. But I am going to now. I'm going to call up Florian and tell him to count me out—and Adalynn, too, to make sure she knows what she's getting into." He looked over at David. "I think I *have* been a bit selfish that way, not thinking what it could mean for her."

"You've got a bit of time for that," David reassured him. "For now, the first order of business: the moment we get home, you are getting out of that dress—"

"Oh?" said Meredith hopefully.

"And straight into a hot bath while I put the kettle on."

"Shame, I thought perhaps you had something different in mind."

"That," said David, letting his voice drop to a growl, "comes later." On impulse, he swept Meredith up into his arms, carrying him without much difficulty. "In fact, the sooner we get there—what?" he interrupted himself as Meredith gazed up at him with a look of utter reverence.

"Do you know how long I've been waiting for you to do that?"

"Probably about as long as I've been trying to convince myself I didn't want to," David admitted. "Incidentally, thank you for the flowers."

"Oh, I thought you didn't like them," said Meredith in relief. Wrapping his arms around David, he leaned in to rest his face in the crook of his neck. "I'm glad you did."

"I like them very much," said David truthfully, "only I didn't catch on at first that they were meant for me."

Meredith didn't raise his head, but murmured, "You thought I'd send myself flowers?"

"Okay, first off, don't you dare act as if that's out of the realm of possibility, and second—no. I thought someone had sent them to you. I never imagined myself as the sort to end up with a secret admirer."

"Course you are. Really," said Meredith indignantly, "how anybody could ever think *you're* unremarkable is beyond me."

"Yes, well, perhaps there is—" David broke off as they reached the crest of the hill.

Waiting on the back deck of Midnight Cottage stood Sylvania Holland and Mrs. Jupiter. In the witch's arms, Bianca began to yip and struggle.

David's good mood faded, replaced with a degree of apprehension. He set Meredith back on his feet.

"Come on," said Meredith. "Whatever's happened, suppose we'd best face it." He took David's hand, and they started toward the house together.

Chapter Thirty

"Well," said David weakly, "I take it you found my note, Mrs. J."

Mrs. Jupiter set Bianca down, and the Chihuahua immediately took off at a run toward them. "I did," she said, "but not before Mrs. Holland came to tell me you were in trouble."

"We were," said David, "but it's all right now. The worst is over, anyway."

Meredith leaned down to let Bianca leap into his arms, cradling her and whispering reassurances as he and David ascended the low stairs onto the deck. David grimaced as he caught sight of their reflections in the sliding doors. They both looked much the worse for wear: his pajama trousers were torn and muddy, his forearm was scraped raw, Meredith's dress was in tatters, and both of them were covered in scratches and smudges of dirt.

"We're sorry to have caused any alarm," said David, "but as you can see, everything is—"

He broke off as voices carried up the hill from the direction of Bednarek's cottage. In the next moment, three new figures came into view as they ascended the path—Bednarek, Cartier, and Kinley, who gesticulated emphatically with the thick sheaf of papers in his hand.

"—according to the Endangered Species Act, not to mention that the

Wood has officially been listed on the National Register of Magical Places since Wednesday. No way in hell are you or anybody else putting a housing development there!"

"Indeed," said Cartier with a placid nod. "In fact, that's just what I came here to discuss with Mr. Bednarek. I take environmental preservation very seriously, you know."

"Yeah, well—well—" Kinley faltered, then deflated. With evident reluctance, he allowed, "I guess we're in agreement there."

"Such big fuss over such little mice," lamented Bednarek. With a resigned shrug, he said, "But I suppose, if they are special mice, is nothing to be done."

Then Kinley caught sight of Meredith and David and rushed over to them, his exclamation nearly drowning out the sound of a vehicle pulling into the driveway. "Oh, *shit*, what happened to you guys? You okay?"

Meredith just had time to let Bianca escape before Kinley seized him in a hug—and then, to David's surprise, pulled him into the embrace as well.

"We're all right," said Meredith, then amended conscientiously, "Unharmed, anyway. You and me will talk later, but short version—you probably owe me that ass-kicking you promised not too long ago."

As car doors slammed shut and footsteps sounded on gravel, the three of them broke apart, though Kinley kept an arm slung over Meredith's shoulders as they all turned.

From around the corner of the house emerged Florian and Adalynn, who both stopped short by the rhododendron bushes.

"Dad?" said Adalynn in surprise, and Cartier raised a hand in greeting as he and Bednarek proceeded along the edge of the deck.

"Oh, for fuck's sake," muttered Florian. He wiped a hand down his face. "Sorry, Ada. I should've known coming here was a bad idea."

Adalynn tilted her head. "What do you mean?"

Kinley's expression hardened. "Hey, you got a problem, man?"

The sound of Florian's scoff was unmistakable, and the expression that passed over his face was unsettling in its familiarity—the same sharp sneer David was used to seeing when Meredith was in one of his rare vicious moods.

Kinley looked as if he wanted to say more, but something unspoken passed between him and Meredith, and he nodded and kept silent.

Meredith stepped forward to face his brother. "*Do* you?" he asked.

"What do you think?" Florian's voice was tight, laden with condescension.

Adalynn frowned. "Of course not," she said. "We were worried when you didn't turn up at brunch or answer your phone."

Florian pinched the bridge of his nose. "No, you know what? Fine. You're right." From where he stood in the garden, he had to look up to meet Meredith's level gaze, and for an instant, hatred glittered hard and fierce in his eyes. "I am *sick* of your shit."

Though Florian's tone was harsh, Meredith didn't flinch. Perhaps it was no more than a flight of fancy, but David would have sworn there was something new and regal in his posture. In spite of the absurdity, in spite of his crown being nothing more than a circlet of sweet woodruff not yet in bloom, David felt as though he really were standing in the presence of the ruler of the Midnight Wood.

"Florian—" Adalynn reached for his hand, but he shook off her touch.

"No, this has been a long time coming." He came a step nearer and made an abrupt, violent gesture in Meredith's direction. "I mean, what the hell kind of stunt are you trying to pull here? First you make a scene at my fiancée's bridal shower—"

"What?" said Adalynn in confusion. "No, there was nothing like—"

Florian went on, talking over her. "You make a goddamn spectacle of yourself parading around like *that* in public, you don't even bother to show up this morning so all anybody talks about is *Oh, where's your brother at*, then come to find you here after you've obviously been out all night doing God knows what, and hanging all over this—"

"Careful." Meredith's voice was a knife's edge.

"*This guy*," spat Florian, his outstretched hand now jabbing in Kinley's direction. "So, what, he's your boyfriend?"

The final word held contempt. Though Adalynn said nothing this time, she now regarded Florian with cool appraisal—a mirror of her father's expression some distance away.

"No," said Meredith, and the moment he reached behind him, David stepped up to catch his hand and stand at his side. "David is."

David couldn't deny taking a certain dark satisfaction in the way Florian looked as if he were about to choke on his own bile.

"And," Meredith went on, "I've had just about all I'm going to take from you."

"*You've* had enough?" repeated Florian in disbelief.

"I have." This time, there was no trace of broken glass, no forced false smile at all, only calm self-assurance. "I had this idea that I was going to tell you off, but it really doesn't matter anymore. I know I'm not blameless when it comes to everything that's happened between you and me, and you can take your pick from about a dozen reasons why I'm not what Mom and Dad wanted, but you're not going to come here and go on speaking to me the way you have been, because I don't deserve that."

"Oh, here we go." Florian ran an exasperated hand through his own straw-blond hair, leaving it spiky and askew. "Playing the victim like usual whenever you can't handle someone calling you out on your selfish bullshit."

"You're right, I have been selfish, actually," said Meredith. "Adalynn, I owe you an apology, for not trying to get you to see what sort of man you're marrying. I know there's no reason for you to take my word over his when we barely know each other, but I still should have tried."

"For Christsake!" Florian exploded, and advanced toward him, but stopped when Kinley, too, came forward to stand at Meredith's other side. Bianca ducked through his legs and stood between him and Florian, growling.

Adalynn's uneasy glance traveled from Florian to her father; a crease formed between her eyebrows. "What exactly would you have told me?"

"He doesn't—" Meredith faltered at last. "He isn't—I mean, if it'd b-been only—I sh-should've—"

"Don't see how you expect to tell anybody anything when you can't hardly talk as it is," taunted Florian, heedless of Maitland Cartier's steely gaze resting upon him.

David placed a hand at Meredith's waist. Kinley gave his shoulder an encouraging squeeze. "Hey, sis, you got this. And we've all got your back."

"If you'll excuse my intrusion," said Mrs. Jupiter, who up to now had observed the proceedings in silence, "I believe I can aid in clearing up a few matters."

All eyes turned to her.

"Now, Meredith," she said, "some time ago I bestowed upon you an enchanted vessel for making persistence-of-memory potion. Did you fill it as I instructed?"

Meredith looked lost. "I d-don't think—"

"That blue glass bottle you were so taken with," supplied David.

"Oh! I did, yeah."

Mrs. Jupiter nodded. "Would you fetch it for me, dear?"

Meredith slipped past them into the house, and David couldn't bring himself to voice a word of protest at the dirt he was doubtless tracking through the living room.

"And, David," said Mrs. Jupiter briskly. "Unless I am mistaken, you have about your person a piece of mind mirror, do you not?"

"I—" David patted down his pockets and produced the shard of glass, though he hadn't remembered returning it there. "I do."

He placed it in her outstretched hand.

Sylvania Holland now pushed herself off the deck rail. "And one of you is still in possession of the ring of revelation I gave to you, correct?"

With some effort, David twisted the ring from his finger and handed it over as well.

"Oh, come *on*." Florian folded his arms. "I don't know what you people are getting at, but my brother, he's—Ada, you don't seriously buy this crap, do you?"

Her voice was strangely distant as she said, "I'm not sure what to think anymore, Florian."

Meredith emerged bearing the vinegar cruet, which he gave to Mrs. Jupiter.

"I doubt you will like what happens next," she said, "though I promise you you'll be better off for it. Still, I'd sooner proceed with your permission than without."

He nodded, face pale but determined. "You have it."

"Thank you. I don't wish to subject you to a full parade of miseries, but I think a few recent events will suffice."

Mrs. Jupiter and Sylvania held a brief whispered conference, exchanged nods, and began to recite an incantation.

The mirror shard puffed into a glittering fog, and was soon permeated by a dim, eerie light that emanated from the obsidian ring. At the same moment, Mrs. Jupiter opened the bottle, poured a generous amount of clear liquid into her hand, and raised her fist to let a small trickle rain down onto Meredith's head. Then she whirled and flicked the remaining droplets into Florian's face, raising her voice along with Sylvania's to drown out his sputtered protest.

This time, the mirror cloud did not dissipate but hung in the air as if frozen in place by the ring's light. It expanded, flowed together, and solidified into a great glass globe floating overhead. Within the sphere, an image took shape, flickering as though from an old film projector: Florian and Meredith standing in the driveway of Midnight Cottage.

The shade of Florian in the sphere spoke, voice crackling but clearly audible as he berated Meredith with the same cruel, hideous words David had seen littering the mind realm. Though he'd already known, it was still excruciating to watch it play out in real time, and he couldn't bear it when past Meredith's eyes fell closed in defeated acceptance as Florian spoke the lie that David was ashamed of him.

David seized hold of the real-and-present Meredith's hand. "I'm *not*," he said, louder than he meant to. "Never."

When sphere Florian snatched the daisies from Meredith's head and flung them to the ground, Kinley started toward the real Florian, but Mrs. Jupiter placed a restraining hand on his arm.

"If he thinks he can get away with that—" he fumed. "Nobody fucks with my best friend like that."

"Just wait," she said, and he reluctantly acquiesced.

David couldn't deny that he felt the same urge, unaccustomed though he was to any violent impulses outside the realm of sport, but giving Florian the beating he deserved wouldn't set right the damage already done. Instead, he squeezed Meredith's hand tighter—a little too tight, judging by the way he winced.

"Sorry," whispered David, letting up on his grip.

Adalynn took a step away from Florian, and Cartier's critical look had solidified into the same one he'd fixed upon Steve Corner the night before.

"Look, I don't know what kind of hocus-pocus garbage you've cooked up, but that's not how it went," insisted Florian. His cheeks had colored an ugly, blotchy pink. "Mere's always been oversensitive. Goes taking everything out of proportion."

No one else said a word, and the scene in the sphere shifted to the living room of Midnight Cottage. Another heated exchange, Bianca's ferocious barking, Florian slapping Meredith's coffee cup from his hand, and green-glazed porcelain shattering against the wall.

David could only kick himself for not having caught on.

Another shift in the sphere—the same room on still an earlier day. Florian paced past the impression of gingham curtains, but this time it was Meredith who spoke first, asking the wary question: "Why'd you go and tell Genevieve you'd asked me to be in your wedding when you never did?"

"Christsake, Mere, you think I *wanted* you involved?" Florian gestured in frustration. "Genevieve had to go running her mouth like usual, so now my fiancée is asking questions about why you never come around, and I do not need this. I swear to God, if you pull any of your usual shit around Adalynn, or in front of her *dad*—"

Meredith raised both hands in a conciliatory gesture. "I won't cause any p-problems, I swear."

"No, you won't," agreed Florian, his voice positively venomous. "You're gonna show up when and where I tell you to, you're gonna lose all this sparkly shit—" He gave the collection of bracelets on Meredith's wrist a contemptuous smack, making him flinch away in alarm, then resumed pacing. "You're gonna keep your dumbass mouth shut, and you are *not* gonna screw this up for me, you got it? The last thing I need is for them to think whatever's the matter with *you* runs in the family."

"But w-w-what—"

"Would you spit it out already?"

"W-what if it *does*?"

Florian whirled back toward him, and even in the flickering light of the sphere, those same red blotches of fury showed up clearly on his face. "*What?*"

"What if you do have kids, and they're n-not quite the way you expect—" Meredith doubled over with a gasp of pain as Florian's elbow slammed into his side. Somewhere out of sight, Bianca barked furiously.

"If you *ever* say a goddamn word about my wife or my future children again—" Florian broke off at the sound of a creaking floorboard.

"David?" called Meredith. The desperate, futile hope in his expression was horrible, and worse was the way it faded in the silence that followed.

David felt ill. This was one of the worst things he had ever done, even if he hadn't known he was doing it, even if he had gone on directly to the front door. What had been thirty more seconds for him must have been endless for Meredith.

"That's enough, I think," said present Meredith. Mrs. Jupiter nodded. At a wave of her hand, the sphere dissolved.

David could do nothing but wrap his arms around him and hug him close. "Meri, why—" His voice broke. "Why didn't you tell me?"

But he had tried to, David realized. That night in the bathroom when he'd seen the bruise and assumed it to be from Brian, Meredith had started to contradict him before David had cut him off.

Meredith kept silent, but leaned back into David and reached up to take his hand.

Adalynn had fled to her father's side, tears flowing down her cheeks. "Florian, I—I don't even know what to say."

"I do," said Cartier, much to David's surprise. "And I think that's just a despicable way to treat anyone, let alone your own sibling. Ada, you're a grown woman and your affairs are your own to manage, but this marriage has no support from me."

"Don't worry, Dad," said Adalynn, "because it won't be happening." She tore the engagement ring from her finger as if she couldn't get it off fast enough, and returned to Florian only to shove it into his hand.

"Ada, listen—"

"There's nothing else to discuss," said Adalynn.

"*Listen*," insisted Florian, catching her by the wrist, "you aren't gonna find anybody else who treats you the way I do, and if you call this off—"

"Let *go* of me."

"—I won't be taking you back, so think long and hard—"

"Hey!" Kinley started forward without hesitation. "The lady said to back off."

David, moving alongside him, said sharply, "We'll have none of that," at the same moment Cartier said in a terrible, imperious tone that never rose in volume, "*Take your hands off my daughter.*"

Seething, Florian let go and took a step back, hands raised. "Whatever. I'm out of here."

"I think that's for the best," said Meredith.

"And you're not welcome back," David called after him.

Chapter Thirty-One

A tense silence fell over them, broken only by Florian's truck roaring down the driveway, tires spitting gravel. Cartier placed a protective hand on Adalynn's shoulder. Bednarek, who'd not said a word since his arrival, looked distinctly uncomfortable at the edge of the crowd. Even Sylvania Holland's usually serene expression had turned solemn.

It was Kinley who spoke first. "That guy's a real asshole. Good riddance, if you ask me." He turned to Meredith, and his voice was gruffer than usual when he said, "If he can't see what a great little brother he's got, that's his loss." With that declaration, he hastened to occupy himself lighting a cigarette, and then, with the air of remembering his manners, he offered the pack to Adalynn.

She shook her head, gazing down the lane as though Florian's presence still lingered. "I had no idea," she said. "Not the first clue. He'd never so much as raised his voice at me until today, but . . ." She trailed off and shook her head again. "I'm sorry. And thank you both."

"No," said Meredith, "it's me who should be sorry." He hesitated, then addressed her father. "And, Cartier—if you hold it against us for not saying anything before, I don't blame you, but please don't take it out on David. He's not responsible for Florian."

That had been the last thing on David's mind, but now he braced himself for the inevitable fallout. He'd made an impression on Cartier, all right, and was about to be dismissed by him personally—either for having broken up his daughter's impending marriage, which he wasn't sorry for, or for not having done so sooner, which he was. Somehow he found that it didn't matter to him now nearly as much as it had a month ago—now that he had his priorities in order.

But what Cartier said was "Neither are you." In response to their evident astonishment, he continued, "Perhaps it comes as a surprise, but I myself know well enough how difficult and complicated these things can be. All the same, I'm grateful for you speaking up when you did, and I'm sure my daughter will be, too, once she gets over the shock. By the way, David," he added, "I realize this isn't the time, but you and I do need to have a chat this week."

So that was it, then. David nodded. "I understand," he said, at the same time Meredith protested, "But you just said—!"

Cartier recoiled as though shocked by the very notion. "Oh, no, you misunderstand me. I have no intention of letting you go, not when I'm going to need sensible, reliable people like you on my team. Especially now that there are some major changes coming to the Corner Store."

"Changes?" repeated David, still trying to make sense of it all. He wasn't being fired. Cartier thought he was sensible and reliable. It was gratifying, to be sure, but again, hardly the matter of grave import he'd previously imagined.

Cartier glanced around. Adalynn had now been drawn into conversation with Sylvania and Mrs. Jupiter, and Kinley was talking to—or, rather, talking *at* Bednarek, undoubtedly giving voice to some of his stronger opinions on landlords.

Satisfied that the conversation was private, Cartier said, "Well, it'll be public news in a few days anyway. Steve Corner is out. I can't say I was impressed with what I saw last night, and it turns out Mr. Pangolin had a number of similar concerns, with quite the paper trail to back them up. It was a pretty lengthy list, all told. But," he said, giving David an amiable clap on the shoulder, "we'll talk more about that later. I imagine you and your partner have some things to discuss now, as do Adalynn and I."

"Mr. Cartier!" called Mrs. Jupiter.

He turned. "Ma'am?"

"Mrs. Holland and I are retiring to my cottage for a cup of tea, if I might take the liberty of inviting you and your daughter along? You've both had quite the stressful morning, and I daresay a nice calming tisane would do you both some good."

"Well, I—" Cartier looked to Adalynn, then to Mrs. Jupiter, adorned with her usual variety of amulets and crystals, and nodded. "I expect you know best."

"And you, too," Mrs. Jupiter told Kinley as the Cartiers followed Sylvania down the path.

He balked at the invitation. "You want me to come to tea with—with that—" David knew with certainty that he was on the verge of saying *capitalist pig*, but Mrs. Jupiter interrupted.

"With the business and community leader who I'm sure is eager to hear more from the enterprising young man who spearheaded the preservation of the Midnight Wood, yes." Mrs. Jupiter shooed him along after the Cartiers.

"*Not you*," she hissed at Bednarek as he attempted to join the procession. "*You* have a few things to answer for yourself. Oh, and I'd nearly forgotten." She produced a jar of healing salve and tossed it to David.

"Thanks, Mrs. J."

She nodded to him, eyes twinkling, and took her leave.

"Ah. Boys." Bednarek shuffled over to them, quite shamefaced. "I admit, my approach to whole business of property sale perhaps neglected to consider bigger picture. Was not kindest way to treat reliable tenants—or friends. After so long, you are both, I hope, my friends. I offer humble apologies. And, Schwarzy, as for your brother—" He narrowed his eyes. "He ever comes back, you tell me and I will—how do you say? Throw the motherfucker out on his ass, no?"

Meredith grinned. "You've got it exactly right," he said, and for once, David had to agree.

"Speaking of property, Mr. Bednarek," he said. "Of course there must be all sorts of red tape involved now when it comes to the question of the Midnight Wood itself, but there's nothing to stop you selling the cottage, is there?"

The landlord's chagrined expression returned. "No, no, I assure you, I do not plan—"

"No," David interrupted, "I meant to us. Hypothetically," he added, casting a searching glance at Meredith. "Just a thought."

"Do you mean it? You'd really want to stay here?" Meredith caught hold of both David's hands. "With the Wood and the Mice and—oh, David, *can* we?"

"I realize there'd be a lot to discuss beforehand," said David, "but if you like the idea, and everything works out—well, Bednarek, what do you say? Would you consider it?"

"That," said Bednarek with his most cherubic smile, "is distinct possibility. You two talk over, and come see me, yes?" He shook both their hands and departed.

AT LAST THE two of them were alone. There were so many things David wanted to say, and they all competed for attention in his mind at once. (Briefly, he wondered whether this was how Meredith felt all the time.)

David exhaled a forceful breath, willing some of the tension to leave his body. Meredith had wandered over to the edge of the deck, looking off in the direction of the Midnight Wood, Bianca at his feet.

David joined him, resting both hands at his waist. "Meri, if I'd known—if any of us had known—"

"I know," said Meredith. "I do, now. It means more than you can know." He sank back into David's embrace and tipped his head back to rest on his shoulder. "Do you know, I thought to begin with I wouldn't be able to bear it, everybody watching all that? I mean, I was quite ashamed—here's me, thirty years old and still scared of my brother like when we were kids. Only now that it's all out in the open, would you believe I sort of feel better? Relieved, in a way."

"Well, I'm glad of that, love," said David, his voice husky. "Come on, then. Let's go inside."

Meredith twisted around to face him and pout. "Not going to carry me over the threshold?"

David huffed out a soft laugh of relief, and the rest of the tension dissolved. This was more familiar territory. "After you've already gone and tracked your filthy footprints all through the house? I should think not."

But he lifted him into his arms anyway and carried him into Midnight Cottage—into their home. It had been all along, even if he'd been too stubborn to see it.

After just enough of a pause for David to close the door behind Bianca and for Meredith to toss his woodruff crown onto the kitchen table ("I *am* going to start the May wine today, I swear it"), they proceeded down the hall to the first-floor bath.

As David fetched more towels from the linen cupboard, Meredith said, "I did mean to tell you eventually, you know. After this morning, I mean, only there were so many things to say—still are, really—and I never expected him to show up like that."

"It's all right," said David. At Meredith's skeptical look, he said, "It is." Maybe David didn't have firsthand experience, but he knew Cartier's words to be true, that it *was* difficult and complicated, and he himself hadn't made it any easier. "Of course I wish you'd felt all along that you could tell me—I wish I'd shown you I was listening. But I certainly don't blame you, and you don't owe me a justification. But right now," he said firmly, "you need a bath."

"So do you."

The insinuation was clear. David cast a doubtful look over the bathtub. "We'd never fit." There was barely enough room for him on his own as it was.

"Shower, then?" suggested Meredith hopefully.

In most cases, David did not particularly enjoy sharing the shower with anyone, no matter what opportunities it afforded, but these were special circumstances. They must be, because he found that he meant it when he answered, "I'd like that."

They shed the remains of their clothing, and as the shower warmed up, Meredith let David comb the worst of the tangles from his hair. Beneath the water, there was no need to speak as they washed the sweat and grime from each other. Meredith's touch was as tender as could be as he lathered soap over David's skin, and he made vague apologetic sounds every time his fingers ghosted over his various abrasions.

When David winced at the water hitting his skinned elbow, Meredith leaned down to kiss it better.

"I appreciate the sentiment, love, but I think that ointment from Mrs. J will be a bit more effective."

David let him do it anyway. Meredith pressed the gentlest kisses to each of his wounds, no matter how minor, and David found himself doing the same in return. Perhaps there was a kind of magic in the innocent optimism of the gesture, or perhaps it was only the psychological reset that resulted from immersing themselves in hot water, but over the next several minutes, the awfulness of thc past hour gradually faded away.

Inevitably, both their hands began to wander, and soon enough their first few chaste kisses turned heated and stinging.

Backing Meredith into a corner, David seized a handful of his steamfrizzed hair and tipped his head back to kiss along his throat, but paused to ask, "Sure you're feeling up to it?"

"I am," said Meredith, and then, with a predatory grin, "Besides, as I recall, I made a promise to you regarding the kitchen table."

"I have been meaning to collect on that, you know." David flicked one of his nipple rings, drawing a hiss from him—at which point he found himself spun around and pressed against the shower tiles.

"Then again," said Meredith, his voice dropping low and sending shivers down David's spine, "I'm not so sure the poor table could stand up to it. Might have to relocate, what do you think?"

David didn't know if he was capable of thinking, not with Meredith dragging his nails down his sides and trailing little bites down his back and the very definite hardness pressing against his ass. "Bed," he managed.

Somehow, after a cursory effort at drying off, they made it across the hall. In no time, David found himself pushed onto the bed so Meredith could resume kissing his way down his back, lower and lower, until he nudged David's legs apart, and then lower still until everything faded into static aside from a single white-hot point of contact.

Over the next eternity, or possibly the next few minutes, David became distantly aware of several things: Meredith lifting David's hips from the bed so he couldn't make contact with the mattress, the sting of nails pressing into his skin, a stream of undignified sounds and broken encouragements in a voice that sounded suspiciously like his own. Tingling sparks danced through his extremities, and if he hadn't been more or less horizontal already, he was sure he would have collapsed.

Meredith stopped.

David came back to himself gradually as Meredith rubbed his back and murmured soothing nonsense. His balls throbbed, everything below his waist ached with need, and his entire body gave the occasional electrified twitch.

"Feeling all right?"

David's voice came out a wordless growl. Finally, he managed, "That was—you are—you'd better only have stopped because you're going to fuck me now."

"I stopped because I thought you might actually pass out," said Meredith, "but yeah, course I will. So long as you want me to."

David could only gesture in the direction of the dresser, but Meredith understood, found the necessary supplies, made short work of putting them to use, and then—

David groaned with relief at the sensation of being filled. Having Meredith inside him was exactly what he needed.

"Oh, God, that's it," breathed Meredith. His movements were slow and shallow, and David needed more. Needed him closer, no matter the sheer impossibility of it. Though Meredith's hands were gentle on his back, his touch seemed to singe David's skin with every caress, and he couldn't get enough.

"Go on," he urged breathlessly. No—in all honesty, David was *begging*. "Go on and fuck me like you promised, so I still feel it all day tomorrow."

"You sure?" Meredith leaned down, and—*God*, he was licking the sweat from between his shoulder blades, which David should have found revolting, but instead, it made him shudder.

"More than sure. *Please*."

"All right, but tell me if it gets to be too much." His movements picked up, hips slamming against David's ass, cock buried inside him as deep as he could go. That was better—and better still when Meredith adjusted his position a short time later.

"There, *that's* it, isn't it, precious?"

In spite of Meredith's insufferable smugness, David could only cry out his approval over and over, and when at last Meredith reached around to stroke him, David simply shattered.

"Oh, *fuck*," said Meredith. It took only a moment more before he tensed and trembled against David, and then neither could hold themselves up any longer, and they collapsed together onto the mattress.

After a time, David found the energy to turn over and draw Meredith into his arms.

“I’ve got to get up,” he protested, though he made no effort to resist David’s embrace.

“Mm, I don’t think so.” David pulled him closer and buried his face in damp hair that still held the faint scent of sweet woodruff. “What for?”

“Practicalities,” said Meredith with surprising delicacy—which he promptly undermined by gesturing downward.

David grimaced. “I understood, thanks.”

“And I’m dying for some coffee. Haven’t had a cup all morning.”

“Oh, I see how it is,” grumbled David, and held him all the tighter.

Meredith laughed and nuzzled at his throat. “What, just can’t get enough of me?”

“No,” said David, and pressed a kiss to his temple. “You know I can’t.”

Epilogue

EIGHT MONTHS LATER

David made his way through the crowded hotel ballroom, following the pull of his bracelet. Flickering electric candlelight played over the stars and baubles adorning the Christmas trees that towered in every corner, and an instrumental recording of a holiday pop song mingled with the low hum of conversation.

Beaming as she caught sight of him, Adalynn Cartier glided past in what had once been intended as her wedding gown, now reimagined in black and crimson, the lace artfully slashed and twisted. Faced with the options of forfeiting her deposit for the wedding venue or postponing her reservation, she had chosen the latter, and opted to throw a formal, if somewhat early, Christmas ball. Meredith had taken to privately referring to it as a not-marrying-Florian party, and David couldn't disagree that was reason enough to celebrate. (Not to mention it had given Meredith a perfectly good excuse to go and buy that emerald-green ball gown after all.)

David continued on his way, catching Mrs. Jupiter's eye as she led Maitland Cartier through a complicated foxtrot, and exchanging a somewhat cooler nod with Genevieve and her fiancé. Stepping around an elderly couple swaying in time to the music, David caught a brief glimpse of Harriet near the opposite end of the room. He waved, and a smile crept over his face as she failed entirely to notice him, caught up as she was dancing with Sylvania Holland.

At last David reached the far side of the room and slipped out onto the terrace. A short distance away, Meredith leaned against the wrought iron railing between two potted cedars and gazed up at the full moon, shoulders bare in spite of the early December chill.

David slowed his approach. He'd intended to take him to task for vanishing after being left on his own for no more than a few moments, but there was an air of melancholy about him that caused the teasing admonition to dissolve unspoken.

Coming up behind him, David slipped his arms around his waist. "Hey, little bird. Feel like telling me what's on your mind?"

"Oh, nothing, really—wait. No." With a rustle of satin, Meredith slipped from his grasp and turned to face him. "Tamara says I've got to talk about these things." Tamara was the therapist he'd been seeing every week since the summer, who'd been helping him sort out how to handle his lower moods. (David had seen one himself for a time, initially in solidarity, but had found that it helped him to talk through a few things after all.)

"Go on."

Meredith traced over the carved dragon motif of his jade bracelet for a moment before he continued. "It *isn't* anything major, only it was getting to be a bit much with all the Christmassy things. This time of year—s'pose it's not really the best memories for me," he admitted.

David caught hold of his hand. "Then we'll have to make some better ones for you, together." He already had a few plans for doing exactly that when they visited his family in Swansea in a few weeks: Early-morning walks under the gray sky of the deserted winter beach. Returning to warm up with tea in front of the hearth, wrapped in a shared blanket.

Christmas dinner crowded around the tiny table that his father insisted served him perfectly well during the rest of the year. (Ruth, now a vegetarian herself, had already insisted on personally making nut roast as an alternative to the traditional turkey.) "And, Meri? Thanks for telling me."

"Course." After a moment of silence, Meredith, in his usual fashion, leapt to an altogether different topic. "Hang on, I thought when you went off a bit ago it was to get more drinks." His gaze traveled pointedly to David's empty hands. "What've you been up to?"

"You'll see," said David, "but you'll have to come back inside before it's too late." He had, in fact, been performing a minor act of bribery upon the DJ, but he didn't intend to give away the game just yet. "Unless you'd rather not, of course."

"Nah, I don't mind anymore. Just needed to get away for a moment, but it's all right now." He took hold of David's hand and led the way back, pausing outside the doors to steal a kiss. It went on long enough to leave him suitably dazed and compliant as Meredith dragged him back into the warm light of the ballroom and into a dance that didn't begin to match the tempo of the current music.

"So when do I find out—" Meredith broke off, distracted from his would-be interrogation as Adalynn and Kinley drifted by in a graceful waltz. The latter appeared slightly terrified, holding on to her as carefully as though she were made of glass.

Then Meredith caught his eye, and Kinley broke into a rare smile.

Once they were out of earshot, Meredith said, "They make a lovely couple, don't you think?"

David started. "*Are* they? A couple, I mean?"

"She finally asked him out this week, and it's about time, too." At David's questioning look, Meredith went on in exasperation, "Oh, really, David, you're hopeless. Haven't you seen them making eyes at each other at the Rat Cellar for ages now?"

In truth, he hadn't. He supposed he'd been too astonished at seeing Adalynn Cartier become a regular at the Rat Cellar to take note of anything further.

Before he could make any reply, the current song faded out, and the DJ announced, "This next one is a special request."

At the first familiar notes of "Non, je ne regrette rien," Meredith's eyes went wide. "You remembered," he whispered.

"Of course I did." David leaned in close. "Happy early birthday, love."

Though the room was filled with strangers and friends and family, their surroundings awash with vibrant colors and opulent fabrics and the twinkle of Christmas stars, for the moment, the whole world had shrunk down to just the two of them in each other's arms, the glide of satin beneath his palms, and Edith Piaf in the background.

David drew Meredith closer and softly sang along.

Acknowledgments

When I first began writing *Into the Midnight Wood* in the winter of 2022, I didn't imagine that anyone would ever be seriously interested in it, and I am still astonished by—and incredibly grateful for—everyone who has proven me wrong and helped to shape this story into the best version of itself.

In particular, I would like to thank:

My agent, Pete Knapp, for believing in this book, as well as Stuti Telidevara, Danielle Barthel, and the rest of the team at Park, Fine & Brower for all their help;

Everyone at Dutton and Penguin Random House who helped bring this book to life, including Alice Dalrymple, Sarah Oberrender, Melissa Solis, Clare Shearer, Lorie Pagnozzi, and especially my editor, Charlotte Peters, for taking such care with this story and these characters;

Laura Barrett, for providing the cover illustration;

Mary Beth Constant, my copy editor; and Leah Marsh and Michelle Hope, my proofreaders;

My UK agent, Claire Wilson, as well as Safae El-Ouahabi and the team at RCW;

Alice Johnstone, my UK editor at Viking;

Rachel, for reading the first draft chapter by chapter as I wrote it (because I'm certain I never would have finished it otherwise);

Simone, for beta reading and contributing a couple important lines that helped set me in the right direction;

Robin, for putting up with me sending ridiculous excerpts with no context;

My former German professors, whom I respect too much to embarrass by sharing their full names here: Dr. L, Dr. R, and especially Dr. H, who first introduced me to the *Galgenlieder*;

And finally, while it would take far too much space to list every single piece of media that inspired something in this book, I can't neglect to acknowledge the authors whose works make direct appearances: Johann Wolfgang von Goethe, Heinrich Heine, and Christian Morgenstern, whose fantastical animal creations have been borrowed to populate the Midnight Wood and its surroundings.